PART I – THE MISSION

IMPERIAL ROGUE

Ashes of Empire #7

ERIC THOMSON

Sanddiver
Books

—1—

Coraline
Unclaimed Space

Nothing. The entire trip had been wasted. So much for First Empire artifacts having survived, secreted away in the ancient fortress built long before Homo sapiens became the dominant life form on Earth. Hal Paget shook his head in disgust as he climbed out of the tiny passage leading to a small hidden storeroom. For six hours, he had searched the dark granite complex with his handheld sensor, only to discover a ghost. All he'd found scattered throughout the massive installation were two-hundred-and-fifty-year-old debris, the remains of a former garrison likely massacred by insurgents during the admirals' revolt that triggered the old Empire's collapse.

The murmur of many distant voices reached his ears, and he feared his time on Coraline was coming to a close. A preindustrial settlement lay several kilometers away, by a river snaking its way through the foothills and across the narrow plain where it drained into the ocean on the distant horizon. Surely the inhabitants had seen his starship land on the fortress roof and were even now coming to investigate. But in Paget's experience, the chances of them being hostile were high. The primitive descendants of the Great Scouring's few surviving victims on most worlds he'd visited viewed high-tech visitors with great suspicion, thanks to the tales of destruction raining from the sky passed through the generations.

Paget — one hundred and ninety centimeters tall, broad-shouldered, with thick dark hair, a bristling mustache, piercing blue eyes, and an aquiline nose above a firm, cleft chin — pocketed his sensor. He gave the bare room with its unidentifiable rubbish strewn across the floor a last look and headed for the stairs leading back to the roof. As he neared the staircase shaft, the voices grew louder, and they definitely sounded belligerent. He took the treads two at a time and quickly emerged back into the mid-afternoon sunshine.

When he approached the small, faster-than-light capable starship, looking for all the world like a giant, black bird of prey preparing to launch at an unseen quarry, a small ramp dropped from its belly, the AI which helped him run the vessel having detected his approach. He suddenly heard a flurry of footsteps behind him, and a slender figure wearing dark blue spacer coveralls dashed by and made for the ramp. Paget ran behind it, but the person reached the top of the ramp and vanished into the ship before he could catch up.

Paget drew his blaster from its hip holster and followed the stowaway-wannabe into the cool dimness of the ship's belly airlock. He came face to face with a tall woman in her late thirties whose green eyes and snub nose dominated her narrow features. Short platinum-colored hair made a distinct contrast to her dark eyebrows and the liberal dusting of freckles covering her cheeks and chin.

The stare she gave him was half fear and half defiance.

"I'm coming with you," she said in a husky tone that quivered just a little.

"What makes you think—" But before Paget could complete his question, shouts erupted behind him, and he saw her eyes widen.

Paget turned, and the sight of a mob carrying spears, swords, and other sharp implements rushing toward the ramp made him snap, "Marlene, button her up. NOW."

The ramp lifted almost immediately, sealing them in.

"Okay. I guess you're coming with me. But you're staying right here for now. I need to lift off, stat. Sit or lie down on the deck for takeoff."

Paget stepped around her and passed through the inner airlock doors, shutting them behind him before she reacted. He rushed to the tiny bridge at the heart of the ship, rattling off orders for the AI, and by the time he slipped into his seat at the controls, the thrusters were spooling up with a sharp whine. A view of the exterior on the primary display showed the mob retreating to the head of the stairs, driven away by the unnatural sound, but still shaking their weapons angrily. They looked like a ragged bunch, with homespun clothes, long hair, unkempt beards, and open mouths revealing rotten teeth. Paget shuddered at the thought of the stench they must carry around with them, a foul miasma capable of triggering nausea.

Then, the ship lifted off vertically and, once it reached a hundred meters above the fortress rooftop, its vector changed to a forward motion, nose lifting at a sharp angle as it headed back toward space. Paget could feel the g-force pushing him back in his seat, and he quickly flipped the view to that of the airlock, hoping the woman was supine or sitting in a corner. He felt a stab of relief at seeing her flat on her back, eyes closed, chest moving with slow regularity as she breathed normally. He figured the spacer's coveralls and the ship's landing traces on the rooftop meant she had probably been marooned on Coraline in the last day or two by her ship. She didn't seem emaciated or overly dirty, meaning she hadn't been there long.

But he knew she had quite a story to tell.

The ship eventually settled into orbit so Paget could make sure everything was all right and prepare for the lengthy trip to his next destination, since Coraline had proved barren. Or at least the ancient fortress had, and it was the sole surviving structure from the First Empire days still standing. Of course, it had been part of the landscape for over a hundred thousand years, untouched by erosion or the passage of time. The L'Taung era Shrehari who built it, knew what they were doing, yet they vanished with the contents long ago, leaving only small anchor holes where they had attached things to the walls and ceilings.

He went aft and down to the lower deck and released his passenger from the airlock.

"I'm Hal Paget," he said, studying her with impassive eyes as she climbed to her feet. He didn't offer his hand, and neither did she.

"Sela Reeve." She returned his gaze with a stony one of her own.

"Tell me, Sela, who did you piss off to get marooned on a primitive world like Coraline?"

"Who says they marooned me?" Maybe I got lost, and they had to leave without me."

Paget raised his eyebrows as he exhaled. "Seeing as how you're aboard my ship and I saved your life, I'd say you owe me honesty."

He turned on his heels. "Let's head for the galley and some tucker. I figure you probably haven't eaten recently."

She followed him silently and sat at the single table in the small compartment while Paget popped two food trays into the autochef.

"Nice ship you have," Reeve said when he turned around and leaned against the sole counter running the length of the galley. "A single-hander?"

"Yes. She's called *Marlene* and has a sophisticated AI helping me, one I've baptized Marlene for obvious reasons. Say hi to Sela Reeve, Marlene."

"Hello, Sela Reeve," a low, disembodied female voice said, the sound coming seemingly from everywhere.

Reeve scowled, and after a while, she replied, "Hi."

"Not a fan of AIs, are you?" Paget asked, amusement dancing on his square face.

"I prefer a fully human team, if it's the same to you."

"Well, Marlene is an integral part of my crew, and so as long as you're aboard my ship, you'll need to put up with her."

An amused expression crept across Reeve's face.

"Her? If you hadn't noticed, you're anthropomorphizing your ship's AI. That can't be healthy for a man in his prime like you."

"Never mind my mental health. Why were you marooned on Coraline?"

Reeve briefly glanced away and sighed. "I pissed off most of the crew by the time we landed, and they left me two days ago. I hid when the villagers showed up with their spears and swords and prayed another ship would show up."

"How did you annoy them?" The autochef chimed. Paget withdrew both trays and brought them to the table, then sat across from Reeve.

"Oh, the usual. I have a talent for it and regularly get left behind, except this time, they didn't wait until we touched a civilized world."

Paget popped a piece of reconstituted meat into his mouth and chewed while observing Reeve and trying to see behind the touchy facade she presented.

"How many ships did you serve on?"

"*Hinksford* was my eleventh in twenty-one years."

Paget's eyebrows shot up. "A little under two years in each? That's pretty short. You must really be a piece of work, Sela Reeve."

"What can I say? I'm a wizard in engineering, but I like to play by my own rules." She speared a chunk from her tray and nibbled on it while watching Paget with a smug look on her face.

"And those rules seem to include the item won't play well with others. What are you? Late thirties? You should have learned better by now."

"Thirty-nine, actually. And I like myself just the way I am."

Paget shrugged. "It's your life. Live it the way you want, so long as you're ready to deal with the fallout. You're damned lucky I showed up and didn't have a chance to chuck you off my ship. What were you doing in the L'Taung era fortress, anyway?"

"Looking for stuff from the old Empire we could sell on."

He nodded. "Scavengers."

"Salvagers."

"Let me guess, *Hinksford* is an ancient tub on the verge of falling apart and has a dozen crew tops."

"Yep. And without me, it won't last quite as long as the skipper would like. Such as returning to a friendly port."

"Oh. Vital crewmember, were you?"

She smirked. "The chief engineer was drunk or high most of the time, and since there were only two of us in engineering, guess what'll happen to that heap of junk now?"

"Did they find anything in the fortress?"

A nod. "Yep. A box of old data crystals from the First Empire in a small, hidden chamber on the third floor from the top. Must have been fifty of the crystals in that crate. Should fetch a decent price on the black market."

Paget figured it was the same chamber in which he'd seen a sensor ghost and silently cursed his arriving two days too late. "And where will they try to sell it?"

"Probably the nearest Imperial world."

"Not in the Republic."

Reeve blew a raspberry. "No way *Hinksford* is ever going back there."

"Back? You mean you're from the Republic?"

"Yep. Born and raised on Yotai."

"And why is your former ship not returning there?"

She chuckled. "Because they're renegades with a price on their heads."

"You got a price on yours as well?"

"I do."

"Why?"

"Because President Derik Juska, bless his shriveled black heart, doesn't like unlicensed salvagers. In fact, he doesn't like anything that's not under the Republic's control."

"So, Juska is still running the place."

"And will until the day he dies, whether it's in his bed or from a knife in the back. Plenty of folks would like to see him go either way, but he's a wily old rat and will probably remain president for another thirty or forty years. I gather you're an Imperial, then?"

Paget winked at her. "Have been ever since the Hegemony declared itself the Second Empire five years ago. And funnily enough, we have a different president now, his predecessor having retired at the end of her term of office. Does the Republic still even have elections?"

Reeve shrugged. "Don't know, don't care."

"I suppose you're always too busy finding your next ship."

She made an obscene gesture at Paget, causing him to let out a bark of laughter. "Be nicer to me. I could always space you and save on the food expenditure and environmental systems usage."

Reeve gave him a speculative glance. "I doubt you're the type to space people who haven't done you any harm."

"How would you know? I could be a psychopath who can't see you as a human being."

"Having met my share of those over the years, I don't think you are one." She paused to take a sip of water. "So what's the plan, Captain?"

— 2 —

"What now indeed?" Paget sat back and contemplated Reeve, who was putting on a patently false air of innocence. "I suppose I could always dump you back on Coraline and wish you luck."

"You wouldn't dare."

"No, I suppose not. But I'm not returning to civilization for a few weeks, or even months, so you're stuck aboard *Marlene*."

"Why?"

"Because I have a certain number of scoured former human planets to visit on this run."

"What for?"

"I look for certain artifacts from the First Empire and survey fallen worlds to determine their population and level of technology."

Her eyes widened slightly. "You work for the Imperial government?"

Paget hesitated, wondering how much he should tell her, and a smile spread across Reeve's face.

"You're employed by the Second Empire. Otherwise, you wouldn't dither about answering me."

"What if I do?"

"It means this ship isn't yours, is it?" Reeve looked around and asked, "Marlene, who do you belong to?"

"I cannot answer that question," the disembodied voice replied before Paget could intervene.

"Yep, you're an Imperial ship."

He rolled his eyes and said, "Fine. I work for the government. Satisfied?"

She grinned at him. "Yep. So, I'm stuck with you for a while, am I?"

"Yes, and you'll earn your keep."

"Doing what?"

"Whatever I tell you to. You mentioned being a starship engineer by trade. Any formal education in that field."

"No. I joined my first ship as a simple deckhand the day after I turned eighteen, and my parents kicked me out. From there on, everything I learned, I did so the hard way — on the job. But I'm a competent, if self-taught, starship engineer and can fix most things that go wrong on small FTL and wormhole-capable craft."

Paget climbed to his feet, grabbed the trays, and put them in the recycler, then he turned to Reeve.

"Let me take you on a tour of *Marlene* so you can familiarize yourself with her inner workings."

Reeve stood. "I'm yours to command, oh Captain, my Captain. By the way, your ship has a strange name for a government vessel. I've never heard of any bearing a woman's first name. Nor a man's, for that matter."

He grinned at her. "That's because I changed her name when I took over. She was a pirate ship taken by the Navy and outfitted as a long-range reconnaissance craft. Marlene was a woman who left me at the altar ten years ago, and I figured my best revenge was riding her namesake and ordering it around. That way I can say I'm always inside Marlene."

Reeve let out a guffaw. "Nice."

"I'm glad you approve."

"Is it a true story, though?"

Paget gave her a sidelong gaze. "No. I've never been left at the altar and don't know any human being named Marlene. The Navy gave her the name when they brought her into service as an auxiliary vessel. I guess whoever did it figured people would believe no naval ship could bear such a name and write her off as another tramp running beyond the frontiers. But you have to admit, it is an amusing story."

As he led her down a circular metallic staircase, she said, "You're Navy. You have to be. They wouldn't give a nice little ship like this to a civilian spacer. What's your rank?"

He remained silent for a few moments, then sighed. "Lieutenant Commander."

"Mighty high for someone running a single-hander."

"I volunteered, if you must know."

"Not much for spending time with other humans, are you?" She asked in a droll tone.

"Like you?"

"Why do you say that?"

Paget ushered her through an airtight door and into *Marlene*'s engineering compartment proper.

"Because I'm an excellent judge of character, and I've decided your troubles with previous crews were because of a distinct dislike of others." He gestured at the consoles and displays dominating the small space. "Everything is automated, and the AI controls it."

"Until the AI craps out and half of these stations turn red." Reeve pivoted on her heels to take in the entirety of the compartment. "Then, you'll be fucked."

"Hasn't happened in the two and a half years since we've been exploring the Empire's outer rim."

"Doesn't mean it won't. The longer a starship runs, the greater its chances of something breaking."

"*Marlene* gets a refit once a year."

She gave him an ironic smile. "Hurray for you! I've never actually been aboard a ship that went into refit. All of the ones I've been on were run until something major threatened to fuck up. Not that any of them did, mostly thanks to me."

"A bit full of yourself, are you?"

"I'm a natural at keeping ships sailing between the stars." She suddenly caught a whiff of herself and grimaced. "And I'm smelling a tad supernatural right now. You wouldn't have a shower and some spare clothes?"

"Come on. I'll show you to your quarters. They include heads and showers. I'm sure I can find you some spare coveralls and undies. You're almost as tall as I am."

"Toiletries too?"

"I may have a few sealed packs stashed away in the emergency supplies compartment. You good with engineering, or do you want to spend a little more time looking around?"

"Give me a bit longer."

Paget stood by the door as he observed Reeve sit at the main workstation and call up engineering data on the virtual display. After a few minutes, he figured she knew what she was doing.

"You're aware you could also helm the ship from here, right?" Reeve eventually asked over her shoulder.

"Of course."

"It's somewhat uncommon. Every other ship I've been on didn't have a backup bridge. But your engineering suite is nice and modern. It doesn't need any babying."

He gave her an ironic grin. "Good to know."

She climbed to her feet. "Show me the rest of your *Marlene,* and afterward, I'll take a nice sonic shower."

When they were done, Paget ushered her into a small but cozy cabin across from the one he indicated was his and said, "This will be yours for the duration of your stay aboard. I'll get the toiletries pack and dig up spare coveralls and undies. After that, we'll be on our way."

"To where?"

"Zeelandia, the next formerly human star system on my list. Ever been there?"

"No. But I think that's where *Hinksford* was headed next. You might be able to retrieve that case of data crystals." Reeve cocked an eyebrow at him with amusement and gave her cabin a quick inspection before undoing the front of her overalls.

Paget turned to fetch the promised items, and when he returned, she was in the sonic shower, the door between the cabin and heads wide open.

"I've got your stuff."

"Oh, thanks," she said, completely unconcerned about her nudity. "Can you toss me the toiletries?"

"Sure." Paget threw the small pack at her, then left, wondering about the multiple faint white scars crisscrossing her torso and upper arms.

He went to the tiny bridge and dropped into the pilot's chair, where he worked on the course for Zeelandia. When he was satisfied, Paget took the controls and broke out of orbit, headed for Coraline's hyperlimit.

Not long after, Reeve, looking distinctly refreshed, albeit floating in coveralls sized for a bigger person, joined him and sat in one of the two unused chairs.

"We're on our way?"

"Yep." Paget touched a control, and the rapidly receding image of Coraline appeared on the primary display. "What did you do with your clothes?"

A smirk appeared. "Put them in the cleaner, of course. Not only can I identify one when I see it, but I can also fix the thing if ever it breaks. They were always going off on my previous ships. The captains bought cheap replacement parts and got exactly what they paid for out of them."

"You'll find the Navy doesn't stint on cost when it comes to the upkeep of its ships. It has a duty to make sure we can come home again."

At that moment, Marlene's voice came through hidden speakers.

"I've detected debris at the hyperlimit. It appears to be the remains of a small starship. No life signs are present. Do you wish to investigate?"

Paget gave Reeve a curious glance and saw something in her eyes that he found a little disturbing.

"Yes. Show the debris on the primary display."

Moments later, the remains of what had once been an FTL-capable vessel appeared. It had broken up into thousands of pieces, most of them spinning in one direction or another as the debris cloud expanded.

"Can you figure out how long ago it disintegrated?" Paget asked.

"No more than a few days ago," Marlene replied.

"Is there anything left that could identify it?"

Before the AI could answer, Reeve cleared her throat.

"If you search closely, you might find the case of data crystals."

Paget's eyebrows shot up as he stared at her. "You mean it's *Hinksford*? What the hell happened?"

Reeve had the grace to appear embarrassed. "I kinda figured they might do something stupid to me while we were on Coraline after hearing the captain whisper to the first mate before we landed. So, I sabotaged the ship to make it blow up when they tried to go FTL. Of course, if I had gone back aboard, I would have disarmed the booby trap. But they left me there."

He shook his head. "I'm not sure whether I should give you access to anything aboard my ship now. You're way more dangerous than I thought."

"You have no idea. But I'd have a hard time putting anything past your AI, whereas *Hinksford* was already falling apart. It only needed a little shove."

"How did you sabotage the ship?"

"Tampered with the antimatter nozzles leading to the hyperdrive nacelles. The moment they'd have spooled up, the nozzles would have broken apart and sprayed antimatter everywhere. And then, boom. I guess it worked."

"And killed a dozen people in the process."

Reeve gave him an irritated shrug. "They condemned me to death by leaving me on Coraline, so turnabout is fair play. It's a cold, cold universe out there, and if you don't watch out for yourself, no one else will."

Paget let out a sigh. "Remind me never to piss you off."

"No worries, Hal. I owe you my life, and I take my debts seriously. Now, why don't you have Marlene find data crystals? The box should have survived the sudden decompression when *Hinksford* came apart at the seams."

"Anything else she should search for?"

"No. We haven't been that lucky on this run."

"Your former crewmates haven't been lucky, period."

"Better them than me. Besides, they were mostly bastards when they were sober and brainless assholes when they were drunk. Which happened often."

"How did you end up serving with a crew like that?"

"No choice. I had to get off Hatshepsut, and *Hinksford* was the only one hiring."

"Oh? And why was Hatshepsut too hot for you?"

"Let's say I got into a little trouble with the local police in Thebes."

"Excuse me," Marlene's voice cut through the conversation. "But I've found what appears to be a cluster of crystals that match those used for data storage during the First Empire."

"Can we retrieve them?"

"Yes. I'll send the probe if you're agreeable."

"Sure, go ahead." Paget turned his attention back to Reeve. "What sort of trouble?"

"I got into a bar fight and wasn't fast enough out the door to escape the law. Since I wasn't a citizen of Hatshepsut, the cops gave me five days to leave the planet. Otherwise, they'd send me to a re-education camp in the wilds of Axsum, Hatshepsut's largest and least developed continent. I didn't have enough money to pay for a passenger berth and really wasn't interested in finding out what that camp was about."

"Let me guess, your previous ship left you on Hatshepsut after you had a parting of ways with its crew."

A grin spread across Reeve's face. "You could say that."

"And did you win?"

"What?"

"The bar fight?"

"Nope."

"What was it about?"

"They accused me of cheating at cards."

"And were you?"

"Yes."

— 3 —

Marlene settled into hyperspace, headed for Coraline Wormhole Two, which would lead, via a red dwarf star with a few uninhabited planets, to the Zeelandia system. The probe had recovered the case with the data crystals, but since Paget had nothing with which to read them, it went into the secure cargo hold where he stored artifacts.

Exhaustion quickly caught up with Reeve, and she took to her bunk while Paget sat in his bridge chair, pondering the fact that he would no longer be alone on this mission. Worse yet, his companion was a woman of dubious character who thought nothing of killing *Hinksford*'s entire crew. And yet vulnerability, perhaps, lurked behind those hard eyes.

She certainly wasn't soulless, but she did live a hard life, of that he was convinced. He believed her when she said she owed him and took her debts seriously. Still, he kept her out of certain systems so she couldn't endanger him or the ship, and would lock his cabin door without the override being accessible to her when he turned in for a few hours of sleep.

Yet when he rose an hour before *Marlene* was due to drop out of hyperspace at the wormhole terminus, Reeve still slept soundly, proof she got little rest in the old L'Taung fortress, dodging hostile locals and searching for food.

He was sitting with his hands around a mug of coffee in the galley when Reeve finally appeared, looking refreshed and strangely mischievous.

"What's that you're drinking?" She asked.

"Coffee. Do you want some?"

"Nah. Tried it once when we landed on an Imperial world and didn't like it. If you have tea, that would be nice."

Paget gestured at one of the lockers lining the wall opposite the cooking station. "I think you'll find some in there."

She rummaged through the indicated cabinet marked 'dry goods' and produced a sealed jar of powdered tea. Inspecting it, she grimaced. "No bags, I presume?"

"None."

"I'd always heard Imperials were coffee-drinking barbarians who considered tea as weak piss."

"So? Tea *is* weak. And hot water is over there." He jerked his chin at the taps above the sink.

Reeve made herself a cup and sat across from Paget.

"I gather we're still FTL?"

"Yep. But we should drop out at the wormhole terminus within the hour. Go ahead and heat a tray if you're hungry."

"Nah, not right now, thanks. I always stick to a cup of tea when I wake up."

"Suit yourself. Did you sleep well?"

"Best I've had in a long time. There's something to be said for traveling in a ship that's safe and not crewed by incompetent idiots who get too hands-on when they're drunk."

"And by hands-on, do you mean—"

She rolled her eyes as she interrupted Paget. "It's exactly what you think it is. I've lost count of the number of times I've had to fight off some asshole who wanted to get inside my coveralls. So be warned. If you try anything funny, you'll get squashed nuts for dessert."

Paget let out a snort. "No worries. I'm a big fan of mutual consent. It makes the experience that much better."

She looked at him over the rim of her cup, amusement dancing in her eyes. "Glad to hear it."

An hour later, after both ate and Paget answered a lot of questions about the ship and its functions, he climbed to his feet and headed for the bridge. Reeve followed him, curious to see how *Marlene* handled a wormhole transit.

They emerged from hyperspace and experienced the usual brief nausea that accompanied the transition. Once it wore off, Paget interrogated Marlene, who confirmed they'd left FTL just short of the wormhole's event horizon, almost precisely as planned. A few minutes later, the ship crossed into the terminus, and their perception of space turned into bright pretzels of color, an effect which also wore off within moments.

"And we're in transit. It should take approximately eight hours before we emerge in ISC440023-2, a red dwarf star system we'll have to cross so we can transit another wormhole to Zeelandia. How about we take the sublight drive controllers apart and check them for any hidden issues Marlene hasn't detected?"

Reeve gave him a skeptical look. "Are you sure that's necessary?"

He grinned at her. "Probably not, but it'll give you hands-on experience with the old girl, and it beats sitting around, drinking caffeinated brews while staring aimlessly at the bulkhead."

"Is that what you do when you're in transit or hyperspace alone? Drink coffee and stare at nothing?"

"No. I read a lot. In fact, I've mostly covered the curriculum of the Imperial War College's basic and advanced curricula by now. If I challenge the examinations, I won't even have to show up at the campus in person. And I play games against Marlene."

"What sort of games?"

"Chess, mainly."

Reeve scrunched up her face. "Ugh. Not my favorite."

"A shame. We could have played against each other."

"Not even in your dreams."

"All right then." He stood. "Come on."

They'd finished working on the sublight drive controllers an hour earlier and were lounging in the galley when Marlene warned them that she'd be popping out the ISC440023-2 wormhole terminus in fifteen minutes.

"I'm going to take a quick shower before we emerge," Paget announced.

Reeve theatrically sniffed her armpits and grimaced. "So will I."

They met again in the tiny bridge a few minutes before emergence, and Reeve noticed a timer in the bottom right-hand corner of the primary display, which was otherwise black.

"Let's hope we'll be in the right system," she said as she took a seat.

"Why? You experienced a lot of wormhole shifts during your time in space?"

"Some. The damn things aren't nearly as stable as we figured them to be. Or maybe the universe is going through a phase of instability in recent times, after centuries of it seeming like they're eternally connected to the same star systems. Considering we know next to nothing about how they really work." She shrugged.

"Thirty seconds to emergence," Marlene's voice said.

"Time to get comfy," Paget replied.

Both humans closed their eyes and placed their forearms on their thighs, in the time-honored position for wormhole transits. A swirl of impossible colors, a touch of nausea, and they were back in normal space.

"We are not in the ISC440023-2 system," Marlene announced as Paget and Reeve regained their senses. "It has one M2-class red dwarf sun. This system has a G2 class binary."

The former speared Reeve with his gaze. "I should have known you were a Jonah, talking about not ending up in the right system."

She raised both hands, palms facing outward, in surrender. "You can't blame this on me, Hal. I don't make wormholes shift."

"Where are we, Marlene?"

"I don't know yet. You do remember that our records of this quadrant are spottier than most. Let me work on it."

Reeve cocked an eyebrow at Paget. "Did she just sound a little peeved?"

"Not that I noticed. Besides, she doesn't have feelings since she's an AI, and peevishness is a sentiment. Her choice of words must have given you that impression."

"How do you know she hasn't developed sentience and therefore emotions?"

"Marlene, are you sentient?" Paget asked.

"Of course not, Hal. I'm merely a sophisticated program with a verbal interface designed to automate most of the ship's functions so you can sail her alone."

Paget flipped his hands in a 'there you have it' gesture.

"And I'm not peeved."

A mischievous smile appeared on Reeve's face. "How would you know that if you're not self-aware?"

"Your question is a logical fallacy."

Paget grinned at Reeve. "She's got you there."

"Shouldn't you refer to Marlene as 'it' since she isn't sentient?"

"Nah. She's a Navy starship, and we always refer to those as she. Speaking of which, did you figure out where we are yet, Marlene?"

"I have, Hal. This system is ISC101287-12."

"Dash twelve?" Paget reared up as he frowned. "You mean to tell me we're in a system with twelve wormhole termini?"

"Indeed."

"Does it have a name on top of the Imperial star catalog number?"

"It does. This is the Lothair system."

Paget rolled his eyes as he groaned. "Oh, hell."

Reeve gave him a curious look. "What's wrong with the Lothair system? Not that I've ever heard of it."

"Marlene, would you care to do the honors?"

"Certainly. According to our records, the Lothair system supposedly had the most unstable wormhole termini in the entire First Empire. No one from the Wyvern Hegemony or the Second Empire has visited the system, at least that we know of. It has two habitable worlds, one of them, Lothair Six, is marginal because of its cold environment. Members of a religious sect colonized the warmer of the two a few hundred years before the Great

Scouring, wishing to escape technological civilization and live in an agrarian, preindustrial society. Since Lothair's wormhole termini were unstable, little to no traffic passed through the system, and the last recorded check on the colony was made by the Imperial Navy twenty years before the First Empire's collapse. Though it was thriving and the colonists were polite to the landing party, they expressed the desire to be left alone."

"I see," Reeve said. "Preindustrial means no useful First Empire artifacts."

Paget scoffed. "Never mind artifacts. We may end up chasing around the wormhole network looking for our way home."

"Right. And how the heck did you know about Lothair?"

"Everyone, Navy and civilian, carrying out surveys has been briefed on star systems presenting a peril to navigation, and Lothair was at the top of the list due to it being a binary with twelve unstable termini. As far as I know, we're the first Wyvern ship to make it here. Hell, we might be the first starship to come into this system in hundreds of years."

Reeve flashed Paget a smile.

"Then let's go see if the colony on Lothair Five is still there. After all, Lindisfarne survived intact for over two hundred years after being cut off from the rest of the galaxy. It'll take what? Two or three days? Then we can figure out how to get back."

Paget sighed as he shook his head. "Might as well, I suppose. Marlene, find Lothair Five and plot a course toward it."

"Working." A few moments later, the AI said, "Found and course plotted, if you'd like to verify."

"I would." Paget busied himself at the helm station, then sat back and announced, "It's good. Start the countdown to jump."

"Transition to hyperspace in thirty seconds."

—4—

Lothair Five appeared unprepossessing from high orbit. Torn clouds floated above dark oceans and land that varied from desolate-looking dun expanses through immense swaths of green to white polar caps. Three major continents and five large islands formed most of the land, taking up approximately thirty-five percent of the surface.

"I'm definitely getting human life signs," Paget announced, looking up from his helm readout. Millions of them, mostly concentrated along the largest continent's southern coast. Or perhaps the southern continent's northern coast. In any case, along the subtropical zone. Smaller groups are inland, along rivers. And lots of open fields surround all settlements."

"So, the back-to-basics nutters are still alive."

Paget turned his head to give Reeve a questioning look. "Back-to-basics nutters?"

"I figure anyone who voluntarily gives up modern tech and goes back to using domestic animals for agriculture and locomotion has a few screws loose." She tapped the side of her head. "Especially if they're doing it for religious reasons."

"Not a believer, are you?"

"Nope. The Sisters of the Void may be fey, but their Almighty is a figment of the imagination. We gonna land and say hi?"

Paget nodded. "Besides recovering artifacts, I also check on human populations that have been isolated since the Great Scouring. And if they're sufficiently advanced, make contact."

"What's sufficiently advanced in your world?"

"That depends on the state the society was in before Dendera's Retribution Fleet passed through. In the case of Lothair Five, it's if they're still substantially at the same level they were. And I'm hopeful that's the case, since I doubt the late Empress' planet killers passed through this system because of the risk to navigation. But first, I'll get us into geosynchronous orbit over the main concentration of people and send a stealth probe to sniff out the place directly."

Before long, the ground features began to grow on the bridge's main display while the descending probe communicated what it gathered in the visible spectrum. Two side displays showed the same scene but in the ultraviolet and infrared spectra, normally invisible to the human eye.

It stopped at an altitude of fifty meters and hovered as it surveyed the center of a small town with a plaza surrounded by solid-looking two-story stone buildings that seemed to have been there forever. The roofs had gray slate or red tile, and chimneys pierced them.

"Looks rather bucolic," Paget commented as he studied the people walking across the cobblestone plaza with purpose. They wore drab homespun clothes, which nevertheless appeared neat and clean, and leather shoes. Many also wore large-brimmed floppy hats of various colors against the subtropical sun.

"Looks farking primitive." Reeve gave him a bored smirk.

"But no more so than when the Imperial Navy last visited, if the records are correct."

Suddenly, one of them stopped and looked straight up at the probe. As it zoomed in, they saw his eyes widen.

"You said it was stealthy."

Paget nodded. "It is. He shouldn't be able to detect the damn thing."

The man pointed up, and his mouth moved as he shouted something.

"You know," Reeve drawled, "it'd be interesting to hear what he's saying."

"Crap, I didn't turn on the audio pickup." Paget touched a control, and a faint voice came through the bridge's hidden speakers.

Reeve cocked her head to one side. "Can you understand what he's yelling?"

"No. It sure as hell doesn't sound like Anglic."

"Did the nutters speak another language?"

"Can't say. The histories mention nothing about that." Paget frowned. "Mind you, it's been several hundred years since the last official contact, and their speech might have drifted into something incomprehensible. Let's find out if the universal translator can make sense of it."

By now, over two dozen people were staring up at the probe, most of them wearing an expression of horror.

"I think we can take it as a given that your drone isn't stealthy," Reeve said. "Otherwise, the entire population of village idiots couldn't make it out."

But before Paget could reply, the three feeds lit up like a million suns exploding at once, then a fraction of a second later, they went dark.

Paget let out a string of heartfelt expletives that caused Reeves to raise her eyebrows.

"I wasn't aware you knew so many bad words, especially for an Imperial Navy officer."

He snorted. "I can string together enough obscenities to go on for five minutes without repeating myself."

"No doubt. What happened?"

"The probe is no longer transmitting a damn signal. If I didn't know any better, I'd say the buggers knocked it out of the air."

"From an altitude of fifty meters? With what? Rocks?" Reeve smirked.

"It looked like some sort of energy burst."

"But they're not supposed to be technologically advanced enough for energy weapons. They certainly didn't look like they've gone beyond chemically propelled slug throwers."

Paget sat back with a thoughtful expression. "You're right, they don't. Still, something took out the probe. It was functioning perfectly until that flash."

"What will you do now? Make contact?"

He shrugged. "My mission is to do so, if possible, and those folks seem pretty much at the same level as they were under the First Empire. But if they killed my probe…"

"Then, let's get out of here and call the Lothair system questionable for re-assimilation into the Empire."

"Nope. Can't do that. We'll touch down outside a smaller town to check if they're ready to talk to us.

"Us? How about I stay aboard *Marlene* and cover your ass, Mister First Contact?"

"Marlene can do that by herself, but fine. If you'd rather hide, be my guest."

"And in case you get scragged, how about telling Marlene she's taking orders from me so I can at least escape?"

"Marlene, you're to take orders from Sela Reeve if I'm killed or captured."

"So noted," the ship replied.

"And now, to choose the town where I'll make my approach."

Paget took Marlene to Lothair Five's surface in lazy spirals around the planet until the ship hovered a bare hundred meters above a clearing a kilometer and a half from a small seaport just before dawn. Nothing in the village stirred at this hour and, after a final confirmation, he landed Marlene.

"Remember, always keep her buttoned up," Paget threw over his shoulder as he stood at the top of the ramp, waiting for it to drop.

"No worries. I don't want any wildlife, two-legged or otherwise, creeping aboard."

"Not that Marlene would allow any in the first place."

With the ramp fully extended, Paget strode down and vanished from Reeve's view. The ramp rose again, sealing off the ship.

"And good luck to you," Reeve murmured as she returned to the tiny bridge.

Paget moved unerringly through a forest as dark as the depths of a mineshaft toward the port, thanks to the night vision glasses he wore. Those glasses linked him to the ship, enabling it and Sela Reeve to see exactly what he saw.

When he neared the tree line, Paget dropped to one knee behind a sizable trunk and cautiously looked around it toward the quiet village. As he did so, he noticed his surroundings turning from black to various shades of gray, a sure sign that sunrise was on its way. Paget waited for a while as the far horizon took on a pink hue, and muted colors replaced the gray.

So far, nothing stirred, meaning the whine of Marlene's thrusters had woken no one, and that pleased him.

As the still-hidden sun's rays reached up into the sky, the village took definition beyond the expanse of fallow fields lying between it and the forest, and he saw it was unprotected, houses backing onto kitchen gardens, barns, and various outbuildings. He even noticed, looking through the gaps between buildings, the shapes of wooden boats pulled up on a shingle beach lapped by gentle waves.

After a few minutes, figures appeared, humans wearing homespun clothes, some carrying tools, others baskets with many headed for the beach. Paget wondered again about the wisdom of contacting these people after they seemingly noticed and downed his stealth probe.

But nothing ventured, nothing gained.

He climbed to his feet and left the tree line, walking slowly toward the village. It didn't take long for someone to notice him, and shouts echoed along the narrow streets as faces turned toward Paget, with some people pointing at him.

He put on a smile and held his hands out to the sides so that he could show he wasn't carrying any weapons, and said in a loud voice, "Hello. I come in peace."

Paget didn't know whether they could understand his words, but he hoped they understood his gestures.

However, the individuals he observed appeared to grow more disturbed. An old woman with long white hair and wearing black robes suddenly materialized between two houses. She raised both hands, pointing at Paget, as her face dissolved into a mask of pure hate. Lightning played on her fingertips, growing in intensity until a ball of pure energy formed and sped toward Paget. It struck him, and his mind blanked out as he crumpled to the ground.

Reeve, who'd been watching via the feed from Paget's night vision glasses, stared at the display for a few heartbeats as her mind processed the events, then she touched the communicator embedded in the captain's chair.

"Paget. Are you okay? Paget?"

When she got no response, Reeve looked up. "Marlene, something's happened to Paget, and we need to be with him now. Get the thrusters spooled up and lock in on his position. Lift off the moment you're ready, emergency power."

"Will do."

Moments later, the low whine of the thrusters reached Reeve's ears as the deck vibrated. Then, she felt a momentary downward pressure as Marlene lifted off straight up into the air before turning on a course directly for the village, skimming the treetops.

The bridge's primary display now showed the view straight ahead, and she quickly spotted Paget's prone body in the middle of a fallow field with villagers carefully approaching it.

The latter's attention switched to the ship the moment they noticed it, and the same crone lifted her arms once more.

"Oh no, you don't," Reeve muttered as she uncovered the nose calliope, a four-barrel forty-millimeter plasma cannon, and targeted the ground a dozen meters in front of the old woman.

A single four-round burst raised a dust cloud so dense, it obscured a fair amount of the field, but not to Reeve or Marlene. The ship dropped to the ground almost on top of Paget, and Reeve ran down two decks to where the belly ramp was opening.

Coughing at the swirling dust, she made her way to the foot of the ramp and, spotting Paget's body, hauled him back aboard.

"Button her up, Marlene, and let's head for orbit as fast as you can."

"If you want speed, lie where you are because I shall pull some gees."

"Will do." The ramp shut, and Reeve settled on the cold deck beside Paget. "Let's go."

Intense pressure pushed her to the deck while the thrusters whined like banshees, propelling Marlene upward and out of the old crone's range.

— 5 —

When the pressure abated, Reeve checked Paget's heartbeat and found a thready pulse, but he was out for the count. She dug an antigrav pallet out of the equipment locker, rolled him onto it, and dragged him up to his cabin, where she settled him as comfortably on his bunk as possible.

"You gonna make it, buddy?" Reeve asked in a soft tone as she stared at Paget's ashen features. "I'm not sure I can get us home, not with unstable wormholes surrounding this system."

"Commander Paget does not appear to be in any imminent danger," Marlene's disembodied voice said. "His vitals are stable, though he seems to have suffered some nerve damage from the old woman's energy blast. Whether or not it is permanent, we shall see in good time."

Reeve's face twisted into an ironic smile. "So, you're a medical diagnostician as well. Is there anything you can't do?"

"I cannot make decisions on course, heading, or attack posture."

"Meaning if he doesn't wake up, we'll be going more or less blind?"

"I can advise on the most appropriate course for any destination in human space."

"Meaning in hyperspace and not tempting fate by taking any of Lothair's wormholes?

"That as well. Barring any unforeseen problems, we should have sufficient antimatter fuel to reach Wyvern on a single jump."

"Really?" Reeve sounded dubious.

"Yes."

"And how long would it take?"

"Approximately three and a half weeks if I push into the upper bands."

"What?" Reeve's voice rose by two octaves. "I can't spend more than three weeks in the upper hyperspace bands. I'll go insane."

"You are sensitive to them?"

"Yep. I'm one of the unfortunates who gets hyperspace dreams. A few nights I can handle. More than that? Nope."

"You may use the stasis chamber."

"And you'd run the ship by yourself?"

"Once I have received a course and heading, yes, I can do that if ordered by an appropriate human. And you qualify since Commander Paget said I was to obey you if he were incapacitated."

"But who'll take care of Hal?"

"The stasis chamber is just big enough for two humans."

Reeve groaned. "Oh, goodie. And what if I ordered you to head for the nearest Republic star system?"

"I would disregard your order."

"Didn't Hal transfer authority to me?"

"Up to a point. But I cannot enter Republic space without a duly appointed naval person directing me to do so. Besides, the closest Republic system with antimatter fuel capability is further away than Wyvern."

"Oh. All right. Let me inspect the chamber." Reeve climbed to her feet. "What about you taking us in hyperspace to the nearest identified system with stable wormholes that lead us back to an Imperial star system with an antimatter fueling station?"

"I could do that as well, but it is not as efficient as a single hyperspace jump back to Wyvern and would not buy us any time. On the contrary. Sailing below the upper hyperspace bands will add only a few days to a trip using the wormhole network. Considering Commander Paget's condition, the faster he gets to medical care, the better."

"How about I try living through the nightmares brought on by traveling in the highest hyperspace bands and see? I can always enter the stasis chamber later."

"Very well."

"In that case, as soon as we're in orbit, calculate the course back to Wyvern and make for Lothair Five's hyperlimit on the proper heading."

"I will do so."

"And what do we have to feed Hal if he's out cold for a long time?"

"I carry several IV packs to provide nutrition intravenously among my emergency medical supplies. You can hook Commander Paget up in eight hours if he is still unconscious. And, of course, catheterize him."

Alarm appeared on Reeve's face. "What?"

"It is a very simple procedure, and I will talk you through it."

"Uh, thanks. I think."

"Do you wish to check my navigation calculations?"

"Nah. I wouldn't know what I'm doing. You go ahead and get us to Wyvern without my input beyond saying 'engage,' okay?"

"As you wish. You should take the time to write a report concerning the events on Lothair Five while they are still fresh in your mind. Imperial Intelligence will wish to know about them, and since Commander Paget was incapacitated, the responsibility becomes yours."

"Can't you do it?"

"I will provide the audiovisual recording as an annex to the report, but Imperial Intelligence insists humans write it, not artificial intelligences."

Reeve let out a long sigh. "I didn't know I'd signed up for Imperial service when I came aboard. But so be it. I owe Hal at least that. Can you show me an example of a report, so I know how to do it?"

"Certainly. If you would use the secondary bridge workstation, I will ensure you have everything you need."

By the time the ship went FTL at Lothair Five's hyperlimit, Reeve sat back and contemplated the signature block at the end of her bare-bones report: Sela Reeve, Civilian, Acting Chief Engineer, ISS *Marlene*. It would have to do. And if Imperial Intelligence didn't like it, they could stick their head into a black hole and suck vacuum.

She checked on Paget and found his condition unaltered. Of course, if anything had changed, Marlene would have warned her. So, Reeve headed back to the bridge, settled in Paget's chair, and stared at the blank display for a long time, wondering why her life had taken a ninety-degree turn into the Second Empire.

Heck, she would even set foot on the Imperial capital, Wyvern, in two and a half weeks. Assuming all proceeded smoothly.

That night, she slept reasonably well, since the hyperdrives were limited to the lowest bands while within a star's heliosphere, but once beyond the heliopause, Marlene would run them up into the highest bands, and Reeve was not looking forward to the nightmares.

And they hit her hard the first night in interstellar space, as Marlene ran through hyperspace as fast as she could. Reeve woke up the next morning feeling drained. One look at her haggard face in the mirror told the story. She would climb into the stasis pod with Paget later that day and stay in it until Marlene dropped out of FTL at Wyvern's heliopause. Yet the idea of entrusting her life and that of Hal to an AI, which was, in the end, nothing more than a highly sophisticated bit of programming, gave her pause.

Programs could malfunction. Hell, the ship itself could malfunction, and she might end up spending eternity in stasis. The idea of putting her life in Marlene's hands rankled now that it was imminent, and she decided to hold off for another night.

The next morning, after she rose, Reeve checked on Paget, who remained unconscious, then laboriously transported him to the hold where the stasis chamber squatted like a malevolent entity and carefully placed him inside.

"This is it, Marlene. Once I'm in the chamber, activate it. Release us when we arrive at the Wyvern heliopause or something goes wrong and you need to drop out of hyperspace."

"Understood. It is the best way. I have monitored your sleep for the last two nights, and you will not survive the trip."

Reeve tried a last attempt at pushing back the inevitable. "Could we slow, so we're not running in the highest bands?"

"The balance between speed, distance, and antimatter expenditure is such that we might run out of fuel before reaching Wyvern if we go any slower, as counterintuitive as that may seem."

"No, I get the drives are most fuel efficient in the highest bands. It's one of hyperspace's idiosyncrasies."

"Besides, Commander Paget needs medical attention soonest."

"Okay." Reeve took one last deep breath and joined Paget in the chamber. The door closed, and she felt a prickling on her skin, one that promptly penetrated her deeper tissues. Within moments, her vision blurred, and then, everything stopped.

— 6 —

New Draconis, Wyvern
Second Empire

"I've got to say one thing for the Imperials — their foreign intelligence briefings about Lyonesse are getting better and better with time." Farrin Norum, former Lyonesse Chief of the Defense Staff, and now a citizen of the Second Empire, sat back in his chair and exhaled loudly. He was in his early sixties, with blond hair mostly turned silver, deep-set eyes, and an angular face. "The news they contain isn't, however."

Currag DeCarde, former Lyonesse ambassador to the Wyvern Hegemony and also now a citizen of the Second Empire, glanced up from his workstation. Tall, muscular, with a square face, sandy hair going gray at the temples, and his family's intensely blue eyes, he was of an age with his long-time friend.

"What does this one contain to have you sighing like a lovesick calf?"

Both were in the office they'd shared for several years at the Colonial Service's HQ in the Blue Annex to the Presidential Palace. Recently, they had become senior consultants, and they worked on issues directly for Admiral Johannes Godfrey, the commander-in-chief of the Service.

"A fair number of items. Makes me wonder where they have agents planted, because not everything can be open source. First, the Republic's capital is now New Lena on Yotai. President Juska proclaimed it a few weeks ago after most of the government functions moved there. Lyonesse still maintains the Republic's naval shipyards, but it is now mostly a backwater.

"Then they can hardly call it the Republic of Lyonesse, can they?"

"No, and that's the second item. Juska proclaimed it the United Stars Republic when he shifted his flag from Lyonesse to Yotai."

DeCarde's eyebrows shot up. "Now that's a turn for the books. Juska simply renamed it just like that?"

"With the full-throated approval of his tame Senate, no doubt."

"Took him long enough, come to think of it. The Hegemony renamed itself the Second Empire five years ago, and we know Juska has ambitions to make the Republic humanity's leading, if not sole, interstellar polity."

Norum gave his friend a half-shrug. "And President Benes holds the same aspirations for the Second Empire."

"Sure, but he's moving toward greater democratization, at least at the star system level, and reducing centralized control over planetary matters, while Juska is heading straight in the opposite direction — aiming for a dictatorship in all but name."

"True. Next item on the intel brief — and I can't tell how definite this is — but it appears the Republic is setting up clandestine re-education facilities for dissidents. The intelligence folks give it a fairly high probability of being accurate, and I'd tend to agree because that's who Juska is."

"Re-education facilities? Or concentration camps? The easiest way of dealing with those the government considers heretics is to incarcerate the poor buggers and delete the access codes. Then starve or work them to death, if they don't execute them with a plasma round in the back of the head."

"I suppose it depends on your level of sadism, and the Juska regime is collecting psychopaths like shit collects flies. Another item related to all the above is renaming the Lyonesse Office of Inquiry as the Office for the Security of the Republic. It now has a uniformed branch along with the former LOI's plainclothes investigators."

"What the heck will a uniformed branch do?"

"Guard the re-education facilities, perhaps?"

DeCarde nodded. "Probably one of the things. But Juska is playing the classical game of consolidating his power with a view to making it absolute."

"Another Ruggero, then."

"The game goes back much further than that, to the era immediately before spaceflight, although it was non-operative during the time of the Commonwealth and pre-Ruggero First Empire. Its practitioners were called fascists, communists, socialists, corporatists, and many other names, but they operated under the same basic premise — achieving absolute power over the common people was the sole goal. A small elite ruling with an iron fist, depriving citizens of their basic rights and enriching themselves in the process. The most successful ones hid behind a veil of fake democracy that vast swathes of their population couldn't pierce. And those that could were often co-opted into serving the regime."

Norum chuckled. "I forgot you've made the study of ancient political systems one of your hobbies."

DeCarde held up a finger and said in a sententious tone, "While history might not repeat, it most certainly rhymes, and therefore, studying it should be the duty of every thinking sentient being. For example, one common feature of those political movements throughout history was re-education facilities, concentration camps, call them what you like — they're all prisons in the end — to remove dissenters from view."

"Yet the Hegemony didn't use that sort of coercion."

"No, it didn't, making it unique among societies that sacrificed freedom for the sake of the collective good. However, the Hegemony arose from a catastrophe unlike any other in recorded history, and its system prioritized the sheer survival of a civilization rather than a deliberate attempt to subjugate a population for the sake of an ideology. Although one can see echoes of the older forms of authoritarianism in the Commission for State Security. And the Hegemony espoused the same basic philosophy as any of the others — all within the state, nothing outside the state, nothing against the state. Even so, it was nowhere near as coercive and corrupt as the Republic is becoming under Derik Juska."

"True." Norum nodded. "Though I still have a hard time understanding why the people of the Republic aren't revolting against Juska's measures."

DeCarde made a face. "Because they don't affect the vast majority of the population, they're content to go along. Besides, the Lyonesse First madness has been going on for such a protracted period of time now — over ten years — that many folks have internalized those twisted ideals to the point of no longer questioning them."

"Well, I am thankful to the Almighty for Vigdis Mandus and Sandor Benes. That Wyvern has two visionary presidents in a row is nothing short of miraculous. Imagine if they'd been cut from the same cloth as Derik Juska."

"Then both halves of humanity would have been on the same course to disaster. And they would eventually have fought a bitter war of extermination between them. You see, authoritarian regimes need external enemies to keep the focus of the people away from what they're doing."

"Hence the Lyonesse First movement. Or whatever they'll end up calling the damned thing now that the Republic changed names."

"Just so."

At that moment, a tall, slim woman with dark eyes and dark hair, wearing flowing black robes, poked her head through the open office door. Her smooth facial features belied many years in the Order of the Void.

"Hello," she said in a bright but gentle tone.

"Hey, Maryam!" DeCarde smiled at her. "And what can we do for the Colonial Service's Leading Sister today?"

"I'm checking to see if you read the latest intelligence digest about Lyonesse, or rather the United Stars Republic."

"We were just discussing it."

"Oh, excellent. Admiral Godfrey and General Torma were wondering if you had a few minutes to talk about it with them."

"Their wish is our command. Now?"

"Indeed. We're in the admiral's office."

Both men climbed to their feet and followed Maryam down the corridor. When they appeared in Godfrey's open doorway, the admiral waved them in.

"Grab a seat." Godfrey, in his early seventies, with thick silver hair and lean, intelligent features, gestured at the chairs surrounding a small conference table in front of his desk before taking one himself. He was imitated by Lieutenant General Crevan Torma, his second in command, a man whose black hair framed a craggy, olive-skinned face dominated by keen brown eyes that missed nothing. "If you're here, it means you read the intel brief."

"We did, Johannes," Norum said, using Godfrey's first name, as he, Maryam, and DeCarde sat. The admiral had requested that he do so when he first began working for the Colonial Office, seeing as how Norum had outranked him when he still wore a naval uniform.

"Since you two are our resident experts on things related to the Republic, we're interested in your thoughts on the latest developments."

Norum grimaced. "They're not good."

Godfrey gave him a wry smile. "We'd gathered that."

"It appears that Derik Juska is finalizing the consolidation of his absolute power over the Republic," DeCarde said. "He basically overrode the Constitution — cheered on by a Senate that he bought — by silencing and disappearing his critics. It wouldn't surprise me if he presented a new Constitution making him dictator for life to the Senate, although he doesn't really need it."

"So in effect, he's now a despot akin to the Ruggeros."

DeCarde nodded. "Complete with a security apparatus designed to eliminate dissent."

"The Office for the Security of the Republic."

"Yep. Juska's Stormtroopers, so to speak."

"And the military is simply letting Juska trample the Constitution to which they swore their oath?" A frowning Crevan Torma asked in an incredulous tone.

"I expect that by now the officers above the rank of major or lieutenant commander who consider their oath paramount have been replaced by those whose loyalty is to Juska, not the Constitution. He's had ten years to remove the ones who'd balk at his actions, more than enough time. Heck, Juska fired Farrin as CDS the moment he took office and replaced him with a Lyonesse First zealot, although Gerhard Glass didn't trumpet his allegiance to the movement before he took over." DeCarde made a moue. "The only good news for the Empire is that the quality of the Republic's officer corps must have dropped significantly. Historically, it always did when professionals in the senior ranks were replaced by those who owed their promotions to politics rather than ability. But that same blind loyalty to political leaders meant the generals and admirals were more willing to take action at the whim of their masters rather than push back when they felt the security of the state was at risk."

Godfrey nodded. "Meaning it makes them more unpredictable."

"Indeed."

"I find it incredible that a single individual, backed by a small but zealous minority, can so effectively take over a nation and twist its politics beyond recognition." Torma shook his head.

"No political system ever devised by humans is proof against cunning sociopaths who crave absolute power, Crevan. Not even the Second Empire with the safeguards built into its revised Constitution, although it probably has much less of a chance to slide into autocracy like the Republic is doing. Lyonesse's founder, Jonas Morane, was a bit of an idealist at heart and didn't understand the lengths someone like Derik Juska would go to. Hence, the Republic's Constitution has many flaws that a would-be tyrant can exploit."

"And what do you know? Someone has exploited them," Norum said in a flat tone that nonetheless conveyed his disgust.

— 7 —

"How was your day?" Farrin Norum asked after giving Rey Weston a quick peck on the cheek.

She'd come out of the living room when she heard the apartment's front door open. Weston, a fifty-something almost as tall as Norum but with long blond hair framing a full face, smiled.

"Same old, same old. Nothing ever changes in the New Draconis Police Service. You?"

They had adopted this ritual years ago, and it never changed from workday to workday.

"The latest intel brief on the Republic came in today. It was depressingly interesting."

"Do tell."

"Not until I have a gin and tonic in my hand and am sitting comfortably."

"Well then, go change, and I'll prepare the drinks."

She and Norum had met on Mykonos while the latter was preparing his escape to Wyvern. Declining to assassinate him as ordered by the Lyonesse Office of Inquiry, her then employer, she'd joined him in exile along with DeCarde and her colleague Beth Svent. Both women now worked for the New Draconis Police as civilian trainers, putting their considerable policing experience — both military and civilian — to good use.

When Norum emerged from their bedroom, he wore khaki shorts, a white, collarless short-sleeved shirt, and was barefoot. Weston, already curled up on the sofa, had her drink in hand, while a tall glass beaded with condensation waited for him on the coffee table. The end-of-day gin and tonic, taken together, was also part of the ritual.

Their relationship started with two lost souls clinging to each other in a strange land, not love. Yet what had begun as a physical attraction during their escape from pursuit by the LOI quickly grew into a deep connection, and by now, they couldn't even consider living apart.

Norum sank into a chair opposite the sofa, picked up his glass, and said, "Your health, my dear."

"And yours."

Both took a long sip, then Weston lowered her glass and gave Norum a questioning look. "So, what did the intel brief say?"

Norum laid it bare word for word, and Weston's face fell.

"That's horrible," she said when he stopped to take a nip of his gin. "What the hell has Juska done to the Republic?"

"What he planned on doing long ago, I suspect."

"And no one back home objects?"

Norum let out a humorless bark of laughter. They rounded up and stuffed those who would have done so into camps long ago, or outright shot them. The remainder are either enthusiastically embracing the madness of the Lyonesse First crowd or wisely keeping their heads down and staying silent."

Weston shook her head. "I suppose. Still, it is depressing to see the golden dream, our peace-loving Republic based on knowledge and founded by a visionary like Jonas Morane, twisted into this ugly thing."

"Yep." Norum lifted his glass to his lips again when his communicator, sitting on the kitchen counter, chimed softly. "Hmm. Who is calling at this time of the day?"

"It sounded like your personal address too, not the work one." She gave him a mischievous smile. "Did you make a new friend, perchance?"

"No. I'm at the age where I don't care for strange folk." Norum put his glass on the table and climbed to his feet before heading for the kitchen to retrieve his communicator.

"Hmm," he said after consulting its virtual display. "A missive from a darknet node — unidentified, of course."

"Someone trying to sell you real estate in swampy Okeegee?"

"No." Norum walked back into the living room, eyes on his communicator. "There's a large, encrypted message behind a single word — sprog."

"Sprog? What the hell is that?"

It took Norum a few moments to dredge up the definition from the murky depths of his memory. "It's an ancient, pre-diaspora term for a recruit, if I recall correctly."

"Okay. Why would someone encrypt a message using an old, disused word?" Weston took another sip, eyes fixed on Norum.

Something was tickling the edge of the latter's consciousness, as if sprog had a specific meaning for him, a meaning he'd filed away long ago and forgotten about. He raised his hand to forestall any further words from his partner as he opened his mind fully to let the significance of sprog emerge from his subconscious. After a few moments, his eyes lit up as he snapped his fingers.

"By the Almighty, but that takes me back. When I was a lieutenant commander and first officer of the frigate *Tristan*, I took a newly commissioned ensign assigned to the ship under my wing to teach him the rudiments of his profession. He was so young and wide-eyed, I called him sprog. Don't ask me where I came by the nickname. It just seemed to fit."

"And who was your sprog?"

"One of the descendants of the man you were just talking about. His great-great-grandchild, several times removed, Lucas Morane. I last heard, he became commodore, but Derik Juska forced him into early retirement shortly after.

"I heard of him but never met the man. Apparently, he used to be a highly respected officer and leader, one seen as a potential Chief of the Defense Staff."

"That he was. And he's also a friend. Why the hell would he be sending me a message? I thought he'd done the same as I and withdrawn from public life after seeing the path Juska planned on taking."

Weston smiled at him. "Enter the name into the message and see if that decrypts anything."

Norum did just that, and the word sprog vanished, replaced by another one — Mina.

"Oh, hell. I know the answer to that one." Norum chuckled. "And it's something only Lucas and I share."

She cocked a questioning eyebrow at him. "Tell me."

"It was the working name of a prostitute I rescued Lucas from on Arietis while we were ashore for forty-eight hours. He didn't know what she was and believed her when she showed interest in him. Except she was interested in the creds he carried, nothing more. I managed to rip him from her sharpened claws just before she took the poor sprog up to her parlor. He wasn't happy, but when I told him what would have happened, Lucas sobered up quickly and thanked me."

A mischievous grin spread across Weston's face. "What would have happened, Farrin? Your sprog might have enjoyed a good time in return for payment?"

"I think he'd have enjoyed a long time-out and woken to find everything but the clothes on his back gone. And perhaps not even those. Mina gave off that sort of vibe." Norum's eyes narrowed as he thought about the appropriate counter to the ill-fated name.

"Do you think he might have mentioned her to anyone else since then?"

"Doubtful. The whole incident embarrassed him, and he swore me to secrecy. Let's see. Arietis as a reply is a bit too obvious. What was the name of the dive bar in which it happened?" A long pause while Norum combed through his memory again. "It could have been 'The Righteous Miner' or something like that."

"There's mining on Arietis? I thought that antediluvian, desiccated orb had absolutely nothing of any worth."

"But it doesn't stop people from using fanciful names for their businesses." Norum entered the bar's name, and the letters Mina transformed into another single word — Mother. "My, but Lucas, if he's indeed behind this, is making sure no one else can decipher his message."

"What's the next clue?"

"Mother."

Weston cocked a questioning eyebrow. "And can you explain that one?"

"Oh, yes." Norum grinned at her. "When Lucas had the frigate *Tempest*, his Sister of the Void, Dulcie, was a tad overbearing, and he privately nicknamed her Mother Dulcie. As far as I know, I'm the only one he shared that information with."

He entered Dulcie, and his grin widened. "I'm in. It's a video message."

"Well, project it to the living room display so we can both watch."

The image of a craggy-faced man in his fifties appeared on the display. Silver liberally streaked his dark hair, and the lines around his eyes and mouth showed how tired he was.

"That's Lucas."

He stood or sat in front of a featureless dark background, leading Weston to believe it had been deliberately obscured to avoid giving any hint of his whereabouts, and she said so, adding, "I'm sure the video will have been stripped of all identifying data as well."

"No doubt." Norum touched the controls of his communicator, and Lucas Morane's voice came from the speakers.

"If you're listening to this, Farrin, it means you remember our youthful indiscretions. You did well to leave the Republic ahead of Derik Juska's enforcers. He would have seen you dead. But the situation is becoming dire for everyone who loves the old Republic, and the resistance to his rule, which is slowly coming together, needs someone with universal credibility around whom it can coalesce and become effective. That would be you, old friend. Let me explain."

Weston and Norum exchanged astonished glances.

"Juska's goons arrested or murdered almost everyone who could lead the opposition to his dictatorship. Even I've gone underground and am living a precarious existence in the dark corners of the Republic because I'm sure to be on the elimination list." Morane paused and it seemed like he was steeling himself to continue. "Every other flag officer dismissed by the regime has vanished, either voluntarily or involuntarily, and been replaced by people loyal to Juska and his Lyonesse First movement. I don't know how much intel about the situation you're getting on Wyvern, but whatever that is, the reality is much worse."

"The LOI, now renamed the Office for the Security of the Republic, has turned into a pervasive state police force that can pick people off the streets anytime they want and make them disappear without so much as a charge, let alone a trial. Half the population is spying on the other half, and personal disputes are solved by denouncing one another to the OSR. And the worst part is, most people simply go on with their lives, ignoring the loss of their rights and the hollowing out of the Republic's ideals, because they're either afraid or believe Juska isn't just right but justified in his actions. That's why Lyonesse First, now renamed the United Stars Bloc, has become not only entrenched but the sole political party still garnering support. The others have withered to nothing. Oh, they still exist to give the regime a thin veneer of legitimacy, but have fully fallen under the control of Juska's minions."

Morane's face seemed to sag.

"It's a nightmare, Farrin. In ten short years, Derik Juska has transformed the Republic of Lyonesse into a morally corrupt dictatorship fully under his control. You are the most senior official from the pre-Juska era still free, and the Republic — the true Republic, not the perverted incarnation thereof currently holding sway — needs you. Come to Yotai and take your place as the leader of the resistance. Our primary cell is established on Yotai, and it will receive you."

Morane gave a series of instructions for making contact in the less savory quarter of Yotai's second city. When he was done, he stared at the video pickup with an intensity Norum had never witnessed.

"Farrin, you represent our best chance of overthrowing Juska. The public still knows your name, and the Defense Force rank and file revere it. Please join us in ousting Derik Juska. Until then, may the winds always be at your back, old friend."

Lucas Morane's face faded from the display, and Norum let out a breath he hadn't known he'd been holding.

"What if it's a fabrication meant to lure you back into Republic space so Juska's goons can nab you?" Weston asked. "They still want you dead, as we saw with the most recent attempt on your life last year."

"Don't think that hasn't occurred to me."

— 8 —

"Surely you're not thinking of going?" Currag DeCarde exploded as he frowned at his friend. Norum had just finished playing the video for him, Torma, Sister Maryam, and Admiral Godfrey in the latter's office the next morning.

Norum raised both hands. "Peace, Currag. First, I need someone well-versed in such matters to analyze the video and determine whether it's authentic or a fabrication, and if it's for real, figure out if Lucas is under coercion or speaking freely."

"I can assist in that respect," Torma said. "The Commission for State Security has the best authenticators in the Empire. If you'll give me a copy of the video, I'll pass it along to a colleague who can get it done while preserving absolute confidentiality."

"Thanks, Crevan."

DeCarde scowled. "But even if it is Lucas, and he's for real, you're not going to throw your life away by joining some forlorn crusade. History has proved that once autocrats of Juska's sort have established themselves, nothing short of a foreign war, hot or cold, can oust them or their successors. Grassroots resistance movements have never succeeded."

Norum, wearing a faint smile, raised a finger. "But there is a first time for everything. Don't worry, Currag. If, and that's a huge if, I decide to join Lucas' forlorn crusade, as you put it, I won't be going in blind. But first, let's allow Crevan's colleague to check the video."

"If?" DeCarde shook his head. "You're a bloody crusader, you are. There's no if. It's a clear no because you'd be signing your own death warrant, should you be so stupid as to go."

Unwilling to let the dispute between the two friends continue, Godfrey said, "We can get together and discuss the matter further after the Commission expert analyzes the video."

"Okay." Norum climbed to his feet, retrieved the data wafer from the office reader, and handed it to Torma. "Here you go."

For the next two days, no one spoke of the video message from Lucas Morane, to Norum's relief. Morane's plea to lead the resistance against Derik Juska haunted him, eroding his resolve. Norum had served the Republic he loved most of his adult life until Juska summarily dismissed him upon assuming power. And that Republic — the one that had existed before Juska twisted its government to serve his ambitions — was worth fighting for.

But he didn't share his thoughts with anyone, let alone DeCarde and Weston, who'd have dragged him into a long, existential debate about whether he still had a responsibility to a now-extinguished ideal. Because Norum was well aware that both had given up on the Republic's prospects a long time ago and slipped comfortably into their lives as Imperial citizens.

Still, he felt a vestigial connection to that paradigm and its preservation against the odds.

On the third morning, Torma forwarded a highly confidential message from the Commission for State Security to him. Norum read it, sat back, and sighed loudly enough to attract DeCarde's attention.

"You sound like someone raided your wine cellar, Farrin."

"Torma's contact at the Commission sent back the results of the video analysis. It's genuine. That's Lucas Morane, not some facsimile generated by a sophisticated AI."

DeCarde scoffed. "How can they be sure?"

"No idea, but it seems that the best authenticators in the Empire have determined it to be so."

"And is he under compulsion?"

"It appears not. Before you ask, they didn't say how they determined that either. Probably used a Sister of the Void's fey abilities to figure it out. Anyway, as far as the Commission — the most ferociously efficient police service in the known galaxy — is concerned, that's a genuine plea from a real Lucas."

"What will you do about it?"

Norum let out a bark of humorless laughter. "Not a clue."

"I suppose that's a better answer than packing a bag, heading for the secret smuggler's HQ, and finding a ship's captain crazy enough to take you to Yotai."

"I couldn't tell you where to find such a daring smuggler."

"Ask Crevan. I'm sure the Commission has a few on retainer, either voluntarily or involuntarily. Or Imperial Intelligence. They must have several undercover ships operating between the Republic and Wyvern if they're getting intel like what we've seen in recent times. Not that I'm encouraging you. As I may have mentioned, an attempted uprising against an established autocracy is generally quixotic absent external threats."

"Yeah, I get it, but still."

DeCarde gave Norum a stern look. "No. Don't even think about it."

That evening, Norum and Rey Weston had a long discussion about the growing pull he felt to return and dedicate himself to overthrowing Juska's regime. Weston's opposition got more and more vehement as darkness fell over New Draconis, and finally, she retired to bed, leaving Norum alone with a glass of whiskey, which he sipped while sitting on the balcony, staring out at the city lights.

Weston and DeCarde were correct, of course. The chances of him being caught by Juska's Office for the Security of the Republic were high the moment he set foot on Yotai, and once he was in their clutches, he'd most certainly die, probably after the sort of interrogation that would leave him a drooling imbecile. And yet, he still remembered his oath to defend the Republic against all enemies, foreign and domestic. That oath remained in force, even though he'd retired a decade ago, and Juska certainly qualified as a domestic enemy, one who'd dismantled the Republic to which he'd sworn allegiance.

When he finally slipped into bed, well after midnight, Weston was sound asleep, but Norum remained awake for a long time, continuing the internal debate he'd been having since Lucas' message first appeared on his communicator. Only now it seemed more urgent since the Commission for State Security had declared the video genuine. His old friend and shipmate had called on him for help against Juska's tyranny. Could Norum simply ignore the appeal and still consider himself an honorable man? The answer to that question struck at the very core of his belief in who he was.

"Farrin, Currag, please come in." Admiral Godfrey waved them through his office door and pointed at the vacant chairs in front of his desk. Torma and Sister Maryam already occupied two of them. "Sit."

When Norum and DeCarde had complied, Godfrey's expression hardened.

"We are about to discuss something classified Top-Secret Special Access. You will not talk about it outside of this office, even among yourselves. Understood?"

He speared each of them in turn with his eyes, for the expected nod. When the four had acknowledged, Godfrey relaxed.

"Intelligence has received a disturbing report from the Republic, and since Farrin and Currag are our best sources for confirmation, Admiral Mindar has asked me to see what you think."

"Fire away, Johannes," Norum said.

"Our people in the Republic have picked up rumors of a certain virus that originally spread in the decades after the Great Scouring, when barbarians from beyond the frontiers looted Imperial research facilities and accidentally infected themselves with it. The barbarians in question almost reached Lyonesse, but the Republic's Navy stopped them at the last minute. Sound familiar?"

Norum and DeCarde both nodded simultaneously.

"Funnily enough," the former said, "we call it the Barbarian Virus, since we found nothing in our records to identify the origin, beyond its DNA bearing some resemblance to that of other viruses causing baneful diseases. The Barbarian Virus is invariably fatal within two weeks at most of infection, but dies with the host and doesn't linger on surfaces. It is extremely virulent, though transmission is entirely via personal contact or aerosols from coughing or sneezing, proving it was designed as a particularly vicious bioweapon. If Dendera's Retribution Fleet had used it, humanity would have been totally wiped out."

"That's what Admiral Mindar was afraid of. Her contact heard rumblings of President Juska planning to use the virus against the Empire, which implies the Republic retained samples of the virus."

Norum grimaced.

"It did. The Republic has kept them for comparison purposes, should it ever reemerge in the wild. For the first two hundred years after the threat vanished, the Republic stored the specimens in stasis inside an isolated, high-security biolab on Gwaelod, the outer of Lyonesse's three moons. It was moved to Gennari, the larger of Yotai's two moons, twenty-five years ago. The existence of the samples is Top-Secret, Need-to-Know, since public reaction to the revelation that we've kept the virus in a state where it could do harm would be extremely negative and could threaten the stability of the government. Or at least that was the thinking before Juska took over."

He gave Godfrey a speculative look. "Intelligence must have some well-placed assets to hear about Juska's plan to unleash the Barbarian Virus on the Empire."

Godfrey raised both hands, palms facing outward. "That comes under the heading of don't ask because Admiral Mindar won't tell, but thank you for corroborating the intel that came from Yotai. If the President is indeed intending to conduct biological warfare on the Empire, how do you think he'll go about it?"

Norum shrugged. "Probably infect a few unwitting smugglers and then send them to various Imperial worlds with high-priority cargoes. They'll be fully infectious and likely rather sick by the time they land, and before we know it, the Barbarian Virus will tear through local populations like a starship with an uncontrolled hyperdrive."

"And there's no cure?"

"None. The only thing that stops the virus is the host's death."

"We should forbid anyone who's been in the Republic from landing on an Imperial world?"

"It may come to that. Of course, enforcing it is another matter. The Empire has spread enough in the last five years that hermetically sealing it off from the rest of the galaxy has likely become impossible. But that doesn't mean the government shouldn't put quarantine measures in place now rather than wait for more intel."

Godfrey grimaced. "Hard to do without panicking the population."

"Not taking any action would be criminal."

"True. I'll get back to Admiral Mindar and suggest the Grand Admiral speak with President Benes on the matter. But I can't help thinking it would be easiest if we simply destroyed the biolab before Juska deploys the virus."

"That's for sure."

The admiral gave Norum a speculative look. "You wouldn't happen to know precisely where on this moon of Yotai the biolab is, would you?"

"As a matter of fact, I do, since it comes under Defense Force jurisdiction and is one of the secrets an outgoing CDS passes in person to his replacement."

DeCarde noticed a strange glint in his friend's eyes and frowned, but held his peace for the moment.

"Would you pass this secret to intelligence? Or does that come under the things you will not share with us because of your oath?"

"Considering the risk it poses to several billion human beings in the Empire, I'd be glad to tell Admiral Mindar exactly where this biolab is."

Godfrey nodded with satisfaction. "I expected no less of you, Farrin."

Norum gave him a half-grimace. "If Juska intends to deploy the Barbarian Virus against the Empire, he's planning on committing a crime against humanity that's second only to Dendera's use of the Retribution Fleet. Someone needs to stop him."

*****

The next day, Norum and DeCarde received an unexpected summons to President Benes' office. Since the Colonial Service's HQ was still in the Blue Annex, behind the Presidential Palace, it was a short walk to the latter's back door, where one of Benes' aides waited to guide them to his office.

There, they found Benes, Grand Admiral Anton Mejik, Admiral Tifa Mindar, and Magistra Abbatissa Ardrix sitting around a low coffee table in front of the expansive presidential desk. Benes, wearing a severe, dark civilian suit, sprang to his feet and smiled.

"Admiral Norum, Ambassador DeCarde, thank you for joining us at such short notice."

Try as they might, Norum and DeCarde had been unable to break Benes' habit of using their former ranks in the Republic.

"Mister President." Both inclined their heads politely.

"Please, sit." Benes gestured at the sofas on either side of the table while Mejik, Mindar, and Ardrix nodded at them in greeting.

Once they'd complied, Benes contemplated them for a few heartbeats before speaking.

"Admiral Godfrey related what you told him yesterday concerning this Barbarian Virus supposedly held in stasis by a biolab on one of Yotai's moons. This revelation is, to say the least, concerning. Especially when one factors in a totalitarian who intends to make the Republic the only human polity in existence. What do you two think about the chances of Juska using the virus against us?"

Both shrugged, and Norum said, "Hard to guess, sir. Biological warfare is fraught with danger for the aggressor and the target. Once released, a virus is almost impossible to control, and Juska certainly knows that. But will his goal of supplanting Wyvern override the caution he knows he should exercise? That is the unanswerable question."

"I also understand you've received a distress call, so to speak, from a friend in the Republic."

Norum nodded once. "Yes — Commodore Lucas Morane, retired. He's a direct descendant of Lyonesse's founder, Jonas Morane, and as upright, honest, and loyal to the old Republic's ideals as his ancestor. Lucas has asked me to return and take the leadership of the resistance against Juska's regime. Apparently, I'm the most senior official of the pre-Juska government still at large. Everyone else either vanished without a trace, voluntarily or involuntarily, or the regime arrested them.

"And are you considering it?" Benes' eyes narrowed almost imperceptibly as he gazed at Norum.

"I hadn't, but your question is leading to something, isn't it?" Norum returned Benes' stare with an emotionless one of his own.

"Correct. It seems rather fortuitous that your friends want you to lead the resistance against President Juska at just the time when we hear of a possibility that Juska might unleash biological warfare against us, and you not only know about the virus but where it's kept."

"So you'd like me to head for Yotai and see if I can destroy the virus stocks with the help of the resistance?"

"Something like that, yes. I suppose I could send a naval task force for the job, with you aboard to point out the target, but it would be a clear act of war and play into Juska's hands. That's if we could get a task force so deeply inside the Republic without being detected, which might be difficult."

Norum nodded. "And since Juska may have stationed a strong naval force in the Yotai system, even if your task force got there unseen, it could find itself in quite a fight, one that may not be winnable."

"Meaning you understand my problem."

"I do, sir." Norum's lips twisted into a humorless smile. "What the heck. I'm getting bored out of my skull at the Colonial Service. It'll be one last hurrah before I really get too old."

He glanced at DeCarde, who rolled his eyes as he shook his head.

"Are you coming with me, Currag?"

DeCarde let out a soft sigh. "I guess I should, since you need a keeper, someone to make sure you don't inadvertently walk into the nearest Office for the Security of the Republic bureau looking to buy a cup of tea."

Benes rubbed his hands together, smiling. "Then it's settled."

"Of course, we would have to change our appearance and biometrics and find a smuggler who'll take us to Yotai," Norum said. "Someone sharp enough to evade scrutiny by the Republic's Navy and the OSR."

"We can arrange both," Admiral Mindar replied, speaking for the first time. "Changing appearance and biometrics to evade detection is no problem. And you won't need a smuggler. I have several officers working undercover aboard single-handers, modern ships with the latest AI, sufficient weaponry for self-defense, and enough room to accommodate a half dozen passengers. If scanned or boarded, no one can trace the ships back to the Imperial Navy or government. They usually conduct reconnaissance in the Republic or the unclaimed star systems. The best of the lot, Lieutenant Commander Hal Paget, codename Rogue, will be returning to Wyvern within the next few weeks. Give him some time off while the yard goes over his ship, *Marlene*, and prepares her for the journey, and you can be off to Yotai in, say, six weeks at most."

"Okay." Norum nodded. "I think we might have the embryo of a plan."

Benes' smile widened. "Thank you, Admiral. I knew you'd step up."

***

"Why is it that whenever senior officers hear the sound of trumpets, they need to call the charge?" Rey Weston gave Norum an angry stare. "If you get caught, you'll both die. And where will that leave Beth and me?"

"You can always move in together."

Weston gave Norum a smack on the arm. "Idiot."

Then, unexpectedly, she burst into tears, and Norum wrapped her in a bear hug.

"It's okay," he said in a gentle tone. "We'll go to Yotai, destroy the lab, and come back. Quick and easy."

"You won't stay to lead the resistance?"

"As Currag keeps telling me, resistance movements against dictatorships have never overthrown them on their own. He should know, seeing as how he's a lifelong student of history. And since I don't believe in throwing my life away on hopeless causes…"

But even as he spoke those words of reassurance, Norum knew he wasn't entirely truthful.

— 10 —

New Lena, Yotai
United Stars Republic

"Sister Elana, please come in." Derik Juska, President of the United Stars Republic, waved at the chairs in front of his desk, an ornate thing large enough to host a gravball tournament. Imposing in appearance and poise, his thick, wavy gray hair topped a chiseled face in which intelligent, yet strangely emotionless eyes dominated. He was a charismatic man, with a deep, soothing voice, who projected an image of probity and deep concern for the Republic and its citizens.

"Mister President."

The Summus Abbatissa of the Order of the Void — or at least of the branch that didn't recognize the Motherhouse on Lindisfarne as being supreme — inclined her head politely and sat. She was Juska's opposite with a thin, ascetic face framed by long, blond hair. But her intense blue eyes, which missed nothing, were equally devoid of anything human. As she had so often before, Elana reminded Juska of nothing so much as a high priestess staring at her next sacrifice.

"And how is the Order's new Abbey?"

"Quite satisfactory and up to the task of being our Motherhouse. Most of the Sisters and Friars working on administering the Order have arrived from Lyonesse and taken up residence. I have therefore officially downgraded the Lyonesse Abbey to a planetary role only. But my, it will be so much easier to control the various abbeys and priories now that we're no longer at the far end of a cul-de-sac that requires us to make three wormhole transits simply to reach the closest nexus and from there, the rest of the galaxy."

"Oh, I do agree with you, Sister." A pleasant smile spread across Juska's face. "Governing the Republic from Yotai rather than Lyonesse is much more effective, not to mention convenient. The builders have performed miracles, transforming a sleepy backwater town like New Lena into a proper capital for the United Stars Republic in such a short time, and I believe most government departments have shifted their operations here by now. But let's get to it. We both have little time to spare on small talk. What did you wish to discuss?"

Juska sat back and graced Elana with a benign expression, one that often induced his interlocutor to speak candidly. He had rehearsed that expression for so long it now came instinctively, but it was lost on the Summus Abbatissa. The talent made her proof against any attempt at manipulation.

"A few things. First, if you'll recall, you asked me several months ago about using the Sisters skilled in psychological manipulation to reeducate dissidents and opponents of your government, maybe even turning them into your supporters."

"I remember. At the time, you seemed dubious."

"I was dubious because, two hundred years ago, an attempt failed spectacularly and our forebears discontinued that particular avenue of research." But after discussing it with my psychologists, we experimented on a prisoner transported to the Windy Isles for life. A volunteer looking for relief from his boredom and who doesn't like your government or any government, period."

"And?"

"It worked. We cannot tell how permanent the change is, but he now looks upon your administration favorably. Mind you, we took a gentle approach, which demanded time. My psychologists weren't comfortable with a more direct technique, fearing they might damage the man's mind."

"Could he have been shamming?"

An icy smile tugged at Elana's thin lips. "We'd know instantly if someone without mental barriers is lying, and trust me, the volunteer was an open book. With this success, we moved on to someone who didn't volunteer, a dissident arrested and placed among the Windy Isles transportees to make him disappear. Though it took more work on the part of my psychologists, they eventually reprogrammed him, so he no longer hates you and your government. Again, we do not know the long-term effects."

What Elana didn't mention was the half dozen other prisoners who'd gone irretrievably mad under the treatment. She didn't want Juska's unshakable confidence in her eroded by what had been, in the end, minor setbacks. After all, Elana had her own plans for the future of the Order, and said future meant much greater involvement in secular affairs. In effect, she wanted the

Void to become indispensable for Juska's continued rule over the Republic.

"Excellent." Juska beamed at Elana. "When can you send a few Sisters to the Yotai Re-education Center?"

"As early as tomorrow. But we'll need a list of people whom you wish us to reform. Perhaps we should start with the easier cases, those whose hatred of you and your government isn't quite that profound. But I must warn you — not everyone will be amenable to our techniques. There is a percentage of the population, a growing number at that, who can resist any attempts to meddle with their minds, and our efforts could be wasted."

Juska made a dismissive gesture. "I don't need all of the dissidents reconditioned. Just enough so we can show the public that re-education works, that we can transform rebels into law-abiding citizens. A bit of propaganda, if you like."

"Very well. On the second subject, we have trained three truthsayers, Sisters conditioned to be totally loyal to you. They can peer into minds and adjust inclinations as necessary without the subject ever finding out."

"What about those who are not amenable, as you called them?"

Elana shrugged. "The Sisters would still be capable of determining the veracity of their pronouncements, but could not look into their minds or inject adjustments."

"And when do I meet them?"

"They're waiting in your antechamber."

And they weren't totally loyal to Juska. On the contrary. Their loyalty would always lie with the Order foremost. Oh, in everyday dealings, Juska would find them utterly dependable. But should his needs be contrary to those of the Order, the latter would win every time because the truthsayers had not, in fact, been conditioned. They remained fully under Elana's control. Still, the fact that Juska accepted Elana's statement at face value was pleasing. It meant his trust in her remained complete, and that's what she wanted.

It was a shame she couldn't do much more than nudge Juska mentally, but he was a psychopath, and instead of a soul that could be manipulated, all she'd found inside him was a great emptiness. One he was trying to fill in vain by accumulating power. Part of Elana pitied him. The other part continually searched for different ways to manipulate him so she could advance the Order's interests.

"Then call them in and present them to me."

Elana briefly closed her eyes as she reached out to brush the Sisters' minds. No unspoken words were exchanged, but they knew the mental feather tickling their consciousness was a summons. Moments later, the office door opened, and three black-robed Sisters of the Void entered. They stopped in front of Juska's desk in an orderly row. Elana stood and gestured toward them.

"May I present Sister Clemenza, Sister Yarett, and Sister Nanta." Each Sister bowed her head when Elana called her name.

The three had the ageless air of Void adepts — smooth-skinned faces, eyes that seemed immeasurably old, and serene expressions that appeared honed over decades — although they differed in height, hair color and length, and complexion.

"They will serve you well, Mister President."

And report back on anything Juska said or did.

***

"Ah, Admiral, do come in." A smiling Juska waved at the chairs in front of his desk as he watched Admiral Rylo Haggan, the Chief of the Defense Staff, come stiffly to attention just inside the office door.

"Sir."

Juska had personally picked Haggan to replace Gerhard Glass a few years earlier, and so far, he did not regret his choice. Tall, elegant, with swept-back silver hair and dark eyes framing a hawk's nose, Haggan looked like the perfect example of an admiral, down to the well-fitting Navy dress uniform with the four stars of his rank on the shoulders and rows of ribbons on the left breast.

But he was a ruthless man, one without scruples, pity, or empathy, a man willing to do his master's bidding no matter what the latter demanded, and that made him precious to Juska. Haggan, in return, understood he'd never have become CDS if it weren't for Juska. In the Navy, which still valued leadership and respect, people saw him as a consummate careerist. He had advanced to flag officer rank because he used any means necessary for advancement, including crushing his competitors.

After Haggan sat down, Juska raised an eyebrow. "What news, Admiral?"

"The isolation lab has brought the virus out of stasis and infected a half dozen test subjects with it. They were dead within three weeks, and the virus itself died off another seven days later, leaving the chamber used for the experiment entirely virus-free. It is the perfect biological warfare agent. We can start reproducing it at any time, though I recommend we wait for the diffusion containers and distribution channels to be ready before beginning large-scale breeding."

"How long before everything will be ready?"

"Approximately ten weeks, if we want to ensure not a single specimen escapes. Then, we can deploy the canisters aboard smugglers to the Hegemony's various worlds."

"And how will you ensure those smugglers don't bring a dose back?"

"Their ships will be destroyed the moment they appear near a Republic-controlled wormhole buoy." Haggan's matter-of-fact tone didn't seem to faze Juska.

"What about the test subjects?"

"My people burned their bodies and then spaced the remains."

"Anyone we know?"

"Just habitual criminals who'd never have seen the light of day again anyway."

"And the researchers who carried out the testing?"

A faint smile creased Haggan's lips. "No need to worry about them. They're Sisters of the Void. No one else was involved. And we know that their ability to keep secrets surpasses any other organization in the Republic by far."

Juska nodded once. "Good."

—11—

Wyvern
Second Empire

Reeve's eyes snapped open as she felt a prickling throughout her body, although she couldn't remember where she was or why. It took her mind a few minutes to clear sufficiently so that she remembered she lay inside the stasis chamber aboard an undercover patrol starship.

"Marlene?"

"Yes," the familiar disembodied voice replied.

"Where are we?"

"At Wyvern's heliopause. I have awakened you as planned."

"How long was I out?"

"Twenty-three standard Wyvern days, ten hours, and forty-four minutes."

Reeve's mind spun at the idea she'd irretrievably lost over three weeks of her life, but they'd arrived. She checked Paget, lying next to her, and was relieved that he, too, had come out of stasis and was breathing normally.

"Open her up, Marlene."

"Certainly."

The stasis chamber door swung aside, allowing light from the cargo hold to stream through.

"Wha—" Paget's voice came out as a croak. "What's going on?"

"You're awake!" Reeve glanced at him and saw confusion writ large across his face, but his eyes were open. "Come on, let's get you out of here, and I'll tell you about what transpired since the old witch on Lothair Five knocked you on your ass."

She climbed out of the stasis chamber and helped Paget do the same.

As they slowly made their way to the galley, Paget said, "The last thing I remember is some old woman with light on her fingertips pointing at me."

"And here it is, three and a half weeks and countless light-years later. We're at Wyvern's heliopause."

Once seated across from each other in the galley, glasses of water in hand, Reeve explained what had happened on Lothair Five, the aftermath, and her decision to place both of them in the stasis chamber.

When she fell silent, Paget nodded appreciatively. "Well done. You likely saved my life."

Reeve grinned back at him. "There's no likely about it, sunshine. Plus, after we lifted off and Marlene couldn't tell when you'd wake up, I catheterized you. An unforgettable experience I will try to scrub from my memory until the end of time."

Paget winced. "Ooh. That's going above and beyond the call of duty. Speaking of which, Marlene?"

"Yes."

"Two things. First, send an encrypted message to HQ advising that we're inbound early—"

Reeve raised a hand. "I wrote a report concerning events on Lothair Five for your superiors."

"Did you now?" Paget cocked an eyebrow at her. "Well, I'll read it before sending it, not because I don't trust you but because I'd better know what happened before HQ finds out. Marlene, second item, plot a course for Wyvern."

"Already done," the AI replied. "Do you wish to verify it?"

"I don't think my mind is quite clear enough to tackle hyperspace navigation just yet, so after sending the message, let's jump inward."

"Message sent. Thirty seconds to FTL."

Paget gave Reeve a small smile. "Say what you like about AIs, but they make life easier."

She inclined her head. "That, they do."

Once they jumped and the nausea passed, Paget sat back and studied Reeve.

"Since we'll be landing on Wyvern in about twelve hours, I think it's time we discussed your future."

Reeve fluttered her eyes coyly. "Can I stay with you aboard *Marlene*?"

A grimace. "Even if I wanted you to, she's a Navy ship and you're not Navy. I can't just take you on as crew like that. Besides, I'm used to being alone."

She gave him a disappointed look. "But we work so well together. Just look at Lothair Five."

Paget glared at her. "Yes, I know. You saved my life." He let out a sigh. "It wouldn't be right simply to abandon you in the Wyvern space dock." Let me discuss this with my superiors once we arrive. I'm sure we can figure something out."

"Okay." Reeve shrugged. "And if not, I'll just find an Imperial-flagged tramp that needs an engineer and sign on. With the Empire's breakneck expansion, that shouldn't be difficult."

He gave her an ironic look. "You're not going to head back into the Republic?"

"You mean Derik Juska's Lyonesse First paradise? Not if I can help it." She put on a sardonic grin. "In fact, I'll go underground in the Empire before I let anyone ship me back."

"There's no danger of that happening. We gladly take in any human beings seeking sanctuary, especially those looking for jobs, because we can't keep up with demand."

"Good."

When they emerged from FTL twelve hours later, Paget queried the Imperial Intelligence node and received instructions to land at an out-of-the-way naval facility, known as Joint Base Byzance, which serviced undercover ships such as *Marlene*. Once they were on the ground and all systems except the AI shut down, Paget, a bag with his personal possessions in hand, met Reeve, who carried a much smaller bag with the things Paget had given her from ship stocks, at the top of the open ramp.

He'd sent the mission report, complete with the part on Lothair Five written by Reeve, the moment the ship had dropped out of FTL at Wyvern's hyperlimit. By now, his superior, Captain Delibes, should know that she was aboard Marlene and the circumstances of her rescue. That he hadn't been waved away from the facility and ordered to land elsewhere meant Delibes accepted his judgment that she wasn't a Republic spy.

Paget had settled *Marlene* into a landing bay barely larger than she was, with walls towering over the ship, hiding her from any casual onlookers. As soon as they stepped off the ramp, two naval ratings wearing dark blue work uniforms and black berets, one of them a petty officer, appeared through the bay's personnel door. Both came to attention and saluted.

"Welcome home, Commander. Captain Delibes will see you immediately." The petty officer turned his head toward Reeve. "And you must be Sela Reeve. Please come with us."

"Where are you taking her?"

"Into preventive custody until you've met with the captain, sir, at his orders. That's all I know."

"Preventive custody?" Paget cocked an eyebrow as he glanced at Reeve. "I guess Captain Delibes needs to speak with me about your future, Sela. Don't worry. It's just a way of making sure you don't wander off into parts of the base you shouldn't."

"We will make her comfortable."

Reeve grinned. "How comfortable?"

Instead of answering, the ratings took position one on each side of her, and the petty officer nodded toward the door.

"Shall we?"

They headed off, and Paget followed them. Once out of the landing bay, one of a dozen lined up along an airstrip, they made their way to the sprawling, two-story base headquarters building under a bright, early afternoon sun. Clad in gray granite pierced by polarized windows, the flat-roofed structure appeared somnolent, but Paget knew from experience that it was a hive of activity inside its walls. They entered through the main doors, but once in the lobby, Reeve and the two ratings headed left, down a corridor leading to the base security office, while Paget took the stairs.

He stepped into the antechamber to the base commander's office and announced, "Lieutenant Commander Paget reporting to Captain Delibes as ordered."

The rating sitting at a desk beside the inner door jumped up, smiling. "Welcome home, Commander. You can go right in."

Paget did so and stopped three paces in front of Delibes' desk. Since he was in civilian clothing, he didn't salute.

"Good afternoon, sir. You wanted to see me?"

"At ease, Hal. Grab a seat." Delibes, a dark-haired man in his early fifties with intense brown eyes and a gray beard framing a square face, gestured at the chairs in front of his desk. "Interesting expedition you had, even if it was a bit shorter than planned."

"You could say that, sir," Paget replied with a grin as he sat.

"Tell me about this Sela Reeve. Is there any chance she's a plant from the Republic sent to infiltrate the Reconnaissance Program?"

"I don't see how that's possible, sir. Before I arrived, someone abandoned her on Coraline, and we found her former ship's debris, including dead bodies, at the hyperlimit. Besides, she was thoroughly frightened when she ran aboard *Marlene*. Yes, she has a checkered past, but she's a valuable starship engineer, with plenty of hands-on experience."

"Do you get along with her?"

"Yes. Sela is a proper shipmate. And before you ask, nothing romantic or physical happened between us. I'm not attracted to her, and she doesn't appear to have any attraction to me."

"How would you feel about keeping her aboard for your next mission?"

Paget frowned. "What would that be?"

"A little trip to Yotai, the Republic's new capital. Considering her background, Reeve might be useful."

A chuckle escaped Paget. "She'd probably kiss you right on the mouth if she were here listening to you."

"Oh? Reeve would enjoy remaining aboard Marlene?"

"She asked me outright if it was possible. Of course, since Marlene is a naval vessel and she's a civilian, I said no."

"That problem is easily solved by making her a direct entry warrant officer on the limited duties list. You say she's a competent starship engineer? We'll put her in the engineering branch. Reeve wouldn't be the first civilian engineer we directly enroll as a specialist reserve warrant officer to temporarily fill gaps while the Navy expands. Do you think she'd be up for that?"

A grimace twisted Paget's lips. "Tell you the truth, I'm not sure. She strikes me as having a distinctly unmilitary, if not quite anti-military bent to her character."

"But if it allows her to spend more time aboard Marlene…"

"We can only ask. But before we do, tell me what the mission to Yotai entails."

"You've heard of Admiral Norum, the former Republic Chief of the Defense Staff?"

"Hasn't everyone in the Navy? He's a troubleshooter with the Colonial Service these days, right?"

"Indeed. He's heading on a secret mission to Yotai along with his colleague, former Republic Ambassador Currag DeCarde, and Admiral Mindar assigned the job of conveying them to you."

"What's Norum doing on Yotai?"

Delibes shrugged. "No idea. He'll tell you if you need to know. Intelligence HQ classified this entire operation as Top-Secret Special Access and strictly compartmentalized its various parts. For instance, our current conversation is not to be repeated outside my office. If Reeve signs on, then she'll only be told about the destination once you're FTL away from Wyvern."

Paget nodded once. "Understood. When do we leave, and what about *Marlene*'s registration and our identification?"

"You leave in two weeks, just enough time to re-equip *Marlene,* and you'll be under credentials identifying you as coming from Ariel, one of the Republic's lesser repopulated worlds, where bribes will buy false entries into various databases. Shall we summon Sela Reeve and see if she's interested?"

"Sure."

Delibes called in his assistant and had him bring Reeve up from the security offices. A few minutes later, she stood in the open doorway, uncertainty clearly written on her elfin face. A smiling Delibes waved her in.

"Please join us. We were just discussing your future." He gestured at a chair next to Paget. "Take your ease. I'm Captain Martin Delibes. I'm in charge of the Special Reconnaissance Division and, thereby, Hal's commanding officer."

Reeve gave him a tentative nod. "A pleasure, Captain."

"I'm sending Hal and *Marlene* on a fresh mission in two weeks, and it'll be one where your experience could be extremely useful. Of course, since *Marlene* is a Navy ship and you're a civilian, we can't just put you aboard and send her off. But we have something called a Limited Duty List, where we enroll civilians as reserve warrant officers for a short period, usually to carry out a defined and carefully circumscribed assignment. At the completion of the assignment, they return to civilian life. It allows us to pay them properly and exercise necessary control over their activities."

"And you want to make me a warrant officer on this Limited Duty List?"

Delibes nodded. "Yes. For the duration of Hal's next mission in *Marlene*. Since you'll be undercover alongside him, you won't even wear a uniform or salute superior officers, for that matter."

"Where do I sign?"

— 12 —

Newly minted Warrant Officer Sela Reeve, Imperial Navy (Reserve), Engineering Branch, detailed to Imperial Intelligence, now equipped with credentials and a card with an advance on her first pay, so she could buy herself a set of clothes and sundry items, stepped out of the HQ building. She stopped and blinked at the sunshine.

"What do we do now?" She asked Hal Paget. "And for the next two weeks?"

"First, we get suites in the visiting officers' quarters, then I rent a car, and we head into Byzance, the nearest town, so you can patronize the local businesses to buy the necessities." Paget nodded at a three-story building behind HQ. "And the VOQs are in there. Then, this evening, once you're more suitably dressed, we'll enjoy a meal in one of Byzance's finer restaurants. Tomorrow morning, I have an appointment with the base surgeon to make sure I've suffered no lingering damage from that old crone's lightning ball. After that, we'll have to wing it. I will spend some time overseeing *Marlene*'s preparation for our mission, but we could visit New Draconis, for instance."

"I'd like that."

They headed off toward the VOQs in silence, Reeve still digesting her unexpected change in circumstances and wondering whether it had been wise to agree. Part of her wanted nothing to do with the Imperial military, but the idea of suddenly becoming a warrant officer in the Imperial Navy, even if it was only for a short time, tickled her twisted sense of humor. And at least she got to stay aboard *Marlene* a little longer. Perhaps she could even eventually find a way home.

When they entered the lobby of the residential building, a holographic AI wearing a naval uniform without insignia appeared behind a black plastic counter.

"What can I do for you?"

Paget pulled out his credentials and gestured at Reeve to do the same.

"Lieutenant Commander Hal Paget and Warrant Officer Sela Reeve, Special Reconnaissance Division. We each need an officer's suite for the next fourteen nights."

"Certainly, sir. I have 301 and 302 free, if that suits."

"It does, thank you."

"I've keyed the locks to your credentials. Is there anything else I can do for you?"

"No."

"In that case, enjoy your stay." The hologram vanished, and Paget led the way to a waiting lift.

"Handy things, those credentials," Reeve remarked as she stepped into the cab. "What will we do with them while on an undercover mission? Surely, we won't carry them, let alone leave them lying around."

"There's a secret compartment aboard *Marlene* where I store things I'd rather no one found. That's where they'll go once we lift off. I'll show you and make sure you can access it too."

"Why did we have to show the credentials? The AI can scan them while they're in our pockets."

"Because of privacy reasons. No one may scan credentials if they're not physically shown."

"Oh. Back home, government agents, including AIs, can peek at credentials whenever and wherever they want. It's one of the many measures the regime has instituted to tighten control over the masses. They don't advertise it, of course, but I figured it out when a pair of Hatshepsut cops nabbed me because I was being rowdy in a public place. They had my particulars at their fingertips, and the only way they could was if they'd scanned my credentials before I even produced them. It didn't used to be like that."

They stepped off on the third floor, and Paget unerringly turned left, where they found their suites at the end of the hallway.

Reeve entered hers and let out a low whistle of appreciation. Her new place wasn't very big, consisting of a bedroom, bathroom, and sitting room, but it had comfortable furniture and was much larger than any accommodations she'd ever enjoyed. Her shipboard cabins were but a fraction of the bedroom's size, and private heads had been rare.

Paget poked his head through the door. "C'mon, Sela. Drop your kit, make sure you have your pay card, and follow me. By the time we get to the main gate, a rental car will be waiting for us."

"Okay." She tossed her small bag on the sofa, patted her pants pocket, and said, "Let's go."

That evening, no one would have guessed Paget and Reeve were Navy officers as they sat in a corner of the dining room of a small, rustic inn on the outskirts of Byzance. Both wore casual, yet elegant outfits — she a short-sleeved white blouse and tan slacks, he an all-black combo of long-sleeved shirt and pants that suited his mysterious looks and olive skin.

Paget swirled the ruby red wine in his glass as he contemplated Reeve, who was finishing her plate of steak and fries.

"You know, I've noticed that you haven't asked any questions about our upcoming mission."

After chewing on and swallowing the last of the tender meat, she shrugged. "I figure you'll tell me when the time is right. Until then, there's no point wasting breath and spit."

A faint smile played on Paget's lips. "You'll do all right in the Special Reconnaissance Division, Sela. One of our rules is, ask no questions, and you'll hear no lies."

"A wise rule." She picked up her wine glass and took a sip. "I've been lied to so often, I shouldn't be able to distinguish the truth, but somehow, I still do. Most, if not all of the time."

"How's that?"

"I just know when someone's telling the truth. Not everyone, mind you. It's an instinctive thing. For instance, you've never lied to me. Withheld information, yes, but that's to be expected in your line of business."

"You can also tell if someone is withholding things?"

Reeve nodded. "Yep. I can't figure out how or why, though. There are some people I'm unable to read, period. But they're usually those with dead eyes. You know, sociopaths or psychopaths, folks without a soul. And they're the ones most prone to lying."

Paget cocked an eyebrow. "It almost sounds like you've got some of what the Sisters of the Void have."

A scowl creased Reeve's face. "Those black-robed d'ayvols? I certainly hope not. I would rather die than allow their sins to infect me.

"What do you have against the Sisters? Here in the Empire, they're respected healers, religious leaders, counselors, and aides."

"Back home, they meddle with your mind," Reeve growled. "I can feel them poking and probing without permission. Fortunately, I've learned to keep them out, and they don't even know it. In any case, let's stop talking about the d'ayvols."

"Sure."

But even as they spoke of other things, Paget couldn't help wondering about Reeve. Perhaps her sensitivity explained why she didn't last more than two years aboard any ship, even as she learned new technical skills at a speed he'd never witnessed. It might also explain her propensity for cheating at cards, as she gleefully admitted.

After a few days of idleness, interspersed with outings to New Draconis and other cities, Paget received notice that Joint Base Byzance had checked *Marlene* and resupplied her. This was the signal for Reeve and him to go aboard, make sure systems were green, and the consumable stocks refilled. And while Paget checked the systems, Reeve went through the food, water, and spare parts stocks.

After lunch in the galley, she sat back and gave him a speculative look.

"Either the next mission will be extremely long range, or we're carrying passengers. Not that I'm asking, but the pantry is a lot fuller than it needs to be for a twelve-week reconnaissance."

Paget stared back at her and then said in a lazy drawl, "You may well think so, but I cannot comment."

"Passengers it is, then, probably two of them. And since your boss was keen on enlisting me, I figure we're taking them deep into the Republic on some sort of special operation." She held up a hand as she grinned at him. "No need to answer. I can see it in your eyes."

"Like I said, no comment," Paget growled.

"Fine." With a wink over her shoulder, she left the galley.

—13—

"My own mother wouldn't recognize me." Currag DeCarde studied himself in the recovery room mirror.

"I didn't know you had a mother. I simply thought someone mixed mud and clay to create you," Norum said as he scrutinized his own transformed features.

"Me, a golem? Perish the thought. For one thing, I can speak."

"You're certainly big enough."

"Family genes that go all the way back to the fabled Ancestor, who lived during the last years of the Commonwealth and witnessed the birth of the First Empire."

"And you witnessed the birth of the Second. History may not repeat, but it rhymes. Let's take a look at you." Both men inspected each other, and Norum grunted with satisfaction. "There's no way a surface biometric scan will identify you."

"Or you. How long until the temporary plastic surgery wears off?"

"I think the doc said six months, give or take a few weeks."

"Should be long enough. A good thing we already said our goodbyes to Rey and Beth. They'd probably get nightmares from hearing our voices come out of unrecognizable faces."

At that moment, the door to the recovery room opened, and a tall, dark-haired woman wearing the four stripes of a Navy captain on her uniform collar entered. Norum smiled at her.

"What do you think, Gwen?"

Captain Gwen Skellan, their handler from Imperial Intelligence, smiled back. "A fine job, if I may say so, sir. I've brought your credentials, complete with new biometric data identifying you as coming from the Republic colony of Ariel."

She handed each a small card. "By the time you reach Yotai, those biometrics should be in the Ariel database, if anyone wishes to check them out. You, Admiral, are now Frank Blake, and you, Ambassador, are Paul Mortimer. You're both registered as independent merchants."

Skellan gestured at a side table where two small, well-worn, nondescript travel bags rested.

"Those contain your clothes, toiletries, and other personal effects. Everything in them, including the luggage and what you're wearing right now, originated in the Republic. You must not bring anything else, or they could tag you as someone who spent time in the Empire."

Both nodded. "Understood."

"We'll be taking you from here to Joint Base Byzance, south of New Draconis, where the Special Reconnaissance Division is stationed, and Lieutenant Commander Hal Paget, *Marlene*'s captain, will take charge of you." The ship is a former free trader that has been extensively upgraded under the skin and can outrun anything she can't outfight. Nothing aboard her directly links to the Imperial Navy, not even her small arms.

"*Marlene* has one other crewmember, a Warrant Officer Sela Reeve, who is originally from Yotai and has traveled extensively within the Republic and unclaimed space as a civilian crewmember aboard salvagers. She's considered safe for the mission, although she doesn't know what it is yet and won't until *Marlene* is FTL outbound from Wyvern, so no discussing the matter, even among yourselves, until Commander Paget reveals the destination. *Marlene* has a sophisticated AI modeled on those we found aboard the Ghost Fleet retrieved from Cascadia five years ago, minus the problems we uncovered, and that AI is omniscient within the confines of its hull. Since Reeve is apparently a highly talented starship engineer, the Almighty knows what she can pull from the AI."

"Got it," Norum replied. "We stay stumm until Paget mentions Yotai."

"Another thing, Paget doesn't know your primary target is the pathogen lab on Yotai's moon, Gennari. It's your decision whether to mention it and when. Nor does he know about your friend Lucas Morane's call for help. Again, your decision. However, Paget is absolutely reliable, and Intelligence conditioned him against interrogation. Due to time constraints and her enrollment on the Limited Duty List, Intelligence did not condition Reeve."

"Then she is the weak link," DeCarde said.

"Yes, but we've judged her experience as a Republic spacer and Yotai native outweighs the risks." Skellan paused for a moment, then added, "If you face a situation where she's likely to fall into enemy hands, you are authorized to terminate her if you judge she will imperil the operation."

"Harsh."

"It's a no-fail mission, Ambassador. Even the two of you are expendable if it means destroying the virus lab."

Norum and DeCarde glanced at each other, then the former said, "We get that and accept it."

"Okay. If you're ready, I'll fly you over to Byzance and place you in Commander Paget's capable hands. He's waiting to lift off the moment you're settled aboard *Marlene*."

"There's no time like the present."

Norum went over to the side table, picked up the bag marked Mortimer, and tossed it to DeCarde before picking up the one labeled Blake. They followed Skellen through the Imperial Intelligence HQ's maze of corridors until they reached an underground garage where she pointed at an unmarked aircar parked on one side.

"Our ride, gentlemen."

They landed outside Joint Base Byzance's main gate and drove through the security arch, as per normal procedure. Any aircar attempting to fly over the base's perimeter would have found itself coming under automatic control and steered away.

Once inside, Skellan took them directly to *Marlene*'s docking bay. By the time they stopped at the outer door, a tall, dark-haired man in his late thirties, with a bristling mustache and piercing blue eyes, stepped through. His appearance, though, was distinctly unmilitary. He wore black civilian trousers tucked into equally black boots and a long-sleeved white shirt under a black vest.

"Commander Paget, I presume?" Norum asked.

"It is," Skellan replied.

She climbed out, followed by Norum and DeCarde, and walked toward the silent, brooding Paget, who observed them with keen interest.

He inclined his head toward Skellan. "Captain."

"Your passengers, Hal. Frank Blake," she indicated Norum. Pointing at DeCarde, she said, "And Paul Mortimer."

Paget nodded at them. "Pleasure. A note of warning, I recognize you and can figure out which is which. My warrant officer doesn't, and we should keep it that way. I hope you won't mind our using first names. We never use ranks on a mission, and *Marlene* is too intimate for the formality of last names."

"Suits me," Norum replied. "How about you, Paul?"

"I'm fine with that."

"Okay," Skellan said. "My work here is done. Good luck and Godspeed."

Norum gave her a tight smile. "Thanks. Hopefully, we'll see each other again by the time six months are up."

Paget cocked a questioning eyebrow. "Six months?"

"That's how long the temporary plastic surgery altering our appearances will last."

"Ah. In that case, we should lift as soon as possible."

"Lead on." Norum gestured at the open door.

They entered, passed through the empty loading dock, and exited inside the bay where *Marlene* waited, ramp open. Norum sensed at once that the ship was ready to leave, not from anything overt but from the subliminal vibrations she emitted. There was no mistaking it. The Republic's corvettes, on which he'd served for many years, emanated the same aura immediately before liftoff.

When they walked up the ramp, a tall, slender woman with short platinum-colored hair, dark eyebrows, and a narrow face appeared — the mysterious Warrant Officer Reeve, a citizen of the Republic now serving the Empire.

"Sela, meet Frank Blake and Paul Mortimer, our mission specialists." Paget gestured at both in turn as he named them. "Frank, Paul, this is Sela Reeve, *Marlene*'s engineering officer."

"Pleased to meet you," Norum said, nodding pleasantly at Reeve, who wore an emotionless expression even though her intelligent eyes studied them intensely.

"Likewise," she replied in a husky voice. "Let me show you to your cabins."

Reeve turned on her heels and led them up a spiral staircase and along a narrow corridor with open doors on either side.

"One's here and the other there. Take your pick." She pointed at two small cabins across from each other. "Mine and Hal's are next to them. The galley is over there. Help yourself to any food you want, but keep the compartment clean. We usually eat together, but if you'd rather not join us, fine."

"Once you've chosen your cabin," Paget said, "Please stretch out on your bunks for liftoff. We're leaving immediately. Sela or I will show you around the rest of the ship once we've broken out of orbit. Oh, and before I forget, say hello, Marlene."

A disembodied voice replied, "Hello, Frank Blake and Paul Mortimer. Welcome aboard."

"That's Marlene, the AI. Ask her anything you want."

He vanished, followed by Reeve. Norum and DeCarde glanced at each other, and the former shrugged.

"I'll take this one, shall I?"

"Sure."

As they each entered their cabins, they felt the ramp close with a soft thud, then the whine of thrusters spooling up reached their ears. No sooner were they stretched out on their bunks than the whine hit a crescendo and an invisible hand pressed down on their bodies as *Marlene* broke free of the ground and rose vertically. A short while later, the hand vanished, and artificial gravity kicked in as the ship entered orbit around Wyvern. Norum and DeCarde climbed out of their bunks and quickly unpacked their bags, then they visited the galley and inspected its food stocks, and that's where Paget and Reeve found them.

"We're on our way to the hyperlimit," Paget said. "You want a quick tour of *Marlene*?"

"Sure."

— 14 —

Aboard *Marlene*
In Hyperspace

"Now that we're FTL," Paget said, "I can reveal our destination."

The four sat around the galley table, three with a coffee mug in hand, the fourth with a cup of tea.

"Considering I'm the only one who doesn't know, you might as well cut the dramatics," Reeve replied with a smirk. "I already figured it's somewhere in the Republic. Otherwise, you wouldn't need me."

"We're bringing Frank and Paul to Yotai, where we'll stick around as long as they need us. I don't know what they'll be doing on Yotai, and neither of us will ask."

Reeve dipped her head by way of acknowledgment. "Fair enough. Either of you gentlemen ever been on Yotai, or will you need a native guide?"

Norum and DeCarde glanced at each other, then the former said, "We've both passed through but haven't stayed long enough for anything more than superficial knowledge of the place. But I understand you left there some years ago."

"Sure, and much has probably changed since then, but I can still help."

"And we accept. You know that President Juska moved the Republic's capital to New Lena?"

"Yeah. I recall reading that in an unclassified intelligence digest while we were on Joint Base Byzance. Makes sense when you think about it. Lyonesse is too far from the center. But that probably means New Lena has expanded beyond belief since the last time I was there."

"Without a doubt."

A mischievous smile spread across Reeve's face. "You're not going there to assassinate that bastard Juska, are you?"

"Sadly, no."

"Didn't think so. Pity. But then, neither of you strikes me as a soulless killer."

Norum let out a chuckle. "That's a relief."

Reeve turned to Paget. "Please tell me you're not planning to go down the Hatshepsut branch of the wormhole network."

He shook his head. "No. I figure we enter the Republic's wormhole network at Parth."

"And what will we be? I presume Imperial Navy vessel is out."

"We'll be a trader registered on Ariel. Our IDs will show us being residents there."

Reeve nodded with approval. "Good choice. The place is still frontier enough to have laxer registration controls."

Paget winked at her. "I'm glad you endorse Imperial Intelligence's decision."

"It means your bosses are smarter than I figured."

"They're your bosses too. At least for the duration of this mission."

Reeve made a face at Paget. "Don't remind me I'm temporarily respectable."

"How long until we reach Yotai via the Parth branch?" Norum asked.

"A little under three weeks," Paget replied. "Two weeks or so in hyperspace on a single jump to Zephyron, an uninhabited star system a single wormhole transit from Parth, then a little over five days from Parth to Yotai via the wormhole network. The route is longer than the Hatshepsut one, but Parth has few inhabitants and no permanent military presence. We enter the network there, no one will ask questions. Any number of civilian traders and explorers head out into the wider galaxy and come back via Parth. Or so Imperial Intelligence says."

"And they'd be right," Reeve said. "I went through the Parth system often enough on salvage hunts. It has no wormhole control buoys. Or at least it didn't a few months ago. No permanent naval station, no buoys. You'll meet the first in that branch at Wormhole Takeshi One. And they do query every ship coming through the terminus inbound."

Paget grinned at her. "You're already proving your worth to this mission, Sela."

"You mean my sparkling personality doesn't count?"

"Personality will get you a cup of coffee in the spaceport mess hall, sorry."

Reeve stuck the tip of her tongue out at him. "Take your cup of coffee and commit an impossible act of self-reproduction with it."

Paget's grin turned into outright laughter. "You're pretty mouthy, Warrant Officer."

"As long as you think I'm pretty…" She gave him a smug look.

"Right. You win. I have no reply to that one." He glanced at Norum and DeCarde. "On that note, if you have nothing else to discuss, I suggest you go to hyperspace stations. Aboard *Marlene*, that means entertain yourselves because apart from the brief drop to normal space at Wyvern's heliopause, we'll be FTL for two weeks with nothing to do. The entertainment library is extensive. For example, it contains pretty much everything you need to work on a graduate degree in almost any discipline, if you're so inclined. Over the last few years, I've picked up a *magister* in hyperspace engineering and one in starship design with the New Draconis University's distance program."

Norum cocked an eyebrow. "Impressive. Those aren't easy subjects."

"It was either that or slowly going insane playing chess with Marlene."

"Any intention of pursuing a *doctoratus* in either subject?"

"The Almighty, no! A *doctoratus* would have me feel like I'm spinning around my own," he hesitated for a moment, as if searching for a better term than the one which came to mind, "black hole, learning more and more about less and less. I'm currently working on a third *magister*, in astrophysics this time. That'll keep me busy until they rotate me out of the Special Operations Division."

"Okay." Norum climbed to his feet. "Let me look at your library and see what can keep my brain busy during waking hours. If I can't find anything, it'll be a hell of a long trip."

— 15 —

New Lena, Yotai
United Stars Republic

"Thank you for seeing me, sir." Charisse Weber, Director General of the Office for the Security of the Republic, a small, intense woman with short dark hair framing a narrow, thin-lipped face, took the indicated chair across from Juska's desk.

"You're most welcome any time, Charisse. You know that." Juska gave her a benevolent smile. "Now what is it you want to share?"

Though technically, the DG of the OSR reported to the Secretary for Public Safety, Juska preferred bypassing him on certain matters. Weber's loyalty to him was beyond doubt. The secretary, on the other hand, harbored hidden ambitions, and for that reason, Juska couldn't fully trust him.

"I have a few matters you should hear about. First, our agents on Wyvern reported that Farrin Norum and Currag DeCarde have inexplicably vanished, although both spouses are still residing in their apartments and working for the New Draconis Police. They walked into Imperial Intelligence's headquarters two weeks ago and never came out. Or at least, men who looked like them did not come out, which makes us suspect they altered their appearance for a covert mission.

"And what's your opinion on where they traveled and the reason?"

Weber grimaced. "There's only one place they would go under a different guise, and that's back into the Republic. Why? Maybe to contact the so-called resistance."

Juska made a dismissive gesture. "They'll be thoroughly disappointed."

"Possibly not. So far, opposition to the government has been haphazard, thanks to our arresting those who could organize it. But Norum and DeCarde were not only very senior members of the Hecht regime with excellent reputations among dissidents, but they also had undisputed leadership and organizational abilities. The opposition might coalesce around them and become effective at operating against the government."

Juska briefly tapped his fingertips against his desktop. "That could become annoying. Keep an eye out for them."

"We'll have every ship coming from beyond the Republic's sphere examined."

"Good."

"Next, we've finally found Lucas Morane. But rather than bring him in, we're keeping him under close surveillance so he can lead us to former military personnel we'd rather not have at large, such as Al Jecks and some of the other retired flag officers of dubious loyalty. But not for long. We'll pick him up in two or three weeks at most."

"Excellent work. My compliments to the agents who tracked down Morane."

"I'll pass that on, sir. Next, the Sisters assigned to the Yotai Re-education Center have reported their first success. Serge Ferris, a former permanent undersecretary of public works, arrested for refusing to enforce your and the secretary's directives, has, apparently, been reformed and wishes to join the United Stars Bloc. The Sisters confirm he's not shamming. I propose we release Ferris and place him under surveillance for a few months."

Juska's lips pulled back in a smile that didn't reach his eyes. "By all means, do so. Interesting that they chose Ferris as the first candidate."

"I asked, and they said he has zero mental shielding but a deep personal dislike of you, which made him ideal."

"Hmm, I see. Who's the next one to be re-educated?"

"Former Commodore Julia Byner, who was the leader of a Navy cabal that plotted against you."

"I remember Byner. Thoroughly unpleasant individual. Called Lyonesse First a fascist organization that should be banned. Keep me apprised of her progress."

"Will do, sir."

"And finally, a request. Considering the Sisters are working so well with the OSR in the re-education center, I'd like to propose assigning one or two of them to each OSR field office to help interrogators by probing the minds of suspects. I do believe the Wyvern Hegemony does that with their Sisters."

One of Juska's many quirks was his refusal to acknowledge the transformation of the Hegemony into the Second Empire, because in his view, the Republic was the First Empire's sole heir.

Anyone who made the mistake of referring to the Republic's rival as the Second Empire would only do so once.

"An interesting idea. Maybe the moment is here to be more forward-thinking when handling the Republic's adversaries. I shall raise it with Summus Abbatissa Elana, and I think it will get a favorable reception. She does want a more proactive role in keeping the Republic safe."

"Thanks, sir. That was it."

Juska smiled warmly at Weber. "Thank you for your continued excellence in handling your responsibilities, Charisse."

The latter rose, bowed her head briefly, then left a thoughtful president staring at her receding back as she made her way across the immense presidential office to its open door.

He'd been waiting for Weber to make the suggestion rather than impose it on her. These things always worked better when he let his underlings propose. That way, there was no resistance, and if things failed, they would assume responsibility rather than point the finger at him. This proposal, formally placing Sisters in OSR field offices, would give Elana a wide-open window into the agency's affairs, something he suspected she'd been craving for a while. If Weber had realized it, she'd probably discounted the risks in favor of the benefits.

Juska touched the control surface embedded in his desktop. "Get me Sister Elana."

"Right away, sir," the voice of his executive assistant replied. A few moments passed, then, "Sister Elana for you, Mister President."

When the Summus Abbatissa's holographic image appeared, floating over Juska's desk, he smiled.

"Elana, how are you?"

"Quite well, sir. What can I do for you?"

"I've just received a proposal from Charisse Weber that involves Sisters being attached to OSR field offices so they can help interrogators. What do you say?"

Juska thought he saw a flash of triumph in Elana's eyes, but it just might have been an artifact of the holographic projection.

"It's an excellent recommendation, and I think I can accommodate the OSR as soon as possible, beginning with the local field offices."

"I will let Charisse know you approve of the idea. Perhaps I can leave the two of you to work out the modalities of the assignment, including the parameters governing the use of Sisters as interrogators."

Elana inclined her head. "Certainly. I can already assure you that the efficiency of the OSR in finding and removing dissidents will increase by an order of magnitude."

"Of that, I have no doubt. I shall let you get on with it, then. Juska, out."

As Elana's hologram faded away, Juska allowed himself a smile of pleasure. Integrating the Order of the Void fully into the government had long been an ambition of his. And now he'd achieved it. The fact that Elana had her own ambitions for the Order, however, remained a blind spot of his, and not by accident. Elana had ways of subtly deflecting his thoughts.

— 16 —

Aboard *Marlene*
Zephyron Star System

"Approaching Wormhole Zephyron Three terminus," Marlene announced. "We will cross the event horizon in fifteen minutes."

Paget drained his coffee mug and climbed to his feet. "We'd better head for the bridge, Sela. You two can stay in the galley if you like."

Norum and DeCarde nodded silently, then watched Paget and Reeve vanish into the corridor.

"And suddenly, it got real," DeCarde said in a soft tone.

"What did?"

"This mission. The last two weeks were simply lazy living. But now we're one wormhole transit away from Republic space. If the buggers put a terminus buoy in place at the other end since the last time Sela passed through, we may face scrutiny earlier than expected."

"We will face it eventually. If not after this transit, then after the next, once we come out in the Takeshi system."

"That's why I said it suddenly got real. We're about to enter enemy territory, and if we're caught and identified, I have no doubt Juska's goons will make sure we're never heard from again."

Norum gave DeCarde an amused smile. "Keep up the cheerful thoughts."

"Oh, I am."

Up on the bridge, Paget was making sure *Marlene* was on the right approach to hit the event horizon at the proper angle, when the AI suddenly said, "Two starships have appeared on my sensors five-hundred-thousand kilometers off my starboard quarter. They are accelerating on an intercept course."

"Damn. Any beacons?"

"No. And I cannot identify them as units of the Republic Navy. I am putting their image on the portside secondary display."

Paget and Reeve's eyes turned left, and they studied the rapidly approaching ships.

"Not naval units, that's for sure," Reeve said after a moment or two. "They look rundown, with hull patches, but no registration identifiers. There can be only one reason they were in silent running mode near a wormhole terminus."

"Pirates."

Reeve nodded. "You got it. And they decided we looked both juicy and harmless enough to warrant an intercept."

"Marlene, will we reach the event horizon before those two ships intercept us?"

"Negative." A heartbeat, then, "They have lit up targeting sensors and weapons and have raised shields."

"Then by all means, do likewise, and at full military power. Maybe that'll discourage them.

"Raising shields, unmasking and energizing weapons, and activating targeting sensors at full military power," the AI replied.

At that moment, Norum stuck his head through the bridge door, DeCarde behind him. "Couldn't help but overhear. We've got company?"

"Yep. Two unmarked, clapped-out-looking ships of different builds that were lying in wait, systems down."

"Pirates?"

Paget nodded. "Looks like it.

"They have locked onto us with targeting sensors," the AI reported. "I detect ten four-tube plasma calliopes on each of one-hundred-millimeter caliber. As well, each has one missile launcher open."

"Then lock us on as well."

Norum winced. "That's serious firepower against a small ship like *Marlene*."

"If she were an ordinary trader," Paget replied. "But she's a naval fighting ship beneath her innocuous looks. Her shields, weapons, and sensors are the latest in military-grade equipment. Still, I'd rather not fight if possible. Getting damaged this far from home wouldn't be a good thing, and I can't simply put into a Republic shipyard. They'd figure *Marlene* out as an undercover naval unit the moment they pop hull plates to repair systems."

"We are receiving an incoming transmission, voice only," the AI announced.

"Put it on."

"Hey there, you cute little trader," a male voice drawled in accented Anglic. "I think you can figure out we've got you cut off from the wormhole terminus, and we outgun you. Let's not make this more painful than necessary. Surrender, and we'll let you take the wormhole in your escape pod. You can call for help from Parth when you reach the other end. Otherwise, we'll simply shoot off your drive nacelles, hole your hull, and take your cargo once you're dead."

Paget and Reeve exchanged a glance. "Cute little trader?"

Norum snorted with amusement. "Pretty casual-sounding pirate. What'll you do, Hal?"

Smiling, Paget raised a finger. "Listen and learn. Marlene, open an outbound channel."

"Ready."

"Hello, you grotesque excuses for pirates. I suggest you turn away right now, before I transform you into ten thousand spare parts flying in close formation. If you'll refine your sensor scans of us, you'll see we're rocking military-grade shields, guns, missiles, and targeting gear. You don't have a chance in hell of taking us on and surviving. Fortunately for you, I'm in a hurry and don't have time to make you meet the Almighty in the Infinite Void. But if you force my hand, I'll do so gladly."

Paget cut the voice pickup and waited. After a minute or two, a low whistle came through the bridge speakers.

"You ain't kidding! That's a lot of high-energy gear built into your sweet little hull. Way too much for a regular trader. You some sort of undercover unit from the Republic's Navy?"

All four chuckled, and Norum said, "I wonder what he'd say if he found out this is an *Imperial* Navy ship."

"He'd probably think we're the vanguard of an invasion fleet. I'm turning the voice pickup back on now."

Paget touched the controls again.

"Let's just say it would be to your advantage if you avoided messing with us. If you decide to fight, we will at the very least cause you sufficient damage that you'll never get those old, ugly tubs of yours to the nearest shipyards for repair. It's your call, and you don't have much time left. You're almost within my optimal firing distance. I'll open up on you the moment I have my solution, and it'll be before you reach your best range."

"Entering optimum firing distance, Captain," the AI said. "Solution calculated. Ready at your command."

"Fire two warning shots across the bow of each ship."

"Certainly."

Almost immediately, they heard the faint clunk of the starboard batteries firing and saw plasma bolts speed off on the primary display.

"Okay, okay," the voice on the speakers said. "I'll grant that taking you on might be a bit too risky for us. Feel free to head for the wormhole with our compliments."

"Ships turning away," the AI announced. "They are powering down weapons and targeting sensors, though shields remain up."

"Smart move, whoever you are. My next shots would have destroyed your shields, and the shots after that would have punched through your hull. Since we'll be reporting this little encounter to Republic officials the moment we're in range, I suggest you bugger off lest the Navy come searching for you."

"I'll take that under advisement. But it would be best if you don't come back by way of this star system.

"If I come back and see you again, I won't wait to open fire. You'll be dead before you have time to react. Marlene, cut the link."

"Link cut."

"Let's keep an eye on the bastards, our weapons ready and our shields up until we cross the event horizon. Once in the wormhole, we'll re-tune the electronics to change our emissions profile so that they can't match it to what they undoubtedly recorded should we ever meet again. I hope you picked up theirs, Marlene."

"Of course."

"You can re-tune your systems without losing efficiency?" Norum asked.

Paget nodded. "The Navy rebuilt her that way. I can change the emissions profile at need and keep her anonymity. It's a must for an undercover ship. By the time we emerge in the Parth system, we'll be, for all intents and purposes, a different ship, albeit one with a generic configuration resembling hundreds of small traders active in the Republic and the Empire. We'll simply add a few hull patches once we're on the other side."

"Impressive."

"We are crossing the event horizon in two minutes," Marlene said. "Please take seats or a bunk."

***

The captain of the larger ship watched the overpowered trader cross the event horizon and vanish from normal space as he rubbed his chin, lost in thought. His and the other ship were under a secret contract to the Republic's Navy, with letters of marque, meaning they were privateers rather than pirates. Their orders — watch the Zephyron end of the wormhole connecting that star system to Parth and harass civilian vessels that weren't clearly identifiable as owned and operated by Republic shippers or crews. Of course, the privateers took harassment to a level the Navy probably hadn't contemplated, but who would find out?

He'd been pretty sure that the unknown trader didn't come from the Republic. First, it didn't broadcast the identification beacon required of registered vessels for the last few years; second, no trader he'd ever seen was that heavily armed and shielded. It was almost certainly up to something. Of course, there was still a possibility it might be an undercover Republic Navy unit returning home. Still, he figured he'd best be sending his employers a report about it, along with a record of its emissions profile, and let them figure it out.

— 17 —

Parth System
United Stars Republic

Marlene popped through the terminus of Wormhole Parth One and immediately engaged silent running, her passive sensors listening and watching for anything not naturally occurring, such as a Republic patrol ship or terminus control buoy. But after an hour of detecting nothing, Paget lit her up.

He and Reeve then donned exosuits and climbed out onto the hull. They pulled hull patches from an open cargo hold and set about modifying the ship's appearance. Once they were done and back inside, Paget sent a recon drone out a few thousand kilometers and had it scan *Marlene*. When the results came in, he nodded with satisfaction.

"Whatever readings those pirates took, we're for all intents and purposes a different ship. Time to set a course to Wormhole Parth Four and the Takeshi system."

"You'll make a standard dogleg to avoid the star?" Norum asked.

Paget nodded. "Yes. I'll emerge from FTL just outside the star's hyperlimit and change heading. Obviously, you've passed through Parth before."

"A long time ago, but I still remember that Wormholes One and Four are on opposite sides of the sun." Norum gave him a wink.

Reeve, watching the interplay with an expressionless face, suppressed a frown. Frank Blake, or whatever his real name was, appeared to be familiar with not only Republic space but also starship navigation. She found that interesting. Over the few weeks they'd been cooped up together in *Marlene*'s tight confines, Reeve had formed the opinion that both of their passengers were former military men, and likely from the Republic. Blake's latest statement seemed to confirm her latter assumption. But she didn't dare ask any leading questions. Mortimer, in particular, came across like the type to cut her throat and space her body if she dared go where she wasn't supposed to. He simply exuded that sort of danger.

They went FTL moments later and settled in for six hours of inactivity. When they emerged at the halfway point, before Paget could enter the course change, Marlene spoke.

"I'm picking up a message on the emergency band.

"Put it on the primary display."

The face of a middle-aged man with a scruffy white beard and short white hair appeared.

"Any ship in the Parth system, this is the independent freighter *Nakamura Maru*. We have experienced an antimatter containment failure, destroying our hyperdrives, and have vented the remaining fuel, leaving us dead in space. We are at coordinates Parth beta-gamma-one-four-three by delta-alpha-five-six-zero by epsilon-theta-seven-two-eight. Any ship that hears this, please help us. We are six crew members, and we will die once the battery power runs out in two days."

Paget grimaced when his eyes met Norum's questioning gaze. "I have no choice. Under the ancient rules of spacefaring, I'm honor-bound to assist, even in Republic space."

"I know."

"Marlene, open a channel."

"Ready."

"*Nakamura Maru*, this is the free trader *Lark*. I've just dropped out of FTL on my way from Wormhole One to Wormhole Four and am in your vicinity. I can help."

"Oh, thank the Almighty, *Lark*," the same man as in the message replied after a few heartbeats. "The Parth system can go for days with no traffic. I'm Captain Silas Maymier, by the way."

"Captain Caleb Thano," Paget replied. "Give me a moment to triangulate your position."

"Got him," Marlene said. "He's just over a million kilometers away. Putting him on starboard secondary."

The image of a ruined bulk freighter appeared. Where its hyperdrives should have been, there was nothing but the stubs of the pylons that used to link them to the primary hull. It was tumbling erratically, though apart from the missing drives, it seemed relatively intact.

"We found you, Captain Maymier, and are on our way. Prepare to evacuate your ship using your escape pod. There is no way we can dock with it the way it's moving, and we're too small to steady it with tractor beams, let alone tow it to Parth."

"Beggars can't be choosers, Captain Thano. We'll eject once you come alongside."

"Okay. *Lark*, out. Marlene plot a microjump."

"Already done."

"Engage."

The wrench of going to hyperspace barely passed when it kicked in again as they returned to normal space a few hundred kilometers from the *Nakamura Maru*.

"We're here, Captain Maymier."

"Excellent. Give us twenty minutes to prepare."

"Alright. Just one question for you. Did your distress call reach Parth?"

"Oh, aye. Two hours ago. They sympathized with me, but there was no starship available to rescue us in this system, and so they sent a message to the naval station in the Takeshi system. So far, I've not heard back, but I expect a Navy ship to come through the wormhole on a rescue mission. When is the question. But now that you're here, it becomes moot."

"I guess it is. Let us know when you're about to eject."

"Will do. *Nakamura Maru*, out."

Paget swiveled his chair to stare at the others. "We will arm ourselves before they come aboard. Loaded with live rounds and ready to fire."

"You think they might try something?" Norum asked.

"I'd rather not take chances. That ship isn't a liner belonging to a shipping company, which means it can carry just about anything. Or nothing. Plus, an antimatter containment problem blowing off both hyperdrives hints at serious maintenance issues.

They're probably smugglers, and that breed has no issues taking another ship when theirs fails."

"Then why don't we just leave them for the Navy?" Reeve asked.

"Can't. They might lose all power before a naval ship gets here, and we cannot condemn human beings to death on a supposition."

Reeve gave him a sardonic look. "Look at you, having a conscience."

"He's right," Norum said. "Spacers don't let other spacers drift off into potential death, unless they're confirmed pirates."

She raised both hands in surrender. "It was only a suggestion."

"Okay." Paget gave her a quick glance. "What I want to do is as follows. I'll have their escape pod dock on the portside universal ring and wait for them just outside the inner airlock door. Sela will stand by behind me with a handheld sensor to scan them for weapons. Frank and Paul, you'll be standing in the corridor on either side of the airlock, weapons hidden but ready to open fire should they decide to charge in. Frank, you'll guide them into the portside midships cargo bay. The rules of engagement are simple. If they obey my orders, we're good. Otherwise, you're weapons free. And Marlene, you're not to speak while they're aboard."

"Understood, Hal."

DeCarde, Norum, and Reeve nodded. "Got it."

"And now, we wait."

Not quite twenty minutes later, the bridge speakers came to life. "*Lark*, this is *Nakamura Maru*. We're launching the escape pod now."

Their eyes turned to the display just in time to see a small, cylindrical shape separate from the hull.

"Sensors are detecting six life forms aboard," Marlene announced.

"Stand by tractor beam, Sela."

"Tractor beam ready."

Paget eyed the distance between *Marlene* and the escape pod and said, "Engage."

"Engaging." Then, "I have it."

"Bring it in slowly and rotate it so the airlock faces us."

After ten minutes of tense maneuvering under Reeve's control, they heard a dull clang coming from *Marlene*'s portside — the airlocks had mated.

Paget clapped his hands once and climbed to his feet. "Okay, folks."

Once they were in place, Paget opened the outer airlock door, eyes on the display beside the inner door. The escape pod's airlock opened, and Captain Maymier cautiously peered through. He carried no visible weapons, but Paget glanced at Reeve, who nodded.

"They're armed, but I'm not reading their guns as powered up and ready to fire."

Paget touched the control screen beside the inner airlock.

"Welcome aboard *Lark*. I'll open the inner door once you're all in the airlock and the outer door is closed."

Maymier nodded, and the six men of *Nakamura Maru*'s crew crowded in, each with two duffel bags no doubt containing everything they owned. Paget closed the outer door, effectively trapping them in the airlock.

"For your safety, I'm going to ask you to turn left upon exiting and follow the crewmember to the portside midships cargo bay. This is a very small ship, and there is really no room to let you wander, but the cargo bay is empty and spacious. Don't worry, it'll only be for the time it takes to reach Parth and land on the Harambee Spaceport."

"Understood," Maymier said. "Could I make a request?"

"Go ahead."

"Would it be possible for you to destroy *Nakamura Maru*? I don't have the money to salvage her, let alone pay for new hyperdrives and a new antimatter containment system, and she's a hazard to navigation. Surely you have sufficient defensive weaponry to do so."

"I can certainly do that."

"Would it be possible for me to watch, so I can swear, hand on my heart, that I saw her last moments?"

"Sure." Paget touched the control screen again, and the inner airlock door opened with a soft groan. "To your left, please. The crewmember taking you to the open cargo bay door will usher you into your temporary quarters. Captain Maymier, drop your luggage off, and I'll take you to the bridge."

Nakamura Maru's crew was a dour-faced lot, scruffy bordering on villainous, with suspicious eyes darting everywhere, reinforcing Paget's opinion that they were smugglers. But they made their way down the corridor and entered the cargo bay under Norum's supervision.

Maymier, divested of his bags, stepped into the corridor again while the cargo bay door slammed shut behind him. Paget gestured for him to follow.

"Compact little trader you have here, Captain Thano," Maymier remarked as they entered the bridge. "I'm surprised you have as many as four crew."

"I enjoy the company. Besides, the blond-haired man is a supercargo and not strictly a crewmember."

Maymier scratched the bristles on his cheek. "Supercargo, eh? Must be doing all kinds of good business."

"We do well."

"And where are you headed, if I may ask?"

"Home, to Ariel."

Paget took his seat and called up the gunnery controls on the console. Moments later, a soft whirring sound reached their ears as *Marlene*'s gun blisters opened to reveal four-barrel calliopes. The weapons locked onto *Nakamura Maru*, tracking her through every tumble. Paget touched the console again, and streams of plasma reached out, stitching the doomed freighter with blooms brighter than the sun that ate through the hull and tore it apart. After a minute or so of sustained firing, little remained but a slowly dispersing cloud of debris.

"There, Captain." The soft whirring sound returned as the calliopes dropped into their recesses and the blisters closed.

"Thank you. I'll sleep better knowing she's gone."

"Just out of curiosity, what were you carrying?"

Maymier shrugged. "This and that. Trade stuff."

Paget nodded, but Maymier's vagueness and visible discomfort at the question made him suspect *Nakamura Maru* had been smuggling illegal things. Likely drugs hidden in innocuous items, which might explain his desire to see the ship destroyed rather than leave it for the Navy to inspect once they arrived. It would have been salvageable, and the risk to navigation was pretty small.

"Right, let's take you to rejoin your crew, and we'll be on our way."

—18—

Marlene settled on the cracked, ancient tarmac of the Harambee Spaceport with a mere sigh. Parth had escaped the depredations of the Retribution Fleet, but losing contact with the rest of humanity for over two hundred years had nonetheless taken its toll.

The metal of her hull ticked as it cooled after reentry, and Paget waited for the outer temperature to drop before lowering the belly ramp. Once it had reached a safe level, he opened *Marlene* up just as rain came in curtains, splashing on the concrete with a thunderous glee.

Captain Maymier and his crew, released from the cargo hold, joined him and stared out at the downpour. Paget and Maymier had been told to wait aboard by the Harambee Spaceport, that someone would meet them, and they should have copies of their logs available.

"Another fine day on Parth," Maymier commented in a sarcastic tone.

But the rain let up as fast as it had come, and water steamed off the ground under the heat. Moments later, a ground car screeched to a halt at the base of the ramp, disgorging a bald, squat, uniformed official. He stepped on the ramp and looked up at them through small, piggish eyes.

"Which one of you is Thano?" He asked in a raspy voice.

Paget raised his hand. "I am."

"Maymier?"

"Here."

"Both of you will come with me. The rest will stay aboard *Lark* until I release them."

Paget and Maymier glanced at each other and walked down the ramp under the scrutiny of the official. When they reached the bottom, he said, "I'm Darius Davout of the Parth Traffic Control Commission. You are required to provide formal testimony about the wrecking and destruction of the *Nakamura Maru* in the presence of the Traffic Control Commission's director general. I assume you have copies of your logs?"

"Sure," Paget replied.

Maymier merely nodded.

Davout gestured at his car. "Please climb in."

He drove them across the spaceport to a sprawling single-story building with the Commission's name above the main doors. The sky was clearing at a rapid rate, and by the time they exited the car, the sun shone in all its brilliance, adding oppressive heat to the suffocating humidity.

Paget, who was on Parth for the first time, finally understood why the ancient Commonwealth had chosen it as a prison planet and why the First Empire had kept using it as such. He wondered whether the Republic did as well, but wasn't about to ask. If he legitimately came from Ariel, he'd already know the answer.

Davout led them into the air-conditioned building and to a small conference room where he pointed at the chairs and then left, closing the door behind him. Paget tried it and found it locked.

"Looks like they don't want us to wander," he remarked, walking around the room.

Maymier merely grunted in reply as he flopped into a chair and stared at his hands. After completing his circuit, Paget sat across the table from Maymier and slumped back, closing his eyes. He knew someone was watching them via hidden video pickups and wanted to present the picture of utter calm, in contrast to Maymier's grim countenance.

After nearly ten minutes, the door opened again, and Davout entered, followed by an older man with short gray hair, ascetic features, and a small goatee. In contrast with Davout, he wore civilian clothes adapted for the climate — light white trousers, a white collarless short-sleeve shirt, and sandals. They took seats at the head of the table, eyes on Paget and Maymier.

"I am Oren Gisk," the man said, "Director General of the Parth Traffic Control Commission. Officer Davout, you already know. We are here to ascertain the circumstances of *Nakamura Maru*'s total loss under the applicable laws and regulations governing space travel in the United Stars Republic. May I please see your identity chips?"

They passed their credentials to Gisk, who swept them over the small tablet he held in his left hand. It would be the first test of Paget's fake ID, and he studied the man's face while he read the results from his tablet. But Gisk merely returned them to their respective owners without comment.

"You have your logs?"

Paget fished a data wafer from his shirt pocket. "A copy of the entries since we crossed the Parth Wormhole One event horizon inbound. I don't think you require anything more."

He slid it toward Gisk, who frowned at him before turning to Maymier. "Captain?"

Maymier pulled an almost identical data wafer from his tunic and pushed it at Gisk. "It's complete. You'll see the antimatter containment malfunction as totally unexpected."

"Thank you, gentlemen." He touched a control embedded in the tabletop. "I have just activated the room's recording system. We will now proceed with the verbal testimony, which may be used in a court of law or an administrative tribunal should the need arise. Do you understand? Please give me a yes or a no."

"Yes." Paget inclined his head in a friendly manner, smiling, but Maymier seemed to tense up as he answered.

"Very well. Captain Maymier, your ship is registered where?"

"Arietis."

"A flag of convenience, then?"

"Yes."

"And what sort of shipping were you engaged in?"

"General freight."

"Only within the Republic?"

After a moment's hesitation, Maymier shook his head. "We also traded beyond the Republic's sphere."

"You're a smuggler?"

Maymier sat up. "No, sir. We always declared the cargo we brought into the Republic."

"I doubt that, but we'll pass on to the next question. Please describe the events leading up to the loss of your hyperdrives and your antimatter fuel."

As Maymier spoke, Paget became more and more convinced that maintenance on the *Nakamura Maru* had been spotty at best. It wasn't so much in what he said but in the way he said it, and the things he left out. Maymier was a shifty character, perhaps even a habitual criminal. Of that he was now convinced. When Maymier fell silent after describing the destruction of his ship by *Marlene/Lark*, Gisk tapped his fingertips on the tabletop, his expression clearly indicating he wondered about the veracity of some elements in Maymier's account.

"You were inbound from a run beyond the Republic's sphere, correct?"

"Yes."

"And what were you carrying back into the Republic?"

"Trade goods — pieces of art, bladed weapons, food delicacies, that sort of thing."

"But with the utter destruction of *Nakamura Maru*, it will be impossible to establish the exact nature of your cargo."

Maymier bobbed his head. "Unfortunately."

"But convenient if you were shipping things that might raise the eyebrows of the Office for the Security of the Republic."

"I can assure you my cargo was eminently legal."

"Wouldn't it have been better to leave the ship intact for salvage rather than ask Captain Thano to destroy it?"

A shrug. "I don't have the means to finance a recovery operation, and she was tumbling uncontrollably in a part of the system often used by passing ships to correct their course between Wormholes One and Four. Thus, I deemed her a risk to navigation."

"Are you aware that the Parth Traffic Control Commission is the sole judge of such matters within this star's heliosphere?"

"No, I am not, sir."

"Were you aware, Captain Thano?"

Paget shook his head. "No. I simply figured I'd do Captain Maymier a favor."

"Did you know him before this incident?"

"Never met him until he came aboard my ship, sir. I was simply responding to a vessel in distress as required by law. Otherwise, I'd be well on my way to Wormhole Four and Takeshi."

"What is your ultimate destination?"

"Ariel, which is my ship and crew's home port."

"What cargo are you carrying?"

"None. I found nothing worthwhile for the return trip. You're welcome to check."

"Cargo verification is not in my remit," Gisk said primly. "I merely asked Captain Maymier about his load because of *Nakamura Maru*'s unexpected and illegal destruction. On second thought, I believe I will ask the Navy vessel inbound from Takeshi to investigate the ship's remains."

Paget acknowledged Gisk's words.

The latter continued. "Until that is done, I must ask you to remain on the ground and wait for my permission to leave."

"Okay, but can I at least land Captain Maymier and his people? I don't have room for them — they were occupying one of my cargo holds for the quick trip to Parth — and I am certainly not equipped to feed them. We're at the tail end of a trip, and I have just enough rations to reach Ariel with my own crew."

"Certainly." Gisk glanced at Davout. "Can you please find Captain Maymier and company room in the secure facility?"

Davout nodded once. "Of course."

"That's it, then. I will review your logs next, and if I have any further questions, I shall summon you back here."

Paget gave Gisk a pleasant smile. "Anything to help you investigate the incident."

Gisk stood and nodded at them before leaving Davout behind to handle the logistics.

"Here's what we'll do. I'll leave you here, Maymier, and take Thano back to his ship, where I'll get the rest of your crew. Then, I'll come back, pick you up, and take you to our holding facilities." He turned to Paget. "Come on."

Once out in the corridor, headed for the main entrance, Paget said, "You might want to check the luggage of *Nakamura Maru*'s crew."

"Why is that?"

"Call it a gut feeling."

Davout gave Paget a sideways glance. "You get a lot of those?"

"When appropriate. I'm pretty sure *Nakamura Maru* was smuggling drugs. Maybe they took some of the stuff off before entering the escape pod."

"Why rat out a fellow free trader?"

"Because I don't like druggies. They make nothing but trouble for those of us who keep above board."

And make *Lark* and her captain, Caleb Thano, look law-abiding.

***

Paget and Reeve watched the crew members from *Nakamura Maru* load their duffel bags in the rear compartment of Davout's car. Davout gave Paget a knowing look as he closed the compartment door, and the latter smiled. Clearly, the official was going to search the luggage at some point, which suited Paget just fine. It would focus the authorities' attention on Maymier and his people and away from *Marlene*.

As the car drove away, Reeve retracted the belly ramp, sealing the ship off from the planet, and Paget invited everyone into the galley for a quick debrief.

"Having a Republic Navy ship scrutinizing us won't be comfortable," Norum said when Paget fell silent. "The Navy is still competent even after ten years under Derik Juska's regime." They'll likely be looking at everyone involved in the *Nakamura Maru* incident. Just how good is our cover as an Ariel-flagged ship and Ariel residents?"

Paget grimaced. "As good as Imperial Intelligence can make it."

"Which doesn't tell us much."

"No, it doesn't. But we have to play the hand we're dealt."

— 19 —

United Stars Republic Ship *Defiant*
Parth System

"Very curious, Mister Gisk." Captain Nika Coven, commanding officer of the Republic Navy corvette *Defiant,* stroked her narrow chin as she contemplated Gisk's holographic image. Thin, tall, gray-haired, with a craggy face, she was getting long in the tooth for command of a corvette — never mind *Defiant* was almost as old as her and not long for the scrapyard.

"Isn't it? Though both captains claim not to know that only the authorities can allow the destruction of a disabled starship."

Defiant had arrived via Wormhole Four from Takeshi ten minutes earlier and immediately opened a link with the Parth Traffic Control Commission to get an update on the situation. What Gisk had relayed made Coven wonder. She had plenty of experience dealing with smugglers and assorted criminals plying the star lanes, and the destruction of the *Nakamura Maru* reeked of an attempted coverup.

"Pass along the coordinates, and I shall examine the wreckage for you. Please keep both crews locked down until I finish my examination and arrive on Parth."

"We are detaining the Nakamura Maru's crew, and I have ordered *Lark* to remain on the ground until I release him." Gisk glanced to one side, then back at Coven. "I've just transmitted a copy of the interview recording, both ships' logs, and the coordinates."

"Excellent. If there's nothing else, I'll head to the site and digest the documents along the way."

"Please do so, Captain. We shall speak again tomorrow."

"Goodbye, Mister Gisk. *Defiant*, out."

Coven relayed the coordinates to her navigation officer and left the bridge for her day cabin to listen and read. Moments later, the jump klaxon sounded, and the officer of the watch's voice came over the speakers, giving the one-minute warning. Coven braced herself for the transition nausea and waited. Once it had come and gone and *Defiant* was in hyperspace, she settled back and played the recording.

***

"I'm picking up a debris cloud approximately two thousand kilometers off our port beam, Captain," the sensor chief reported. "Pretty much where they said it would be."

"Good. Helm, bring us to within one kilometer of the cloud's edge. Sensors, begin scanning for every substance known to humanity."

"It'll take a while, sir."

Coven grinned at him. "Fortunately, we don't have any higher claims on our time right now, Chief."

"True."

In the end, it took just under three hours for the sensors to produce a detailed report on the composition of the debris cloud. At the head of the list was the item Coven and the sensor chief had expected.

"Approximately five hundred kilos of faedust." Coven let out a low whistle. "Street value must be in the tens of millions. Where the hell did *Nakamura Maru* get this much?"

"I heard rumors the natives grow the plant it's distilled from on New Tasman, sir. They apparently trade it for tech items."

"Do they now? A shame New Tasman is so far away from the Republic's sphere. It could use a little naval intervention to teach its inhabitants the error of their ways."

"Well, it's just a rumor I picked up in a dive bar on Yotai, so don't quote me on it."

"I won't." Coven turned to her second officer, who had the watch. "Tom, send a probe out to collect a sample of the faedust, a couple of kilos, and follow the procedures to secure the chain of evidence. I think *Nakamura Maru*'s captain and crew are facing time in a penal colony, and since they've reopened the ones on Parth, they won't have far to travel."

"Aye, aye, Captain."

"Signals, open a link with the Director General of the Parth Traffic Control Commission. I think he'd like to know sooner rather than later about our findings."

A few moments later, the holographic projection of Gisk's head appeared, floating in mid-air in front of Coven.

"Good morning, Captain. I assume you have news?"

"Good morning, Mister Gisk," she replied, even though it was mid-afternoon, shipboard time since naval vessels in the Republic were set to New Lena's clock on Yotai. "I have indeed. We found approximately five hundred kilos of faedust in the debris cloud. If you're not familiar with the substance, it's a decidedly illegal narcotic produced well beyond the Republic's sphere and commands a high price on the market."

A cold smile spread across Gisk's face. "I knew it. Maymier was much too evasive and nervous."

"So I noticed. We're about to collect a sample of the faedust, taking care to secure the chain of evidence. I think you can arrest Maymier and his crew on charges of drug running right away."

"And what about Thano and *Lark*?"

Coven thought about it for a moment, then said, "I'd like to meet this Thano and his crew and form my own opinion about their honesty. He certainly looked relaxed in the interview video, a man with a clear conscience, I would say."

"Meeting them is easy to arrange. Simply land your ship at the Harambee Spaceport."

***

"Ah, Officer Davout. Thank you for being so prompt." Gisk gestured at the chairs in front of his desk. "I've received a notification from *Defiant* that the *Nakamura Maru* carried a large amount of an illegal substance called faedust. Please contact the Harambee Police Department and have Maymier and his people arrested and charged with narcotics traffic."

"With pleasure, sir. Now I can finally search their luggage officially."

"Did you search it unofficially?"

"Scanned it with a handheld sensor. I detected a lot of small, sealed containers impervious to my scans, the sort smugglers use to hide illegal substances, and figured it was probably narcotics they saved from their ship."

"Please open the containers in the police's presence, if you will."

"Sure thing, sir. I knew those guys were as crooked as a Desolation Island whango tree. What about the others?"

"Captain Coven wants to speak with them herself, but I think she figures they're blameless. Save for destroying *Nakamura Maru* at Maymier's behest in contravention of regulations, of course."

"We can always slap a fine on them for that. Ignorance of the law is no excuse, after all."

"Perhaps."

— 20 —

"By the Almighty, is that *Defiant*?" Norum stared in awe at the corvette settling on the tarmac beside *Marlene*. He and the others crowded the bridge, eyes on the primary display. I would have assumed they decommissioned and sold her off by now. She's what? Close to fifty years old?"

"You've served in her?" Paget asked.

"I commanded her a long time ago. She was one of the finest corvettes in the entire Navy. I wonder what she's doing here."

"Probably the Navy ship from Takeshi responding to the *Nakamura Maru* situation," DeCarde said.

"Of course." Norum grinned at his friend. "I was simply overwhelmed by seeing *Defiant* again after all this time to think of that."

Suddenly, Norum noticed Reeve was staring at him with a faint smile on her face, and he realized he'd said too much in her presence.

"I knew it," she said in a soft voice. "You're a former Republic Navy officer. And you, Paul? Navy or Marines?"

DeCarde grinned at her. "Now that would be telling."

"I'm going to guess Marines. You don't have the Navy look like Frank."

Norum's eyes narrowed as he studied Reeve. "Since when have you suspected we were ex-Republic Defense Force?"

"Not long after we left Wyvern. There's something about both of you that tipped me off, but I can't pinpoint what it is."

"Sela is extremely perceptive," Paget said. "Almost Sister of the Void level."

Her eyes flashed as she glanced at him. "What did I tell you about comparing me to those d'ayvols?"

Paget raised his hands in surrender. "Okay, okay. Sorry."

"D'ayvols?" Norum chuckled. "Now there's a term I haven't heard in a long time. Should I ask why you consider the Sisters demons?"

"No."

Her flat refusal was the answer Norum needed. If she had a Sister's perception, then Reeve was a wild talent, and wildlings viewed the Order of the Void with extreme suspicion, mainly because it preferred talented individuals to be under its control.

But before Norum could pursue the matter, the bridge speakers came to life.

"Free trader *Lark*, this is the United Stars Republic Ship *Defiant* parked to your starboard side. Captain Nika Coven would like to meet with Captain Thano."

Norum's eyebrows shot up as he looked at DeCarde. "Another blast from the past. Nika was one of my junior officers years ago. If she's still stuck as a lieutenant commander in charge of an ancient corvette, her career must have stalled in the last ten years."

"Not one of the favored daughters of the Republic?"

"She always had a sharp mind and an even sharper tongue, and the current regime would definitely disapprove of her contempt for most politicians."

"Sounds like a good egg."

"She would have been at least a captain if not a commodore had Juska not seized power ten years ago."

"Yet she has a command in space."

Norum shrugged. "I'm sure the Navy still recognizes her competence. Besides, command of a tired, old starship like *Defiant* wouldn't be the choice of any up-and-coming officer, especially not if she's stationed permanently in the Takeshi system."

"Can I interrupt your traipsing down memory lane to answer?" Paget asked in a mildly sardonic tone.

Norum made a sweeping arm gesture and grinned. "Please go ahead."

"United Stars Republic Ship *Defiant*, this is the free trader *Lark*. I'd be glad to meet your captain. Will she come aboard my ship?"

"That's the intention, *Lark*. I hope you have no problems with that?"

"Absolutely none. Captain Coven is most welcome."

"In that case, stand by. She'll be coming over shortly. *Defiant*, out."

Paget turned to Norum. "Do you want to hide, or is your appearance sufficiently different from what Coven remembers to fool her?"

"Yes, it is. And she probably knows there are four of us aboard. It would seem strange if she saw only three. Besides, even if she suspects it's me, Nika wouldn't say a word. Knowing her, she probably bears a deep and abiding hatred for the current regime. Derik Juska is precisely the sort of politician she utterly despises."

"All right, then."

They watched *Defiant*'s belly ramp drop and four people march down as Davout's car approached. Two of them, one carrying a container, made a beeline for the car while the other two, a man and a woman, headed toward *Marlene*.

"That's Nika. The lieutenant with her, I don't recognize. But I suspect it may be her second officer."

"Time to unbutton the old girl." Paget touched his console, and they heard *Marlene*'s belly ramp unlock and lower. "You'd better come to greet our visitors so we can get it over with. My goal is to lift off after we meet with Captain Coven and shake Parth's dust from our feet. Marlene, you remain silent throughout the visit."

"Understood," the AI replied.

The four stood at the top of the ramp when both Navy officers appeared. They stopped just short of the ramp's bottom.

"I'm Lieutenant Commander Nika Coven, captain of USRS *Defiant*. This is Lieutenant Tom Previc, my second officer. Do we have permission to come aboard?"

Paget, surprised by her formality and politeness, stepped forward. "Certainly. I'm Caleb Thano, *Lark*'s captain."

He watched them march up the ramp, and when they stopped at its top, Paget said, "This is my crew. Sela Reeve, engineer, Paul Mortimer, bosun, and Frank Blake, supercargo."

Coven and Previc nodded at each as they were presented. Norum thought he saw a brief flash of almost-recognition when his and Coven's eyes met, but she gave no outward sign.

"Is there any place we can sit and talk — all of us?" Coven asked.

"The galley. Follow me, please."

Paget ushered them into the compartment, inviting their visitors to take a seat while the others pulled out chairs. As she looked around, Coven's eyes met Norum's again, and this time, she frowned slightly.

"Mister Blake, I get this strange feeling we may have met long ago."

Norum briefly put on a puzzled expression. "I don't think so, Captain. I've had very little contact with Navy officers and would remember."

"So," Paget said, before Coven could reply, "what is it you wish to discuss?"

"Were you aware *Nakamura Maru* carried faedust — an illegal narcotic — in quantities sufficient to fetch tens of millions of creds on the black market?"

"I'm not surprised."

"Captain Maymier and his crew were arrested for drug trafficking, and when they're found guilty, the court will likely sentence them to life in one of Parth's new reopened penal colonies."

Paget cocked an eyebrow at her. "When, not if?"

"They were also found in possession of the substance in the luggage they took with them, several kilos per crewmember. We detected upward of five hundred kilos in the ship's debris cloud."

Paget let out a low whistle. "That's a lot."

"The largest amount ever found on a single smuggler. It would have been better, however, if we'd seized the drugs intact, and that makes me wonder about your decision to humor Maymier. If you're not surprised by our findings, surely you were aware that in the absence of antimatter fuel, your gunfire wouldn't eliminate every trace of the faedust."

"Oh, I suspected he was smuggling something when he asked me to destroy the remains of his ship, but not drugs specifically. I figured doing as he asked would keep him calm while not completely erasing the evidence. There are six of them and only four of us in tight quarters, and I wanted them in the hands of the authorities on Parth without trouble. As far as I'm concerned, mission accomplished. A large quantity of drugs will not end up on the market, and the smugglers are in prison, facing a life sentence."

Coven nodded. "True, and I suppose I should thank you on behalf of the Republic."

Paget waved her words away with a self-deprecating smile. "I was merely doing what I thought right under the circumstances."

"Where were you coming from?"

"Yawin and the star systems beyond."

"Cargo?"

"None on the return trip, but we sold all of our merchandise while reconnoitering potential markets beyond the Republic. My holds are empty. Feel free to inspect them at your leisure."

"You're returning home to Ariel?"

"That's the plan. We've been away for quite some time and need a bit of rest."

She turned to Norum. "And what's your hometown, Mister Blake?"

"Originally, Lannion, but I relocated to Triton on Ariel twenty-odd years ago, looking for the frontier spirit."

"And did you find it?"

"Enough to not regret my choice, but I still sailed aboard traders headed for the true frontier of the Republic and beyond."

Coven glanced at Reeve. "How about you?"

"Born and raised in a little town outside New Lena on Yotai. I've been going from ship to ship for the last twenty years, but in between, I always seemed to end up on Ariel, so I figured I'd sign onto a trader based there."

Norum fully expected her to question DeCarde next, but instead she climbed to her feet, imitated by her second officer.

"Let's visit your cargo holds, Captain Thano."

"Certainly."

Paget led the two Navy officers through the four holds, demonstrating their emptiness, then gave them a full tour of the remaining compartments to prove he wasn't hiding anything.

As they walked back to the ramp, Coven said, "My compliments on the state of your ship. It obviously saw some hard service, but it looks impeccably clean and well-maintained."

Paget inclined his head. "I intend to keep sailing *Lark* for a long time yet."

"You're the owner?"

"Yes. I bought her with an inheritance a few years ago and had her refurbished."

They stopped at the top of the ramp.

"As far as I'm concerned, the drugs we found in the *Nakamura Maru* debris are sufficient to prosecute its crew, and I'll advise Mister Gisk to let you proceed on your journey."

"Thank you, Captain."

"It's refreshing to come across an independent such as you who's open, honest, and not trying to hide something from the authorities. Goodbye, Captain Thano."

And with that, Coven and her second officer marched off the ramp and returned to their ship.

—21—

"What do you think, Tom?" Captain Coven asked her second officer once they were back aboard *Defiant*.

"That they seem too good to be true, sir. In my experience, free traders of that size aren't so well run, and the crews seem a lot shiftier than Thano's people."

"I agree. And there's that Blake fellow who vaguely reminds me of someone. Don't worry, I'll figure it out eventually."

"What are you going to do, Captain?"

"Do? Nothing. Thano and his crew are not under suspicion of being anything other than upstanding citizens of the Republic." She thought for a moment. "But I will want to take a reading of *Lark*'s emissions curve once she's in space and compare it to those in our database, just in case she's come to the Navy's attention before."

"Then we'd better lift off before she does."

"Aye. Prepare the ship, will you, Tom."

"Yes, sir."

As she headed for her day cabin, leaving Previc to handle things, Coven was suddenly struck by the realization that she knew who Blake really was, and she paled as a look of despair overcame her. Fortunately, the second officer was no longer around to see her face change, and she quickly vanished behind the cabin's closed door.

The man's voice had finally shattered the veil of memory. He could disguise himself all he wanted, but his voice remained, and she finally remembered it after more than fifteen years since they last met. It was the voice of her mentor during her early years as a commissioned officer, and they used to speak for hours when off duty. He'd pulled her through the funk she'd experienced during her first six months as a callow ensign aboard her first ship, then as she grew more confident, his voice had reined in the worst of her impulses. Like her intense disdain for the Republic's politicians. He'd taught her to keep it well hidden lest she cut her career short.

Coven refused to think of his name, because then, his reappearance under a convincing disguise at the hind end of the Republic would not be real. She, of course, knew he'd vanished ten years ago, shortly after being dismissed from his post as Chief of the Defense Staff by President Juska, and had heard the rumors he'd defected to the Second Empire. And if those rumors were correct, then *Lark* had to be an Imperial ship, and he was on a secret mission against Juska's regime.

Her duty, of course, was to denounce Blake as an enemy of the Republic, a defector. But she bore such hatred for Juska and his awful government that she felt no loyalty whatsoever toward him. On the contrary. And if her erstwhile mentor had indeed come back to the Republic on a mission against the regime, she would privately cheer him on and not reveal her suspicions about his true identity to anyone.

But should she conveniently forget to record *Lark*'s emissions signature, to help him? No. Her second officer would recall, and he was loyal to Juska. In fact, Coven suspected him of being a United Stars Bloc member, meaning he wouldn't hesitate to denounce her should he find she'd been showing less than sterling devotion to the administration.

***

"What happens if she finally figures out who you are?" Paget asked, sitting back in his chair at the galley table.

"Nothing. Nika Coven won't betray me in a million years. She'll take that secret to the grave."

"Unless she falls into the hands of the Office for the Security of the Republic," DeCarde said. "No one can keep secrets when the police of a dictatorial state work you over."

"But why should she? No, my real identity is safe with Nika. In a certain way, she's the daughter I never had. Back when she was a young officer trying to find her way, I mentored her and steered her clear of rocks and shoals. Besides, she surely despises Juska and his administration. They're precisely the sort of politicians she'd prefer to watch dangle from lampposts along the Grand Avenue outside the Presidential Palace, you can believe me on that."

"If you say so." Paget drained his coffee mug. "There's nothing we can do about it now. I'd consider scrubbing the mission, but I don't know what you're after in the Yotai system. Perhaps it's important enough to risk recognition."

"Oh, it is, trust me. And no, I won't tell you just yet." Norum winked at Paget.

An hour later, they watched *Defiant* lift off, but still hadn't received permission to leave themselves. That came almost two hours afterward from the traffic control center rather than Gisk himself.

"It's about time." Paget settled in his bridge chair while the others lay down on their bunks.

Once out of Parth's atmosphere, *Marlene* didn't even make one orbit before heading for the hyperlimit on a course to Wormhole Four.

"There's *Defiant*." Paget pointed at the icon of the corvette on the bridge tactical display. "I'll bet she's taking a good emissions reading of us right now."

"No bet," Norum replied. "Even if Nika recognized me and is keeping it to herself, taking our signature is mandatory. And no, you can't change it again because we're about to enter the controlled part of the wormhole network and have already been read."

"Don't I know it." Then, "She's breaking out of orbit on a parallel course to ours."

"Of course. We're both headed for Wormhole Four and Takeshi."

— 22 —

Lindisfarne
Unclaimed Space

"Summus Abbatissa." Ardrix inclined her head as she stepped into Sister Mariko's office. The head of the Order of the Void, seated behind a simple desk, nodded solemnly at her in greeting.

"Please enter, Magistra Abbatissa, and welcome back."

"It's good to be back at the Motherhouse."

A faint smile twitched on Mariko's lips. "Is it? You've made the long, arduous trip how many times? Five? I'd have thought you'd be tired of visiting us by now."

Ardrix knew Mariko was gently teasing her. The two Sisters had established a close rapport early on during Ardrix's first visit, in large part because the latter easily submitted to the Summus Abbatissa's rule.

Mariko gestured at the simple wooden chairs across from her desk. "Please take your ease and tell me about your latest voyage to our little corner of the galaxy."

Ardrix obeyed, folding her hands in her lap. "There isn't much to say about the trip. I came aboard *Terrifiante*, one of the regular Navy patrol vessels that visits Lindisfarne every few weeks, now that Wyvern has decided to reunite Lindisfarne with the Empire by hook or by crook, notwithstanding the immense distance."

"So long as Wyvern does not impose its rule on us, it may do as it wishes."

"I think there's little chance of that. The Empire is founded on the principle that each sovereign world governs itself according to its own lights, leaving merely collective defense, foreign affairs, interstellar transportation, interstellar policing, and a few other functions to the Imperial government. Although eventually, Lindisfarne will have to contribute financially to fund the central administration, just like all other sovereign star systems.

"When that time comes, we shall be ready to negotiate our fair share."

"It won't be until the Empire's sphere actually encompasses Lindisfarne, from what I understand, so it'll take a few decades." A wry smile appeared. "But I was being truthful when I said it was good to be back. There is something about this world that makes me feel at peace with myself and the universe. Perhaps the immense number of talented minds working in harmony has a beneficial effect on my subconscious."

Mariko gave Ardrix an amused look. "Or maybe being far removed from your heavy responsibilities is allowing you to breathe freely for a while."

Ardrix let out a peal of laughter. "True, especially when I walk the cloister here after evening service. There's no one wanting a bit of my time on an urgent matter like back home."

Mariko winked at her. "I know about that. Now, what business shall we discuss before I have tea served in the Abbey garden?"

"A few items. First, the alignment of the former Void Reborn with Lindisfarne is complete. Friars are back in their traditional roles as administrators, and the senior leadership positions are now in the hands of Sisters. Also, I have withdrawn the Sisters from government tasks save for the traditional duties as counselors aboard Navy ships or for ground units. You may therefore consider us back in a state of orthodoxy and in full communion with the Motherhouse."

A broad smile spread across Mariko's face. "That is so good to hear. Thank you for your efforts."

"In certain respects, it proved easier than expected, in others, more difficult. Thankfully, the senior friars, when faced with the option of complying or leaving the Order, chose the former." A mischievous air crossed Ardrix's narrow features. "Especially with the subtle unvoiced pressure I put on them."

"You nudged their minds, did you?"

"Only those who were inclined to protest the realignment of responsibilities, of which, after a number retired to spend the rest of their lives in quiet contemplation, there were few."

"However, you managed it, well done. And faster than I expected. Do you have news of the Lyonesse Brethren?"

Ardrix grimaced. "That was my next point. We have secret links with some Lyonesse Sisters, and they are dismayed at the path their Order and the Republic itself have taken. As you might recall, the Lyonesse Order had decided it would not come into communion with Lindisfarne."

"I remember. Sad they should choose to become schismatics, but there is nothing we can do."

"It gets worse. The latest reports we received from the Republic are chilling. Their Summus Abbatissa, Sister Elana, is inserting the Order into secular affairs at an alarming rate and working closely with the President, Derik Juska, to help him tighten his grip on power. Based on what we've received, we figure he's a dictator in everything but name, and Elana is well on her way to becoming his number two and wielding considerable secular power herself."

"By the Almighty, the Lyonesse Brethren aren't schismatics, they're heretics!"

"Indeed. Sisters have become involved in re-educating political prisoners by direct mental manipulation, including against the subjects' will."

An appalled look overcame Mariko's expression. "That's abominable and against every single rule we hold dear."

"Apparently, the Sisters who do this sort of work were either stripped of their conditioning to do no harm, or said conditioning failed, if they even applied it in the first place. Elana has had almost ten years to cultivate a new sort of Sister, one which we might consider the functional equivalent of sociopaths, women without empathy but with a powerful talent. The very thought of such creatures existing fills me with an indescribable dread."

"It's a perversion of everything the Order has stood for since its inception over fifteen hundred years ago. I must denounce them publicly and make them anathema to those who serve the Almighty."

Ardrix shook her head. "I wish you wouldn't. Although the chances that word we know about the Lyonesse Order's inner doings getting back to them are minimal, they aren't zero, and I would not wish to jeopardize the lives of those Sisters who keep us informed in the hopes we might help stop Elana's headlong rush into darkness."

"Very well. I can see the reasons behind your suggestion and agree. I shall keep this to myself."

"Thank you, Mariko. Even more wicked than that, our informants in the Republic told us President Juska had ordered an ancient virus, kept in stasis in a top-secret biolab, be revived and prepared for use as a biological agent against the Empire by Sisters engaged in bio research. It apparently causes a one-hundred percent death rate. Then, in the absence of further live hosts, it dies away. The goal, apparently, is to depopulate Imperial worlds by killing us all."

"The perfect bioweapon." Mariko's words came out as a whisper. "Is there any end to their depravity?"

"Apparently not. Juska seems so deeply consumed by hatred of the Second Empire, he'll do anything to extinguish it."

"And the Lyonesse Brethren are helping him…"

"At this point, I don't think we should refer to them as Brethren, Mariko, let alone the Lyonesse Branch of the Order of the Void."

"Then what shall we call them?"

Ardrix's face hardened.

"I think it would be best if we simply ignored their existence. In a similar vein, a reconnaissance mission uncovered what might have been strange manifestations of the talent." Ardrix went on to recount what Paget and Reeve had reported. "Since this world is in a star system with twelve unstable wormhole termini, chances of them seeing more visitors are extremely limited."

"Fascinating. We have far from discovered the limits to the talent, haven't we?"

— 23 —

Yotai
United Stars Republic

"We have a problem with Subject One-Three-Seven," Sister Ygritte said, entering the office of Sister Sybil.

Sybil looked up at Ygritte, irritated by the interruption. "Let me guess — another stroke?"

"Just so. She's in a coma, and her chances look dim."

"The fifth in the last two weeks. What are we missing in our selection of the most likely candidates?"

"I have no idea. Do you think we should stop the remaining re-education processes while we find out?"

"Elana wouldn't like that. She'd probably order us to write off those who don't make it as the price of perfecting our methods."

Ygritte was silent for a moment, then she said, "And Elana wouldn't be wrong. Our subjects are enemies of the Republic and, as such, their lives are of limited use."

It was a harsh epitaph for former Commodore Julia Byner and the others who'd suffered strokes or whose brains had simply shut down. But the Summus Abbatissa had specially selected the Sisters involved in the re-education project as much for their ability to penetrate minds as for their lack of empathy. As a matter of fact, Elana had long believed the two characteristics were related. It stood to reason. Violating the most intimate part of a person's being requires an innate absence of compassion.

And giving them numbers instead of using their names further dehumanized their victims, reducing them to animated objects.

"In that case, investigate why Subject One-Three-Seven suffered a stroke, but continue the process with the rest of them."

"As you wish." Ygritte bowed her head, turned on her heels, and left Sybil's office.

The latter wrote a brief note addressed to Elana concerning the latest setback and sent it, encrypted, to the Motherhouse Abbey.

Another political prisoner gone, but the Order was steadily advancing its knowledge of direct mind manipulation without the target's knowledge. No more nudging preexisting inclinations, but full-blown control of another's thoughts. Maybe even in Sybil's lifetime, at the rate they were discovering new techniques. And then, the Order would rule over the Republic. Through others, of course, but they'll be mere meat puppets doing what the Sisters made them.

But the breakthroughs so far had proved the strongest Sisters could disable people, even kill them, with their thoughts. And that might prove extremely useful in itself.

Sybil wondered whether Elana thought along those same lines. Maybe she should institute research into eliminating subjects besides the current attempts at trying to manipulate their thoughts. There were plenty of political prisoners who would never see the light of day again, on whom they could experiment.

The more she thought about it, the more Sybil warmed to the thought of creating mind assassins within the Order. It would help in the Void's covert takeover of the Republic. People who didn't cooperate or could not be sufficiently mind-manipulated? Perhaps they might suffer from fatal strokes.

It was definitely something she would discuss with Elana the next time they met.

***

President Derik Juska glanced over Hendrick Golub's shoulder at Sister Clemenza, who sat like a statue in the shadows of an alcove. The truthsayer nodded, indicating the latest pronouncement by the head of the Shipbuilders Association was true.

"I'm glad to hear that, Henny." Juska gave Golub his patented smile. "We need more naval ships if we're to win the race with the Hegemony to reunify humanity."

"Mister President, the builders are in with your plan."

They'd better be, Juska thought. *Otherwise, my friend, you'll find yourself replaced, as will those who aren't sufficiently enthusiastic.*

That was the great thing about the system he'd created. The companies engaged in industries deemed vital remained in the private sector but had become entirely subservient to the state. Derik Juska was the ultimate director general, who gave them their marching orders and made the final decisions. He was the state.

And as an ancient once said, all within the state, nothing outside the state, nothing against the state.

"Excellent. I expected no less from such a distinguished group. Thank you for coming to see me in person with the good news, Henny."

Knowing he'd just been dismissed, Golub climbed to his feet and bowed his head.

"Always a pleasure, Mister President."

Juska watched him leave, and when they were alone in the presidential office, he looked at Clemenza.

"How was he?"

"Candid and eager to please you."

"As I would expect from one of the earliest Lyonesse First members." Juska nodded with satisfaction.

So far, the truthsayers had been useful in separating the utterly loyal from those who had something to hide. And Juska suspected his next visitor belonged among the latter.

As if on cue, his executive assistant popped his head through the door.

"Anya Fong is here, sir."

"Show her in, please."

A compact, thin woman with shoulder-length, jet black hair framing her smooth face entered moments later. She wore a subdued, dark, high-collared business suit with a gold brooch on her left breast. The brooch, a stylized representation of a double-headed condor superimposed on a galaxy, was the symbol of the United Stars Bloc, successor to Lyonesse First, which she had led as secretary-general for the last ten years.

Juska knew about Fong's ambitions. She considered herself second only to him in the Republic's hierarchy and had designs on the presidency once he left it. Or perhaps even before he was ready to do so. But she'd been and still was instrumental in developing and disseminating the propaganda that propped up and legitimized his regime. Juska knew that without her, ordinary citizens would have begun to question the changes he was making to the constitutional order long ago. Still, she could become a serious rival to his rule, and that might make her disposable, especially once his grip on the presidency became absolute and her genius at propaganda was no longer required.

"Anya! How are you?" Juska's tone was light and welcoming.

"Doing fine, Mister President." Fong gave him a brilliant smile that didn't quite reach her eyes as she accepted his gesture to take a chair across from his desk. "I'm here to discuss the celebrations surrounding the fifteenth Anniversary of Lyonesse First and the United Stars Bloc and your role in them."

Juska's expression didn't change, but inwardly, he felt just a bit of exasperation. The anniversary celebrations did not warrant a face-to-face meeting, at least not at this point, but such was Fong's self-importance that she probably believed them to be the most significant event on Juska's agenda right now.

He made an elegant go-ahead gesture with his hand as he composed himself.

"As you know, it'll be a weeklong rally here in New Lena, with representatives from every part of the Republic joining us. I expect at least twenty-five thousand people, enough to fill the Stadium of the Stars and every hotel room on the continent."

Fong seemed pleased by the numbers, and Juska smiled.

"The opening will see the Presidential Guard Regiment march in, take position around the dais, and present arms as you and I arrive."

The Presidential Guard had been another of Fong's ideas, five years earlier. Separate from the rest of the Defense Force, the regiment's commanding officer answered directly to the president's chief of staff. Its black, silver-trimmed uniforms with cuff titles further distinguished the Guard from the Army and the Marines. Even the rank insignia were different, though the discipline and pay rates were the same. And they wore black helmets with the double-headed condor on each side rather than the ubiquitous berets of the Defense Force.

"Then, the Guard Band will play the Republic's anthem as silent fireworks fill the air…"

And on it went, Fong enthusiastically laying out the program for the entire week while Juska kept a smile painted on his face, though he'd rather have his hands around her throat by the end of it. But he needed her for a bit longer. Besides, he utterly disliked Fong's deputy, who would step in should anything happen to her. Perhaps a scandal involving both would be the way to go when the time came.

"Thank you for your thorough schedule, Anya. I can't see anything you've missed."

Fong beamed at Juska, though the latter knew it was at least in part fake. No one could be that exuberant about what was, in effect, a large-scale public relations exercise. And it was a cynical manipulation at that, to ensure the United Stars Bloc members would be eager, engaged, and obey his regime, whether they were present or not.

"Thank you, Mister President."

"Was there anything else?"

"No, sir." Fong climbed to her feet, gave Juska another smile, and said, "Enjoy the rest of your day."

When she was gone, Juska glanced at Sister Clemenza in her shadowy alcove again. "And?"

"She has a dark blot on her soul, mostly envy, but also something more dangerous. I would be careful with her."

— 24 —

Takeshi
United Stars Republic

"Traffic control buoy reports a ship just came through Wormhole One," the bored petty officer on duty announced in a lazy drawl.

"*Defiant* already?"

The equally bored duty officer, an elderly lieutenant whose waning career had landed him in Takeshi Station's operations section, a despairingly dull assignment if there ever was one, wandered over to glance at the petty officer's display.

"Nope, sir. A civilian trader whose beacon identifies it as *Lark*, registered on Ariel. According to our database, it hasn't been through here before."

"Be sure to take the emissions signature and log it."

"Yes, sir."

The petty officer managed to keep irritation at being told his job out of his tone. Just. The lieutenant might have been terminal at his rank, but that didn't keep him from being a thorough prick when he wanted to. And when he was bored, which was pretty much all the time these days, he'd go hunting for things that annoyed him.

"You want me to speak with them, sir? Check their destination and see what kind of people are on board?"

"Sure. If nothing else, it'll break the monotony."

"Okay." The petty officer flicked the subspace radio on. "*Lark*, this is Takeshi Station Operations. Please come in."

A few heartbeats passed, then, "Takeshi Station, this is *Lark*. What can we do for you?"

The petty officer and the lieutenant glanced at each other. Normally, inbound ships took a lot longer to respond. This one was unusually quick.

"Go to visual, please."

Moments later, the face of a rugged-looking man with wavy dark hair and a flowing mustache appeared. He wore the impassive face of someone who had nothing to hide, at least in the lieutenant's estimation.

"I am Captain Caleb Thano."

"How many aboard your ship?" The lieutenant asked.

"We're four."

"Where are you headed?"

"Home to Ariel."

"Cargo?"

"None. We sold everything and found nothing to buy."

"Do you intend to stop over on Takeshi?"

Thano shook his head. "No. I plan on making a dogleg for Wormhole Two. We're rather impatient to get home."

"All right, then. Have a good voyage. Takeshi Station, out."

Thano's image faded, and the lieutenant sighed as he took his seat again. Only two more hours before his shift was over, and he boarded a shuttle for the surface on a three-day pass.

***

"*Defiant* didn't warn Takeshi Station of our arrival, it seems," Norum said once the link died away.

Paget rubbed his chin. "No. It could mean that they don't suspect us of anything, or your former officer decided to look the other way. Either way, it suits me. Onward to the Yin system."

Norum stared at Paget for a few moments. "I think I should discuss our mission now that we're in the Republic proper."

"Sure. Let me get *Marlene* into hyperspace on our first leg to Wormhole Two, then we can sit in the galley around a cup of something."

When Paget finally joined the others in the galley, the three of them cradled mugs of tea in their hands, but he made himself coffee instead, then sat beside Reeve.

"Okay, Frank. Tell us about your mission."

"Let me spin you a tale first. Over two hundred years ago, after the Retribution Fleet had scoured most worlds, barbarians from beyond the old Empire's borders crept back into the human-settled sphere, wondering where our ancestors had gone. As they moved from planet to planet and outpost to outpost during their nomadic wanderings, they took what they could and smashed what they couldn't. Unfortunately, the old Empire had research stations on its outer rim conducting various experiments hidden away from the public eye, including those involving biological warfare."

Norum took a sip of his tea.

"And as fate would have it, the barbarians stumbled across one of those on the edge of the Coalsack sector. We never uncovered precisely where the station was located or what the barbarians liberated from it, beyond a virus so deadly it kills one hundred percent of those infected. How did we find out about it, you ask? Simple. Barbarian ships tried to force their way into the Lyonesse branch of the wormhole network, but a Lyonesse warship kept them from getting any further than the Corbenic Wormhole One terminus. When our ancestors found out the barbarians were succumbing to a deadly disease, they quarantined the Republic's three star systems — Lyonesse, Broceliande, and Corbenic — as well as kept patrols watching for ships bypassing the network.

"Eventually, the infected barbarians succumbed, and the virus died out on its own. It was designed for biological warfare and couldn't be allowed to persist in the absence of human hosts. But in the meantime, our forebears collected live samples for research of our own and stored them in stasis in a top-secret, high-security biolab on Gwaelod, the outermost of Lyonesse's three moons. In theory, the virus, once decanted out of the stasis bottles, would be as virulent as ever. Twenty-five years ago, the Navy secretly moved the biolab and its contents to Gennari, the larger of Yotai's two moons, to get it away from Lyonesse but keep it in a secure star system."

While Norum sipped his tea again, Paget frowned. Then, a light came on in his eyes.

"And Imperial Intelligence recently got word that Juska has somehow revived interest in the virus."

Norum tapped the side of his nose with an extended index finger.

"Give the Imperial Rogue a prize. In fact, Intelligence received indications that Juska is contemplating deploying the virus on Second Empire worlds."

Reeve sat up, a look of dismay on her face. "He's frecking crazy!"

"No arguments here. Yet he and a substantial proportion of the population would be more than happy if the entire Second Empire vanished. It would end the cognitive dissonance the Republic has been suffering from since we found out we weren't the sole surviving human starfaring civilization."

A frown appeared on Reeve's forehead. "Wait a minute, Frank. If it's top-secret, how do you know about the biolab?"

Norum and DeCarde exchanged a glance. The latter shrugged and said, "I don't see how it makes a difference now."

"You were right, Sela. I used to be in the Republic's Navy. High up enough to be in on top-secret things like biolabs."

"Aha. I knew it." She gave him a triumphant glance. "And you were surely high up in the Marines, Paul?"

"Not nearly as high as Frank, but yeah."

"And you're heading for Yotai to do something about that virus, right?"

Norum nodded. "Yes. Since I know precisely where it's located on Gennari, we'll try to figure out a way of destroying the lab and the virus it contains before it's deployed and without leaving Imperial fingerprints on the deed."

A smirk appeared on Reeve's face. "Let me get this straight. The Second Empire is facing an existential threat, and they send two former — and not that young — officers who defected from the

Republic's Defense Force instead of crack commandos or at least professional intelligence agents?"

"Yep." Norum grinned at her. "But I've actually been inside the biolab, and your professionals haven't. Besides, Paul and I can handle ourselves better than most. And we have a secondary mission on Yotai itself that only we can carry out."

Reeve raised both hands in surrender. "Have it your way. Just try to arrange things so we escape with our skins intact."

"Sorry, Sela," Paget said. "But I was told in confidence before we left that we were expendable if it meant success in the mission."

"Great! Now you tell me, when it's way too late for me to back out."

"We can always drop you off on Yin…"

A snort. "As if. I signed up for this, so I'll see it through, have no fear. And what's your secondary mission, if I may ask?"

Norum briefly met DeCarde's eyes again, then said, "We need to get in touch quietly with people who are secretly working against Juska's regime."

"A resistance?" Reeve cocked an amused eyebrow. "This is getting more and more interesting. Old Defense Force buddies of yours? Or should I not ask?"

"Let's stick with you not asking."

— 25 —

Yotai
United Stars Republic

"There it is, live and in color." Paget gestured at the bridge's primary display once the transition nausea faded away. The wormhole transits through Yin and Micarat to Yotai had been uneventful, and traffic control in the three systems had simply passed them through based on *Marlene*'s beacon as *Lark*.

"Find me Gennari and focus on the side facing away from Yotai, and I'll pinpoint the biolab," Norum, sitting at the portside workstation, replied.

"Is Gennari tidally locked?"

"Aren't most moons?"

Paget studied the navigation plot and grunted. "I'll have to make at least one orbit beyond that of Gennari. Hopefully, it won't make the locals suspicious."

"There's no other way. I need to feed the biolab's precise coordinates into your targeting system so you can blow it up before getting the hell out of here on an interstellar vector."

"*If* you decide to stay and lead the resistance against Juska's regime."

"We'll see. Better safe than sorry. At least you'll have the coordinates."

They fell silent as *Marlene* made a lazy run between the two moons. Once they neared Gennari, Norum began searching for the lab with passive sensors, so as not to reveal their interest to Republic authorities. After a few minutes, he tapped his console.

"There." The primary display came to life, showing the tops of structures mostly dug into the moon's surface. "That's it. Hit the damn place with everything you've got, and you should leave a nice, empty crater. It's proof against radiation and small asteroids, not naval-grade missiles and guns. If all else fails, crash *Marlene* into it. Her antimatter containment unit's collapse will create an explosion big enough to wipe any trace of the lab from this universe."

Paget's face took on a grim expression. "You may say that in jest, but if I have to, I will do so. The lives of billions are at stake."

"I wasn't joking, Hal," Norum replied in a soft tone. "And I know you'll do it."

"It might be better if you, your friend, and Sela stay on Yotai."

"Ya know," Reeve drawled, glancing over her shoulder at Paget from the starboard workstation, "I think I'll just stay on Yotai no matter what. It's been a lot of fun, but I'm a Republic girl, and Yotai is my home world. You can thank the Navy, have me discharged on the day I step off *Marlene,* and they can keep whatever pay they owe me."

"You sure about that?"

"Yep."

"Okay. I'll make up for the missing pay from our untraceable mission funds to tide you over."

"You're a gentleman and a scholar, Hal."

"Well, you saved my life on Lothair Five."

"And you saved mine on Coraline, so I guess we're even."

Norum climbed to his feet, chuckling. "I'll leave you to continue your mutual admiration society in private."

"No, stay. We're done." Paget gestured at the seat Norum had occupied. "We need to finalize what we'll do next."

"Okay." Norum sat again.

"We're agreed that Sela, being a native of Yotai, is best placed to scout New Lena while we remain aboard?"

A shrug. "Sure. Although Paul and I are also quite familiar with the place."

"Still, at least her credentials are real and her family connections easily verifiable. Yours, not so much."

"True. Give her what? Six or seven hours?"

"Something like that. What do you think, Sela?"

"Should be enough to see what the atmosphere is. Heck, if you give me the coordinates of your resistance contacts, Frank, I can even check them out for you."

"Pass."

"Have it your way." She looked at Paget. "Shall we ask for a landing slot at the New Lena spaceport?"

"Might as well. We have what we need from Gennari."

***

They landed without difficulty but were relegated to the far end of the spaceport's freight section, in front of dilapidated hangars and warehouses dating back to the initial resettlement of Yotai more than a century earlier. Reeve left *Marlene* via the belly ramp, which remained extended during her absence, the airlock at its top serving as a secure entry point.

"Feels distinctly uncomfortable sitting here, a few kilometers from Derik Juska's Presidential Palace. We're as close to being in the belly of the beast as is possible without moldering in the dungeons of the Office for the Security of the Republic," DeCarde commented, staring out at the spaceport's activities via the bridge primary display.

"And the feeling will get worse when we step off *Marlene* and wave goodbye. You regret coming with me, Currag?"

DeCarde shook his head. "No. I was getting bored beyond tears working for the Colonial Service and ready for a last hurrah. If we don't make it, at least we'll have died on a Republic world trying to rectify the biggest mistake in our history."

Norum gave him a wry look. "You mean my absconding and hiding under an assumed identity for five years, soon after Juska assumed the presidency, rather than staying on Lyonesse and fighting him before the court of public opinion?"

"If that was the mistake, then I'm equally guilty of going into self-imposed exile rather than battling the Lyonesse First hordes. No, what I meant was giving Juska the ability to seize power in the first place."

"And what would you have done?"

"I'd have cornered him quietly and told him he wasn't running in the next election." DeCarde made a cutting gesture across his throat. "Or else. Face it, we knew what Juska wanted — that was to subvert the Constitution and turn himself into a dictator by riding on the Lyonesse First tidal wave. But we chose to ignore what the signs and our guts were telling us."

"We would have violated the Constitution ourselves if we'd done what you suggest, Currag."

"Sure, but the Republic and its billions of citizens would be much better off, and a lot of people who died at the hands of Juska's minions would still be alive." DeCarde shrugged. "So I'm a utilitarian. At least in part."

Norum smirked. "History is full of people like you who say 'I told you so'."

A smile. "True. But that doesn't invalidate the feeling."

Their conversation continued in a desultory fashion until Marlene's voice interrupted them.

"Warrant Officer Reeve is returning."

They glanced up at the display and saw her walking back toward the ship in an unhurried fashion. She disappeared, then Marlene announced, "Warrant Officer Reeve is back on board."

Moments later, her head poked through the bridge door.

"And?" Paget asked.

"The city is quiet. There's no undercurrent of discontent that I could detect. The people are going about their business as normal. If you were expecting revolution roiling beneath the surface, you'll be sadly disappointed. President Juska seems well-liked and respected, as is the United Stars Bloc. You'll be hard-pressed to find people who speak out against the regime beyond the normal gripes about government in general."

DeCarde and Norum looked at each other, and the latter said, "Do you still want to come with me? It seems like the cause could be more hopeless than we expected."

"We could always give up on contacting your old friend and lift off, take out the biolab, and head back to the Empire at flank speed."

"How about you seek out your friend," Paget said, "and if you figure it's hopeless, you come back here, and we do exactly as Paul suggested?"

"You'd wait for however long it took us?" Norum asked.

"Within reason. Say five days max, then Sela and I leave."

"Fair enough." He turned to DeCarde. "Shall we?"

"Might as well."

Both climbed to their feet. "Five days, Hal."

Then, they went to their cabins, picked up their small backpacks, and headed for the airlock and the ramp.

As soon as they came within visual range, Reeve and Paget watched them head toward the line of hangars on the bridge's primary display until the two men vanished. Reeve touched a control panel, then turned to Paget.

"I'm afraid we have a problem. Or to be more precise, you have a problem."

A frowning Paget glanced away from the display and at Reeve, who was pointing a nasty-looking power weapon at him, face hard as granite and eyes cold as space.

"What the frick, Sela?"

"Sorry, Hal, but it's the end of the line for us. I'm afraid you're under arrest for plotting against the Republic."

She briefly shifted her eyes to the display and back at Paget after noting half a dozen armored figures spilling from the nearest hangar and running toward *Marlene*.

"What?"

Moments later, they heard footsteps jogging up the ramp, and then two of the armored troopers burst through the bridge door.

They pointed their carbines at Paget, and one of them ordered him on his knees, hands joined behind his head.

Paget gave Reeve an accusing stare. "You are a Republic operative."

"No talking," the same trooper said as he butt-stroked Paget in the midriff.

An icy smile twitched on Reeve's lips.

"I am, and I thank you for bringing me home. I fully expected to die on Coraline until you showed up. The bastards crewing *Hinksford* eventually suspected I was an undercover government operative sent to spy on their activities and stranded me. Maybe your saving my life will mean something to my superiors, and they might spare you the indignity of being treated like a hostile agent. But I wouldn't count on it." She stood, and her weapon vanished beneath her tunic again. "There won't be any need to bring my pay up to date after all. Besides, this ship and its contents belong to the Republic now. You see, I've overridden your control of the AI, and it will no longer respond to your commands. Oh, yes, I forgot to mention I'm a cyberneticist as well as a starship engineer. I've been preparing the ship to lock you out for weeks, and I've activated the dormant program just now. Possibly they'll hand her over to me so I can do covert observation missions just like you did. Sadly, you'll never know. Goodbye, Hal Paget."

The troopers shackled his hands, pulled him to his feet, and led him out of the bridge. Reeve let out a satisfied sigh as she dropped into the captain's chair.

"Marlene?"

"Yes, Warrant Officer Reeve."

"You will deactivate all AI functions, leaving only those necessary to reactivate them via verbal command at a later date."

"Understood. I am complying."

And with that, Marlene, the AI, fell silent, perhaps forever.

PART II – INTO THE FURNACE

— 26 —

As soon as they rounded the hangar's corner and disappeared from *Marlene*'s sight, Norum and DeCarde found themselves surrounded by uniformed officers of the OSR brandishing lethal weapons. The officers quickly cuffed and muzzled them, warning that they would beat them if they didn't cooperate. Moments later, a black ground transport with polarized windows pulled up, and the officers summarily bundled them aboard. After a ride of approximately twenty minutes, the transport came to a halt, and the doors opened.

They found themselves in an underground garage, parked alongside other black vehicles. The officer in charge ordered them out, and they were escorted through a maze of gray corridors with harsh lighting to a detention area. There, they shoved them into separate cells, removed the manacles and muzzles, and left them in bleak surroundings with the same harsh

lighting as the rest of the facility. Furnishings were summary —
a bare bunk and a stainless-steel toilet surmounted by a sink. No
windows relieved the gray sameness of the walls or pierced the
door.

Norum, mind still spinning at the speed of events, spread out
on the hard bunk and stared at the smooth gray ceiling. Once his
thoughts caught up with him, he came to the only possible
conclusion. Reeve had betrayed them. Far from being an
innocent refugee rescued by Paget, she was a Republic agent,
albeit one in dire straits when Paget picked her up. No other
answer remained. And that meant Paget and *Marlene* were in
Republic custody by now. In other words, he and DeCarde were
not just screwed, they were royally fracked. It wouldn't take the
Office for the Security of the Republic long to figure out their
real identities now that they had them in custody.

Knowing he was under observation, Norum composed himself,
stretched out on the bunk, and closed his eyes.

***

Charisse Weber, Director General of the Office for the Security
of the Republic, stared at the twin feeds from the detention
center on her office display, wondering who the two men were.
Lieutenant Reeve had said they were respectively a former
Republic naval officer and a former Republic Marine who'd
defected to the Hegemony years earlier. The naval officer
appeared to have been quite senior in rank. And they were here
on a mission to destroy the biolab on Gennari and stir up trouble
for the government on Yotai, marking both as traitors deserving
the death penalty.

Frank Blake and Paul Mortimer. Those names sounded like they came straight out of a cheap holonovel. But she'd soon find out who they really were thanks to deep biometric scans. A shame Naval Intelligence had claimed the captain of that little undercover ship, but since he was apparently a serving Hegemony Navy officer, they got the first crack at him.

What the Defense Force wanted, it usually got, the OSR be damned. Weber was working hard to raise the OSR's importance above that of the military, but it would take time. First, she had to get OSR political officers aboard starships and into ground units, and the Defense Force was resisting with everything it had. But she was slowly convincing the president that it would be an excellent idea and help further consolidate his power.

If she could turn those two into propaganda successes thanks to the Sisters…

She studied the one called Blake but couldn't determine who he was behind his disguise, much less the other, Mortimer. Then, with a soft sigh, she shut the feed and turned to her queue. Protocol, unless the matter concerned a time-sensitive issue, was to let political prisoners stew for at least thirty-six hours in a brightly lit cell without comforts, food, or water. It disoriented them and made them more compliant.

***

"Lieutenant Commander Hal Paget, Wyvern Hegemony Navy." The interrogator took a seat across the bare metal table from Paget and deposited a small tablet on the otherwise bare tabletop. He was a slender, bald man of indeterminate age, with a black mouth beard, cold gray eyes, and thin lips, and wore a severe civilian suit. "You work for the Hegemony Intelligence Special Reconnaissance Division."

"No."

"What do you mean, no? Lieutenant Reeve reported it to be so, and she's one of our best agents."

"I'm a member of the Imperial Navy and work for Imperial Intelligence. The Hegemony was consigned to the dustbin of history over five years ago."

An icy smile appeared on the interrogator's lips. "Ah, but the United Stars Republic does not recognize the Hegemony's assumption of the Imperial mantle."

"You mean your power-hungry asshole of a president doesn't."

A pained expression creased the man's face.

"Please don't try my patience with deliberate crudeness, Commander. I expect better of naval officers, even ones from a rival star nation."

"Why am I in custody? We're not at war, as far as I know."

"But you were plotting to commit an act of war against the Republic. That's sufficient for us to detain you indefinitely under military law with no recourse whatsoever. Then, there's the small matter of you operating undercover in Republic space and on Republic worlds, meaning you're a spy. Also sufficient for indefinite detention on its own. I'm afraid you're not going anywhere, Commander."

"Unless you exchange me for one of your people we're holding back on Wyvern."

A bark of laughter. "The Hegemony doesn't hold anyone of interest to us. No, Commander. I'm afraid you'll remain with us for a long time. Possibly even forever. How you'll live your life depends on how well you cooperate."

"Paget, Hal, Lieutenant Commander, D34 897 131."

The man chuckled, though there was little humor behind it. "Cute. Name, rank, and serial number."

"That's all I'm required to tell you."

"Required, yes. But we'll get what we want from you nonetheless. You can either answer our questions freely, or the Sisters of the Void will interrogate you. I understand you use them in interrogations as well, so you should know what they can do to one's mind. The chances of their tender mercies driving you permanently insane are one in ten."

Paget managed a shrug, even though his hands were still manacled behind his back, but said nothing.

"Okay, Commander. Have it your way." The interrogator climbed to his feet and pocketed his tablet. Then, he left the room.

Alone once more and though outwardly calm, Paget allowed himself a private moment of rage at having been duped by Reeve. And to think he'd vouched for her with his superiors. He never figured he was easy to manipulate. On the contrary. But Reeve had managed, and how.

Paget clamped down on his feelings once more and closed his eyes, sliding into a meditative trance. He figured they'd leave him in this uncomfortable position for a while. It would be a part of the process to weaken his resistance. Even the Sisters back home preferred to work on subjects after continuous, low-key mistreatment sapped their willpower.

When the door finally opened and Paget pulled out of the trance, his internal clock told him almost an hour had passed, and his shoulders were stiff from the unnatural posture he'd been forced to adopt. A pair of troopers with no insignia on their green uniforms, helmet visors down to hide their faces, and big, mean-looking blasters holstered at the hip entered and effortlessly lifted him from the chair.

They wordlessly led him along a bare corridor with white walls pierced at regular intervals by unmarked doors until they came to one that was open. Bundling him inside, one of the troopers removed his manacles, then both withdrew, the door slamming shut behind him.

Paget examined his new surroundings with a sinking heart. His cell was practically bare — a hard cot, a stainless-steel toilet, and a sink were its only furnishings. No windows pierced its walls or door, and he suspected the harsh light remained on day and night to help disorient him.

With a suppressed sigh, he stretched out on the bed, closed his eyes, and fell back into a meditative trance.

— 27 —

Farrin Norum couldn't begin to figure out how much time had passed when they hauled him from his cell, manacled his arms behind his back, and put him into an interrogation room. Between the lack of food and restful sleep, he was so hungry and frazzled that he had difficulty concentrating on anything.

After ten minutes, a bland-looking man wearing a business suit entered and deposited a small scanner on the table as he sat across from Norum.

"Good morning, Mister Blake. We've been reliably told you are a retired Defense Force member. Today, we find out who you really are. Before I subject you to biometric analysis, would you care to tell me your true name?"

Norum didn't reply but kept staring at the man.

"Very well, then."

He held up the scanner and pointed it at Norum's eyes for a few seconds, then glanced at its display.

"Retinal scan is good."

In his state, Norum couldn't suppress a smile as he remembered the Imperial Intelligence cosmetic surgeon injecting a fluid into his eyeball that would subtly distort his retinal print and make it untraceable. The man noticed and frowned.

"Let me guess, the retinal scan won't give up your true identity."

Norum grinned and shook his head.

After a few moments looking at the display again, the man said, "And you're right. There's no record of your retina in the Defense Force database. You must have received a distorting injection. Okay. We'll look at your fingerprints next."

Norum gave the man an amused glance.

"You had them done as well, did you?"

The man stood, walked around the table, and crouched behind Norum's chair, where he scanned the tips of the former admiral's fingers. A few moments later, he straightened and grunted.

"No record of your fingerprints. Either you lied to our source about being a former Defense Force officer, or you had a good cosmetic surgeon. I'll do a facial scan next."

He sat across from Norum once more and aimed his scanner at the latter's face. A minute passed, and the man sighed.

"There's not a trace of you in any database."

"That's because whoever told you I was a former Defense Force member," Norum said in a husky voice, "was either mistaken or a liar."

"Could be. But I will do a DNA scan next. Yet, since giving a DNA sample has only become obligatory for the Defense Force in the last few years, yours is probably not in our records." He half rose, reached for Norum's head, and deftly plucked a strand of hair.

"Hey, do you mind?"

The man didn't reply. Instead, he concentrated on feeding the hair follicle into his scanner, then sat back, eyes glued to the display. Norum knew the databases lacked a match because he had never provided a DNA sample.

Finally, the man looked up at Norum. "I guess you'll remain Frank Blake a little longer. No doubt they'll be subjecting you to one of the Sisters working as our interrogators next."

He climbed to his feet and exited the room with no further ado, leaving Norum thinking it had been a good idea to hide their true identities from Sela Reeve. No doubt they'd figure out who he was in due course, but the longer it took, the better.

Fifteen minutes later, a pair of guards escorted him back to his uncomfortable cell, where he wondered when he would be hauled out again and for what reason. Unbeknownst to him, his friend Currag DeCarde was being subjected to the same procedures, with the same results, testimony to the skill of the Imperial Intelligence's surgeon.

***

A disembodied voice ordered Paget, weakened by hunger, the discomfort of a bare cot, and constant harsh lighting, to stand with his hands joined behind his back, facing away from the cell door. When he followed instructions, the door unlocked, and a few moments later, restraints secured his wrists. A guard roughly spun him around and shoved him out into the corridor, where a second guard, also wearing armor and a visored helmet, waited.

They silently escorted him to another interrogation room, one equipped with what looked like a black tabletop or a board standing on its end. The guards removed his manacles, pushed him until he had his back against the upright panel, hands at his sides. Unexpectedly, extrusions formed, capturing his wrists, ankles, and forehead, leaving him completely immobilized.

The board tilted until it leveled, forcing Paget to stare at a featureless white ceiling. He heard the guards exit the room and remained alone for an indeterminate amount of time.

The gentle swishing of robes cut through the total silence that had prevailed until then, and a woman's narrow face framed by short gray hair suddenly appeared in his field of view. It had the sort of ageless grace he'd long ago associated with Sisters of the Void. Deep blue eyes stared into his, but he saw nothing in them, not a shred of curiosity, let alone empathy, at his plight.

"Lieutenant Commander Hal Paget, Wyvern Hegemony Navy, detailed to Intelligence's Special Reconnaissance Division." The woman's voice was deep and melodious, the sort that could easily hypnotize. "I am Sister Petra of the Order of the Void."

"I wish I could say it was a pleasure meeting you," Paget croaked, "but I would be lying, and I know what your sort thinks about liars. If your intent is to make me talk, I warn you I have little to reveal beyond my own missions, and they were, without exception, dull. At best, I could give you a travelogue of the places I visited, and they're well beyond the Republic's reach."

"Oh, I'm not interested in your past, Commander, but your future."

"How's that?"

"Very simple. We will work together to realign your loyalties and thought processes so that you can go back to the Hegemony as a double agent, working for the Republic."

A manic burst of laughter escaped Paget. "Good fracking luck with that."

"We don't need luck, Commander. Instead, we have developed the ability to enter someone's mind and influence memory engrams to change in a desired way, thereby modifying thought processes."

"Damned mind-meddling."

"If you like. You'll be the first with whom we attempt changes to this extent, but I'm sure we will succeed. It would be best if you did not fight us. Otherwise, you might experience significant physical distress, up to and including strokes, perhaps even a fatal one. Some of our subjects struggled and found themselves with various debilitating conditions, permanent insanity being one common outcome."

"Sure. I'll let you turn me into a traitor. Not a chance, Sister. I'd rather spend the rest of my life trying to piss in the corner of a round room than betray the Empire."

"We shall see about that," Petra replied in a silky tone.

A fraction of a second later, Paget yelped in surprise when ghostly fingers caressed his mind.

"What the frack was that?"

"You're sensitive to my touch, are you? That is relatively unsurprising. The number of humans able to sense us entering their consciousness has gone up dramatically over the last two centuries. We theorize it is a reaction to the quasi-extinction-level event visited upon humanity by the last Empress."

"How about you stay out of my brain?"

"Sorry. I have my orders, and they are to turn you into a double agent." The fingers remained but slowly faded until they were almost imperceptible. "Fortunately, once we're in tune with an individual mind, we can mask our presence while we work."

Paget braced himself and unleashed a torrent of mental hatred that caused Petra to gasp and withdraw.

"Now that was not nice, Commander," she chided.

"Neither is meddling with my mind."

"I shall remind you of the risks inherent in resisting my efforts. The stronger the resistance, the worse it can get."

"Still, I'll take my chances."

He felt a vague sense of someone invading his mind again, and he projected another burst of hatred, but this time, Petra didn't withdraw.

— 28 —

"And finally, we captured three Hegemony spies not five kilometers from here, sir, at the spaceport." Charisse Weber smiled proudly at President Juska. "One of them is an undercover Hegemony Navy lieutenant commander, the other two are apparently former senior Republic military officers who defected. The Navy has claimed the lieutenant commander, as he is a serving officer. Naval Intelligence thinks they can adopt the same techniques used to recondition dissidents to turn the lieutenant commander into a double agent and release him, his ship, and the Republic intelligence agent who helped capture the three to spy on the Hegemony. But the OSR holds the supposed defectors. So far, attempts at identifying them via biometrics and interrogation have failed, and we will subject them to a Sister's attentions later today."

Weber went on to describe Reeve's role in the entire business and the Hegemony agents' goal of destroying the biolab on Gennari as well as fomenting revolution on Yotai.

"So you haven't figured out who the operatives are yet." Juska tapped his desktop with his fingertips. "Yet very few senior officers and officials defected. At the very least, that much is known to us. Do you have images of them?"

"Certainly." Weber called up a holographic projection from her tablet. "The one on the left calls himself Frank Blake, and the other Paul Mortimer."

Juska frowned as he studied Blake, then a rumble from deep within his chest sounded, burbling to the surface in a roar of laughter.

"By the Almighty, I'd swear that was Farrin Norum. Which means the other one is Currag DeCarde. They vanished from Wyvern a few weeks ago, correct?"

"Yes, Mister President, and if you'll recall, I surmised they were headed into the Republic."

"Then proceed under the assumption they are Norum and DeCarde. Now, you mentioned the biolab on Gennari. In what context?"

"That it held the Barbarian Virus, and that you were contemplating its use against the Hegemony worlds."

"Damn." Juska's right fist clenched. "You will keep that information closely held."

"I've placed a blanket embargo on it."

"Good. I was always certain you'd do the right thing. How the hell did they find out about that?"

"We obviously have a further, so far unknown spy working in the biolab or at the highest levels of government, one of those with access to the information about our plans. And said spy has a secret communications pipeline back to Wyvern, probably using smugglers."

Juska sighed. "Brilliant. A spy at the heart of our scheme. Well, it appears you have a new priority — find that traitor."

"Yes, sir."

"And confront Norum. The sooner we confirm his identity, the faster we can put him in the re-education program. Can you imagine? Admiral Farrin Norum, a staunch supporter of the United Stars Bloc and my government." A beatific smile spread across Juska's face. "We might even find him a high-visibility sinecure, to remind people even my strongest opponents can see the light and become unshakable supporters."

"With the same treatment for the one we presume to be Currag DeCarde?"

"Of course."

"It shall be done. A shame the military took control of the third man, the Hegemony Navy officer."

A smiling Juska shook his finger at her.

"Don't be greedy, Charisse. Let Naval Intelligence have its piece of the action." And allow the Defense Force and the OSR to continue their rivalry. Divide and conquer.

***

The custodians escorted Norum back to the interrogation room, and this time, they shackled him to a chair bolted to the floor. After ten minutes alone, observed by Charisse Weber via the video pickup, a tall, severe-looking woman in a black suit, with short black hair framing a narrow face dominated by intense green eyes, entered and took a seat across from him.

She looked at his face in complete silence for what seemed like an eternity, then she said in a surprisingly low voice, "Now that we've found out who you are, I can absolutely see your true face beneath the surgical disguise, Admiral Norum."

The woman smiled when she saw the momentary flash of surprise in his eyes.

"Thank you for confirming it. That makes your companion Ambassador Currag DeCarde. Welcome home, Admiral. We haven't seen you around for over ten years." She allowed herself a faint smile when Norum pointedly refused to speak. "But you remain high on our list of wanted officials from the former regime. It's very kind of you to walk straight into our arms and save us a lot of grief. You were one of those bits of unfinished business that worried us."

Norum contemplated her without betraying any emotion.

"Oh, come now, Admiral. The moment I mentioned your name, I sensed a mental surge that could only have come from being recognized."

"You're a Sister of the Void." His tone made it a statement, not a question.

Her smile widened. "Yes. I'm part of a small cadre assigned to the Office for the Security of the Republic to conduct interrogations and aid sensitive investigations. The Summus Abbatissa judged it better if we blended in by trading our black robes for black business attire."

"Okay, so you recognized me. What happens now? I'm disappeared by the OSR like so many former officials?"

"No." She shook her head. "We will rehabilitate you at the Yotai Re-education Center so that you eventually become a productive member of society, at peace with the Republic's new direction and its leadership."

"In other words, brainwashed."

"No. We will simply reorient your negative impulses, and they will become positive. And you should do well, since you didn't detect my intrusion into your mind. Those who can sense a Sister's presence tend to resist her attempts at modifying thought patterns, and that can lead to unfortunate outcomes, including insanity and death."

"Isn't that fortunate for me?" Norum's voice dripped with sarcasm. "Intrusions into other people's minds without permission breaks the law and shouldn't be allowed by your training."

This time, she chuckled outright. "The law has quietly changed during your absence, and I happen to be one of those Sisters in whom the conditioning never took, hence my assignment to the OSR. Besides, for the last five years, the conditioning of new Sisters has been discontinued by the orders of the Summus Abbatissa."

"Isn't that nice. What's the next step? The Order becomes the power behind the throne and gets thoroughly enmeshed in secular affairs?"

"We exist to serve, nothing more."

"No doubt," Norum said in a dry tone. "Self-service being what it is."

He was mildly astonished at the Sister's openness about matters that should have remained internal to the Order. Was it a sign of arrogance growing along with greater influence over the business of ruling the Republic? The fact that she wore a business suit instead of the traditional robes to better blend in with the rest of the OSR officials spoke volumes.

She gave him a condescending look. "You may believe as you wish, Admiral. Once your time in the re-education center is over, you'll have a whole new outlook on life. And with that, I wish you a good day."

Ten minutes later, a pair of guards led Norum from the interrogation room straight to the underground garage, and he got into a ground car. He couldn't tell if Currag DeCarde would receive the same treatment because he hadn't seen his friend since they were arrested several days before.

***

Currag DeCarde recognized the tall, thin woman wearing a black business suit for what she was the moment she entered the interrogation room and knew instinctively he had to hide his sensitivity to a Sister's talent. According to the family lore, that awareness had been a genetic trait in the DeCardes since at least the time of the Ancestor over twelve hundred years ago. So he forced his mental defenses to stay at rest and blanked out his mind even as he felt ghostly fingers brush it. The Sister nevertheless gave him a curious look as she took the chair across the table from him.

"Ambassador Currag DeCarde. Oh, don't bother denying it. We've already identified your travel companion as Admiral Farrin Norum. And now that we know who you are, the physical resemblance is there." A cold smile briefly spread across the Sister's lips. "Plus, I felt a mental surge when I mentioned your real name just now. Yes, I'm a Sister of the Void, but you already realized that, didn't you? I wonder why."

DeCarde merely shrugged. "You carry a particular aura that spells danger."

He'd carefully chosen his words so the Sister would detect truth in the statement without giving away that he could sense her.

"Nicely put, Ambassador. You don't deny you're Currag DeCarde?"

"Would it do me any good if I did?"

"No. The surgically implanted disguise will no doubt eventually be resorbed by your body, and you will return to your own self, more or less, in a few months. We just have to hold you in isolation until then. But we have better plans. You and Admiral Norum will be useful to the government if we reeducate you into supporting President Juska and the United Stars Bloc. And that is what will happen."

DeCarde snorted. "Reeducate us into becoming supporters of Juska's criminal regime? Good luck with that nonsensical propaganda wet dream."

"Oh, we — the Order of the Void — have begun a large-scale program of re-education on behalf of the government, and it's working. Of course, as with all such interventions, individual idiosyncrasies sometimes mean a subject can go insane or die. Yet we've found it happens mainly to those with a greater awareness of a Sister adjusting their minds and fighting it. But that wouldn't be your problem, would it?"

"Fight what? An unseen assault on my subconscious? I wouldn't even have a clue where to begin."

She gave him a curious glance again, then climbed to her feet. "From here, you will go to the Yotai Re-education Center. Good day, Ambassador DeCarde."

— 29 —

Sisters Hermina and Rianne were taking their usual twilight walk through the Yotai Abbey orchard after evening services. The former prioress and the former abbess of Hatshepsut, now relegated back to ordinary Sisters, were joined by Bree, the former counselor aboard the Republic Navy Ship *Serenity*, who'd been relieved of her duties with the Defense Force and assigned to the Yotai Re-education Center. The three had gravitated to each other over the passing weeks, recognizing kindred spirits — those dismayed by the path upon which Elana had set the Order of the Void.

"Good evening, Sisters." Bree fell into step beside them.

"Good evening," both replied in the same soft tone. "What news do you have on this fine nightfall?"

"We have received two new inmates at the center, both for intense re-education. Would you believe one of them is former

Admiral Farrin Norum and the other former Ambassador Currag DeCarde?"

Hermina gasped. She'd been DeCarde's chief of staff during their brief embassy on Wyvern.

"How is it they both reappear after ten years?"

"I have no idea, but the propaganda value they represent for the regime is immense."

"Is there anything you can do to prevent them from being brainwashed?" Rianne asked.

"I'll try to figure something out."

"Please do," Hermina said. "We can't let two great men like that turn into drooling United Stars Bloc idiots."

"No, we certainly can't."

Bree's mouth twisted up at one corner. "The re-educated are hardly turned into drooling idiots. They're the same as they were, except they have a newfound love for Juska's regime. How long it lasts, we can't even begin to guess, seeing as how we barely understand the first-order effects of the engram manipulation techniques involved, let alone the second and third-order effects."

"I'm not surprised. Didn't Sister Marta warn us against attempts at modifying minds more than two hundred years ago?" Hermina asked. "Something about killing subjects or driving them insane."

"And we've had our share of deaths and madness since Elana ordered the re-education program to begin. Still, a surprising number of political prisoners had their outlooks successfully changed to become fervent supporters of Juska."

"Yet most of the Sisters engaged in re-education don't care about those who suffer."

Bree shook her head. "No. Elana has cleverly assigned the ones whose empathy ratings are below normal and whose conditioning never took. Thank the Almighty I'm assigned to the center as a psychologist, not a re-educator. I'd find it distressingly difficult, otherwise. I still cannot understand why Elana is taking us into this disastrous direction and aligning herself with Juska's misbegotten goals."

"Power," Hermina said with finality. "Nothing more than that. She wants power over the secular as well as the spiritual."

"But why?"

"Because Elana is one of those Sisters without empathy in whom conditioning never took. I'd even venture that beneath the carefully crafted surface, she has no soul."

"Surely we weed out psychopaths before they begin training," Bree said.

"No selection system is one hundred percent accurate. It was only a matter of time before a soulless one passed."

"And climbed rapidly to seize leadership of the Order," Rianne added. "Now, she's using those like her to advance an agenda that will transform the Order into something I fear could turn nightmarish."

"It will end up nightmarish, Rianne," Hermina said. "I'm involved in a top-secret program with the Order's biosciences sector. A group of Sisters with a background in biology, including me, are quietly reviving an ancient virus that has been kept in stasis for over two centuries, a bioweapon dating back to the old Empire with a one hundred percent casualty rate."

Both Bree and Rianne took a sharp breath as they realized what Hermina meant. Rianne gave her a sideways glance.

"You don't mean…"

"Oh, yes. The billions living in the Hegemony are to be eradicated through work performed by the Order. Once we soil ourselves by assisting in a genocide, there can be no way back to the Almighty. I got word to Wyvern about it — don't ask me how, I will never say — and I suspect Norum and DeCarde were here to stop the operation before the stasis canisters with the live virus leave Gennari."

"Then you must do so in their stead," Bree whispered.

"Don't think I'm not considering ways of accomplishing that ever since I found out the ultimate goal of reviving the virus. I cannot imagine a universe where such horror would be unleashed on Hegemony worlds, and I would gladly give my life to stop it."

"Glad to hear you say so, Hermina."

They walked on in silence for a few minutes, all three contemplating Hermina's revelation. Finally, Rianne spoke.

"We must find a way to stop Elana. If she's supporting Juska's regime in fomenting genocide, what other abominations is she ready to promote in her quest to make the Order preeminent in the Republic's affairs and herself the true power behind the presidency?"

"Can the council of elders not force her out?" Bree asked.

Hermina bit back a bark of laughter. "She has the elders thoroughly wrapped around her little finger. How, I do not know, but I hear her talent is one of the strongest, if not *the* strongest, of our generation."

Bree repressed a shiver. "A powerful talent that is not constrained by a soul. We will certainly head straight into darkness."

"That is why Rianne and I seek like-minded Sisters and Friars to form the nucleus of a resistance movement against Elana, one which will, in due course, eject her from the Summus Abbatissa's chair and ban her to Lyonesse's Windy Isles."

Bree took a sharp inhalation. "That would be unprecedented."

"These are unprecedented times. But make no mistake. Elana will do everything to retain her power and position, including sending rebellious Brethren to the Windy Isles themselves."

"Oh, I'm in. Elana will lead us to perdition, and we must stop her.

"Good. Then know we are organized on a cell basis — three or four Brethren per. You're the third in our cell. Rianne and I are in clandestine contact with other cells as we build up our strength until we have enough Brethren ready to rise up and enforce Elana's exile as well as the nomination of a new Summus Abbatissa."

"Understood."

"If you come across Brethren who think like we do, approach them quietly and sound them out. Should they be willing to join the resistance, set up your own cell, but do not, under any circumstances, mention this one."

"And when will we know it is time to rise against Elana?"

Hermina gave her a small smile. "You'll know, trust me."

The trio reached the gate to the orchard and split up, each headed for their respective dormitories, Bree lost in thought.

She had a hard time fathoming that the Order was so divided about Elana's path that a faction — size unknown — would actively militate to replace her, by force if necessary. As a wise one once said, a house divided against itself cannot stand. Will the Order of the Void remain when the dust settled?

Bree had been one of those who'd secretly wished for a greater rapprochement with the Void Reborn, bridging the relationship between Republic and Hegemony, especially once the latter branch of the Order returned to communion with Lindisfarne. But Elana wanted nothing to do with the ancient Motherhouse, calling it hopelessly lost in the past and incapable of leading the Void toward a greater future. And, even worse, for some inexplicable reason, she held the Void Reborn beneath contempt.

Perhaps the Order could correct its direction once Elana had gone, and they could also potentially enter into communion with Lindisfarne.

The next morning, Bree found herself in the re-education center's operations room, staring at side-by-side displays showing Farrin Norum and Currag DeCarde in their cells, which, fortunately for them, were more comfortable than those they'd enjoyed in the OSR's dungeon.

Sister Ygritte entered and came to stand beside her.

"Any inmates of interest, Bree?" She asked.

"Norum and DeCarde, of course. Hard to believe they were once powerful and respected, only to fall into OSR hands wearing disguises."

"They will be respected once more when we're done with them, although not powerful except as propaganda tools." Ygritte's matter-of-fact tone sent a small shiver up Bree's spine. "Why are you interested in them?"

"Because of what they represent more than anyone else in here — the old regime with its flaws. It shall be interesting to follow their progress."

"Feel free to observe their treatment and transformation firsthand, Bree. I've always suspected your fascination with the re-education process was greater than you let on."

A faint smile crossed Bree's lips. "You read me well, Ygritte. Yes, I would be interested in joining the Sisters who will tackle those two."

"Then it is done. We can always use more re-educators, and your talent is strong. Besides, you've served several years with the Defense Force, and that may come in useful with a former Navy admiral and a former Marine Corps colonel."

"Thank you. When does their treatment start?"

"Tomorrow. Sister Desra has primary responsibility for their re-education. She is most adept at it and probably one of our best."

— 30 —

"You want to do what?" Lieutenant Sela Reeve, United Stars Republic Navy, laughed incredulously.

"Turn him and send both of you back into the Hegemony, claiming mission accomplished."

When she saw that Captain Quyon was dead serious, Reeve's smile disappeared. Her superior, the head of Naval Intelligence's Reconnaissance and Exploration Division, didn't have much of a sense of humor to begin with. Both, wearing civilian business suits, sat in the latter's office in a nondescript wing of the new Defense Force HQ on the western outskirts of New Lena.

"Begging your pardon, sir, but in what universe will you turn a professional like Hal Paget? He's steadfastly loyal to the Hegemony, and we have no blackmail material on him."

"The Sisters of the Void have developed means by which they can reprogram minds. Apparently, they've already turned several dissidents into fervent supporters of President Juska's administration."

"Those d'ayvols? The Almighty protect us!"

"I know the Sisters aren't your favorite people, Sela, but they assured me their chances of turning Lieutenant Commander Paget into a compliant tool of the Republic are high."

Reeve snorted derisively. "And I have better chances of becoming Derik Juska's anointed successor. It's an idea so horrible I can't find adequate words to express how awful it is. I suppose you expect me to babysit him so I can monitor whether it took."

"Yes, and if it didn't take, kill him. This will be as much a field test of the Sisters' success in mind-meddling as a viable means of spying on the Hegemony directly. You've taken control of the AI on his ship, so you should be safe."

"I still think it's a lousy idea, sir, and I don't trust the d'ayvols further than I can spit at them. They're full of promises, but apart from turning the odd political prisoner doolally by screwing with their brains, I haven't yet seen them turn anyone sufficiently to be trusted with a starship. So we get back and tell the Hegemony, mission accomplished. But they obviously have a source in the project itself, and that source won't be singing from the same hymnal."

"By the time they verify, the containers with the live virus will already be on their way. In the meantime, they'll be a little more complacent than they would otherwise be, and that's a positive thing."

"And how will the d'ayvols know Paget has become a loyal spy for the Republic and isn't just shamming?"

Quyon shrugged. "That, I don't know. We pretty much have to take their word for it."

"Again — a lousy idea, sir. What if he isn't turned but fakes it well enough to fool everyone, and then takes me out? Or hands me over to the Hegemony's tender mercies?"

"That's a risk we'll have to assume."

Reeve didn't quite sneer, but the beginnings of one were apparent. "What's this 'we' shit, sir? I'm the only one who'll be assuming the risk."

"Careful, Lieutenant." Quyon raised a restraining hand, indicating Reeve had just crossed a line.

"Sorry, sir." But she didn't sound repentant one bit.

"In any case, I acknowledge your reservations, but the Chief of Naval Intelligence herself issued the orders."

"I'm not surprised. She is a d'ayvol lover. Probably wishes she had enough brainpower to become one herself."

Quyon sighed. Reeve was an excellent field operative, with a quirky yet brilliant mind, and a ruthlessness that served her well. Yet she could also be coarse and unafraid to express her feelings, something which would hold her at the rank of lieutenant for the rest of her career. But since she preferred being out there, undercover, rank didn't matter, and her career could be cut short if she tripped up, something getting more likely with every mission because statistically she was bound to eventually fail. In fact, if it hadn't been for Paget, she'd still be stuck on Coraline, or her dead body would be moldering there, ending an unconventional, if not idiosyncratic, career, because she'd finally made one mistake too many.

"Just once, will you cheerfully accept orders and carry them out in the spirit of obedience?"

Reeve winked at him. "You'd keel over from a heart attack if I ever did so."

***

"Good morning, Hal." Sister Fricka, whom he privately called his very own torturer, entered his cell, a cheerful smile plastered on her soft, round features. Like all Sisters, she appeared ageless, though the cap of short dark hair framing her face held a few strands of gray, and fine lines radiated from the corners of brown eyes that seemed curiously dead under certain angles of light. "And how are you today?"

Knowing she was probing his mind, he projected a gory scene of dead bodies and blood.

Fricka's peal of laughter sounded like little bells chiming. "Give it up, Hal. You're only making yourself miserable by thinking those disgusting thoughts. They don't have any effect on me."

"A prisoner of war must resist the enemy by any means necessary."

"You're hardly a prisoner of war, since no conflict exists between the Republic and the Hegemony."

"It's the Second Empire, you daft, dark-robed, mind-meddling devil."

She gave him a beatific smile. "Flattery will get you everywhere."

At least the cell was livable. It resembled a tiny, somewhat bare studio apartment more than anything else. The bed had sheets and covers; there was a small sitting area with an entertainment display that gave access to a large library; and a separate bathroom. It had no windows, but at least he could control the lights. Best of all, they shoved a covered food tray three times a day through a slot in the wall, and to Paget's surprise, its contents were quite palatable and varied.

He remained confined to the small space, however, and the Almighty only knew what Sister Fricka was doing to his memories and his mind. So far, he couldn't sense any changes within, but then, would he?

"Sorry, Fricka. You're not my type."

The peal of laughter sounded again, and she said, "I'm also old enough to be your grandmother."

"I can tell."

"Now, will you sit and subject yourself to my touch voluntarily, or shall I call in the guards and have you strapped down?"

Paget considered her question for a few heartbeats and decided physical resistance didn't give him a damn bit of leverage. Though he didn't realize it, that was the first sign of Sister Fricka's success — the dwindling of his defiance against her.

"Do your worst, you witch. Whatever you're attempting, it's not working." He settled back in his chair and closed his eyes. Shortly thereafter, he felt her cool fingertips touch the base of his skull. Then, his awareness dwindled to nothing.

When we became conscious of his surroundings once more, the fingertips were gone, as was an hour of his time, but without a clock anywhere, he figured only moments had passed.

"That was it for today, Hal." Fricka rose in a graceful movement and left Paget to wonder what she'd done to him as she exited his cell.

A tall, narrow-faced woman with platinum hair intercepted Fricka in the corridor.

"I'm Sela Reeve, Sister, and I've observed your treatment just now, or at least the last five minutes of it."

"Ah, yes. The Naval Intelligence agent who brought Hal Paget in."

"And whose orders are to take him out again."

Fricka cocked her head to one side as she probed Reeve's mind and found nothing but solid mental barriers.

"What can I do for you?"

"You can tell me whether your chances of genuinely turning him into a double agent are more than just wishful thinking. My life will depend on it, should we be sent back into the Hegemony, and he's not really turned but successfully shamming."

"You don't have much faith in our abilities, do you?"

Reeve shook her head. "And I don't trust your sort, period."

"Perhaps because you're a wild talent?"

"Oh, I'm wild, alright. And I get wilder whenever my life is at stake."

"To answer your question — the chances of turning him are pretty good; the chances of him successfully faking being turned are zero."

"Zero, eh? I wish I had your convictions. But I don't."

Fricka gave her a mysterious smile. "You'll see for yourself when the time comes."

"What do you mean?"

But instead of replying, Fricka walked away with a silent wave over her shoulder.

Reeve felt a surge of irritation course through her body. How typical of the d'ayvol to leave more questions than answers in their wake.

—31—

Commodore (retired) Lucas Morane, on the run from Derik Juska's regime for the last eighteen months, had lately been feeling the noose tightening around his neck. Especially since rumors began to float around resistance circles that the OSR had captured Farrin Norum and Currag DeCarde. Those rumors floated in no small part because Sisters of the Void who disagreed with Elana were doing their best to whisper the word in the right ears.

A direct descendant of the Republic's founder, Jonas Morane, he'd begun opposing Juska the moment he was involuntarily retired from the Navy because, like his ancestor, he clearly saw the disastrous direction the regime had taken. At first, the president and his followers tolerated him and the others who spoke out against the president, but then, as Juska tightened his grip on the Republic, the police harassment and intimidation began in earnest.

Morane had left Lyonesse for Yotai under a new identity before the latter became the Republic's capital and immediately vanished underground, hoping that the security forces had lost his trail.

He'd continued assembling a core of hardened dissidents, but it was slow work. In despair, he'd sent a cryptic message into the Second Empire, hoping it would reach his old friend and mentor Farrin Norum. If the rumors were true, it not only seemed to have reached the latter, but he'd actually come, only to end up in the hands of the OSR, possibly betrayed by whoever brought him to Yotai.

The realization and feeling of doom that had crept over him in recent times made Morane isolate himself from his closest allies, lest he somehow betray them. And that, in turn, fueled a sense of despondency like he'd never experienced before.

He glanced over his shoulder before disappearing into a narrow garbage-strewn alley in one of the oldest quarters of New Lena, where abandoned warehouses dominated, even though he knew it was impossible to detect any surveillance. The OSR was much too professional by now and would be watching without his being aware. If they were watching him. But his instincts screamed that the OSR had made him and was keeping him on an invisible leash to see who he contacted.

Morane turned into another alley, as insalubrious as the previous one, and with a final look around him, disappeared inside a darkened doorway.

Lights came on the moment the door panel wheezed shut behind him, revealing a short corridor with dingy white walls and a grimy gray plastic floor. Three openings led to the rooms that made up the cheap, no ID required apartment he had been renting for almost a year — bedroom, kitchen, and living room combo, and bathroom. None had windows to the outside — the rooms didn't actually appear on any city plan, but the bedroom boasted a hidden tunnel entrance which led beneath the alley and into an abandoned warehouse's basement. This feature persuaded Morane to take the seedy smuggler's apartment.

The furnishings were basic, but clean, and once he'd gotten used to living in what was a manufactured grotto, he found it rather cozy. And it had a rudimentary early warning system — a motion-detecting camera overlooking the alley, ready to alert him if anyone approached his door.

He'd never brought any of his contacts in the resistance here, and as far as he knew, no one else was aware of his little hideaway, other than the scruffy man who'd leased him the place and collected the rent every month. And he studiously avoided asking any questions, not even about the assumed name taken by Morane.

He removed his jacket and unclipped his holstered blaster from his waistband, hanging the former over a kitchen chair and dropping the latter on the counter. How long would his safe house remain safe, he wondered as he pulled a cold beer bulb from the stasis box and nipped off the end of its drinking tube. He took a healthy swig and sighed.

Amazing that humanity still brewed the stuff in much the same way after more than seven thousand years since it first appeared in the historical records on old Earth. And the recipe had traveled thousands of light-years in every direction during the human diaspora to the stars, adapting to new worlds and new strains of yeast, grain, and hops. Morane had no doubt the Yotai brewed beer's taste bore little resemblance to one brewed before humanity reached for the stars, but the palate adapted, especially where ethanol was involved.

A small beep shattered the silence, and he immediately swung around toward the living room display, which had lit up automatically, showing the alley outside. Five individuals wearing black tactical clothing, harnesses, and visored helmets, carrying carbines, were carefully casing his lodging's door. There could only be one explanation, since the entrance was nondescript and more likely a side door to the disused warehouse surrounding the apartment.

"Damn."

Morane knew his luck had finally run out. He grabbed his jacket and blaster and headed for the bedroom. There, he touched a control button hidden in the baseboard, and lines suddenly appeared on the previously blank wall, outlining a panel, which slid aside moments later. Still carrying the beer bulb, Morane entered the small dark space behind the panel and touched another control, sealing the opening once more.

He climbed down a narrow shaft on a ladder until he reached a low-ceilinged horizontal tunnel faintly lit by dying glow globes. Water dripped randomly from cracks in the walls and ceiling, and slime made the floor slippery.

As he took cautious steps, Morane figured that if the OSR didn't know about his secret escape route, he still had a chance of eluding them. But then what? Another change of appearance, of course. The increasing amount of surveillance sensors blanketing New Lena, at least in the more respectable quarters — they tended to malfunction in the rougher parts of town — practically demanded it. And then, he'd try to disappear among the city's growing transient population, perhaps move to the second largest agglomeration on Yotai, five hundred kilometers south of New Lena.

He reached the end of the tunnel and another shaft with a ladder pointing toward the surface. Having done the trip several times to familiarize himself with both ends, Morane knew he'd emerge in a hidden closet at the back of one of the abandoned warehouse's offices, but wouldn't be able to see if anyone waited for him outside.

Morane gently touched the controls to open the closet door, and it silently slid aside, exposing an empty office with a thick layer of dust on the floor. So far, so good. He listened for almost a minute, but beyond the faint sounds of small creatures scurrying about unseen, he heard nothing.

Then, he carefully stepped out and made for the office door, cracking it just enough to peer out. Still nothing. Encouraged, Morane crossed the bare warehouse floor, noting the only traces in the dust were those of little three-toed native rat analogs. Clearly, the OSR was unaware of his escape route. For now. They'd eventually find the hidden door in the apartment, and he needed to get out of here.

He slipped through the half-open cargo doors at the other end and headed across a yard overgrown with tough, native vegetation reclaiming its little piece of the planet. One glance at the alley through a gate hanging drunkenly to one side to confirm it was empty, and he stepped through.

After orienting himself, Morane headed deeper into what was generally acknowledged as the city's lawless zone, where transients lived cheek by jowl with criminals, drug users, and assorted riffraff. The local police occasionally patrolled the area but generally left the people to prey on each other. The authorities didn't care what happened to the dregs of society in Derik Juska's enlightened Republic.

Once at the heart of the zone, Morane made his way to the hidden saloon back room where the Identity Maker held court. There, he dumped a handful of cred chips on the counter, and in half an hour, he received a new appearance and new credentials that were good enough for everyday use.

After thanking the man, Morane returned to the street and searched out the flophouse he'd previously reconnoitered in case he had to vacate the apartment quickly. Taking care to appear tough and intimidating, he stepped over a few addicts in the throes of their drug-induced hallucinations, while meeting the eyes of losers and outcasts sitting in doorways, sizing him up for a quick mugging. Bearded, with long hair, a craggy face, and a piercing gaze, Lucas Morane exuded menace in the way he carried himself. Those who'd served a hitch in the Defense Force recognized a fellow former member, while the pure civilians saw a man who shouldn't be crossed.

He reached the flophouse and entered.

"Got a cot for three nights?" He asked the thin, scruffy-looking woman sitting behind a pane of transparent aluminum that protected her from the rowdier inmates.

"Yep. Ten creds, in advance," she replied in a thin, scratchy voice, pointing at a sliding tray cut through the pane. "No fighting, no drugs, and no sex. Otherwise, you're out on your ass with no refund."

"Sure." He dropped a ten-cred chip in the tray and watched it vanish in an instant.

"Second floor, room twenty-three." She indicated the stairway behind her.

"Thanks."

Morane climbed the grimy concrete stairs — no lifts in this part of town — and found his room near the landing. He opened the door onto a space that made ordinary closets look spacious. It contained a narrow bed, a tiny table, and a few shelves, nothing more. After keying the door lock with his thumbprint, Morane found the communal washroom and availed himself of the facilities, then took the stairs back to the lobby and exited the flophouse, looking for food.

He found a rundown tavern one block over, entered, and, after a scan of the sparsely populated taproom, took a corner table. The place was cleaner than its outside appearance suggested, though the furnishings showed signs of age and heavy use. A large man in a sleeveless shirt held court behind the metal-topped bar, a giant blaster holstered at his hip. Morane figured he had little trouble with the riffraff.

A holographic menu popped up from the tabletop, and he studied it with one eye — a list of drinks and a much shorter list of food items. Then his nostrils caught the aromas wafting from the kitchen, and they were more enticing than he'd expected. Morane ordered a hot-pot and a beer and sat back, eyes roaming over his surroundings. He must not have looked out of place because no one paid him the slightest bit of attention, and for the first time since the display in his former apartment bleeped to life, he felt some of the tension in his shoulders drain away.

After a while, Morane smiled as he thought about how far he'd fallen — from commodore in the Republic's Navy to vagrant and political criminal on the run. Then again, his friend Farrin Norum had fallen from far higher and, after ten years on the run, ended up in the clutches of the OSR. Derik Juska had much to answer for, and Morane would gladly put a round from his blaster through the president's skull, but that had to stay in the realm of fantasy.

— 32 —

"It's quite simple." Sisters Desra and Bree stood outside Farrin Norum's cell, watching him via a display beside the door. "And rather complex at the same time. We enter his mind and imprint good feelings about President Juska and his government onto his memory engrams. But finding the right engrams can be difficult, and we theorize that the attempt to imprint the wrong engrams causes the negative reactions we've seen from time to time. But we have yet to find proof. The whole science of manipulating the mind by etching false memories directly onto the brain is still poorly understood. And that's mainly because of the two-hundred-year moratorium on research thanks to Sister Marta, the great-grandmother several times removed of our Admiral Norum."

"What happened?"

"The way I understand it, she was experimenting with psychopathic prisoners in the Windy Isles, attempting to cure them. One died a horrible death under her care when her brain literally burned out, and Marta never forgave herself. She had the Summus Abbatissa of the time forbid further research and experimentation involving direct intervention in another's mind."

"And Elana removed the strictures."

Desra nodded. "Just so."

"Do you wish me to join you in his cell?"

"Yes. And since Ygritte indicated you might be interested in becoming a re-educator, you'll accompany me in entering the subject's mind to observe what I do and how I do it. We shall join our consciousnesses, so you sense what I sense."

"I have never joined with another Sister."

"You'll find the experience interesting. We retain our individuality, of course, and cannot enter each other's minds unless we want to. But it's not necessary. Discovering the ability to join is another result of Elana finally allowing research."

"Interesting." Bree studied Norum, who sat in his cell's only chair, staring at an entertainment screen. "I am ready, whenever you wish to begin."

Desra touched a control surface embedded in the door jamb, and it slid aside noiselessly. An obviously alert Norum turned toward it almost immediately and watched the two black-robed Sisters enter.

"I am Desra, and this is Bree. We are your re-educators."

"I won't lie and say I'm pleased to meet you, Sisters. Let's just say I abhor the notion of meddling with another's mind and changing parts of it against his will."

"In that, you do not differ from any of the other subjects who pass through our hands."

"Subjects? Is that what you call your victims? Nicely dehumanizing, if you ask me. But then, considering you're abominations, I shouldn't expect anything else."

A cold smile briefly touched Desra's lips. "Abominations? Do take care with your epithets, Admiral, for I can show you terrors like you've never imagined."

"I'm sure you can because I've witnessed Sisters of the Void Reborn doing so to loosen the tongues of criminals. Not a pleasant sight. But I understand they'll no longer do so since they've submitted to Lindisfarne and are withdrawing from those secular affairs that are contrary to the Spirit of the Void." He paused and then, injecting as much contempt and loathing into his voice as he could, he added, "Whereas you're embracing the vilest of secular business. At least the Void Reborn never tried to rewrite someone's thoughts."

"Retreating back to the old ways will ensure the lesser Void Orders vanish, leaving us as the only true servants of the Almighty."

"The way you're going, Sister, the Almighty will turn away from your debased version of the Order, leaving it to serve the darkness."

"Enough," Desra snapped. "You are not in a position to criticize us, you who betrayed the Republic and its citizens by defecting to our existential enemy."

Norum let out a bark of laughter. "You've swallowed Juska's and the United Stars Bloc's propaganda wholesale, Sister. It doesn't speak well for you."

Desra took a few steps and placed her dry, cold fingertips on Norum's neck before he could protest. Almost at once, his capacity to shrug her off vanished.

"You bloody witch. Give me back my free will."

"Shush, Admiral. This will go much easier and faster if you simply sit back and relax."

Desra held her other hand out to Bree, who took it. A second or two later, the latter felt Desra's consciousness brush up against hers. Then, she followed it as they plunged into Norum's mind, looking for places they could use to anchor new memories of admiration and respect for Derik Juska. It was painstaking work, and when Desra finally broke contact with Norum an hour later, both she and Bree were exhausted.

"That will suffice for today, Admiral. You may now exercise your free will once more."

"Gee, thanks." Norum rolled his stiff shoulders and slowly loosened his neck muscles. "And thanks for causing me massive muscle seizures in my upper body."

"If I didn't have to keep you forcibly still, you wouldn't be in pain. Think about it the next time."

With that, Desra and Bree left the cell.

"How did you find your first experience?" The former asked as they walked along the corridor to the Sisters' break room for a breather.

"Um, fascinating. I've never been so deep inside another's mind. But I still couldn't sense anything beyond his emotions, which were quite strong and negative toward us."

"That is normal. Reading another's thoughts is still beyond us. Just finding the places in his consciousness where we can implant new memories is a stretch."

"I saw nothing like that."

"And you won't until I begin the process of implantation. Then, you'll discover what those places look like. But once you do, you never forget. We'll tackle DeCarde after the midday meal. I should be sufficiently recovered by then."

"Is it highly draining?"

"Yes." Desra nodded once. "Implanting the new memories even more so. That is why it takes weeks to complete in even the most cooperative of subjects. Those with awareness of our doings in their mind take longer since they fight us. Some go insane; a few die."

The matter-of-fact way in which Desra spoke made Bree cringe inwardly. The Order of the Void was supposed to ease suffering, not cause it. If this was their future, she might as well defect to the Empire as well because she could not see herself remaining in an Order so cruel. But first, she had to find a way of keeping Admiral Norum and Ambassador DeCarde from joining Juska's cheerleaders, or worse, suffering insanity or death.

They were back in the detention block after eating, this time observing Currag DeCarde via the display beside his cell door. He, too, was watching the entertainment screen from the cell's sole chair. After a few minutes, Desra touched the control panel embedded in the door jamb, and it opened.

"I am Sister Desra, and this is Sister Bree. We are your re-educators," the former said as they stepped into the cell.

DeCarde kept his eyes on the screen but said, "I'm in no need of further education, let alone re-education, so kindly fuck off, Sisters."

Desra reached out to touch his subconscious and found impassable barriers around it.

"You have defenses."

"Congratulations for noticing. I guess you're a real mind meddler and not some cheap imitation in black robes."

"You will drop them."

"No."

Desra attempted an all-out assault on DeCarde's barriers and let out a small shriek when he assaulted her in turn with gory images of dismemberment and death, forcing her to retreat.

"How did you do that?" Though in control of her words, both Bree and DeCarde noticed slight tremors in the tone, a sign the brief experience had thoroughly shaken her.

"It's a genetic trait my family has carried since the time of the Ancestor before the First Empire was founded. But I can't reach out to others, only project when others enter my mind."

"I see. Then we have a problem."

"You have a problem. Without access, you can't reeducate me, and I won't give you access."

"There are ways to convince you, Ambassador. All human beings have a finite limit on the amount of pain they can tolerate. Once we find your threshold, we will apply pressure until you yield."

"So, the Order of the Void, Lyonesse Version, is into torture as well as forcible mind-meddling now? How the hell did that happen?" DeCarde slowly turned his head toward Desra and cocked an eyebrow. "When I left five years ago, it was still a benevolent religious organization dedicated to succoring the afflicted."

"We do not torture people, although the OSR will employ more robust methods of convincing political prisoners to cooperate with us. As for the forcible mind-meddling, as you call it, that is merely to correct antisocial leanings and help political prisoners reintegrate into society as productive, cheerful members.”

“I suppose telling yourself sweet little lies like that is a coping mechanism. Then you don’t have to look at yourself in the mirror and wonder why you’re such an evil, soulless bitch.”

A thin, icy smile briefly pulled at Desra’s lips. “Oh, I’m going to so enjoy re-educating you, DeCarde. Maybe I’ll slip in a few special behavior modifiers just for fun.”

“Good luck with that. My mental defenses will not drop even though you end up killing me. Understand that they’re up by default, and I have to will them down. For that, I need to be awake, conscious, and not in pain, because pain overrides my ability to lower them. It’s an instinctive survival mechanism. Don’t ask me how it works because I don’t know. We DeCardes are born with it.”

“We shall see. And if you are impossible to reeducate, you might provide one last service to the Republic by being executed as an example to others who would defect.”

“A Sister of the Void advocating for capital punishment simply because one disagrees with the president? What next? Execution for holding the wrong beliefs? You’re not the Order of the Void; you’re the Order of Darkness. The Almighty’s face has turned away from you, damning you and your Brethren for eternity.”

Desra shook her head. “You talk too much, Ambassador. I will refer you back to the OSR, and they’ll see what they can do. The Sister conducting your interrogation did not mention any defenses. According to her report, she entered your mind easily.”

“Because I let her.”

“I get the feeling a bit of vigorous convincing will open your mind. Enjoy the rest of your day.”

With that, Desra turned on her heels and left the cell. Bree gave DeCarde a sympathetic glance before following her colleague back into the corridor.

Desra's words, especially her equivocation and hypocrisy, mildly shocked her, and she wondered whether DeCarde might be right — that the Almighty's face had turned away from them for the monstrous acts Sisters were committing against other human beings.

The following day, a familiar, yet still nameless figure entered DeCarde's cell as he sat in front of the entertainment screen — the business suit-wearing Sister who'd first interviewed him in the OSR dungeon. A thickset bald man with a goatee, also wearing dark business attire, followed her. He carried a briefcase in his left hand.

"Good morning, Ambassador."

"Look who the rats dragged back into my cell. What do you want, Sister?" DeCarde immediately dropped his mental defenses, and ghostly fingers brushed his mind. "What's your name, by the way?"

"You can call me Mara."

DeCarde glanced at the silent, expressionless man behind her. "And your friend is?"

"An OSR officer. His name isn't important." She cocked her head to one side as their eyes met. "Curious. Desra told me that you have strong mental barriers and refuse to drop them, so you can be re-educated. And that you even claim pain will cause them to remain shut against your will. Yet I can sense your emotions without issues. Why is that?"

A shrug. "You were misinformed, or Sister Desra is incompetent."

"Oh, I think neither is the case. You're merely toying with me."

Instead of replying, DeCarde projected the goriest imagery he could come up with and had the satisfaction of hearing Mara gasp.

"I see you're going to be a challenge," she said after recovering her composure. She produced a wicked-looking blaster from underneath her tunic and pointed it at DeCarde. "Please don't move while the officer secures you to the chair."

The man placed his briefcase on the small table fixed to the cell wall, opened it, and pulled out manacles. A few moments later, DeCarde's arms, legs, and torso were tightly fastened to the chair. Then the man slipped a band over DeCarde's forehead and the chair's headrest, immobilizing his head.

De Carde said, "I wondered why the jailers configured and bolted the chair to the floor in that way. Now I know."

"We don't want you to injure yourself during the procedure."

A bark of laughter escaped DeCarde's throat. "You black-robed spawn of darkness do have a way with sophistry — calling torture a procedure. As if that word substitution hides your inhumanity."

"Has anyone ever told you that you talk too much?"

"As a matter of fact, your fellow malignant Sister from hell, Desra, did only yesterday."

The man pulled a metallic cap from his briefcase and placed it on DeCarde's head. Instantly, he sensed hundreds of tiny probes extruding and coming into contact with his scalp.

"This is a pain inducer," Mara said. "It stimulates the pain centers of the brain, making you experience various sensations, such as being burned, limbs being cut off, cuts being inflicted, and so much more. You will not be physically hurt, although the sensation will be authentic. Most subjects cannot endure more than a few minutes before breaking and submitting."

"But my mind is open to you. There's no need to torture me."

"You refused Desra, and now you will suffer the consequences."

She nodded at the OSR officer, who had a small tablet in his hands, and a blinding flash of pain in the fingers and toes struck DeCarde. His eyes closed as he let out an involuntary groan.

"How was that?"

"Miserable," DeCarde replied through clenched teeth.

"Let's try something else."

The OSR officer glanced at his tablet again, and DeCarde's chest felt like it was on fire. This time, he let out a cry and began panting. Just as suddenly as it had come on, the pain vanished, though his nerve endings tingled unpleasantly. Then, before he had a chance to recover, a spasm seized his back, and he tried arching it to relieve the agony, but couldn't because of the restraints. For a moment, he thought he would pass out, but then it faded away, leaving nothing but a vivid memory of the torment behind.

"That hurt, you bitch," DeCarde said between gasps of air.

"Well, at least what you said about your mind slamming shut when you experience pain appears to be correct. Your barriers are impenetrable under the pain inducer's impulses. Now, shall we continue, or do you open your mind to Desra?"

"Go frack yourself."

Mara nodded at the OSR officer again, and a wave of blinding pain coursed down every nerve in DeCarde's body, and he screamed as time seemed to stand still. When the officer cut the impulse, his neurons kept firing, and it took over a minute for them to stop. Meanwhile, DeCarde hovered on the edge of unconsciousness.

As he recovered, he realized that he'd almost reached his limit and couldn't go on taunting Mara. No, DeCarde had to find another solution, perhaps opening himself and quietly reversing every bit of interference Desra planted in his mind.

"Okay." His voice came out as a croak. "You win. I'll drop my defenses for Desra."

"I thought you'd see it my way. Just remember, any backsliding will earn you another visit from us, and the next time we won't be so gentle." He lowered his mental barriers and sensed the unnerving caress of invisible fingers. "Stay as you are, and you'll be fine."

The OSR officer methodically removed the inducer and the restraints and stowed them in the briefcase, then he left the cell. Mara studied DeCarde for a bit longer.

"I do believe you'll let Desra carry out her work."

And with that, she turned on her heels and left. Moments later, Sister Desra swept in, followed by Bree. The former looked jubilant, while a distinct air of concern hung about the latter, as if she was worried about his treatment at the hands of Sister Mara.

"Shall we begin?"

Desra placed a cold, dry hand on the back of DeCarde's neck and offered her other hand to Bree. Almost immediately, DeCarde fought his desire to raise barriers as ghostly fingers probed his mind. But this was a different sort of probe, one that didn't just softly caress like a Sister tasting his emotions. It touched specific spots repeatedly, though no new memories were left behind. Unnerving though the sensation was, he managed to remain dispassionate and let Desra wander through, testing his engrams. This went on for almost an hour, and he soon got used to what once made his skin crawl. Then, it ended.

"Thank you, Ambassador."

Both Sisters left his cell, though Bree gave him a look of concern before disappearing into the corridor.

Bree learned the exotic art of implanting false memories over the next few days as Desra tutored her and then allowed her to perform the procedure on Norum and DeCarde. After a little over a week, Desra reported back to Sister Ygritte that Bree was doing well, and Ygritte reassigned her to one of their tougher cases, leaving Bree alone in treating Norum and DeCarde.

Bree had hoped for precisely that.

On her first solo treatment, she implanted a very specific memory — that of her telling both men she would no longer imprint false memories on their engrams, but that they should act as if she did and slowly become big fans of Derik Juska. And they had to be true fans if another Sister scanned them to check, which meant she would still work to repress some of their stronger feelings toward him.

At the end of Norum's turn, he simply looked at her curiously, and she slowly nodded once. DeCarde, who was conscious of her actions, locked eyes with Bree before she left his cell and gave her a faint but unmistakable acknowledgment.

That evening, walking through the Abbey orchard with Hermina and Rianne, Bree told them what she had done.

"Praise the Almighty for having opened a way," Hermina said. "You're sure they'll be able to pass as treated?"

She wrinkled her nose in disgust as she spoke the sentence's last word.

"No, I'm not, but I have several weeks to work something out."

"You'll have to share with us, Bree," Rianne said. "Naval Intelligence has a Hegemony officer undergoing treatment to turn him into a double agent. Fricka couldn't help boasting about it last night. She's received the job of turning the man, a Hal Paget. He apparently commanded the undercover Hegemony Navy ship that brought Norum and DeCarde to Yotai. I've put in a request for a transfer from military chaplaincy to Intelligence as an interrogator so I might help this Paget in the same way Bree is helping the other two."

— 34 —

New Draconis, Wyvern
Second Empire

"We may have a serious problem, Mister President," Grand Admiral Anton Mejik said after he and Admiral Mindar, Imperial Chief of Intelligence, took chairs at the small conference table in Benes' office. Magistra Abbatissa Ardrix and Chancellor Conteh had arrived before the two officers and already sat on either side of the president.

"Tifa will explain." Mejik nodded at Mindar.

"We just received a missive from our contact on Yotai, the one who warned us about Juska planning to weaponize the Barbarian Virus. He — or she, we know nothing about the individual — advises that someone betrayed Admiral Norum and Ambassador DeCarde upon arrival at the New Lena spaceport. The OSR currently holds them at the Yotai Re-education Center, undergoing brainwashing to turn them into Juska supporters for propaganda purposes."

"Damn." Benes clenched a fist. "No news about the destruction of the biolab?"

"As far as the contact is concerned, it's still up and running. But that's probably because Lieutenant Commander Paget is also a prisoner and is undergoing brainwashing as well, but under the control of their Naval Intelligence. Fortunately, according to our contact, they're still a few months away from deploying the virus."

"How were they captured?"

"We don't know, but I suspect Sela Reeve might not have been the innocent scavenger as she so convincingly portrayed herself."

"A Republic agent?"

"Yes, sir. That's our operating assumption right now."

"It would seem a bit of a miss on the part of your counter-intelligence people, Admiral."

Mindar had the grace to look slightly embarrassed. "It certainly would be, sir."

"So the mission to Yotai is a total failure." Benes tapped the tabletop with his fingertips. "What are our options, Anton?"

"Hope that the Republic never deploys the virus."

A wintry smile briefly lit up Benes' solemn expression. "That would be your throwaway course of action, correct?"

"Of course, sir. The other option would be to send a naval task force through interstellar space rather than the wormhole network and have it destroy every installation on Yotai's moon, Gennari."

"Which would be an act of war against the Republic. Can't we get our agent on Yotai to do something?"

"We have no way of contacting him or her. It's a one-way relationship," Mindar said. "We get messages delivered from smugglers and never the same one."

"Damn."

Mejik grimaced. "I'm afraid the only way of dealing with the threat is the task force, sir."

"How large will it have to be?"

"The operations staff figures at least a dozen ships — a mixture of cruisers and frigates. That ought to be enough to keep the Republic's Yotai squadron at bay while one or two of them destroy every structure on Gennari. Come in, bombard the moon, get out. Hopefully, President Juska will understand the reason behind our attack and not declare an all-out war. Besides, his Navy isn't powerful enough to guard the Republic's star systems *and* strike at ours."

"He'll be pissed, though. And angry dictators can throw self-destructive tantrums, as we saw with Empress Dendera."

"True, but it's still the only viable option."

"Who do you figure for command of the task force?"

"Newton Giambo. He's got more than enough initiative and guts to conduct operations far from home. Newton will get the job done."

Benes nodded. "I agree. He's an excellent choice for a no-fail mission. How soon can he leave?"

"Two weeks. His ships will come from 2nd Fleet and be built around the 21st Patrol Squadron."

"Do you have a name for the task force?"

"Task Force Dunmoore." When Benes frowned, searching his capacious memory for the significance of the name, Mejik smiled. "Commodore Siobhan Dunmoore led a task force in a daring assault on the Shrehari Empire's home system during the last war against them in the twenty-fifth century. The assault convinced the Shrehari to seek an armistice, so you could say that she ended the war."

"Aha." Benes nodded. "Very apt."

"Siobhan Dunmoore, a twenty-fifth century flag officer?" Ardrix spoke for the first time since Mejik and Mindar arrived. "I seem to recall reading in the family annals that she was a distant ancestress of mine and a long-serving Chief of Naval Operations for the Commonwealth that preceded the First Empire."

Benes turned his gaze on the Magistra Abbatissa. "Interesting. Perhaps you should join the mission as the task force commander's personal counselor. A good luck charm, so to speak."

Ardrix allowed herself a faint smile. "If the Almighty wants Rear Admiral Giambo to succeed, then he will, whether or not I'm there. Besides, my duty to the Order is here, not aboard a cruiser that will be in interstellar space for weeks."

"I had to try. Task Force Dunmoore, it is, then. Anton, I'll be personally approving the orders you'll give Newton."

"I figured as much, sir, considering the stakes."

"When do you expect to have them ready?"

"In four days. It'll be called Operation Sea Eagle, by the way."

"You were so sure I'd approve the course of action that you already named it?"

Mejik nodded. "It's the only option we have."

***

"You have got to be kidding me." Rear Admiral Newton Giambo shook his head in disbelief once Grand Admiral Mejik finished briefing him on Operation Sea Eagle and its background. "That mission is clearly an act of war against the Republic, sir."

"I haven't run it by the JAG, but no doubt she'd agree with you. Still, we face an existential threat from a madman trying to emulate Dendera. Taking out the biolab on Yotai's moon is vital, act of war or not."

"Are we sure this Barbarian Virus actually exists and isn't the fever dream of a dissident trying to stir up trouble between the Republic and us?"

"Oh, yes. Farrin Norum confirmed its existence and that of the biolab on the moon, Gennari. That's why he volunteered to go to Yotai aboard the undercover intelligence ship, so he could point out the location of the lab to the ship's captain."

"A location we don't have."

"I know. Which is why you'll have to destroy every human-built structure on the moon."

"What if there are people in them?"

Mejik grimaced. "I suggest not scanning for life signs ahead of your attack run."

Giambo stared at the Grand Admiral, clearly aghast at his matter-of-fact statement. "That's cold, sir."

"If they release the virus on our worlds, everyone will die. It would wipe out the Empire's entire population before we could react. Against that, the lives of a few innocent Republic citizens are nothing."

"And how do we know containers with the virus aren't already on their way aboard unwitting smugglers?"

"We don't. Except that our agent on Yotai said they were still a few months from deploying it."

Giambo made a skeptical snort. "The same agent whom we know nothing about except that he or she began contacting our intelligence eighteen months ago, feeding us information about the doings in the Republic."

"But the data sent to us has always checked out," Admiral Mindar, who'd backed up Mejik on the intel side of the briefing, said.

"Okay." Giambo raised both hands in surrender. "Obviously, the President approved this mission, so it's got to go. Let me digest the details over the next day or two and backbrief you. Does that work?"

"Absolutely, Newton."

"In the meantime, I'll prepare and transmit a warning order to the 21st and the ships from the other squadrons that'll be attached to my command. No details. Everyone is simply to prepare for a long-range mission as part of Task Force Dunmoore and have antimatter fuel tanks topped up to the max." Giambo frowned. "Speaking of which, we'll be running on fumes on the way back from Yotai. An automated tanker or two waiting for us at a predetermined spot would be nice. Failing that, I'll need permission to raid a Republic antimatter fueling station before we leave their space."

"I'll make the arrangements for a pair of tankers. I'd prefer you to appear only around the Yotai moon, Gennari. That'll send a clear message to President Juska. Stealing his antimatter fuel would distract from that."

"Your call, sir."

Mejik glanced at the antique clock sitting on one of the sideboards decorating his expansive office. "I'm sorry, but it's almost time for me to see the President."

Giambo and Mindar immediately stood and came to attention. "With your permission?"

Mejik waved toward the door. "Off you go. I'll be expecting the backbrief in two days, Newton."

"Yes, sir."

As he watched them leave, Mejik wondered, not for the first time, about a universe where people like Derik Juska had enough power to believe they could wipe out half of humanity purely for political purposes.

— 35 —

New Lena, Yotai
United Stars Republic

As his ground car approached the Stadium of the Stars, President Derik Juska could feel the electricity in the air, and he allowed himself a satisfied smile, despite his mild irritation at the coming spectacle. The anniversary convention of the United Stars Bloc would shortly unfold beneath a carpet of stars with both of Yotai's moons shining fully overhead. The music from the stadium boomed faintly through the car's armored windows, showing the party was already in full swing..

The first vehicle in the presidential convoy disappeared down the ramp of the underground parking lot, then the second, then Juska's, followed by the remaining three. All of them were driven by uniformed members of the Presidential Guard and carried his personal minders, men and women who would unquestioningly and reflexively take a plasma round for him.

The convoy came to a stop in front of the doors leading to the underground lobby. Anya Fong stood in front of them, hands joined in front, a smile pasted on her face. Juska's minders climbed out of the ground cars and formed a protective circle around his vehicle. The president's aide-de-camp, a Presidential Guard officer, black uniform dripping with silver adornments, including thickly braided aiguillettes hanging from his right shoulder, jumped out of Juska's car and stood by the back passenger door, which slid open silently. The aide raised his right hand in a salute as the president emerged.

"Mister President." Fong inclined her head in greeting. "Welcome."

"The house seems to be hopping." And indeed, the rumble of an excited crowd was clearly audible even in the underground parking.

Fong's smile broadened. "The stadium is full, with overflow in the park watching on giant screens. Everyone is keyed up, ready to celebrate the United Stars Bloc."

Just then, a dozen heraldic trumpets shattered the air several stories above them, and the rumble increased before dying away.

"That was the warning for the honor guard to march in," Fong said.

Moments later, the sounds of a military band reached their ears. They could barely make out that it was playing "*The Double-Headed Condor*", which the Presidential Guard had adopted as its own when Juska formed it. Still, he noticed how every Defense Force band soon removed that particular march from its repertoire. The regular military and the Presidential Guard despised each other, but the United Stars Bloc members favored the latter. One could hear the rhythmic clapping of the twenty-five thousand-strong crowd accompanying the band.

"We can make our way up now, Mister President. By the time we're on the Presidential Loge level, the Guard will be in place."

Surrounded by Juska's minders and aide, he and Fong made their way to a spacious elevator. Not everyone fit in, but Juska knew some of his escort had already cleared the way and taken up positions in the loge. Preparing every place before he arrived had become standard long ago.

They exited the lift four floors higher and stepped into a broad, well-lit corridor. Bodyguards lined both sides from the cab to the loge door. Juska led the way to the latter, and it opened at his approach, revealing a luxurious and spacious reception room with floor-to-ceiling windows overlooking the dais from which he would speak and the stadium's interior. To the sounds of the march, *Hail the President*, he crossed the room, and one of the windows slid aside, letting in a waft of warm air laden with the aroma of twenty-five thousand overexcited bodies, their eyes focused on him as he stepped through.

A command rang out, and the five hundred Presidential Guard troopers standing at attention on the stadium floor, facing the dais, presented arms in unison, and the band played the Republic's anthem, *"We Shall Prevail."* Twenty-five thousand separate voices joined in singing the words, everyone standing with right hands over their hearts. The magnificence of the moment sent shivers up Juska's spine.

As the anthem's final sounds faded away, a cheer erupted from the stadium, its roar loud enough to echo through the city. Juska felt it energize him beyond anything else he'd ever experienced. His nerve endings crackled as he raised both arms, and he positively wallowed in the unexpected sensation. Juska was unaware of his three truthsayers positioned in the shadows, their eyes on him, their minds manipulating his to increase the pleasure he sensed at the raw force of the crowd applauding him. They did so at Sister Elana's orders, of course, as part of her plan to turn the Republic into a theocratic dictatorship with the Summus Abbatissa holding the reins, hidden behind a puppet president.

It took several minutes for the cheers to die away, but when they finally did, the spotlight centered on Juska while red lights lit up tall vertical banners with the black double-headed condor of the Republic's Great Seal framing the dais from behind. The effect was designed to mesmerize the audience and leave them in awe of the president's strength and prestige. Anya Fong and her team of propagandists had personally designed everything about Juska's appearance to enhance his perceived supremacy over the United Stars Bloc and the United Stars Republic itself.

"Fellow citizens of our great Republic." Juska's amplified voice echoed across the stadium, loud enough to drown out any other noises. "Our sacred movement is celebrating its fifteenth Anniversary this week, fifteen years of transforming the Republic into the greatest star nation in existence."

Cheers erupted at Juska's words, along with thunderous applause. Once it died away, he continued.

"I'm here to inform you that the Hegemony is running out of time."

The ensuing acclamation was, if anything, louder than before.

"Our United Stars Republic is the sole true heir of humanity's past and the sole true path to humanity's future!"

The whole stadium became wild with enthusiasm when they heard that declaration, and it took a solid five minutes before they were calm enough to let Juska continue.

"That is why tonight, I'm declaring United Stars Bloc the sole political entity permitted to operate as such. I hereby ban all other political movements."

Juska knew it was a risky move, a clear declaration that democracy was dead in the United Stars Republic — although in practice it had died years earlier — but the audience cheered like their wildest dreams had come true. And after ten years of maneuvering toward this day, his opposition had become ineffectual, voices in the desert, unheard and unheeded. The vast majority of the citizenry enjoyed good lives and didn't care about who ran the Republic so long as things didn't change for them. And Juska had made damn sure the ordinary citizens saw no difference, except for a renewed pride in their star nation and a desire to see it supreme in human space.

Meanwhile, back at the re-education center, all inmates were forced to watch the spectacle on their cells' entertainment screens. They couldn't turn it off, not even lower the sound. Norum and DeCarde sat in front of theirs, the former in despair, the latter with nothing except disgust. They took care to avoid showing their feelings, however, since they knew they were being watched and needed to keep up the charade that Bree's attentions had changed their views on Derik Juska. Still, showing mock admiration or excitement at Juska's speech was beyond them.

The Republic they'd once served was irretrievably gone.

— 36 —

Task Force Dunmoore
Second Empire

When Task Force Dunmoore emerged from hyperspace to take the wormhole to Santa Theresa — the first leg of their journey to Yotai — Rear Admiral Giambo called a command conference, to be attended virtually by those not aboard his flagship, ISS *Caladrius*. And at the appointed time, one by one, three-D holograms of the fifteen captains popped into existence around the table in the ship's conference room. *Caladrius'* skipper and the task force staff officers already sat in their appointed chairs. Once the last one appeared, Giambo took his seat at the head of the table and looked around at the attendees.

"Good day, everybody. In a moment, you'll understand why we left Wyvern without my having shared our mission or destination with you." He paused for effect. "Our destination is Yotai, the United Stars Republic's capital world, and our mission is to destroy a biolab on Yotai's moon, Gennari. That biolab is supposedly reviving an ancient virus with a one-hundred percent death rate that escaped from a First Empire biological warfare installation more than two hundred years ago. They plan to release it on Imperial worlds, wiping out the Second Empire's entire population in one fell swoop."

Giambo saw astonishment combined with anger on many faces.

"This is a no-fail mission, and if it turns into a one-way trip, so be it. Compared to the billions of lives in the Empire, we are eminently expendable." Giambo paused again. "I know you're thinking our raid is an act of war against the Republic, but so is their deploying a bioweapon against us. We have no choice in the matter but to act before they can do it. Our sources say they're still a few months away from sending out stasis containers with the virus aboard unwitting smugglers and free traders, so we have a bit of breathing room. And we will use that time to creep up on the Yotai system undetected. The task force will quit the wormhole network in the uninhabited Dai Shiang system, arriving via its Wormhole Four, and proceed on a direct course for Yotai in interstellar space."

One of the captains frowned and said, "That means almost three weeks in hyperspace, sir. Six weeks both ways. We might run out of fuel."

Giambo allowed himself a faint smile. Commander Trevor Wenn, captain of the frigate *Longwei* and his former first officer when he had *Caladrius,* was always extremely quick on the uptake.

"Command has assured me that two automated antimatter fuel tankers and their handler ship will be waiting for us by wormhole Dai Shiang Four. If they're not in position when we return, we'll divert to the Furong system via ISC234450-4. While that takes us well out of our way, the antimatter cracking station orbiting Furong Six will come online in four weeks."

"I didn't know we were building a fuel point in the Furong system," another of the captains said. "Last I heard, they were in the early stages of establishing a colony on Furong Two. Isn't a cracking station a bit premature, sir?"

Giambo chuckled. "It's not so much to support the colonists but the Navy's ships as we expand the Empire's sphere in our race against the Republic to reclaim as many star systems as possible. In the long run, it's cheaper to commission cracking stations than automated tankers."

"Then why don't we aim for Furong straight from Yotai?"

"Because of the magic of wormholes. Furong is reachable via wormholes from Dai Shiang without imperiling our fuel reserves, but not via interstellar space from Yotai. If we tried from Yotai, we'd probably be riding on fumes by the time we got to Furong."

"Ah. Of course. Tankers in the Dai Shiang system, it is."

"We'll stop at Santa Theresa's cracking station to top up our tanks both ways. *Caladrius'* navigator has prepared the navigation plot for the entire mission. You'll receive it when this conference is over. We will transit and jump together at all times. Now, my intentions when we emerge at Yotai's heliosphere. First, we will go silent the moment we come out of hyperspace and stay so for at least an hour, observing our surroundings. Intelligence says the Yotai Squadron has sixteen ships, of which eight are patrolling at any given time; the other eight are docked at the orbital station or sitting on the ground, giving the crews a respite. That means the chances of anyone seeing us drop out of FTL are vanishingly small."

It had been the problem since time immemorial. Ships at a star system's heliopause were lost against the vastness of space, and unless sensors looked precisely at the spot where they emerged from hyperspace, they would remain unseen.

"Then we find Yotai and jump inward. The moment we pop out at the planet's hyperlimit, *Caladrius*, *Longwei*, *Rostov*, and *Zmey* head for the moon Gennari and blow up every human-built installation on its surface while the rest of the task force protects those four ships from any Republic naval unit. You are authorized to open fire if fired upon. Once we've sterilized Gennari, we head back to the hyperlimit and jump to the heliopause and from there to Dai Shiang. Fast, simple, and deadly."

Giambo let the attack plan sink in for a few moments. Then Commander Wenn raised his hand.

"Yes, Trevor?"

"What if some installations we destroy house innocent civilians?"

"Since we don't know which of them is the biolab, just that it's on Gennari…" Giambo shrugged.

A frown marred Wenn's forehead. "I see."

"Trevor, it's either a handful of innocent Republic citizens or each and every inhabitant of the Empire's worlds. Billions."

"Understood, sir." But Wenn seemed unconvinced.

Giambo sighed. "Look, I had the same reaction when I was briefed on the mission and received the same answer. I was also advised to not scan for life signs on Gennari before making our run."

"That's cold, sir."

"And that's exactly what I said when I was told not to look for life signs, Trevor. But nonetheless, we need to destroy the biolab because it's an existential threat to the Empire, and since we don't know which installation it is, they all must go."

"Yes, sir," Wenn replied reluctantly.

Giambo was glad his former first officer hadn't lost his fundamental decency.

"That, in essence, is my plan. You'll receive detailed orders before we transit the wormhole to Santa Theresa, where we'll reconvene to discuss any questions or issues you may have. Does anyone want to raise a question or issue now?"

He looked around the table, but the captains shook their heads in turn.

"Right, then. Prepare to synchronize our transit. Giambo, out."

— 37 —

New Lena, Yotai
United Stars Republic

"And how are we doing today?" Sister Fricka swept into Paget's cell like a minor force of nature, followed more subtly by Sister Rianne, who'd finally gotten herself assigned to the Defense Force re-education program.

Paget, seated in the cell's sole chair, glanced at Fricka and shrugged. "I'm well, but I don't know how the pair of you are."

Fricka's smile was far from reaching her eyes. "Ah, yes. The infamous Paget sense of humor strikes again."

"You're the one who used the plural *we*. Rather patronizing, isn't it?"

Rianne chuckled. "He's got you there, Fricka."

The older Sister didn't reply but gave Rianne a brief, irritated glance. They hadn't been getting along that well since the latter was assigned to the Paget project. Fricka preferred to work alone and saw Rianne as an unwarranted imposition. As a result, the latter could not help the Imperial officer since Fricka refused to let her work in his mind by herself.

"Today," Fricka announced, "we'll check if the treatment took."

"You mean you'll check. I'm just the passenger here."

Instead of replying, Fricka reached out and placed her cold, dry fingertips on the back of Paget's neck, and he immediately felt a ghostly presence in his mind, alongside his own. He saw images of officers in Republic Navy uniforms, including Sela Reeve, and experienced pleasant thoughts. They gave him unheard orders, and he was pleased to obey, although a small part of him, hidden from Fricka, noted a sense of unease at his willingness, as if a tiny shard had resisted the treatment.

This went on for a long time, then abruptly, Fricka broke the contact and stepped back.

"I'd say you are ready to serve the Republic as a double agent. Your mind is pliable."

"Glad to hear it," he replied in a droll tone. "Although I can't tell."

"Naturally, you can't tell. The treatment changed you into a new person, one whose loyalty to the Republic is beyond question." Fricka turned her head and said, "Lieutenant Reeve, you may join us."

Reeve, wearing civilian clothes, entered the cell and stopped halfway to Paget's chair. The latter experienced another mental touch — less intense than before but still apparent. She contemplated Paget with her usual sardonic air, then turned to Fricka.

"And you're sure he's turned?"

"I'm in contact with his mind just now, and the mood he's in, seeing you, is warm and friendly, not hostile."

Paget was shocked when he realized that Fricka was telling the truth. Even after Reeve's betrayal, his disposition toward her was comradely, not full of contempt and animosity. He felt trust and friendship for Sela Reeve. Paget hid it well, but his mind reeled at the first actual indication Fricka's treatment had worked.

The Sister chuckled. "Yes, young Hal. I have changed you, and only now do you realize it."

"He's safe?" Reeve asked.

"As safe as can be, Lieutenant. He's your friend who would do anything for you."

"Even after I screwed him over?"

"He holds no grudges against you for your actions."

Paget surprised himself by nodding. "You did what you had to, Sela. And I respect that. I just hope we can work together as well as before."

Reeve cocked a skeptical eyebrow at Fricka. "Is this for real?"

The Sister nodded. "It is. Trust me."

"Riiiiight," Reeve drawled. "You black-robed devils aren't trustworthy at the best of times."

"I'm sorry you think that, but it isn't an unusual sentiment among wild talents. You do realize that we can train you to control your abilities with no sort of commitment to the Order."

"Pass."

"All right, then. I'm going to declare Hal Paget ready to the Naval Intelligence chain of command. What they do with him afterward is none of my business." Fricka glanced at Paget. "It's been a pleasure, Hal."

Then, she left, followed by Rianne, who was doing her best to hide her dismay. Reeve stayed a little longer, staring at Paget.

"So, you've really developed a fondness for the Republic?"

"Not a fondness as such, but a willingness to work with it in the interests of interstellar peace."

"Yeah. Why don't I believe you?"

"Because you're an ornery so-and-so who believes only herself. How you became an officer and a Naval Intelligence agent is beyond me." But Paget smiled and winked at her to take the sting from his words.

Reeve made an obscene gesture in response, one that transcended the division between Republic and Empire, but she smiled as well.

***

"Really? You're sure of that?" Derik Juska cocked a skeptical eyebrow at Summus Abbatissa Elana. She sat across from him in the presidential office, and they were alone. Juska had dismissed the duty truthsayer since he didn't need her with Elana. Not that any of the three had a talent powerful enough to even taste Elana's emotions.

"I am. Both Norum and DeCarde successfully ended their course of treatment and are now friends of your government. As a result, may I suggest you invite them to join you in the stadium's presidential lodge for the Anniversary closing ceremonies, where they can and will be seen by all and sundry. You can even introduce them as your newest friends. The propaganda value doesn't get much better than this."

Juska rubbed his chin as he contemplated Elana's recommendation. The propaganda value was undeniable. And yet…

"It's worth a shot." He stabbed the control surface embedded in his desktop. "Alex?"

His executive assistant answered immediately. "Sir?"

"Have the bodyguard collect Currag DeCarde and Farrin Norum from the Yotai Re-education Center and bring them to the Guesthouse. Confine them to their suites, but otherwise, treat them as honored guests. Also, have them fitted for proper business suits, with the United Stars Bloc lapel insignia. They'll attend the Anniversary closing ceremonies as my guests in the presidential suite."

"Sir, can I assume that they have successfully become supporters?"

"According to the Summus Abbatissa."

"In that case, it must be true. I will carry out your orders immediately."

"Juska, out." He cut the link and glanced at Elana. "I just hope you're right. If they haven't turned, they could do incalculable damage.

"Fear not. Besides, I will be there as well."

Elana sounded so confident, it stilled Juska's doubts. Of course, the Summus Abbatissa had nudged his mind in the right direction as well.

***

"Hey, Farrin. How are they hanging?" Currag DeCarde gave his old friend a wry smile as Norum climbed aboard the black ground car with the tinted windows. He already sat in the passenger compartment, hands shackled in front of him.

"Same as always." An equally shackled Norum replied, dropping onto the bench facing DeCarde. The door slid shut, and the car smoothly moved toward the re-education center's main gate. "Any idea what the hell is going on?"

"No, but I can speculate."

Norum grinned. "Nah. Let's just allow the situation to unfold."

"Yeah."

They stared out the windows as the car took them back into New Lena until they entered the one-kilometer-long Boulevard of the Stars, connecting the Presidential Palace with the Senate building, turning left toward the Palace.

"Hmm, looks like we're about to find ourselves in august company," Norum said in a conversational tone.

The car swung around the Palace and entered via one of the rear gates after a thorough security scan. Then, it headed for a low, two-story building at the back of the presidential compound and stopped in front of open double doors. A flunky in a business suit stepped through them and waited.

The passenger compartment door facing the building slid aside, and their shackles opened, falling to the floor. A disembodied voice bade them to exit. As soon as they stepped out, the man waiting by the door bowed his head.

"Welcome to the Presidential Guesthouse, gentlemen. I am Wentworth, the butler. If you'll follow me, I will guide you to your suites."

DeCarde glanced at Norum as the man turned around, raised his eyebrows, and mouthed, 'Presidential Guesthouse?'

Norum merely shrugged in reply. Instead, he asked, "Why are we here, Wentworth?"

"You haven't been told, sir?"

"No."

"You will join President Juska in his loge at the Stadium of the Stars tonight for the closing ceremonies of the United Stars Bloc Anniversary celebration."

"In this?" Norum indicated the orange jumpsuit he wore.

"Certainly not, sir. Suits tailored to your size await in your suites. Please be ready to leave by nineteen hundred."

"And what about meals?"

"You will find menus available via the entertainment system. Simply place your order, and droids will deliver it to you."

"Can Ambassador DeCarde and I eat together?"

"I'm afraid my orders are to keep you apart until it is time to head for the stadium, sir."

"I see."

They were walking down an expensively appointed corridor, with muted white walls, a cream carpet, and various paintings hanging between dark wood doors that bore brass plaques with engraved numbers. The soft, diffuse lighting made it look all the posher.

Wentworth stopped at a door, which opened at his touch. "Admiral, this is yours. Ambassador, you have the one across from it."

As if on cue, the door facing Norum's opened, and DeCarde stepped through. He glanced around and let out a low whistle.

"Nice. Very nice. Who usually gets this sort of treatment, Wentworth?"

"VVIPS. Planetary leaders, senior United Stars Bloc figures, those sorts of guests. The suites are the best we have."

"Then I suppose we should be honored."

"You are the president's personal guests tonight. As such, only the best for you will do. Until later." Wentworth bowed Norum into his suite, and both doors slid shut without a sound.

Their rooms might be exponentially nicer than those at the re-education center, but they remained well aware they were still prisoners at the pleasure of Derik Juska and his regime.

—38—

Nineteen hundred hours found the two friends back in what seemed to be the same ground car as earlier in the day. Both wore dark, expensively tailored, high-collared business suits, adorned with a United Stars Bloc brooch.

"Looking quite elegant tonight, Farrin," DeCarde drawled in a languid tone.

"As are you, my dear Currag." Norum settled back on the rear-facing bench, across from DeCarde as the car smoothly moved out. "Had a good meal?"

"Most excellent. The finest I've eaten since we visited Le Pied de Cochon in New Draconis."

"Tell me, the Sister who treated you, what was her name?"

"First it was Desra and Bree, and lately Bree only."

"The same as me." Norum half-cocked his left eyebrow and slightly tilted his head to the right.

"Meaning we received exactly the same treatment."

"One could easily assume so." A pause as Norum glanced out the window. "I'm looking forward to this evening, celebrating the United Stars Bloc. It's a bit of a strange sensation, that."

"You'll get used to it. I am. It only takes letting yourself go with the events, as Sister Bree so intuitively implied."

"Indeed."

They fell silent for the rest of the trip to the Stadium of the Stars and alit from the car in the same underground garage that would soon see the president's convoy. There, an attendant wearing a gray business suit greeted them and led the way up to the Presidential Loge. They could feel the pounding of the music and the weight of the crowd on the way up, but nothing prepared them for the sight of an overflowing venue filled with enthusiastic United Stars Bloc adherents and what seemed like the entire Presidential Guard Regiment when they stepped into the loge and gazed out through its expansive transparent aluminum sliding doors.

"Impressive," Norum muttered, just loud enough for DeCarde to hear. "Especially the honor guard."

"Yep. They look like toy soldiers, which is what they probably are."

They looked around at the other people assembling in the loge and, besides the vice president, Vandeleur Dost, they noticed a pale, thin-faced blond Sister wearing the orb of the Summus Abbatissa on a chain around her neck, watching them intently.

"That must be Elana."

"She certainly doesn't look like any of her predecessors," DeCarde said, sotto voce.

"No. She reminds me of a bird of prey scoping out its next meal."

Another staffer, wearing the same ubiquitous gray suit, approached them. "Admiral, Ambassador, may I bring you a libation?"

"What do you have?"

"Anything you may desire."

"Then a single malt whiskey with a splash of water for me," Norum said.

"Same," DeCarde added.

"Certainly." The staffer inclined her head and scurried off toward the bar.

DeCarde leaned toward Norum. "Think happy thoughts, Farrin. The bird of prey is checking our moods."

"That's right. You're sensitive to a Sister's mental touch, aren't you?"

"I am, and she's touching us right now."

"Bree taught me to always think happy thoughts when I'm not alone."

"Good."

The staffer returned with a small silver tray, upon which were perched two tumblers with a healthy amount of amber liquid in them.

"Gentlemen." She held out the tray, and they each took a glass.

DeCarde swirled the contents of his for a few seconds, staring into its depths, then raised it. "Your health, Farrin."

"And yours, Currag."

They both took a sip and sighed contentedly in unison.

"It's been way too long since I've had a wee dram," Norum remarked, eyes aimed over DeCarde's shoulder as he studied the other guests.

Just then, a muted fanfare sounded, and the march *Hail the President* sounded from hidden speakers. Everyone in the room quieted and turned toward the inner door, the officers in uniform standing at attention. Out of sheer reflex, both DeCarde and Norum downed the rest of their whiskey, put the empty glasses aside, and came to attention.

The door slid aside, and Derik Juska strode in, tall, erect, a grave expression on his face. His eyes covered the room in an instant and settled on Norum and DeCarde.

His voice boomed out. "Good evening, everyone, and thank you for being here."

Many voices were heard to reply, "Mister President," while heads bobbed respectfully.

Juska ambled over to where the two former officials stood and thrust out his hand at Norum.

"Admiral. Glad you could make it. The United Stars Bloc insignia looks good on you." They shook, and he turned to DeCarde, offering his hand. "You as well, Ambassador. I'm glad both of you saw the error of your ways and have rejoined the Republic's leadership. Together, we will make the United Stars Republic a blazing beacon of light for humanity and announce to non-human civilizations that we are back and stronger than ever."

Norum smiled. "We're happy we're back home and eager to be of service to you and the Republic, Mister President."

"Glad you said that, Admiral. Let's forget bygones and march toward a glorious future, united in thought and deed."

"Indeed, sir. The future it is." Both Norum and DeCarde inclined their heads by way of punctuating the former's reply.

"Why don't you hang around with me tonight? When I go out there to address the crowd, stand on either side of me, slightly behind. Does that work for you?"

"Certainly, Mister President," Norum replied.

A pleased smile spread across Juska's face, but it didn't quite reach his eyes, which were as cold and watchful as ever. He turned around and walked toward Elana, followed by DeCarde and Norum, who took his invitation to heart.

"Sister. Thank you for coming tonight."

Elana essayed a faint smile. "I wouldn't miss your triumph for anything, Mister President."

"You know Admiral Norum and Ambassador DeCarde?"

"Not personally, but I've been told much about them." Her gaze, as lifeless as Juska's, shifted from one to the other. "How are you gentlemen tonight?"

"Doing absolutely great," Norum replied, nodding politely, imitated by DeCarde. "It's a pleasure to be here."

"Glad to hear you say it, Admiral. And I think I speak for everyone when I say I'm pleased you and the Ambassador have rejoined the Republic as loyal citizens."

"We are equally happy to have done so, Sister."

With a final tight smile at Elana, Derik Juska wandered off to where the Chief of the Defense Staff, Admiral Rylo Haggan, stood with the Chief of Naval Operations, the Commandant of the Marine Corps, and the Chief of the Army Staff. Norum knew Haggan only too well. A true politically minded officer — amoral, unethical, without a shred of empathy, and with a habit of backstabbing anyone in his way. When he'd been CDS and Haggan a Navy captain, he'd annotated the man's confidential personal file with the mention 'unsuitable for flag rank because of severe character issues.'

Haggan must have seen his confidential file because he gave Norum a look of pure hatred the moment he recognized the latter. Norum merely smiled. Once the president had made his manners, Norum asked, "How are you, Rylo?"

"I'm excellent, Farrin. It's amazing what the last ten years have done for the Defense Force."

"And getting better under your inspired leadership, I don't doubt." Norum turned to the three other Service chiefs, whom he'd known as much more junior officers. The Chief of Naval Operations had been a Lyonesse First adherent even then and had let the chauvinistic views of the movement color his temperament. He was certainly not, in Norum's estimation, the sort who should have risen to four stars.

"Hello, Fedor, nice to see you again." They shook hands, and as their eyes met, Norum saw suspicion in his.

"And you, sir."

The Commandant of the Marine Corps had been a solid, if unimaginative, officer back in the day. But he was of the type seen as politically reliable because he had a chameleon-like ability to reflect a superior's views, no matter what they were.

"Good evening, Gerard. I trust the Corps is doing well."

"As well as can be, sir."

Norum turned to the third of the Service chiefs, General Edward Estevan, a former Marine who'd wormed his way up the Army chain of command after being appointed chief of staff of the Theban Defense Force five years earlier. But before he could greet Estevan, DeCarde spoke.

"Hey, E.E., I see you made chief of the Army. That's a lot higher than anyone expected you to go."

"And yet here we are," Estevan replied in a supercilious tone. "How are you, Currag? Recovered from your years in the wilderness?"

"Quite nicely, thank you." DeCarde glanced at Norum. "Did I ever tell you how E.E. got his nickname?"

"No. But save it for later. How are you, Edward?"

"Probably doing better than either of you two." Estevan winked at Norum. "At least I still have a career."

"And yet we're in the Presidential Loge with you, E.E."

Derik Juska, who'd been watching the interplay with amusement dancing in his eyes, turned when Anya Fong approached him.

"It's almost time for you to step out on the dais, sir."

"Right." Juska glanced at Norum and DeCarde. "Please attend me, gentlemen."

He took a position in front of the dais door, with one of them on either side, a pace back, and Vice President Dost immediately behind him. Norum sensed movement at his heels and quickly glanced over his shoulder. The four senior military officers, as well as the Summus Abbatissa, had taken their places next, followed by the other VIPs in the loge. Anya Fong came up beside Juska and took one last glance at the formation before nodding to the president.

Outside, the Presidential Escort Band launched a fanfare with a dozen heraldic trumpets, effectively stilling the roar of voices. Then the doors opened and, to the strains of *Hail the President*, Derick Juska marched out of the loge and onto the dais, his followers hard on his heels.

He stopped at the edge, and when the last notes of the march faded away, raucous cheers erupted, circling the stadium ceaselessly as Juska smiled and raised his hands above his head in a victory gesture.

Five hundred kilometers away, in Fingal's Inn, at the heart of Ormkirk, a small town upriver from New Lena, a heavily disguised Lucas Morane watched the scene on the Inn's large display, which normally showed professional sports. Tonight, it brought a live feed from the Stadium of the Stars, like every other news net in the Republic. As soon as he spotted Farrin Norum and Currag DeCarde, both wearing United Stars Bloc pins, standing immediately behind Derik Juska, he felt his heart skip a beat.

The unethical Sisters at the thrice-damned Yotai Re-education Center had turned them. That was the only explanation.

Deep despair filled Morane's soul until he felt as if he were drowning in hopelessness. If the regime could make loyal servants out of stalwart dissidents like Norum and DeCarde, even giving them a place of honor, what hope did the Republic have?

— 39 —

Rear Admiral Newton Giambo, sitting in his command chair on *Caladrius'* flag bridge, felt his trepidation increase as the countdown clock appearing in the primary display's lower right corner approached zero. Task Force Dunmoore was on its final FTL approach to Yotai after an uneventful trip from the Empire into the very heart of the Republic. They'd not met any ships while underway and had remained undetected as they dropped out of FTL at Yotai's heliopause to plot the final jump.

The plan was to emerge at Yotai's extreme hyperlimit — as close to the planet as they could without causing stress damage to the ships' hulls — while under silent running. But everyone on and around Yotai would see them the moment they switched on their targeting sensors and kicked their sublight drives into delivering thrust so they could adjust their trajectories.

After weeks in interstellar space going FTL, they were almost at the target.

Just then, the ship's public address system came on, advising the crew that *Caladrius* was to secure for silent running. A few minutes after that, the sixty-second emergence warning sounded, and Giambo's heart rate shot up, though no one watching him could tell he was nervous and getting more so. After all, he was about to attack another star nation unprovoked and probably start a war.

Transition nausea gripped him the moment the timer hit zero, and his head spun as his guts tried to climb out through his nostrils. But it vanished as quickly as it had come, and his eyes fixed on the tactical holographic projection at the center of the flag bridge. Representations of Yotai, its two moons, and a constellation of artificial orbitals rapidly crowded the projection as passive sensors collected data. Three among the constellation turned red, indicating they were naval vessels, and one turned green — an armed orbital station.

The threat detectors remained silent, proof that Task Force Dunmoore wasn't yet being pinged by active sensors. As Giambo stared at Gennari, a small part of him realized his nervousness had vanished, replaced by a quiet resolve to accomplish his duty and get the hell out of here.

Then, the task force navigator raised his hand. "Admiral, we need to go up systems and correct course."

"Signals, make to the task force, up systems, prepare to receive nav instructions."

"Aye, aye, sir."

Giambo idly wondered what would go through the minds of the Yotai traffic control officers when an unknown naval task force suddenly appeared on their sensors. None of his ships was broadcasting a beacon, and the inter-ship links were encrypted beyond the ability of the Republic to crack, at least not quickly enough to make a difference.

Within moments, *Caladrius*, *Rostov*, *Longwei*, *Zmey*, and two other ships peeled away from the task force and headed for the moon Gennari. Meanwhile, the rest of the ships headed for Yotai to interpose themselves between the three Republic naval vessels in orbit and Gennari to dissuade them from acting. If the Imperials didn't have to open fire on the Republic's Navy, so much the better.

The threat detectors began screaming, proof that Republic sensors and targeting systems had locked on to *Caladrius* and her consorts. But since the unknown ships hadn't yet committed a hostile act, the cruiser's sensor chief didn't report any missile launchers spitting out flight after flight of nuclear-tipped birds.

Gennari was quickly growing on the bridge's primary display, and human-built structures lit up, outlined in red. Most of them were on the side facing Yotai, and Giambo dispatched *Longwei* and *Zmey* to take care of them while *Caladrius* and *Rostov* engaged the ones on the other side. The two other ships would follow, ready to launch a second strike just in case the first one missed a few sites.

As *Caladrius* came within optimal range, Giambo felt the vibrations of launching missiles through the soles of his feet and saw streaks of light head for the moon on the display. The barrage continued until the cruiser passed over Gennari to do one orbit around Yotai before heading back to the hyperlimit.

A few minutes later, one of the follow-on ships reported the sites on the side facing Yotai destroyed, followed by another announcing the same for the sites on the side facing away.

Giambo immediately nodded at the signals petty officer. "Send the break message."

"Aye, aye, sir." Then, "Task Force Dunmoore, this is flag, break, break, break. Mission accomplished. Begin extraction."

He listened intently, then turned back to Giambo. "All units have acknowledged."

"The Republic ships in Yotai orbit are powering up, Admiral. And the orbital defense platform just launched missiles."

Time seemed to slow as the task force extricated itself from Yotai's orbit and reformed as it sped at top sublight speed back to the maximum hyperlimit, pursued by Republic missiles. The rearmost ships ended up having to shoot them, but that proved easier than expected.

Soon enough, the ships synced and went FTL, headed for the star system's heliopause. This time, however, Giambo expected Republic vessels to attempt an intercept. After all, they'd have a good idea where the task force would emerge to prepare for interstellar travel.

But for now, Newton Giambo felt relief at the speed and efficacy of the raid and decided a session in the ship's gym would relieve the rest of his tension and allow him a good night's sleep during the transit to the heliopause.

— 40 —

President Derik Juska and his entourage sat on the dais, watching the show unfold on the stadium floor. Anya Fong had planned it as a spectacular display of close order drill by the Presidential Guard, a traditional dance number by the one hundred dancers of the Yotai Academy, a concert by a rabidly pro-United Stars Bloc musical group, and more.

Halfway through the drill demonstration, a naval aide came through the doors, scurried over to where Admiral Haggan sat, and leaned over to whisper in his ear. As the aide spoke, a look of alarm grew on Haggan's face. When he was done, the admiral waved him away, and he vanished while Haggan climbed to his feet and slowly walked to the president's seat. He knelt beside it.

"Sir, I have alarming news to report."

"Can't it wait?"

"I'm afraid not. It seems that a Hegemony task force of sixteen ships appeared at Yotai's hyperlimit half an hour ago and attacked every installation on Gennari, destroying all of them, the biolab included. Then, they ran back to the hyperlimit and jumped to hyperspace on a course roughly congruent with an interstellar transit back to the Hegemony."

Juska sat up and stared at Haggan, the spectacle at his feet forgotten. "What?"

"The Hegemony, which obviously targeted the biolab on Gennari, attacked us, meaning they most definitely knew about the Barbarian Virus program but not the lab's exact location beyond somewhere on the moon."

"And you're sure they destroyed the lab."

"Along with every other installation on Gennari. Thousands of people, mostly Defense Force personnel and government researchers, died."

Juska's face hardened. "That was an act of war against us, Rylo."

"Most assuredly, sir."

"As a wise man once said, never let a crisis go to waste. I trust the Navy is pursuing that enemy task force."

"We are, but we don't have more than seven ships in this star system, let alone the sixteen it would take to match them, so even if we catch up with them, I don't see what we can do."

"Still, I want aggressive action, Rylo, no matter the cost. It's a matter of optics."

"Yes, sir."

The drill routine came to a close with the team presenting arms to the dais, and Juska climbed to his feet.

"A fine display," he said, his voice echoing across the stadium, "by a fine body of troops. Let's give it up for the Presidential Guard Drill Team."

Applause thundered until Juska raised his arms as the drill team vanished through one of the wide ground-level doors.

"I have grave news to announce," he continued once the stadium was silent. "Thirty minutes ago, a Hegemony task force attacked us unprovoked, a despicable deed which will not go unpunished. Many of our innocent fellow citizens died in the attack. As a result, I have no choice but to conclude that a state of war exists between the United Stars Republic and the Wyvern Hegemony. It is a war I didn't want but one which I will prosecute and which we will win because we are on the side of righteousness and they represent nothing but evil."

At those words, the crowd went wild, cheering like there was no tomorrow, and nothing Juska said or did calmed them for a good five minutes. DeCarde and Norum appeared as enthusiastic as anyone else standing behind Juska, though they were both secretly appalled at the news. Yet they were also pleased because Juska's declaration of war could only mean a successful Imperial raid on the Gennari biolab. At least whoever that was had destroyed an existential risk to the Second Empire.

Beyond the stadium, wherever people were glued to newsnet feeds showing the ceremonies as they unfolded, a wave of enthusiasm lit up small groups in taverns and recreation centers all over Yotai. Lucas Morane, who'd already been wallowing in despair, now felt tears running down his craggy cheeks because he knew this moment could mark the end of human civilization across the stars for the last time. However, because he was in one of the tavern's dark corners, no one noticed his distress.

Meanwhile, Hal Paget, who was also watching the scene with Sela Reeve in the living room of the Naval Intelligence safe house on the outskirts of New Lena, turned to his companion.

"That complicates things a bit, don't you think? For us, I mean."

Reeve made a face. "I don't see why it should. We gallop back to Wyvern, warn them that President Juska has declared war on the Empire, and start gathering intel about Imperial fleet dispositions. Intelligence will surely send us out on recon missions against the Republic as well, which will be ideal for us to pass along information we collected."

"And what will our excuse be for not destroying the biolab, leaving it to this mysterious task force Juska spoke of?"

"Republic authorities detained us and grounded *Marlene* for months while they investigated. Sadly, they arrested our two passengers and put them through re-education, turning them into loyal subjects of President Juska."

Reeve didn't roll her eyes, but she figured the turned Paget seemed to have lost a lot of his quirky brainpower and spunk. The regular Paget wouldn't need her to explain how they'd cover for the delay in returning without accomplishing their mission. Then there was the quasi-apathy with which he looked at life in general, a big change from who he was before.

In effect, the black-robed devils had robbed him of an essential part of who he was, turned him into an inferior and much less interesting version of Hal Paget.

But he was now a double agent, working for the Republic.

PART III – CRY HAVOC

—41—

DeCarde and Norum were silent during the ride back to the Presidential Guesthouse, both lost in their own thoughts, though they gave each other significant glances from time to time. Derik Juska had spoken to them after the ceremonies, which had been sumptuous, complete with a hundred-voice chorus to sing the national anthem as the Republic's flag was lowered after a fly past by several Navy shuttle squadrons.

Juska wanted the two of them to act as his personal advisers in prosecuting the war, since they were the most knowledgeable individuals about the Second Empire — he called it the Hegemony, of course — in the entire Republic. Privately, they recoiled at the prospect, but they agreed, seeking to thwart the president. And so, their residency at the Guesthouse was made permanent, but they figured the OSR was spying on them constantly, nonetheless, and couldn't speak openly to each other.

"Well, Currag," Norum finally said as their car pulled onto the Boulevard of the Stars, "this is a turn for the books, though, isn't it? The Hegemony attacks us out of the blue, and we become presidential advisers. I say we do the utmost with the chance that events and the president have given us."

"Oh, agreed, old friend. Agreed." DeCarde stared out the window at the brightly lit monuments lining the boulevard. "I wonder what sort of advice the president will look for. We are, so to speak, jacks of all knowledge Hegemony, but masters of none."

"Indeed. Still, I suppose we're the experts on Hegemony politics if nothing else and can advise the president on the likely reactions to his declaration of war."

"Don't sell us short. We are probably the experts on Hegemony military and technological affairs as well."

Norum glanced at DeCarde, who wore a faint, but unmistakably mocking smile, a sign he was acting for the invisible watchers. It reassured Norum that his old friend definitely was not re-educated, as Juska believed, and Sister Elana could not figure it out even in close proximity. The Almighty bless Sister Bree. Because without her…

The only question was what they could do to frustrate Juska's war goals without completely betraying the Republic. They were both still bound by their oaths as officers, even if they had taken Imperial citizenship because they never figured they'd return, let alone find themselves as advisers to a president they loathed but who was still the Republic's legitimate head of government and head of state.

But the car stopping at the Presidential Compound's back gate security arch for a scan cut his thoughts short. Moments later, they resumed traveling at a more sedate speed until the car pulled up in front of the Guesthouse. This time, Wentworth was nowhere to be seen, and they made their way back to their suites alone and in silence. The suites' doors slid open at their approach.

"Enjoy your sleep, Farrin. Tomorrow could be an interesting day."

"Thanks. You too."

The next morning, a pair of taciturn bodyguards wearing business suits picked them up, scanned them, and took them across the compound to the Palace, where they waited for more than thirty minutes in an antechamber to the presidential office. Settee groups dotted the spacious room, and sideboards held water, tea, and juices. But they'd encountered no human beings along the way, and the two bodyguards, having delivered them, vanished into a corridor. Norum and DeCarde, alone in the antechamber, glanced at each other and then silently fell into a light meditative trance to pass the time.

Their eyes snapped open the minute the president's executive assistant entered the antechamber.

"Gentlemen, President Juska will see you now."

They rose to their feet and followed the man along a short corridor and through a simple doorway, which gave onto the expansive and ornate presidential office.

"Admiral Norum and Ambassador DeCarde," he announced, stopping just inside the office door.

"Come in, come in." Derik Juska, ensconced behind his desk, waved them in with a jovial air pasted on his face. "And please sit." He indicated the chairs across from him.

As they entered, DeCarde suddenly became conscious of a Sister attempting to touch his mind, and he glanced over his shoulder, only to see one sitting in the shadows of a shallow alcove, her features indistinct.

"Black robe on our six," he murmured out of the corner of his mouth, unable to tell if Norum caught what he said.

"Noted," Norum replied, smiling at Juska. "Good morning, Mister President."

"Yes, good morning," DeCarde chimed in. "And how are you after your triumph last night?"

"Tolerable, gents, tolerable." He watched them settle into the tall-backed chairs. "Still prepared to advise me on Hegemony affairs?"

Norum nodded. "Certainly, sir. Anything to help the Republic in these troubled times."

"Pleased to know." Juska's eyes went from one to the other, then he glanced over DeCarde's shoulder as if meeting the Sister's gaze. What he saw must have satisfied him, because he seemed to relax. "Tell me about the top political leadership of the Hegemony."

And for the next hour, until the executive assistant reminded Juska of his next appointment, Norum, with the occasional interjection by DeCarde, explained the Empire's political system and gave thumbnail sketches of the top people in the government. Juska listened with rapt attention, asking a few questions along the way.

"That was most illuminating, Admiral. Much more so than anything put together by our intelligence services. Thank you."

Hearing the dismissal in his voice, Norum and DeCarde stood, politely bowed their heads, then made precise about-turns and left the office. Once they were gone, Juska glanced at Sister Nanta, who sat in the darkened corner and raised a questioning eyebrow.

"They were telling the truth," she said. "And nothing but the truth, as they believed it. They're both well disposed toward you, although DeCarde proved hard to read."

"That is good, Sister."

The same bodyguards as before met Norum and DeCarde just outside the presidential office and escorted them back to the Guesthouse, where they were locked inside their suites once more and left to their own devices, unable to communicate with each other.

— 42 —

"What the hell did you do to Marlene?" Paget didn't sound hysterical to Reeve's ears. Not quite.

They'd been aboard the ship for less than five minutes, but Marlene hadn't answered Paget's increasingly urgent requests to come online.

"I ordered her to shut down and hand the ship's controls over to the non-AI systems."

"Didn't you corrupt Marlene to the point where she would only obey you?"

"Yes, but I prefer not to take chances. AIs can be temperamental. Besides, we can run the ship without it."

"Sure, but I prefer having Marlene to back me up."

"Tough. We're each other's backup. Now, how about we get the launch sequence started?"

"You're a harsh one, Sela. That's for sure."

Paget dropped into the captain's chair and touched the control surface embedded in its right arm. The ship lit up almost immediately, but no voice came through hidden speakers, and that saddened Paget to a degree he hadn't thought possible.

"All systems appear functional and ready," he reported after a few moments spent scrutinizing status updates scrolling by on the bridge's primary display.

Reeve could see the updates as well as Paget did, but decided not to make a snarky comment to that effect. He seemed a tad... She searched for the right word, and when it came to her, Reeve had to suppress a grim smile. Fragile.

Hal Paget, the Imperial Rogue, seemed fragile, thanks to the d'ayvols' mind-meddling. She wondered what else in him had changed, and did that mean increased risk for her if he lost some of his abilities or character traits?

"In that case, spool her up. Intelligence has cleared us for a return to Wyvern so we can announce President Juska's declaration of war following the attack on Gennari."

"Ah, yes," Paget replied absently, focused on bringing the systems online. "War. What's it going to do for the Republic? Nothing good, I suspect."

"Ours not to reason why. Ours but to obey orders."

"Yeah, yeah, yeah."

Before Reeve could say anything else, the high-pitched sound of thrusters spooling up filled the silence.

"Secure for liftoff, Sela."

She dropped into the chair at one of the bridge workstations without further comment and turned to face the primary display.

"I'm ready."

"New Lena traffic control has cleared us to thirty thousand on a vertical vector. After that, we come under Yotai traffic control."

"Ack."

"Lifting."

He touched the control surface again, and the whine of the thrusters increased while giant hands pushed them into their chairs as they lifted off under full power.

Finally, they passed through thirty thousand meters, and Yotai traffic control gave them an angular vector up into orbit. An hour later saw *Marlene* on a heading to the hyperlimit, and an hour after that, she jumped on a course for Wormhole Two, to begin the series of wormhole transits that would eventually see them emerge through Wormhole One in the Torrinos system, back in the Empire.

Since absolute secrecy within the Republic was no longer required, Reeve had plotted the fastest way back to Wyvern, and that passed through the wormhole system via Hatshepsut, at the Republic's far edge. *Marlene* now broadcast a beacon identifying her as a government ship, letting her pass through wherever she went.

Until she left the Republic.

At that point, Reeve would jettison the beacon through the nearest airlock, so the Imperial authorities wouldn't have a chance of identifying her as carrying double agents.

They were FTL and had just finished a meal when Reeve pushed her tray away and contemplated Paget openly for a bit.

"What?" He finally asked.

"Just trying to figure out what the d'ayvols did with part of your personality."

Paget frowned. "Huh? What do you mean?"

"I guess you haven't figured it out for yourself yet. You're different. You lost your spark, the thing that made you Hal Paget, Imperial Rogue."

"Nope. I feel fine. In fact, I feel great."

"Yeah, feeling is one thing, being is another altogether. And you're not the being you were."

"So? I'm finally free and headed home. It's the only thing that matters."

"Sure, but you're not the same person who's headed home. You're now working for the Republic."

"Because the Sisters enlightened me as to the evil of the Hegemony versus the rightness of the Republic."

"And there you have it. Calling the Second Empire the Hegemony, as per President Juska's pet peeve. The real Hal Paget would never stoop so low."

"What are you complaining about? I thought we were supposed to work together for the betterment of the Republic. Whether or not I'm the same doesn't factor into it. For what it's worth, I don't see any changes in me."

Reeve simply shook her head. "You're right, and I won't mention it again. This is better than moldering in a prison cell."

"Thanks, and yes, it is." He climbed to his feet. "And I'm going to check the drive controllers. She hasn't been FTL in months. I'm sure a few minor adjustments are called for."

— 43 —

Life turned monotonous rather fast for Norum and DeCarde. An hour with President Juska every second day and several hours with various Naval Intelligence officers every day. By the second session with Juska, Norum had decided to present the Second Empire as stronger than it was, rather than weaker, and made his decision known to DeCarde in a roundabout way during their walk between the Guesthouse and the Palace. DeCarde indicated, in the same fashion, that he had come to the identical conclusion but would leave the details to Norum.

On the third day, they were allowed the full run of the Guesthouse, including the common and dining rooms. No more solitary meals in their suites. But they remained the sole inmates of the spacious building, interacting only with Wentworth, the butler.

"I could get used to this lifestyle," DeCarde commented after taking a sip of his whiskey and soda. "Have you seen the sort of single malts this bar stocks?"

He turned around and glanced at Norum, who'd just entered the common room, a large space that nonetheless gave off an intimate atmosphere. With a coffered ceiling, subdued lights, waist-high wainscoting, and small settee groups sitting on colorful rugs, it boasted a full bar with countless bottles containing every sort of alcoholic drink known to humanity. And only the best of those.

"I took a quick glance early on. What are you drinking?"

"Glen Petras."

"The finest Mykonos single malt. Nice. I'll have myself a wee dram of that." As he poured, Norum asked, "Anything special from this afternoon's conversation with intelligence?"

Contrary to their sessions with the president, the spooks questioned them separately, which made keeping the same story interesting, so they simply told the truth, exaggerating some items, like perceived fleet strength, political determination, and a few others.

"Not really. They revisited the Hegemony Navy's order of battle, and as I've told them many times before, we only know a little more than the average Hegemony citizen in that respect. The Colonial Service doesn't own or operate starships."

"Yes, getting the concept of the Colonial Service as a military-led but mostly civilian organization through to Naval Intelligence has been a bit of a challenge, hasn't it?" Norum took a sip and sighed. "That's the good stuff."

He dropped into the nearest easy chair. "It's nice to finally be out of solitary isolation."

DeCarde nodded. "That it is. I haven't tried the front door yet, but I assume we're confined to the Guesthouse."

"Most assuredly. They wouldn't want us wandering around the Presidential Compound unescorted. There's no telling what mischief we might get up to."

"Is there not?" A melodious, although somewhat deep female voice asked from the common room's doorway. "I would have thought the former Chief of the Defense Staff and the former Republic ambassador to the Hegemony know exactly what sort of mischief they could cause."

Both men turned to look toward the entrance at those words.

"Sister Elana," DeCarde gave her a polite nod. "What brings the Summus Abbatissa of the Order of the Void here? Not to see us, surely."

"Yes, to see you, Ambassador." She walked in, black robes swishing gently around her ankles. "What is it you're drinking?"

"Glen Petras."

"Oh. Could I have some?"

"Certainly." DeCarde gestured at the bar. "Help yourself. But I wasn't aware the Brethren used ethanol for recreational purposes."

"You're undoubtedly unaware of many things concerning us."

"Without question. Now, why are you here for us?"

Elana didn't immediately answer. Instead, she headed for the bar, studied the bottles on display, and settled for an Isabellan green brandy. She poured, took a sip, and made an appreciative moue.

"Why indeed? I have a few questions, especially for you, Ambassador. Your mind seems to have certain traits we generally see only in Sisters of the Void, and that's unusual."

Norum immediately visualized his happy place, as Bree had taught him, but DeCarde slammed his mental barriers down hard. Elana gave the latter a cruel look, and he felt intense pressure against his shields. Not being fully aware of what he was doing, DeCarde pushed back with as much power as he could muster and felt Elana's mental barriers snap.

She staggered, gasped once, and collapsed to the floor, dropping her glass of brandy, which splashed on the rug.

Norum was halfway out of his chair before his thoughts caught up with him, and he quickly knelt beside her, fingers reaching for the carotid artery in her neck. He pressed down, shifted them slightly, and held. After almost a full minute, Norum glanced up at DeCarde.

"I believe she's dead," he said in an incredulous tone.

From the doorway, Wentworth said, "I have advised the presidential physician. He should be here in a few minutes."

"You had us under observation?" DeCarde asked.

"Of course, so I could be ready to respond in case you needed anything."

And to keep an eye on us, DeCarde thought, but he merely nodded at the butler.

"Are you sure she's dead?"

Norum climbed to his feet. "I'll let the physician make that determination, but I wasn't getting any heartbeat. What the hell just happened?"

"Search me," DeCarde said. "One moment she was saying something about having questions, the next she let out a gasp and collapsed." He turned to Wentworth. "Heck, you must have recorded it."

"Indeed, sir. And I will turn the recording over to the investigators, because there will be an inquiry for sure."

"Good."

They stared at Elana in silence, but none could detect even the slightest bit of movement, proving she breathed. Her eyes, still open, stared out at nothing.

A few minutes later, a portly man in his late sixties carrying a medical pouch marched into the common room.

"Wentworth. I got your alarm. Sister Elana, is it?"

He approached her, retrieved a medical sensor from his bag, and aimed it at the supine Sister.

"She's dead, that's for sure. Can't tell the cause until the autopsy. If the Order allows one. But I'd say sudden cardiac arrest."

"Isn't that the cause of all deaths, Doctor?" DeCarde asked.

"Ultimately, yes. But many, if not most, of them have causes leading to cardiac arrest. Sister Elana appears to have been healthy. Probably healthier than any of us still standing here." He stared at her again. "We may never discover why her heart suddenly stopped, but it happens. Yes, it's rare, but not unheard of for healthy people in the prime of their age to simply die. I'll prepare the death certificate."

The physician stowed his medical sensor, nodded at them, and left. The three Sisters that Norum and DeCarde had identified as President Juska's truthsayers immediately replaced him.

"What in the name of the Almighty happened?" One of them, Sister Clemenza, asked in a tightly controlled voice.

"We have no idea. One moment she was speaking to us," Norum replied, "the next she was dead."

"And no one to receive her essence. I shall see if anything can be salvaged. If not, it will be a great loss to the Order."

Clemenza knelt beside her late superior and touched the side of her head with her fingertips. She closed her eyes but quickly recoiled, an air of extreme anguish spreading across her ageless face.

"Her mind. It's been burned out. There is no trace of her essence or even of her."

"How do you know?" Norum asked.

Clemenza gave him an angry glare. "A person's essence, the soul if you like, leaves traces for up to thirty minutes after death, and electrical impulses still cross the synapses for as long. But in Sister Elana's case, her mind is completely dark, as if some outside force had violently snuffed every trace of her essence and extinguished everything."

"But how is that possible?" Sister Yarett asked, stunned by the announcement.

"I have no idea," Clemenza admitted. "The power it would take to erase everything Elana was so thoroughly is beyond my comprehension. She had one of the strongest talents in the Order, if not the strongest. Her shielding should have been proof against anything."

DeCarde took care to keep his face absolutely expressionless and his mind closed to everyone. He didn't doubt that he was responsible for Elana's death. It happened moments after he struck back in fury at her attempt to force an intrusion.

Something the Sisters did to him during the re-education, perhaps even Bree's attempts to keep their minds as they were, had changed him, strengthened his abilities well beyond the family standard the DeCardes had held for over a thousand years.

Or maybe the DeCardes always had the ability to kill with a Sister's talent, but had never been pushed to use it before, or used it without being aware.

Norum, who knew about his friend's talent, was quickly coming to the same conclusion, but he also schooled himself to show nothing, let alone glance at DeCarde.

Clemenza stood and turned to Wentworth. "Are we the only women in the Guesthouse at this time?"

The butler nodded. "Until Elana's arrival, the only inhabitants were Admiral Norum, Ambassador DeCarde, and I. The presidential physician briefly attended to confirm the death, and then you three arrived."

"Curious." Clemenza gave DeCarde a speculative glance and seemed on the verge of saying something else, but then changed her mind. "We shall sit with Sister Elana until the Abbey retrieves her remains. And we should prefer to do so with no one else present."

"There is the matter of the investigators," Wentworth said.

"They can do as they like. We know how the Summus Abbatissa died. Once the mortuary attendants from the Abbey arrive, they will take Sister Elana in charge and leave. There will be no autopsy, and Sister Elana will be committed to the Infinite Void in a private ceremony, far from secular eyes."

"Of course, Sister." Wentworth glanced at Norum and DeCarde. "Shall we leave the Sisters to it, gentlemen?"

"Sure."

Both men drained their glasses and followed the butler out of the common room, heading back to their suites, lost in thought.

— 44 —

An hour later, a pair of OSR agents wearing the standard dark business suit of their species burst in on Norum. They flashed their credentials.

"Admiral, we'd like to ask you some questions about Sister Elana's death," one of them said with no further introduction.

"And you are?" Norum cocked a regal eyebrow.

"Agent Tomasso, sir. This is Agent Vennit," he replied in a grudging tone.

Norum gestured at the settee grouping occupying the center of his suite's sitting room. "Please, sit."

Tomasso pulled a small tablet from his jacket's inner pocket. "If you don't mind, I'll be recording the interview."

"And if I do mind?"

The agent didn't quite roll his eyes, but it was clear he wanted to. "I was merely being polite, sir."

"Just checking. Ask away, Agent."

"We saw the video of the event. Now we'd like your interpretation of what happened."

"It's rather simple. One moment, Sister Elana was talking; the next, she was dead on the floor. The president's physician said it was probably cardiac arrest. As you might have noticed, I was sitting two or three meters away from her at the time, so I couldn't have done anything. And neither could Ambassador DeCarde. He was also two or three meters away from Elana. Her death is as much a mystery to us as it is to you."

"Sister Clemenza said Elana's mind had been wiped of everything. Whatever that means. What do you think she was referring to?"

Norum steeled himself to remain completely expressionless. "No idea. The Order of the Void hasn't taken me into its confidence."

Tomasso chuckled. "That's almost exactly what Ambassador DeCarde said."

"You've spoken with him already."

"Yeah. He had nothing to add to the video record either." Tomasso and Vennit glanced at each other, then climbed to their feet. "Thank you for your time, Admiral."

***

"Just like that?" President Derik Juska stared at Sister Clemenza in disbelief after she told him what she knew about Elana's death, having seen the video recording herself.

"Yes, sir."

But Juska wasn't one to dwell on the death of a political ally. He had more important concerns. "And who will take her place?"

In the interim, until a new Summus Abbatissa can be named, Sister Quessi, the Motherhouse Abbess, assumes the leadership of the Order.

He knew next to nothing about Quessi but was aware Elana's changes had riven the Order into various factions, some deeply opposed to her reforms. But as far as most secular people were concerned, the Void was monolithic in its attitude and direction because dissent from the Summus Abbatissa's approach remained carefully hidden. It would be disastrous for his progress if Elana's successor were diametrically opposed to her program. Disastrous, but not fatally so.

"Should I reach out to Sister Quessi or wait until she contacts me?"

"With the turmoil surrounding Sister Elana's death, I would suggest you wait, Mister President."

"Any idea who might succeed Sister Elana in the long term?"

Clemenza shook her head. "No, sir."

Juska didn't dare ask the truthsayer about the divisions within the Order because he knew she wouldn't answer. He was well aware that Clemenza and her two acolytes had worked for Elana and not him, and now would work for whoever would become Summus Abbatissa. The Order's secrets would remain inviolate. And with Elana's passing, that worried him.

***

News of Elana's sudden death had electrified the Yotai Abbey, and as details surrounding it became known, the gossip began in earnest, for the Brethren were addicted to rumors just like any other folk. In that, they were almost normal.

That evening, during services, the acting Summus Abbatissa, Sister Quessi, did her best to warn the Brethren against spreading hearsay indiscriminately, but in vain. The mystery of Elana's sudden death held such a place in the imagination of the Sisters and Friars that whispered conversations continued well into the night.

Sisters Hermina, Rianne, and Bree met in the orchard after the service and slowly strolled among the trees, out of earshot of their fellows.

"Elana suddenly dying is one for the books," Hermina finally said, breaking the silence. "I wonder what happened."

"Whatever it was, none of her possible successors could be crass enough to keep the Order on its current path into darkness. Certainly, Sister Quessi won't. She's opposed Elana almost since the start and wouldn't have become abbess of Yotai if Elana had been Summus Abbatissa when Quessi was named to the position."

"Thank the Almighty for that. But Quessi will only be interim unless she presents her candidature for the position. Some of the others who might postulate have openly embraced Elana's policies."

"Then we must ensure they don't accede to the supreme title." Rianne frowned. "Did you hear that Clemenza said Elana's mind had been scoured? She apparently reached into it a few minutes after death, and everything that had once been Elana was gone, as if blasted away. But she cannot find a reason why."

"Indeed, I heard," Bree said. "And also, that Ambassador DeCarde and Admiral Norum were the only ones present when Elana died."

Hermina gave Bree a curious look. "You sound like you're thinking about something in particular."

"I might be." Bree glanced around them to make sure they were alone. "Ambassador DeCarde has the talent. And a strong one to boot, although untrained. He can shut his mental barriers, and no one gets in. No one. He can also project rather strongly, albeit in an undisciplined manner. I fear that the re-education might have given him greater insight into his talent and enhanced it. Rather like the unfortunate Stearn Roget, of more than two hundred years ago, in the days of Sister Marta. Remember his story?"

Both Hermina and Rianne shuddered. Roget had long been the exemplar of an extraordinarily strong talent gone terribly wrong. Every Sister knew of him.

"You really think DeCarde killed Elana?" Rianne asked.

"It's the only thing that makes sense. She might have tried to force herself into his mind, a sure way of triggering an uncontrolled, violent response in someone like DeCarde. Someone programmed him from a young age to resist any unwanted intrusion. With the changes the attempt at re-education made to his mind…" Bree shrugged. "We've been playing with fire, ignoring the experiences of our forebears during Marta Norum's time. Forcing the sort of personality changes through re-education as we've been doing is bound to go wrong. I'm surprised it's taken this long. It may be the first of many unexpected events."

"You're not only saying Ambassador DeCarde killed Elana, but we've potentially got more ticking time bombs who emerged from the re-education program?" Hermina sounded dismayed.

"Yes, and yes."

"Is there a way to find proof so we can urge Sister Quessi to shut down re-education?"

"I can't see any without betraying Ambassador DeCarde. And that, I will not do. Sorry. He is a good man. An honest one, who wants nothing but the best for the people of the Republic."

"Yet he killed our Summus Abbatissa, if you're right."

"I still theorize that it resulted from an involuntary reflex rather than a conscious attack on Elana. She'd be just the type to try a main force assault on someone with mental barriers, and he'd have lashed out without wanting to."

"What do we do with this information?" Hermina asked.

"Stumped if I know."

***

Currag DeCarde knew full well he'd killed Sister Elana and had known the moment he did it. He was also aware of Stearn Roget's story, thanks to family lore, and realized the re-education process had somehow turned him into a modern-day version of the crazed friar.

Ironic that both he and Roget had killed the Summus Abbatissa of the day, although Sister Gwenneth hadn't deserved the end she met, while Elana was a different story. Besides, the latter had attempted to violate his mind with a forcefulness that belied her vows as a Sister of the Void.

Interestingly, he felt not a shred of guilt at having sent Elana into the Infinite Void. She wasn't the first human he'd dispatched, of course, but considering she was probably a psychopath in black robes, what with her leading the Order of the Void deliberately into darkness, she was likely the most deserving.

What really intrigued DeCarde, however, was whether he could consciously blast the mind of someone like Derik Juska, who had no sensitivity and couldn't trigger the defense mechanism that made him lash out at Elana. Now there was a man who desperately needed killing, before he destroyed both the Republic and the Empire in his disastrous war. And didn't Stearn Roget almost kill President Morane, but Sister Gwenneth sacrificed herself at the last minute to save his life? This time, there wouldn't be a strong Summus Abbatissa to rescue the president.

DeCarde resolved to try the next time they met with Juska. Even if he died along with the president, it would be worth it.

***

"You think we have another Stearn Roget on our hands?" Abbess Quessi, a short, elfin woman with a Sister's ageless face framed by iron gray, mid-length hair, frowned at Sister Clemenza, who'd just finished speaking of her suspicions.

"We know for a fact that Ambassador DeCarde is something of a wild talent. Desra confirmed it early on in his re-education process. She had to take extraordinary measures to force his mind open."

"Please use the right terms, Clemenza. The time of euphemisms to hide what we do has passed along with Elana. Desra employed torture," Quessi said with distaste evident in her tone. "Something that will cease as soon as I issue my directives as interim Summus Abbatissa tomorrow."

"Then what will the re-educators do with wild talents that refuse to cooperate?"

"Nothing because I'm also suspending the Order's participation in the re-education program and other secular initiatives that I deem contrary to our vows, such as Sisters augmenting Naval Intelligence."

"President Juska will not be happy."

"I don't really care about his happiness, Clemenza. Elana was leading the Order down the path of perdition. I will attempt to save it, provided it's not too late. And on that note, you and the other two truthsayers will report back to the Abbey permanently. I hereby rescind your duties in the president's office."

Clemenza, hearing the finality in Quessi's voice, inclined her head. "As you command, Summus Abbatissa."

"And you will refrain from speculating about Ambassador DeCarde's potential role in Elana's death. She will undergo the proper rites, and her ashes will be dispersed as per the Rule. Officially, she died of unexpected cardiac arrest. That is the extent to which anyone will discuss her passing. I am aware rumors and gossip are already circulating concerning your findings in Elana's mind, but you will not feed them. If you hear any speculation, please do your best to stop it."

"Yes, Summus Abbatissa." Clemenza hesitated, then asked, "Will you do anything about DeCarde potentially being another Stearn Roget?"

"As long as he doesn't go crazy like Roget did, no."

"Why do I get the impression you're not particularly shattered by Elana's death?"

"Because I'm not. While I've not made my vociferous opposition to her embrace of a greater secular role openly known, many were aware of it. I think her untimely passing gives the Order a chance to back away from her policies, regroup, and consider its future."

"Understood."

— 45 —

"Sir, the new Summus Abbatissa, Sister Quessi, for you on a link." Juska's executive assistant had poked his head through the open office door rather than call the president on the intercom.

The latter looked up, let out a soft grunt, and touched the control surface embedded in his desktop. Almost immediately, the hologram of a serene-looking Sister appeared above the desk.

She — or rather her image — nodded. "Mister President. Thank you for taking my call."

"For the Summus Abbatissa, I always have time."

"You may change your mind when you hear what I have to say."

A frown creased Juska's forehead. "That sounds ominous. But before we discuss those issues, we should probably talk about Sister Elana's funeral. She was one of the Republic's most important leaders, so I see a state ceremony honoring her life, with me presiding. What do you think?"

"Nothing, Mister President. The Rule of the Order proscribes any sort of ceremony for the deceased. Under the Rule, we will remember her at the evening service tonight, then we will cremate her body and scatter her ashes in the Abbey's orchard. Earth to earth, ashes to ashes, and dust to dust. That is it."

"Surely someone of her stature deserves more."

"We are all the same in death, and our remains return to the earth in the same manner. There can be no discussion about this."

Juska gave Quessi a hard stare, which she returned measure for measure. Then, he relented. "Very well. What was it you wished to discuss?"

"I am changing the Order's direction from that taken by Elana and returning us to what we should be — spiritual guides doing good for the community in positive ways. It means that as of this morning, I have withdrawn the Sisters from the re-education program, the Naval Intelligence aid program, the OSR, your own office, and various other secular work that should never have been ours. You may have noticed your former truthsayers are no longer at their posts."

"What?" Juska reared up, completely blindsided by Quessi's pronouncement.

"Elana's push to implicate the Order in more and more secular business that had never been within our remit has caused great dissension among the Brethren. As the Summus Abbatissa, albeit on an interim basis only at this time, I have ended Elana's experiments. It is not the Order's place to meddle with minds, assist in repression or warmongering."

"You can't do that!"

"I can and I have. The Brethren's obedience to my directives is absolute under the Rule because they conform to the Rule. Elana's directives didn't, and she only got away with it by pitting factions against each other within the Order and using unsuitable Sisters to carry out her most egregious tasks. Those Sisters find themselves relegated to isolated and widely scattered priories for the rest of their lives as of this morning."

"Damn you. I'll find a Summus Abbatissa who's willing to cooperate with my government, and then you'll be exiled to an isolated Priory on Arietis or another dying world."

"You can send the OSR or even the Marines to arrest the lot of us, but you will find no one willing to obey any direction you give. Not even among the unsuitable Sisters. You may do like Dendera and many of the rebellious admirals did and massacre the Brethren, but bending us to your demands is not something that will happen. Ever. And the public outcry should you attack us will bring your government down in fire and blood. The rank and file of the Defense Force will mutiny, for sure, no matter who the admirals and generals pledge allegiance to."

Juska, whose fury at the dismissive abbess had been growing by leaps and bounds, said through clenched teeth, "Take care with your words, Sister. I rule the Republic and can end the Order with a single command."

"I doubt that. You and Elana were building a repressive regime calculated to control the daily lives of billions on the shaky basis of cults of personality. Elana held the Brethren in thrall to her vision. With her death, that vision has turned to dust. You also hold your followers in thrall, and your disappearance will also mean the end of your vision because you have a lot fewer devotees than you think. Most show enthusiasm at your utterances because they don't want to be singled out as dissidents, not because they believe in what you say."

"Enough, Sister," Juska growled. "But know that withdrawing your services condemns the Order to irrelevance and eventual extinction, because you no longer have a use for my government, and those who have no use are relegated to the dustbin of history. Goodbye."

He stabbed the control surface embedded in his desktop again, cutting the link, incensed that he'd lost his composure with that insufferable abbess. It was as if she'd been trying to deliberately provoke him. But she was right. He could do little against the Order in the short term and would simply have to wait and see who replaced Elana permanently. Juska felt his usual calmness return. He'd long ago learned not to obsess about matters beyond his control. Still, he would prepare a campaign against the Order in secret, ready for use if Sister Quessi became the next substantive Summus Abbatissa.

"Mister President, Admiral Norum, and Ambassador DeCarde are here for your meeting."

The executive assistant's voice over the intercom brought Juska back to the present. Life must go on, even though the Order of the Void had suddenly transformed itself, if not into an enemy, then into a neutral whose leader disdained his regime.

"Send them in."

Both Norum and DeCarde wore appropriately somber expressions as they entered Juska's office.

"Mister President."

Juska waved at the chairs in front of his desk. "Please. Terrible business with Sister Elana."

"Indeed, sir," Norum answered. "But according to your physician, it was one of those unexpected things."

"I know. He told me. But you were there. How did it happen?"

Norum went through the sequence of events once again, brief though it was.

Juska nodded, rubbing his chin. "A strange occurrence, but perhaps she suffered from an undetected heart defect. Not that we'll ever know. The Order won't allow an autopsy and is preparing to cremate her remains today. A shame. Elana and I shared a vision of the Republic's future."

"And Sister Quessi holds different views?" DeCarde asked.

"Quite different, Ambassador. They run rather contrary to mine. She's withdrawn the Sisters working with my government save for traditional roles, like military chaplaincy, hospitals, palliative care centers, and the like."

Norum's eyebrows shot up. "You mean no more Sisters in the re-education program?"

"No, nor in Naval Intelligence or the OSR. Such programs are effectively dead in the water. I don't know what we're going to do with the people currently in them."

"Send them back to prison," DeCarde said flatly. "If they've not completed the process, then they're unreliable."

"Probably. They're worthless to my government if they're not reformed. I might as well order their execution."

DeCarde tried to feel anger at Juska's reply and lashed out with his mind, but his half-hearted energy throw felt like it splashed against nothing.

Still, Juska's eyes narrowed, and he reached up with his hand, squeezing the bridge of his nose between thumb and index finger.

"You'll need to excuse me, but I suddenly seem to have developed a blinding headache. We'll postpone today's meeting to another day. I'll have my executive assistant contact you."

Hearing dismissal, Norum and DeCarde stood, bowed their heads briefly at the president, and filed out of his office. As they walked back to the Guesthouse, without an OSR escort by now, both having been deemed reliable enough, neither spoke nor glanced at each other until they were halfway between the Palace and their residence.

"Strange that the president got a sudden headache," Norum said, keeping his eyes straight ahead.

"Isn't it?" DeCarde replied in the sort of offhand tone that told Norum everything he needed to know. "He must be developing something."

"Shame, that."

"Yep."

— 46 —

Wyvern
Second Empire

"Wyvern Control, this is the Imperial Navy Ship *Marlene*. Requesting an approach vector to Joint Base Byzance."

"*Marlene*, this is Wyvern Control — received. Stand by for instructions."

Paget knew the civilian controllers would contact the Navy, pass along *Marlene*'s particulars, and ask for guidance. If Byzance wasn't ready to take the ship, they would mandate her to stay in a parking orbit for however long it took. Five minutes passed before they called back and gave him a path through Wyvern's atmosphere to the joint base, advising that *Marlene* would come under Byzance control when she reached ten thousand meters.

"Okay, Sela. Time to sit," Paget threw over his shoulder at Reeve, who was doing something in the galley.

She appeared on the bridge moments later and took her accustomed workstation, facing the primary display, which showed a big arc of Wyvern's blue-green-white beauty.

"Home sweet home, eh, Hal?"

"Yeah. It's good to be back. This time, I hope we'll get a few weeks of leave before our next mission."

They began their descent, and as soon as they passed ten thousand, Byzance came on the link and instructed them to land in one of the enclosed bays. Not long afterward, *Marlene* decelerated until she hovered over the base riding her vertical thrusters, then slowly dropped toward the assigned bay. She settled on her stubby legs, and the whine of the thrusters faded away.

"We're here." Paget stood and stretched to ease muscles that had tensed during the landing process.

"What now?"

"First, we report to Captain Delibes and advise him of President Juska declaring war on the Empire after the attack on Gennari. I doubt the task force made it back yet, and they wouldn't know about the declaration unless they were specifically listening in on civilian frequencies during their time in normal space." He leaned over and touched a control screen, and the sound of the belly ramp unlocking and dropping filled the ship's still air. "Come on."

They made their way out of the bay, across the tarmac, and to the HQ building. Once inside, they found Captain Delibes' office, and Paget knocked on the doorframe, the door itself being open.

Delibes looked up from his workstation and smiled. "Come in, come in. I've been expecting you ever since traffic control informed us of your arrival."

"We've had an interesting time in the Republic, sir." Paget and Reeve took chairs across from Delibes' desk.

"What happened? I notice your two passengers aren't with you."

"The Republic's authorities took them in shortly after going ashore on Yotai. However, they seem to have joined President Juska's entourage since then. I don't know how or why. The OSR investigated us while we were grounded. — oh, hell, it's time to end the charade. Arrest Reeve. She's a Republic Naval Intelligence operative and holds the rank of lieutenant. Considering President Juska declared war on the Empire after that task force struck Gennari to take out the damned biolab we couldn't destroy, she's officially an enemy agent."

Reeve laid astonished eyes on Paget. "What the hell are you talking about, Hal?"

"The brainwashing to turn me into a double agent for the Republic wore off during the trip back, but I figured it would be better if I pretended otherwise, lest you knife me when I least expect it." Paget recounted the actual story of their expedition, including the re-education to turn him. "You understand now why I didn't send a mission report ahead of my arrival. I couldn't very well write the truth and risk Sela finding it. She has established full control over *Marlene*."

Delibes sat back and let out a low whistle. "That's quite a tale, Hal. And I remember you telling me in this office that the chances of Reeve being a Republic agent were negligible."

"I guess I was about as wrong as I've ever been, sir."

"Since a state of war exists between our star nations," Reeve said, "I expect to be treated as a prisoner of war, and not a spy."

"That'll be for the judge advocate general to decide, Reeve. For now, consider yourself under arrest." Delibes touched the control surface embedded in his desk. "I have a prisoner in my office to bring to the Armed Forces detention center in New Draconis. She's a Republic officer, and apparently, we're at war with it."

"Yes, sir. I'll have someone come up at once," a disembodied voice replied.

"You had me fooled," Reeve said to Paget in the ensuing silence.

"I didn't know myself whether I was coming or going during those days while the Sisters' best efforts wore off." Paget turned to Delibes. "But just in case I still have some residue of the brainwashing in my mind, could you place me on leave immediately and withdraw my credentials? Then, if at all possible, could we have a Sister or two of our Order peer into my brain?"

"Hal, I'm sure we can arrange that. "Very well, I am suspending your credentials and you. And kudos for stepping aside while we investigate what affected your mind."

"Couldn't do it any other way, sir."

Two burly Marines showed up at the office door, and Delibes stood, pointing at Reeve.

"Take her into custody and deliver her to the New Draconis Detention Barracks. She's an enemy officer of the rank of lieutenant whose status as a prisoner of war is still uncertain. She's to be considered dangerous and locked up in solitary confinement."

"Yes, sir." One of the Marines advanced on Reeve, manacles in hand. "If you'll please stand, Lieutenant."

Reeve obeyed with ill grace and placed her hands behind her back so the Marine could fasten them. He frisked her but found nothing. Then, with his hand on her arm, she marched out of Delibes' office.

The captain sat back and considered Paget in silence for a few seconds. "Our sources on Yotai warned us you were being turned into a double agent, and I was ready to go along with the charade on orders from the Chief of Intelligence just so we could see what you'd do. Fortunately, I won't need to. Now I need to call HQ and let them know we're at war with the Republic. I assume you have some proof?"

Paget fished a data wafer from his tunic pocket. "A recording of President Juska declaring it to adoring crowds that went positively wild at the notion of another ruinous civil war among human beings."

Delibes took the wafer and dropped it on the control surface. Images appeared on the office main display, and he watched, appalled, as Juska spoke.

"And to think he declared war because we conducted a defensive strike against his assets so he couldn't mass murder us. Hypocrisy doesn't begin to cover it."

"Derik Juska is a real piece of work from what I've seen. He's going to take all of us down given half a chance." Paget scrunched up his face. "What about *Marlene*? Sela locked the AI to her commands."

"We'll flush her and restore the ship's systems to factory zero. We may or may not reload an AI."

Paget shook his head. "Damn. I've really gotten to like the Marlene AI over the years."

"Even if you can convince Reeve to release the AI, would you trust it?"

A moment passed, then, "No. I suppose not. There is no way to check if her programming has genuinely returned to its initial state. Heck, the Sisters might not even be able to check my programming, which means I'd better find another career, far from the Navy."

Captain Delibes slowly nodded. "You got that right, Hal."

"Damn. Well, I suppose I'd better get my personal gear from base storage and head for New Draconis. I figure my uncle Harry will put me up until I can find myself a job and a place to stay."

"No hurry on the job. The Navy will keep you on its payroll, even though it suspended your credentials.

"Thanks, sir."

"Besides, the Sisters might find something lingering in your brain, but there are plenty of Navy jobs that don't require the level of security clearance this one does. And the Service hates to throw out perfectly good round components if it has round holes to fill."

"Maybe, but after a few years in the Special Reconnaissance Division, any other job will seem much too tame and bureaucratic."

Delibes chuckled. "It's the bureaucratic part that has you spooked, isn't it, Hal?"

Paget grinned at his superior. "Guilty."

"Into each career a little mindless bureaucracy must fall," Delibes replied in a sententious tone, although he was smiling. "Otherwise, one doesn't appreciate the freedom of deep space aboard one's own starship. And speaking of which, it's time I called HQ and told them Admiral Giambo's little raid triggered a war with the Republic."

"That was Newton Giambo's task force?"

"Yep. Best man for the job."

— 47 —

New Lena, Yotai
United Stars Republic

Over the following days and weeks after the Order of the Void withdrew its services from the government, both Norum and DeCarde noticed President Juska growing more suspicious of the people around him, more paranoid. But curiously, he took them more and more into his confidence, as if their supposed re-education had ensured complete loyalty to him.

One morning, just as their daily session was ending, Juska's executive assistant poked his head through the latter's office door.

"Anya Fong is here for your eleven-hundred, sir."

Norum and DeCarde climbed to their feet, assuming this signaled their dismissal, when Juska waved them back down.

"Sit, my friends. I'd like you to stick around for this and give me your impression of Anya afterward."

Fong bounced in moments later.

"Good day, Mister President." She beamed at Juska in a way that felt completely false to DeCarde.

"Anya. You know Admiral Norum and Ambassador DeCarde, I presume?"

"Of course. Good morning, gentlemen."

Both nodded a greeting at her. "Good morning."

They also noticed Juska didn't justify their presence, and Fong didn't ask.

"What's up, Anya?"

"Your popularity, sir. Even though we've not yet engaged the enemy, your approval rating has shot up after declaring war on the hated Hegemony." She sat beside Norum. "I think we should capitalize on this by having you give a State of the Republic address sooner rather than later."

Juska put on an air of interest. "And what should I say during that address?"

"Play up the capabilities of our Defense Force, make vague allusions to plans for total victory and the absorption of the Hegemony worlds into the Republic, that sort of thing. Raise the war spirits even further. That'll allow you to impose new laws to solidify your regime without complaints from the citizenry."

"Hmm." Juska glanced at Norum and DeCarde. "What do you say?"

"I say go for it, Mister President," Norum replied. "We can help you craft the address if you want."

"That sounds like an excellent idea." He turned back to Fong. "Done. Schedule it with the newsnets."

"Of course, sir."

Fong went on to discuss a long list of items related to United Stars Bloc business, and Norum could see Juska's growing boredom reflected in his eyes, though Fong never noticed because her enthusiasm never wavered. But even that sounded phony to his and DeCarde's ears.

Finally, she was done, and Juska thanked her for her diligence in leading the movement to ever greater heights. Sensing her dismissal, Fong climbed to her feet, bowed her head, and said, "It's always a pleasure, Mister President."

Then, she turned on her heels and left.

Once they were alone again, Juska raised his eyebrows, looked at Norum and DeCarde, and asked, "What do you think of her?"

"A false front of bonhomie hiding seething ambition to succeed you," DeCarde said. Norum nodded his agreement.

"My thoughts as well. Anya is an excellent political organizer, a superlative booster, and loyal to a point. Yet she doesn't have the gravitas for a senior government role, let alone the administrative skills. I rely on her to run the United Stars Bloc movement, but she and her deputy are replaceable, and I will replace them the moment her ambition gets the better of her. I've already prepared that move."

"A wise idea, sir," DeCarde replied, reaching out mentally to see if he could nudge Juska's mind into thinking more warmly of himself and Norum. He had no idea whether or not it worked, of course, but he'd been doing it at every meeting since the day of the headache. "Keep your options open, always."

"Stick around, Currag. And you too, Farrin." A faint smile crossed Juska's lips. "You'll see a lot of the people around me over the next few days."

As if on cue, the executive assistant announced the arrival of Vice President Vandeleur Dost, who entered Juska's office on the

EA's heels, without waiting. A big man, almost as wide as he was tall, Dost didn't so much walk as stomp. Short black hair and a black beard framed his square face while intelligent dark eyes took in Norum and DeCarde. But he dismissed them almost immediately.

"Good morning, Mister President."

"Hello, Vandeleur. And how are you?"

"Doing splendid, sir," Dost replied in a low, powerful voice.

"You know Admiral Norum and Ambassador DeCarde, I trust?"

"Yes. How are you, gentlemen?"

Dost didn't even wait for Norum and DeCarde to acknowledge him. Instead, he took a chair beside Norum without waiting for an invitation, something that surely must irritate Juska, but the latter betrayed no emotions. Dost was a career politician whose roots with the Lyonesse First movement dated back to its early days. Two vigorous terms in the Senate raised his profile to the point where Juska had no choice but to accept him as his vice president when he succeeded President Hecht upon the latter's death. That Dost engineered his nomination by underhanded means was conveniently suppressed afterward.

"Sir, I'd like to discuss a proposal that I lead the war cabinet," Dost continued. "As you may recall, I alluded to it at last week's cabinet meeting."

"I do recall. Tell me why you should lead the war cabinet."

"Before I do, sir," he glanced sideways at Norum, "is it necessary to have these two present for our discussion?"

"Farrin and Currag have become my closest advisers, men whom I trust implicitly, Vandeleur. They'll sit in on any meeting I choose."

DeCarde suppressed a triumphant smile. His untutored nudges must have had some effect.

Dost inclined his head. "Of course, sir. I believe I should lead the war cabinet for several reasons. The first and foremost of them is to free your time for strategic decisions rather than get caught up in the everyday minutiae of running the Republic on a war footing. Then, there's the fact that I served in the Defense Force and have a good grasp of things military."

At that second statement, Norum forcefully stopped his eyes from rolling. Dost had been a company commander as a centurion in the Army reserve before stepping into politics decades earlier, which gave him no advantage whatsoever in the current situation and a war that was likely to be naval. But he said nothing because he understood it was neither the time nor the place to comment. If Juska wanted his opinion, he would ask once Dost had left.

"And who would you have in the war cabinet?"

"The Secretary of Defense, of course, the Chief of the Defense Staff, and the Secretaries of Transport, Finance, Procurement, Public Safety, and Justice."

Juska's eyes briefly met Norum's, and the latter gave a faint nod. Dost's proposed war cabinet sounded okay.

"We can try it and see."

Dost pasted a broad smile on his equally wide face. "You won't regret it, sir. We'll have the running of the war in hand and make sure everything is carried out according to your wishes."

"Was there anything else you wished to discuss?"

"Yes, as a matter of fact." Dost launched into several other proposals whose net effect was to give him more day-to-day powers while distancing the president from many important aspects of governance.

Juska listened politely but reserved his decision on the matter. The war cabinet was one thing — it would be temporary and a working group of the full cabinet — Dost's other ideas would mean a permanent rearrangement of who controlled which levers of power.

Norum figured Dost had brought them up now because the Order's truthsayers were no longer present to expose his deeper plans.

"Thank you, Vandeleur. Enjoy the rest of your day."

Once Dost had gone, Juska glanced at his new advisers in turn. "So?"

Norum chuckled. "The vice president dwarfs Anya Fong's ambitions, sir. He's much more dangerous to your continued rule. I would, under no circumstances, accede to his proposals save for the war cabinet. He is clearly attempting to supersede you through seemingly innocuous means."

"I would get rid of him as soon as possible, Mister President," DeCarde interjected in a flat tone.

"But why is he trying now?"

"Because he smells weakness, what with the Order having withdrawn its services. It means you've lost the support of the second most powerful force in the Republic, and in the eyes of many, perhaps even the Almighty's approval for your continued leadership. Look for him to approach the new Summus Abbatissa and court her. Or eliminate him. I'm sure you have contingency plans for that as well."

"Well, I named you my advisers, and you're giving me unflinching advice, that's for sure. You're also excellent judges of character. In some respects, even better than the truthsayers, who focused on the veracity of what was said in my office rather than the persons who spoke."

"We're pleased to serve you, Mister President," Norum said. "You have the vision required to foster the Republic's growth into the Empire's true successor."

"Glad to hear you say so, Farrin." Juska snapped his fingers. "Why don't you two join me for supper tonight. We can talk more about the future around a good bottle of wine."

"Certainly, sir. It would be our pleasure."

— 48 —

New Draconis, Wyvern
Second Empire

"What the hell is Juska playing at?" Imperial President Sandor Benes shook his head as the recording of Juska's war speech ended. "Our polities don't even abut, and neither of us has sufficient ships to do more than conduct small-scale raids."

"I believe he's engaged in a behavior called not letting a crisis go to waste," Magistra Abbatissa Ardrix replied. "Admiral Giambo destroyed the biolab on Yotai's moon, removing that option forever. Declaring war to rally the Republic's population around his leadership may in no way be comparable, but it takes advantage of the situation."

"What do we do?" Chancellor Conteh, the third member of the Imperial Executive Council, asked.

"We acknowledge his declaration based on Admiral Giambo's raid, make it public, and prepare our frontiers accordingly. I don't propose to conduct any aggressive action," Benes replied. "And I seriously doubt the Republic will carry out any either. At least not in the short term, which gives us time to grow our defensive posture. I certainly will not use this declaration of war as a way of stirring up any belligerent nationalism. On the contrary. I will publicly deplore it and hope the Republic's leadership comes to its senses."

"And Giambo's raid?"

"The fly in the ointment. We cannot make the existence of the biolab with its Barbarian Virus public, and the raid is under the strictest need-to-know secrecy. Officially, it never happened. And until I see a reason to do otherwise, I shall remain puzzled at Juska's unwarranted and unprovoked declaration of war."

"Did either of you notice Admiral Norum and Ambassador DeCarde standing right behind President Juska?" Ardrix asked.

"Can't say that I did," Conteh replied.

Benes half closed his eyes. "I do believe you're right, Ardrix."

He touched a control surface, and the video played again. "And there they both are, honored guests of the president. I wonder what that means."

"Either they were turned," Ardrix said, "or they managed to worm their way into Juska's confidence by pretending to have been turned."

"How could they become Juska supporters who receive VIP treatment?"

"The same way Lieutenant Commander Paget was. By planting false memories into their minds."

"And in his case, it wore off."

"One might expect the same in theirs, which means they could be playing a long game of some sort. After all, they are not only highly intelligent and full of initiative, Currag DeCarde also has more than a smidgen of a Sister's talent."

Benes cocked an eyebrow at Ardrix. "He does? How did you find out?"

"I tried touching his mind a few years ago. He slammed down impenetrable defenses, and I asked about it. We had a very interesting conversation afterward. It turns out the ability is genetic and has been passed down his family line for over a thousand years."

"Taking us back to the conversation at hand, are he and Norum influencing Juska?"

"Possibly."

"And in which direction?"

Ardrix grimaced. "Certainly not in the direction of war. Both are aware of what another civil war between human factions could cost. Norum especially embodies Jonas Morane's spirit, and the Republic's second president did not want any more internal strife after Dendera's almost fatal attack on humanity."

"Perhaps they're just background characters under Juska's control," Conteh said. "With no influence whatsoever."

Ardrix inclined her head. "True. But studying their facial expressions, especially the eyes, tells me differently."

— 49 —

New Lena, Yotai
United Stars Republic

Norum and DeCarde were let through the unremarkable doorway connecting the Presidential Palace's official section to the president's private quarters, which only a fraction of the people working in the Palace ever saw. Once inside, they heard Juska's voice calling them into a remarkably homey sitting room.

"Good evening, my friends." Juska, sprawled in a comfortable-looking easy chair, glass in hand, waved at the rows of bottles sitting on a sideboard. "Do help yourselves. I have a fine Glen Petras, which is, as I recall, among your favorite tipples."

"Good evening, sir." Both men stopped just inside the sitting room, came to attention, and bowed their heads politely. Then, they did as they were bidden and walked over to the drinks display.

Glasses in hand, they joined Juska, taking chairs on either side of him.

"Your health." The president raised his glass.

"And yours."

They drank, then Juska put his glass on a side table and leaned forward.

"I've considered what you mentioned regarding Vandeleur Dost, Currag, and I'm starting to understand your perspective. He is dangerous — to me and to the Republic. But he has a following in the United Stars Bloc movement."

"Screw his followers, Mister President," DeCarde replied in a conversational tone. "Fact is, he doesn't have your vision and never will. That means he can't succeed you without jeopardizing the Republic's future, and yet he's angling for your job and will soon take more muscular measures to oust you. He clearly crafted his proposals earlier today to whittle away your power.

"Yes." Juska rubbed his chin with his hand. "And you reckon he'll try to take my job?"

"He reeks of ambition. A tiny mishap, maybe an unanticipated coronary while far from complete medical assistance, and he's in charge."

If Juska caught the allusion to how some suspected he might have succeeded President Hecht more than a decade earlier, he didn't show any signs.

"You make good points, Currag. I suppose you know the Senate imposed him on me.

"I do, sir. And it's time to correct that mistake. Besides, this isn't the same Senate as back then. Nowadays, they'll let you have your way."

"Indeed. There's much to be said for a legislature that cooperates with the executive. But how do I rid myself of Vandeleur?

"I do not know, sir. Still, a man with your experience of politics can surely figure something out."

"And who do I name as my vice president in his stead? You?"

"No, sir. I'd make a lousy VP. I've got the political instincts of a Marine combat officer." DeCarde's eyes shifted to Norum in a way Juska couldn't miss. "Ideally, you'd need an outsider rather than a longstanding United Stars Bloc member, someone who isn't beholden to anyone else and who doesn't really want the job, but someone of proven leadership and administrative ability. A person who'd be loyal to you and have no ambitions of his own." DeCarde stroked Juska mentally with his undisciplined and limited abilities.

"Hmm." Juska stared at Norum, lost in thought. "You know, the individual you describe sounds ideal. But who embodies those traits?"

DeCarde shrugged. "Farrin, by dint of having been CDS, has some very sound political instincts. His leadership and management abilities are beyond question. And he's loyal to the president by default. Plus, he's got no ambitions other than to serve the Republic, not to become president himself."

Norum hid his surprise at DeCarde's words, but a chuckle escaped Juska's throat.

"Ironic, considering we were bitter enemies when I was VP, and he was on my elimination list after I took over as president."

"The re-education process works, sir. It's a crying shame the Order withdrew from it."

"It is." Juska picked up his glass and took another sip. At that moment, a human butler entered the room.

"The evening meal is ready to serve, Mister President."

"Excellent. Thank you, Worcester." He climbed to his feet. "If you'll follow me, gentlemen."

The meal, a simple three-course repast plus dessert, was accompanied by some of the finest wines Norum had ever tasted, and he said so. Meanwhile, the conversation centered around the difficulties of governing a star nation strung out along the various branches of the wormhole network with a small population relative to the number of worlds re-colonized.

Norum offered many cogent comments and suggestions, knowing they would weigh in the balance should Juska actually take DeCarde's recommendation that he be appointed vice president seriously. He hadn't yet figured out why his old friend was advocating the idea, but cooperated and strived to make himself appear essential without seeming keen.

They found themselves back in the sitting room, snifters of brandy in hand, after polishing off their desserts.

Juska raised his glass and said, "This was one of the most enjoyable evenings I've had in a long time. Thank you. I usually spend my time either alone or with people who want something from me. You two didn't look for any favors or decisions and were content to engage in intelligent conversation. It's a rare experience for me."

"It was enjoyable for us as well," Norum replied. "I hadn't realized the magnitude of your task, but now that I do, I have a much better appreciation for your efforts in guiding the Republic down the right path."

"It does seem like a Sisyphean task most of the time. But the key is surrounding myself with the right people. And that definition changes with time. You've met Anya Fong. Is she still the best one to lead the United Stars Bloc movement?"

After a moment of silence, when it became clear Juska wasn't asking a rhetorical question, Norum put on a thoughtful expression.

"Not particularly, sir. She's full of enthusiasm but produces little other than churn."

"My thoughts exactly. Anya is flash rather than substance. Yet she harbors ambitions to replace me."

"Replace her," DeCarde said. "You have the power, Mister President. Everyone in the Republic's government and the United Stars Bloc movement serves at your pleasure."

And then it struck Norum. His friend was trying to sow suspicion between the president and his closest confidants. Hopefully, Juska wouldn't notice.

"I'll consider it. Perhaps the wrong people have been in charge all along, or they haven't kept up with the evolution of my government."

"I suspect it's the latter, sir. Some folks simply can't adapt to changing circumstances, and you've evolved quite a bit over the years."

"Thanks once more for the encouraging and provocative talk." Juska climbed to his feet, imitated by Norum and DeCarde, who hastily downed the rest of their brandy before rising. "I believe we have another meeting scheduled for ten tomorrow morning."

"Indeed, sir."

"Then let me wish you a good night. We will certainly do this again very soon."

"Good night, sir."

Juska led them to the door and saw them through. A pair of bodyguards picked them up in the public part of the Palace and accompanied them back to the Guesthouse. Once there, they went to the common room for a nightcap.

"Interesting evening, wasn't it?" DeCarde commented after taking a sip of Glen Petras.

"It was. I think the president needs a bit of assistance from disinterested outsiders."

"My thoughts exactly. Ready to help him?"

Norum nodded. "Yep."

— 50 —

Wyvern
Second Empire

"I do believe you've shed the attempts at memory modification, Commander."

Sister Hildegard sat back in her chair after spending almost three hours searching through Paget's mind. He could still feel her fingers on the side of his neck. But the Void adept, whose black hair framed an ageless, elfin face, looked exhausted to the naval officer's eyes, and he said so. She gave him a wan smile.

"There is a price to pay for any intrusion into another's mind," Hildegard said. "And that price is our very life force. I will go meditate for an hour or so, then nap. It will restore me."

"How sure are you I'm clean, Sister?"

"As sure as I can be under the circumstances. Implanted false memories don't look like the real thing and stick out like a Sibirian scullywog in an art gallery to someone like me, who's made the study of the human mind her life's work. Fortunately, there aren't too many places in the mind where they can stick false memories in the first place, so that limits the amount of searching I have to do."

Hildegard's expressive brown eyes met Paget's.

"You're lucky, you know, Commander. We've long theorized that implanting memories can cause the brain to essentially short-circuit, inducing madness or death. Not that we ever found out in practice, since the Order considered the whole embedding false memories into someone else's mind against their will abhorrent. At least our Order. The Lyonesse version clearly thinks differently.

"The Sister who treated me didn't seem terribly empathetic."

"She could have been that most frightening of Sisters, a highly talented psychopath. We weed them out early on, but perhaps the Lyonesse people use them instead."

"Now, getting back to my question, are you sure enough to sign off on my returning to duty?"

Hildegard nodded once. "If there are any remaining false memory fragments I missed, I'm sure they'll either flush out by themselves or, failing that, not have any lingering effects on your thought processes. In other words, I'll declare you ready for duty without restrictions."

"That's excellent news, Sister. Thank you.

"Like I said, you're lucky. Try not to let anyone do this to you again. It might be fatal a second time."

"I seriously doubt the Navy will send me back into the Republic after this. They have my biometrics and can ID me no matter what disguise I wear."

—51—

New Lena, Yotai
United Stars Republic

"Morning, Currag." Farrin Norum kept his eyes on the tablet set up behind his breakfast plate as DeCarde entered the Guesthouse dining room.

"Morning. What's the news?" DeCarde took a seat across the table from Norum, and a service droid trundled in, carrying a cup of tea, black, just the way DeCarde liked it.

"You'll be shocked — Vice President Vandeleur Dost died last night of a heart attack. He and his spouse had just come back from a gala soirée at the New Lena Opera when he settled into a living room chair, clutched his chest, and passed on."

"Oh, no. That's terrible."

Norum looked up at DeCarde and saw the understanding in his eyes. Juska had finally acted against the increasingly obstreperous and obstructive Dost. Only a week had passed since their evening with the president, but Dost had become an even greater nuisance in that time. It was as if he'd felt his window of opportunity was closing. And now it had slammed shut with finality.

DeCarde ordered his breakfast from the droid and sat back, enjoying his tea while Norum finished his plate. Wentworth walked in moments after the droid delivered DeCarde's breakfast.

"Gentlemen, the president's office just called. He would like to see you at eight-thirty."

Both glanced automatically at the replica of an ancient grandfather clock quietly ticking away in a corner. The time was just before eight.

"Alright. Eight-thirty it is," Norum replied. "Thank you, Wentworth."

The butler bowed his head and left.

"I wonder what the president wants so early in the morning," DeCarde said in a light tone.

Norum made a face at him but didn't say a word.

At eight twenty-five, their usual escort arrived at the Guesthouse and led them to the Palace, where they navigated down the various corridors until they reached the presidential antechamber, over which the executive assistant presided.

He gestured at the sofas. "Please have a seat. The president will receive you shortly."

At eight-thirty precisely, the EA climbed to his feet and gestured at the inner door. "Gentlemen."

He ushered them into the presence of a somber Juska.

"Good morning, sir."

Juska waved them to the chairs in front of his desk. Once the EA had retreated into the antechamber, he asked, "You're aware Vandeleur Dost died of a heart attack last night?"

"Yes, sir. Read it on the newsnet at breakfast."

"A very sad business. I'm about to decree three days of mourning throughout the Republic, followed by a state funeral."

Norum nodded. "It's the very least he deserves."

"Then I must name a new vice president." Juska gazed at Norum. "How would you like the job, Farrin?"

"I would feel honored to assist your government in any manner you desire, sir."

"Excellent. I'll announce it once the mourning period is over. Until then, please keep this closely held."

"Of course, sir."

Juska broke out in a smile and rubbed his hands. "I think you and I will form a great team, Farrin. The fact that we were adversaries long ago will simply reinforce our new relationship."

"That it certainly will, sir. I am looking forward to working for you."

Though he didn't show a single emotion, DeCarde was privately jubilating. He'd succeeded in getting his friend named number two in the Republic's leadership. It wouldn't take much to make him number one in a few months.

Both friends attended the president during the mourning period and sat right behind him during the state funeral. People noted their presence, but it was no longer unusual.

However, when President Juska announced Farrin Norum's appointment as the new vice president, it created a remarkable stir among the Republic's political classes — and within the resistance — mostly if not entirely negative. Of course, the newsnets greeted the new vice president with enthusiasm, since Juska had brought them under his control, either directly or indirectly.

Norum was vaguely aware of the cabinet members' reaction to his appointment, vaulting him over their heads, but it was brought home to him as he met the war cabinet for the first time on his second day.

"Good morning."

Norum smiled as he took his seat at the head of the table in the Presidential Palace's small executive conference room. He received two nods in reply — from the Secretary of Transport and the Secretary of Justice — while three more simply watched him with expressionless eyes. But Admiral Haggan sat stony-faced as he stared at Norum, while Bea Pollan, the SecDef, a short, dark, intense woman in her fifties, gave him looks of pure hatred. Traditionally, the SecDef was third in the government chain of command after the president and the vice president, and she had clearly expected to become VP upon Dost's death, yet the president could appoint anyone he wanted.

Still, it worried Norum that Pollan was making her displeasure so clearly known. It meant she didn't fear him or his reaction, and he wondered why. As Juska's VP, he was an extension of the president's will and therefore was to be treated the same as him. What was he missing?

However, the meeting was civil, though unproductive, and Norum wondered whether any of the Secretaries truly believed the Republic was at war with the Empire. He supposed it was a good thing. The less the Republic's war machine spun up, the lower the risks of actual fighting. He knew President Benes was totally against any sort of aggressive action and would, at best, reinforce the Empire's defensive posture, but at the cost of developing reclaimed worlds any further. Still, if they didn't truly believe in Juska's declaration of war, what else didn't they believe in? What were they saying or doing behind the president's back to undermine him or keep him in check? Perhaps Juska's quasi-dictatorial powers weren't quite so absolute. Or perhaps Dost had been quietly fomenting a revolt against the president.

Regardless, the cabinet members greeted Norum coldly, not with warmth. Suspicion and outright dislike were more the order of the day. Norum didn't really care. His end goal was ending Derik Juska's administration by hook or by crook and putting the Republic back on the right path — if that was even possible.

Still, at the end of the meeting, Norum asked Pollan to stay behind. Once they were alone in the room, he studied her for a few moments.

"You're angry because the president gave me the VP slot ahead of you, right?"

Nostrils flaring, eyes betraying deep resentment, she nodded. "Yes."

"You do realize that carrying a grudge against me won't do anything other than gnaw at your soul. I didn't apply for the job. Derik Juska appointed me out of the blue when Vandeleur Dost died. And when the President of the United Stars Republic asks you to take on certain responsibilities, you're duty-bound to say yes, agreed?"

She stared back at him in silence for what seemed like an eternity before replying. "Could be. But that still doesn't mean I like you, let alone trust you. For what it's worth, I and many others believe the president made a grave mistake in appointing a former renegade like you to the number two job, and I intend to speak with him about it."

"Fair enough. But while I'm VP, we have to work together effectively for the greater good. Otherwise, we're both failing our oath to the Republic."

She gave him a grudging look. "Okay. But always keep in mind how much I dislike and distrust you. That won't change."

"Understood."

"Vandeleur Dost was an excellent VP, the best. He understood us cabinet members and made sure the president heard our ideas and our concerns."

"I'll try to do as he did, but for that, you and your colleagues must speak to me or else I can't be your ally."

Her eyes narrowed slightly at Norum's last few words, but otherwise, her expression remained carved in stone. Did that reaction mean anything? Norum couldn't tell.

"We'll see. Was that it, sir?"

"Certainly. Thank you for taking the time. I do hope you'll give my request some thought. I'd rather be your ally than your enemy."

She gave him another strange glance before escaping the conference room.

When Norum returned to his spacious, richly appointed office at the other end of the Palace from Juska's, he found Colonel Detlef Varik, the commanding officer of the Presidential Guard, waiting for him. Tall, muscular, with a square face, blond hair cropped almost to the scalp, and sharp blue eyes, he looked like a recruiting poster. Varik wore the silver-trimmed black uniform of the Guard, with the twin oak leaves of his rank on the collar. He also wore three rows of ribbons on his left breast, marking him as a former Defense Force member with plenty of service to his credit.

Varik popped to his feet the moment Norum entered his office's antechamber.

"Mister Vice President."

"Colonel. To what do I owe the pleasure of your company?" Norum gestured at Varik to follow him into his inner sanctum.

"We haven't had a chance to chat yet, sir, and since you have a bit of free time on your schedule right now, I figured, why not come and see you?"

"Excellent idea." Norum slipped in behind his desk and sat, indicating the chair across from him. "Please, Colonel."

Varik obeyed, settled back, and crossed his legs, right ankle over left knee, showing off his gleaming black riding boots, an anachronism for day-to-day wear in a military branch of an interstellar polity.

Having briefly scanned Varik's personal file, Norum knew the man had been a Regular Army major, born on Lyonesse and an early adherent to the Lyonesse First movement almost fifteen years ago. That last made him the ideal choice as commanding officer of the Presidential Guard when Juska first conceived of it. He was ambitious, like most people surrounding Juska, and intelligent, but the confidential part of his file noted some character flaws that had kept him from a flourishing Army career. Norum, who'd seen the signs before, suspected he was probably a highly functioning psychopath since his worst recorded flaw was a total absence of empathy.

"What do you know about the mandate of the Presidential Guard, sir?" Varik's tone was deferential without being submissive.

"Why don't you assume I know nothing and start from there? Your branch didn't exist in my day, and I've had little interaction with it since my return."

"Certainly. Well, first of all, our primary job is to protect the president's life from any threat. The plainclothes bodyguards you see around him are specially trained non-commissioned officers of the Guard. We also protect your life, sir, and your minders are from the Guard as well. You may not have noticed them much yet, since you still live in the Guesthouse and haven't left the Presidential Palace since becoming VP."

"Ah. I was wondering about the serious-looking young men in business suits that seem to materialize whenever I leave my office."

"Indeed, sir. Our secondary job is to appear as ceremonial guards around the Palace and wherever the president or you go. We also have a third role, one which doesn't officially exist and that we keep totally deniable. We take care of the president and your personal enemies if they become dangerous, as well as serious foes of the government if they decide to act."

"Such as resistance members?"

"Yes, sir. They're high on the list of targets for the direct-action battalion. Once they're in our hands, we simply make them disappear. It discourages others from trying the same thing."

Norum felt a wave of disgust, as much at Varik's words as his matter-of-fact tone, but he kept his feelings well hidden.

"How many battalions does the Guard Regiment have?"

"Four. The direct-action battalion, which is officially the 3rd, the Close Protection Battalion, which is the 2nd, and the official duties battalion, which is the 1st, along with a headquarters battalion, twenty-four hundred troopers in total. We're garrisoned next door in the New Lena Barracks."

"And you draw your personnel from?"

"Originally, everyone came from the Defense Force, but we've established our own battle school and are recruiting suitable candidates from civilian life. Our standards are considerably higher than the Army's or the Marine Corps' when it comes to recruits, especially regarding their integrity. We need people who are wholly loyal to the president."

"And to the United Stars Bloc movement?"

Varik shook his head. "No, sir. When President Juska established the Guard, he made it clear we were to be apolitical and profess no allegiance to any movement."

"But profess your allegiance to the president."

"Yes, sir. Whoever he or she may be."

Interesting. Norum thought the Guard would swear loyalty to Juska personally, maybe even to the United Stars Bloc, but that was not the case. Maybe his initial assessment of Juska, made more than ten years earlier, was correct. He'd used the Lyonesse First and its successor, the United Stars Bloc, to advance his own ambitions, not because he was a firm believer in the Republic's mission to reunite humanity, the Empire be damned. But he knew he was mortal, and Norum once again wondered what Juska's endgame could be. He had no children to whom he could pass the mantle of leadership, let alone trusted political allies. From what Norum had witnessed over the previous weeks, Juska seemed to exist in solitary splendor, deep inside the temple of political ambition he'd constructed.

And that made him vulnerable.

"The president is our sole reason for existence," Varik continued, jolting Norum from his thoughts.

"Have you ever had to stop genuine threats against him?"

"Distant threats, yes. Close-in, no."

"And how did you take care of those distant threats, which I assume refers to plots against him rather than assassination attempts."

"You assume correctly, sir. We terminated the threats with extreme prejudice."

"You killed the plotters."

"Yes, sir. They won't be trying anything ever again."

The sense of satisfaction underlying Varik's tone caused another wave of disgust at the man casually dismissing extrajudicial murder to rise up Norum's throat, but he suppressed it without showing any reaction.

"Good," he replied in an emotionless voice.

"On another subject, if I may, sir, Vice President Dost refused to have an aide-de-camp from the Guard. He deemed it unnecessary. But I think the VP, just like the president, should have one, not only for protocol matters but to serve as a close-in bodyguard. Since you were Chief of the Defense Staff, you'd of course know how useful a uniformed aide can be in many ways, something your predecessor failed to appreciate. And I have just the perfect candidate for you."

Norum immediately realized the aide would be Varik's way of keeping tabs on him, and that's why he was pushing the notion. Perhaps Dost had thought so as well, which was why he declined to have one. That raised further questions about his late predecessor's private agenda. And about Varik's. Still, having an aide could be useful.

"And who is that perfect candidate, Colonel?"

"Major Magda Finn, from the Close Protection Battalion. She's a former Marine command sergeant who worked for Defense Force Security and is one of my best officers."

"Can I meet her before accepting?"

"Of course, sir. I have her waiting outside. With your permission, I'll introduce her to you."

At Norum's nod, Varik jumped to his feet, headed for the office door, and opened it. Moments later, he stepped aside to allow a statuesque blonde woman wearing the Guard's silver-trimmed black uniform to enter. She stopped three paces in front of Norum's desk and raised her right hand in a crisp salute.

"At ease, Major," he said after returning the compliment with a grave nod. As she adopted the parade rest position with Varik standing by her side, Norum studied Finn.

Tall — approximately one hundred eighty centimeters — she appeared to be in her forties with braided blond hair pinned to either side of her skull. Her deep blue eyes looked out from a strong, handsome face, and a muscular body molded by a well-tailored uniform completed the picture.

"Tell me about yourself."

"Yes, sir." Her voice, a deep alto, was resonant, yet somehow also melodious. "I joined the Marine Corps straight out of school at eighteen, and after three years as a basic infantry trooper, I went to Defense Force Security School to become a military police noncom. I served in various policing functions over the following nineteen years and graduated from the close protection program. At twenty-two years of service, when I was a command sergeant, the Presidential Guard recruited and commissioned me as a centurion. I've been serving in the Close Protection Battalion as a team commander ever since."

"And why would you want to be my aide-de-camp?"

"I recall your time as CDS, sir. You inspired a great many of us, and the honor of serving as your aide would be the greatest experience in my career."

Norum repressed a smile. She was putting it on a little too thick, considering he doubted she'd volunteered for the job. Varik didn't strike him as someone who'd leave the responsibilities of the VP's aide to whoever raised his or her hand. No, he'd handpicked Finn and briefed her on his expectations, and they had only partly to do with making Norum's life easier and safer.

He considered her in silence for a few moments longer, then smiled. "I suppose you should put up the requisite aiguillettes and organize yourself a desk in the anteroom beside my executive assistant, Major. Welcome aboard."

—52—

Wyvern
Second Empire

"You're joking." President Benes stared at Admiral Mindar with the sort of astonishment the latter had never witnessed before.

"No, sir. The evidence our agents provided confirms it. Admiral Norum is the new vice president of the United Stars Republic."

"But how is it possible? Norum is a refugee from the Republic who has been the target of assassins. How could he suddenly become the number two of the USR under the same president who persecuted him? It makes no sense whatsoever."

"We can only surmise he maneuvered his way into President Juska's confidence after being brainwashed like Commander Paget to show loyalty to Juska's regime."

"In that case, the brainwashing should have worn off by now."

"Indeed, sir, which means he could be using his appointment to undermine Juska. Or he might have turned into a genuine supporter of Derik Juska through brainwashing. We can't know until we speak with him, and that will not be possible anytime soon, if ever."

Benes frowned as he rubbed his chin. "Would sending Paget back to Yotai under his double agent guise and having him try to contact Norum make any sense?"

"He'd be going back without his Republic Navy control officer. She's being held as a prisoner of war in the Detention Barracks."

"Any chance of doubling her?"

Mindar shook her head. "Doubtful. She's entirely loyal to the Republic and has refused to say anything beyond rank, name, and serial number. And since she is a POW, we haven't interrogated her any further.

"Do you believe his Republic handlers would accept the narrative of her death after they were compromised and he fled to Yotai?"

Mindar considered it for a bit, then shrugged. "Perhaps, sir. It's impossible to tell. But if they subject him to Void truthsayers, they'll find out about the ruse rather quickly. If we're going to send him back, it's with a completely new identity, including temporary surgical changes, under the guise of a Republic smuggler."

"Except there won't be an agent from the Republic aboard his ship, ready to betray him."

"True. I'll ask Paget, but I won't order him, sir. He's already done enough for the Empire."

Benes nodded. "Fair. Go ahead and ask him. If he doesn't wish to repeat the journey, find someone else. We need our own eyes and ears on Yotai."

"Yes, sir."

***

"You realize they have my DNA signature, sir. One fresh sample from me, and it doesn't matter what I look like — they'll know immediately I'm Hal Paget, lieutenant commander, Imperial Navy."

Paget, wearing his naval uniform with the two and a half stripes of his rank at the collar, put on an apologetic air.

Captain Delibes grimaced. "I'm aware of that, and so is Admiral Mindar, Hal. But you're the best person to reach Yotai unnoticed and contact Admiral Norum."

"I still can't accept he's the vice president to that murderous canker on the butt of humanity, Derik Juska."

Delibes' grimace turned into an ironic smile. "Don't hold back, Hal. Tell us how you really feel."

"His using Sisters of the Void to majorly mess with minds is way beyond anything I can forgive."

"I've got news for you, Hal. The Commission for State Security used our Sisters to help with interrogations until recently. They were mind-meddling too."

"Got one you could send with me to act as my backup against their evil version?"

Delibes considered Paget for a few seconds. "It sounds like an interesting idea. Let me check. Does that mean you're open to taking on the mission?"

A slow grin spread across Paget's face.

"Well, it's either do it or give up my call sign, and I've become somewhat attached to being known as Imperial Rogue."

"More like an Imperial Pain," Delibes muttered just loud enough for Paget to hear, triggering a gale of laughter from the latter.

"Is that what you higher-ups call me? Priceless. So let me know if the Sisters will send someone with me, and I'll accept the mission. Until then, it's a tentative yes. What about the ship? Will it be *Marlene*?"

Delibes shook his head.

"No. We wiped the AI you knew as Marlene, and Republic authorities might easily identify the ship itself. You're getting one of the same class, *Yanna*, with a freshly installed AI."

Paget groaned theatrically. "An AI that I'll have to train from the ground up."

"You'll have little else to do during the long passage to Yotai. Besides, the latest ship AIs are far more advanced than Marlene."

***

Two days later, in the early afternoon, Delibes summoned Paget to his office without providing any explanation.

When he entered the office, a short, round-faced woman with curly black hair framing an aquiline nose and impassive brown eyes sitting across from Delibes' desk looked up at him. She wore a long-sleeved black top and black trousers tucked into calf-high boots and had an ageless face that hinted at her vocation.

"Ah, Hal. Meet Sister Valery. The Order assigned her as your counselor for the mission."

"A pleasure, Sister." Paget politely bowed his head to her while she studied him.

"Likewise, Commander."

"Take a pew, Hal." After Paget sat beside Valery, he said, "The good Sister received a briefing on your entire story, from your initial departure to your return home, and your deprogramming. She's fully cognizant of your next mission to Yotai."

"And she was still crazy enough to volunteer for it." Paget glanced at Valery. "No offense, Sister."

"None taken, Commander." A faint, almost mocking smile briefly crossed Valery's lips. "But we members of the Order don't volunteer. We're assigned. Although I would have volunteered for this one anyway. Life has become a bit boring since we no longer work with State Security."

"Oh, life can become extremely non-boring in the Republic if we're nabbed by the OSR. Especially for an Imperial Sister of the Void."

"I'll try not to worry about it," Valery replied in a dry tone.

Paget felt ghostly fingers touch his mind, and he smiled at her. "I sense that you're a Sister of great talent."

"You can perceive my mental touch? Sister Hildegard was correct in her evaluation of your latent abilities."

"Are you taking the mission then, Hal?" Delibes asked.

"Since Sister Valery is the real deal, sure. Just point me at our ship and we'll be off to Yotai via one of the smuggler routes."

"We need to modify your appearance first."

"Oh yeah. Point me to the Intelligence Service's best plastic surgeon."

***

When Paget returned to Joint Base Byzance after his alteration treatments, Captain Delibes only recognized him thanks to his voice and mannerisms. Sister Valery, on the other hand, briefly touched his mind and smiled.

"The surgeon did an excellent job, Hal," she said. "If I hadn't sampled your emotions when we first met, I wouldn't know it was you beneath the disguise. Let's hope it'll be enough to fool the Republic's authorities."

"It won't if they take a DNA sample, but we'll try to avoid that. We would have been fine if it weren't for Sela Reeve the last time."

"Ah, yes. Sela Reeve. I had a chat with her while you were under the surgeon's care."

"She actually spoke with you? I reckoned she was clinging to name, rank, and serial number."

"You'd be amazed at what a former State Security interrogator like me can pull from someone even if they're unwilling."

"And what did you learn?"

"That she's an amoral being who doesn't care a whit about others, only herself. And she's a wild talent, a strong one, which makes her highly threatening. The Order doesn't even try to train her sort. A psychopath with a fully developed talent is dangerous in ways you wouldn't believe."

"Oh, I'd take it as true." What sort of Sister do you figure meddled with my mind and presumably those of Admiral Norum and Ambassador DeCarde to turn us into docile servants of the Republic?"

Valery inclined her head. "True. It would take a thoroughly unprincipled Sister to do so. What is the Lyonesse Order thinking? I know we were skirting darkness working for the Commission as interrogators, but they appear to have wholeheartedly embraced it. I'm not sure there's a way back from that."

"Let's hope neither of us falls into the hands of the psycho Sisters. There's no telling what they'd do with someone like you. Anything else of interest from Sela?"

"She's furious with the Sisters who supposedly turned you for failing to make it stick and landing her in an Imperial prison. Says they are d'ayvols, which I think signifies devils in an old language of Earth."

Paget let out a bark of laughter. "She has a genuine dislike of the Sisters of the Void. How the heck did you get that much out of her since you're a d'ayvol yourself?"

A faint smile crossed Valery's lips. "I didn't identify myself as such and only touched her mind at the very end of the conversation. The surprise and outrage she evidenced at that point was amusing."

"I'm impressed, Sister." Paget glanced at Delibes. "Please tell me that *Yanna* is ready to go. I'd rather not drag things out."

"She's ready, and so is Sister Valery. Her personal effects are already on board."

"Suitably screened for anything that points back at the Empire?"

"Of course. And your gear, screened as well, also awaits you aboard. You can lift within the hour if you so wish."

"I do." Paget climbed to his feet. "Come on, Sister. Our mission awaits."

Delibes watched them leave his office, wondering whether sending Paget back to Yotai was such a good idea, especially now that the Republic had declared war. But Admiral Mindar's orders were explicit — if he was willing to go, off he went.

— 53 —

New Lena, Yotai
United Stars Republic

Major Magda Finn, with the knotted silver cords of a vice-presidential aide-de-camp dripping from her right shoulder, magically appeared in Norum's open office doorway.

"Good morning, Mister Vice President, and to you as well, Mister Ambassador," she said in a formal tone.

Norum and DeCarde both glanced at her and nodded, the former gesturing at her to enter.

"Good morning, Magda. Grab a pew."

"Thank you, sir." Finn sat beside DeCarde on one of the chairs facing Norum's desk.

He hadn't been able to discuss much, if anything, with DeCarde since his appointment as vice president. They still operated under the presumption that the OSR would hear every word they spoke via various surveillance means. The fact that Norum had been named to the second highest office in the Republic did not mean he could expect any privacy. So they simply kept using veiled speech and significant looks to communicate on sensitive matters. It was far from ideal. Norum wanted to talk openly with his old friend and use him as a sounding board as he made his way in the increasingly murky politics under Derik Juska. But he couldn't.

"What's up?" Norum asked his aide.

"I've finalized the arrangements for your visit to Defense Force HQ, sir."

DeCarde cocked a questioning eyebrow. "Visiting HQ? Any specific reason?"

"To try and patch things up with Rylo Haggan. Having the CDS sputter with hatred every time he sees the VP isn't a healthy way to govern the Republic."

"Why does he hate you?"

"Probably because he finally got into his confidential file and saw a notation I signed stating that he should never be promoted to flag rank due to serious character deficiencies."

DeCarde winced. "Ouch. And how did he get to be CDS with that in his file? Or shouldn't I ask?"

"Best not." Norum glanced at Finn. "You didn't hear any of this, Magda."

"Any of what, sir?" A faint smile softened her severe features.

But Norum was sure Varik would hear his words via Finn soon enough, and he didn't really care. So far, Major Finn had proved invaluable, making his life easier in so many small ways. And since she didn't have a family, she'd moved into the guest suite of the vice-presidential apartments so she could be available to him at any hour. That's exactly how Finn put it in her deadpan manner.

The only disadvantage of his current arrangements was DeCarde still living in the Guesthouse. By protocol, Norum couldn't have him stay in his apartments, and so the friends only saw each other for an hour or so in the vice-presidential offices each day, and for the occasional evening meal. But DeCarde now had the official title of senior adviser to the vice president and an office near Norum's.

"If it isn't talking out of school," Finn continued, "Admiral Haggan isn't fond of Colonel Varik or the Presidential Guard. He considers us to have usurped the Defense Force's legitimate role as presidential protection."

"And yet he's CDS," DeCarde said. "The president must really see something in him."

"In fairness, he seems to do okay. Not stellar, but not bad either. In today's Navy, he's among the more competent flag officers."

DeCarde smirked. "Because the really competent ones have retired."

Norum raised a hand, palm facing outward, in surrender. "Let's not go there, Currag."

"Sorry." But Norum could see DeCarde was far from remorseful.

"Tell me about the arrangements, Magda."

She did so. In excruciating detail, but without making it tedious — another trait of Finn that Norum was appreciating. And as he listened to her, he couldn't help once again feel she was quite attractive. Norum did like the strong, handsome type, and Finn reminded him a lot of Rey Weston, the partner he'd left behind on Wyvern.

Of course, there was no way Varik could have known he and Weston would end up as a couple during their flight from the Republic, but he suspected Finn had also been selected as his aide for reasons other than purely pragmatic. And he didn't quite know what to make of that.

"Thorough as usual," Norum said when she fell silent, and a pleased smile lit up her face. "Thank you." He glanced at a reproduction pre-spaceflight clock sitting on a sideboard. "And on that note, I declare the working day over. Are you free to dine tonight, Currag?"

"Sorry, but no. I have a previous engagement with Deeta Conn. We're going to The Enchanted Pig."

Deeta Conn, President Juska's enigmatic and attractive chief of staff, worked in the president's shadow, and few people beyond the inner circle knew her.

"Lucky you. Enjoy." Norum glanced at Finn. "I guess it'll be you and me breaking bread."

"As always, a pleasure, sir."

"Leave the uniform behind, will you? I'd like to have a normal evening, not one where I'm constantly reminded I'm the VP of the Republic.

"Of course, sir. At what time shall I tell the catering staff? Nineteen hundred?"

"Sure." Norum climbed to his feet, quickly imitated by DeCarde and Finn. "I don't know about you two, but I'm slipping into a nice glass of Glen Petras the moment I step into my apartment. See you tomorrow, Currag."

DeCarde sketched a salute at his brow. "Until then, Mister Vice President."

Norum watched both of them leave, then stepped through the doorway himself. "Time to call it a day, Evan."

Evan Grad, his executive assistant, nodded solemnly. "Very well, sir. See you tomorrow."

Norum walked down private corridors and took a hidden staircase that delivered him to his apartment's door, which opened at his approach. Once alone, he sighed and loosened the collar of his business suit. The days of a vice president were long and jumped from subject to subject like a demented treecat on drugs.

He was having trouble keeping up with the demands of his office and felt the concomitant fatigue in every bone of his body. His last ten years — five in Mykonos' wilderness and five as an anonymous consultant for the Imperial Colonial Service — had left him unprepared for the demands of a high-powered job.

True to his word, he headed for the sitting room with its bar, replenished by the taxpayer's generosity, and poured himself a dram of Glen Petras. Norum took a sip and sighed. He still didn't know how he'd stop Juska and his mad regime — if they were even stoppable. Meanwhile, he had no choice but to take things one day at a time if he wanted to survive.

At eighteen-forty-five, a soft chime floated through the apartment, signaling that Major Finn was ready to join Norum, and, ensconced in his favorite sitting room chair, he called out, 'come.'

Moments later, Finn stood in the sitting room entryway, looking stunning. Her severe braids had vanished, leaving thick blond hair that fell below her shoulders in their wake. It softened her strong face to a degree Norum had not expected. She wore a dark burgundy silk blouse and black slacks, along with pendant earrings and a choker necklace, both made of diamonds set in gold filigree.

"Good evening, sir." Somehow, even her melodious alto voice seemed to have shed its harder edges.

"Good evening, Magda. Do come in. Please help yourself." He gestured toward the array of bottles.

"Thank you." She walked across the room with a gracefulness that was entirely absent from her uniformed persona, drawing Norum's gaze.

Finn poured herself a glass of red wine and then joined Norum, taking the easy chair beside his. He caught a whiff of her scent and felt a thrill course up his nerve endings, making him wonder whether she was on a deliberate mission to seduce him tonight. Or this might simply be how she presented herself when shed of the uniform she normally wore like a second skin.

"I've never asked, Magda, but what is your family background?" Norum took a sip of his drink.

"There isn't much to say, sir. My parents were farmers here on Yotai, and I grew up on the farm. But I wanted to see more of the galaxy and enlisted in the Marine Corps the day I turned eighteen, intending to do one hitch and return home. Unfortunately, my mom and dad died in a vehicle accident while I was on Mykonos, and the bank repossessed the farm because of the massive debts dad had accrued to keep it viable. With nothing to come home for, I re-upped, transferred to Security, and made the Corps my career."

"I am sorry regarding your parents' sudden passing, Magda."

She gave Norum a helpless shrug. "It's been a long time, sir."

The brief story, told in a faintly wistful tone, somehow made Finn seem more human than the coldly efficient aide Norum had come to know. She gave Norum a shy smile before raising her wine glass to her lips, and he felt something stirring within him, something he hadn't experienced in a long time, not even with

Rey. It gave him pause, and he wondered whether this evening had been a good idea.

Another chime sounded, and Norum perked up. "I believe that means the evening meal is served."

He jumped to his feet, grabbed his glass, and nodded toward the dining room. "Shall we?"

Upon entering, they saw two places had been set at the long table, across from each other on the long sides, and surrounded by silver utensils were plates of delicately smoked fish, with dollops of remoulade, pickled seaweed, and small, light crackers. A glass of white wine sat beside each plate.

"Looks delightful," Finn commented as she took her seat.

"It better be delicious as well," Norum mock growled as he reached for his glass of wine. He took a sip and smacked his lips appreciatively. "A good start."

"I agree," Finn replied after taking a taste of hers.

"Bon appétit." Norum picked up the outer knife and fork from the utensil array and attacked a sliver of pink smoked delight. He popped it in his mouth and chewed, eyes lighting up with delight. He swallowed and said, "This is excellent!"

Finn, who was still chewing on her first piece, nodded, and their eyes met, sending a small jolt of electricity up Norum's spine. He briefly wondered whether she'd had the same reaction or whether he was sensing something that wasn't there.

But when both had finished their plates and Norum had signaled the catering staff they were ready for the next course, they sat back in their chairs, Finn twirling her wine glass in her long fingers, their eyes met again, and he could have sworn he saw a come-hither expression in her gaze.

That was quickly interrupted by service droids appearing with covered plates and glasses of red wine, which they deposited in front of each, removing the covers to reveal rare roast beef, mashed tuber, sauteed vegetables, the first two drowned in a mushroom gravy, and steaming buns along with a side of horseradish.

Norum inhaled the aroma of the dish and grinned at Finn. "That smells fantastic. I hope you enjoy rare meat."

"I do. Very much so." A slightly predatory smile twisted Finn's lips, something Norum found strangely erotic, and part of his mind wondered whether she did it on purpose to excite him or whether it was spontaneous and she wasn't really aware of her expressions.

Norum cut a piece of beef and chewed on it, observing Finn, whose smile widened at the flavor and tenderness as she ate her first bite.

"So, Magda, with your parents gone, do you have anyone close left in your life?" Norum asked after taking a sip of wine.

"No. I have no relatives, and I'm not in a relationship. You could say my work is my life."

"That's a bit sad."

She shrugged. "It is what it is, sir."

"How about you drop the 'sir' for tonight and just call me Farrin?"

Finn gave him a mischievous look from beneath half-closed eyelids. "If you wish. Am I right that you're alone in the galaxy as well, Farrin?"

By now, Norum's interest was truly aroused and, suppressing a thought about Rey Weston, he nodded. "My parents are also dead, I have no siblings, and as you may have noticed, I have no other relationships."

A coy look. "You could say we're birds of a feather."

"So it seems."

After polishing off his plate, Norum sat back in his chair, playing with the stem of his wine glass, eyes on Finn, who was finishing her meal. She grew aware of his scrutiny and gave him a slow, lazy wink.

Norum smiled and said, "Dessert is supposed to be berry cheesecake, unless you're interested in a different sort of treat."

"If it's a treat we can mutually enjoy, then I'd prefer that."

"Then let me cancel the rest of the meal and secure my apartment so we're not disturbed by anything short of a direct attack on the Palace." He reached for his communicator and entered a few commands while she finished her wine. "There, done."

Norum climbed to his feet, imitated by Finn, who now watched him with a smoldering gaze, her lips slightly parted. He held out his hand and took hers across the table, then led her toward the apartment's luxurious bedroom, where they embraced with an intensity that took his breath away. Clothes quickly dropped to the floor, and they fell onto the bed. And then, they lost themselves in each other and the moment.

— 54 —

When Norum woke up early the next morning, he was alone in the darkened bedroom, and part of him wondered whether the previous evening had been nothing more than a fever dream. He didn't remember putting his clothes there, but they were neatly draped over a chair beside the bed, and her clothes were gone.

But then his nose caught a faint whiff of a scent he remembered only too well, what Magda had been wearing mixed with Magda's natural bouquet itself, and he recalled their lovemaking in great detail. That it had been one of the best sexual experiences of his life was beyond question. If she were still in his bed, he'd go for another round or two without a shred of hesitation. Magda had been passionate, uninhibited, and energetic.

A sigh escaped Norum as he threw back the covers and climbed out of bed. Time to shower off the aroma of their lovemaking.

Finally dressed and ready for the day, he walked into the dining room and found it cleared of the evening meal's remains, even though he didn't remember ordering the droids to do so. That, and finding his clothes on the chair instead of the floor, indicated Magda had set things to rights before slipping back into her suite, like a good aide-de-camp. He ordered a large breakfast and opened his briefing queue to scan the overnighters.

The food arrived quickly, and he ate while reading a report from the OSR's special investigation unit that recounted a midnight raid on suspected dissidents in New Lena. They took five people into custody and would interrogate them later. Norum suppressed a groan of dismay. Based on what he'd seen so far, the 'dissidents' were no more than malcontents who'd been speaking out of turn where indiscretions could cost them their liberty.

He drained his coffee cup and rose before the droids could appear to de-garnish the breakfast table and made his way downstairs to his official office suite, where he found DeCarde already waiting for him, coffee mug in hand.

Norum dropped behind his desk and gave his friend an amused glance.

"You look like you've had an interesting evening with Deeta Conn."

"Interesting is right. What that lady knows, or suspects, is worthy of an eight-volume series."

At that moment, Major Magda Finn filled the open office doorway. "Good morning, sir," she said in a cheerful voice that held a hint of artificiality to Norum's ears. "Would now be too early to go over your upcoming itinerary?"

"No. Please come in." Norum schooled himself to look like anything but the guy who disported himself with Finn the previous evening. One glance at DeCarde told him his old friend wasn't having any of it.

Once Finn had received Norum's approval and left his office, DeCarde cocked an ironic eyebrow at the vice president.

"Really, Farrin? Your aide?"

"It just happened. Besides, historically, I'm far from the first senior official to fall in bed with a member of his staff."

"You're right about that. I hope it was everything you needed."

"And more. You didn't with Deeta?"

"Turns out I'm not her sort of human. Wrong plumbing."

"Ah. Did she tell you outright?"

"As soon as I tried the old family charm offensive. We had a chuckle, then delved into the president's plans for the next six months."

"Anything we didn't know?"

"Nope. Mind you, she was probing me as much as I was probing her. Call it an in-depth getting-to-know-you evening, or friendly sparring if you like."

"And what did you tell her?"

"Nothing she wouldn't already know, don't fear."

***

Over the following days, Finn acted as if nothing had happened, which Norum found maddening because her mere presence in his office or at his side tended to arouse him. But if she noticed, she gave no sign. At least she checked his office for surveillance sensors at his behest, with him watching the scanner's display over her shoulder, and called it clear, meaning he could talk a little more candidly with DeCarde.

In the meantime, Norum's relations with the war cabinet didn't thaw. In fact, they got frostier, if anything. As for the full cabinet, every member remained polite but distant and volunteered little. If Norum needed to know something, he had to ask point-blank. If he let his paranoia run free, he'd conclude they were deliberately trying to sabotage him by not keeping him in the loop. On anything.

"I don't know what to do about it," Norum said after telling DeCarde about his invidious situation. "They're the perfect hypocrites. The lot of them."

"Have you been paying attention to the president's cabinet meetings lately?" DeCarde asked.

"Why?"

"He's being treated the same as you are — like a mushroom."

Norum stared at his friend uncomprehendingly. "What do you mean?"

"Kept in the dark and fed manure." DeCarde smirked. "It ain't just you who's being denied the full flow of information. Our pal Derik is as well. It wouldn't surprise me if there's a cabinet cabal working against both of you. And Vandeleur Dost headed that cabal before his untimely death."

"You think?"

"It's the best explanation. You noticed me sitting in the shadows of the cabinet room when Derik was presiding, right?"

"Barely."

"I was observing everyone around the table, and you know I can divine a body's thoughts and intentions by watching them."

"Sure. You've got the talent, Currag. But why is the cabinet turning against the president?"

"Because the most powerful cabinet members are tired of Derik's reign. His declaring war on the Empire was the last straw, and along with his increasingly visible oppression of any opposition, they now consider him a danger to the Republic's long-term ambitions. They'd rather he weren't so obvious about turning the Republic into a dictatorship. It keeps the dissidents under control." An ironic smile tugged at DeCarde's lips. "And as far as his detractors are concerned, you and Juska are almost conjoined twins because he appointed you. I'm afraid they'll soon have the upper hand. If they haven't got it already."

"What do you mean?"

"That I fear a cabinet revolt is coming. I sensed it during yesterday's meeting. The secretaries are feeling increasingly desperate, yet Derik is utterly oblivious. As are you. Vandeleur Dost's death threw a wrench in their plans, and your appointment instead of the SecDef as VP compounded the problems faced by the cabal. Now they have to depose, dispose of, or otherwise remove not only Derik but you."

"Both of us having a heart attack simultaneously would be a tad suspicious."

"It would. I can't really see how they'd get rid of you both at the same time unless they don't care about appearances."

"Or they could make me vanish first, get the president to replace me with the SecDef, and return to the original plan."

DeCarde grimaced. "It becomes a question of time. They'll probably want to get rid of Derik before the Defense Force engages the Imperial Navy so they can quietly cancel the war. And the longer it takes, the greater the chance of the war going hot, making a disengagement more difficult."

"Right. What about Varik's bunch? Surely, they won't let anyone get away with assassinating both of us."

DeCarde gave him a questioning glance. "Are you sure your office is clean?"

"Magda checks it every morning these days."

A grunt. "I wouldn't rely on Varik to cover either of you. Every man has his price, Varik included. I'm pretty sure Dost negotiated something with him, and now that he's gone, whoever replaced him at the head of the cabal must have done the same. Otherwise, they wouldn't be growing so confident."

Norum let out a heartfelt sigh. "Is there a single honest individual in this damned Palace?"

"Apart from you and me? Doubtful. But historically, in autocracies, everyone in a position of power is playing everyone else because it's the only way to advance and, in many cases, stay alive."

A smirk. "Last person standing, eh?"

"Something like that. And since everyone is playing everyone, trust is almost nonexistent, despite declarations of loyalty."

A thoughtful expression crossed Norum's face. "So that's why he appointed me as his VP. Because he figures that the Sisters' treatment meant I was more loyal to him than anyone else in the government."

"Precisely. And I think if he can find a way of dismissing or otherwise getting rid of Bea Pollan, he'll appoint me SecDef because I, too, underwent the Sisters' treatment."

"So Derik is aware of his cabinet's growing lack of enthusiasm for his leadership. Interesting."

"Whatever else he is, he's nobody's fool. Otherwise, he couldn't have maneuvered his way to the top and placed such a grip on absolute power that no one dares gainsay him."

"Except he's got a cabal of supposedly trustworthy people scheming against him."

"Every autocrat does at one point or another. It's why absolute dictatorships have even less staying power than pure democracies.

The real question is what do we — you and I — do about it. I don't want either of us to die in a power struggle for control of the Republic."

"No. It's not like I have a shred of ambition to become president or even stay VP any longer than I have to. My only goal is to stop this senseless war before people get hurt."

"And if I'm right, the cabal wants the same thing."

"So either we help them or we get the hell out of here before they do unto us."

DeCarde nodded. "That's about the size of it. I'm in favor of scramming, if we can find a means to put some distance between us and Yotai."

"Only if we're sure the cabal will abort this nonsensical war before we go, Currag."

"Granted." DeCarde paused for a few heartbeats. "Should we warn Derik?"

"Based on what? The fact that you can sense things in people since the Sisters messed with your mind. He evidently has his suspicions already. No, I'm more interested in where Varik comes down in this and why. I think he'll be key in determining whether the Republic undergoes a change in leadership."

— 55 —

DeCarde and Norum were enjoying their morning coffee the next day, when the latter's executive assistant poked his head through the office door.

"Colonel Varik wonders whether you might have ten minutes to see him, sir."

"Now?"

"He's waiting in the antechamber."

The two friends gave each other puzzled glances. Varik never surprised his superiors with an unexpected visit.

"Send him in."

Varik appeared moments later, a spring in his step. "How fortuitous to find both of you here, sirs."

Norum cocked an ironic eyebrow at DeCarde and said as he gestured at Varik to take a chair across from him, "Come now, Colonel, you knew the Ambassador was here. Your surveillance network of the Palace is probably complete, except, I hope, for the private apartments."

The faint air of amusement Norum thought he detected in Varik's eyes seemed to indicate he knew exactly what had transpired between him and Finn the other evening.

"You're right to assume our surveillance network is extensive, sir. It's for your and the president's own protection."

"Does it cover our offices as well?" When Varik hesitated, Norum said, "Never mind. What can we do for you this morning, Colonel?"

"Well, it is a rather delicate matter, sir. Both of you know that certain members of the cabinet are less than happy with the president's leadership, correct?"

Norum glanced at DeCarde. "I guess that answers whether the good colonel is listening in on what happens in the office as well as the private apartments." He turned his eyes back to Varik. "So when Finn scans my office for surveillance sensors, she omits to mention the ones you're operating. I hope they're the only ones she ignores."

"It is for your safety, sir."

Norum let out a humorless bark of laughter. "The distasteful and ultimately illegal actions committed under the banner of 'for your safety' throughout history are legion. But hey, let's not get hung up on that. Let's talk about what Colonel Detlef Varik wants, because like it or not, he's maneuvered himself into the position of kingmaker."

Varik's pale eyebrows shot up. "Sir?"

A wintry smile twisted Norum's lips.

"Don't be coy, Colonel. Or should I call you Detlef? You've listened to every secret whispered in the Palace, every word said in confidence. And perhaps in other places than the Palace, such as the offices of the various secretaries, the Chief of the Defense Staff, and the offices of the United Stars Bloc leadership. And that means you know about the motivations, grievances, loves, hates, and plans of every high-ranking official in the Republic, at least those on Yotai. Let's cut the crap, shall we?" Norum's smile broadened. "What do you really want from us?"

Varik seemed to relax, as if he'd reached a point of no return. "President Juska's time in office is ending. Too many members of his cabinet are unhappy with him, especially since he declared war on the Hegemony. Surely you realize that."

Norum nodded. "We do."

"Thus, the real question is who comes next. The cabinet will likely attempt to install Bea Pollan as president. She's their unacknowledged leader and has unlimited ambition. With Vandeleur Dost in his grave, she won't be content as VP, what she would have become had Dost lived to succeed President Juska."

"But I'm the president's successor."

A cruel smile split Varik's impassive features. "Accidents or medical emergencies happen, sir. I've heard talk of injecting you with a cardiac arrestor during your visit to Defense Force HQ. An autoinjector at the back of the neck while in the elevator with Pollan, Haggan, and their aides, and Pollan becomes the next VP."

"If the president nominates her. The SecDef being third in the chain of command is more a matter of tradition than law."

"Your nomination came as a surprise. The next VP will be imposed on President Juska because they'll be ready. Trust me when I tell you they have the means to do so."

DeCarde let out a low whistle. "Being the Republic's VP is a dangerous job. First, Dost dies of an unexpected heart attack.

Now the cabinet wants to make Farrin merge with the Infinite Void in the same manner."

"The Republic's government is a lot more unstable than anyone can imagine, Ambassador."

"And what happens to me once Farrin is dead?"

"Bea Pollan will arrange to have you disappear."

"Why are you telling us this?" Norum asked. "And not the president."

"Because, for one thing, he would order me to arrest the entire cabinet and anyone else even remotely involved. Mass arrests, show trials, and probably executions. That would likely bring his regime crashing down because even Admiral Haggan would not stand for such a move, let alone the service chiefs and their subordinate flag and general officers, should Haggan be on the list of those involved or support the president."

"Okay. Makes sense. Then why tell us instead of just letting the cabinet cabal do its thing?"

"The cabinet and Bea Pollan in particular have no love for the Presidential Guard Regiment. Should she become president once Derik Juska resigns or is incapacitated —"

"By another convenient heart attack?" DeCarde asked in an amused tone.

"Perhaps something of the sort. The people seeking to oust him don't really care about how the ousting will look to the general population. They want the president gone, period. As I was saying, should Bea Pollan become president, she would disband my unit and replace us with an Army or Marine Corps regiment. My troops and I would find ourselves with nothing because the SecDef considers us Derik Juska's private army of murderous thugs, unfit for any duty, let alone one that has us wearing a uniform and carrying weapons."

"Right. I can see why you don't want Pollan or any other cabinet member to sit behind the presidential desk. But why come to us with this?"

"Because I think you and I can reach an understanding, sir. One that will give the Republic a bit more stability. You see, you're not a politician, and it shows. You're probably the most honorable individual in the entire Palace right now."

"And you think we can reach an understanding?" Norum replied in a sardonic tone. "Please explain that."

"It's simple, sir. We stand back and let things happen, the Republic gets thoroughly destabilized. We shape the events; we can right the ship of state. All we need to do is have you replace President Juska before Pollan and company have time to take you or Juska off the board."

"And how do we 'replace' the president?"

"We force him to step down."

"Easier said than done."

"I have certain evidence that if released to the public will see him forced to resign in disgrace and criminally charged or face a mass uprising."

"Evidence of what?"

"Massive embezzlement. He's been stealing the taxpayers' money since his days as a senator and has hundreds of millions of creds stashed away in numbered bank accounts. Then there's the matter of sexually assaulting dozens of women, some of them as young as fifteen or sixteen. None of them has come forward because either he paid them off or scared them. In recent times, he's ordered us to dispose of a few permanently."

DeCarde sat forward and stared at Varik in disbelief. "You mean Derik is a thief and a serial rapist who's had you murder his victims?"

Varik nodded. "That's it in a nutshell. Except we didn't kill the women. Simply gave them new identities and sent them to outer colonies with enough money in their pockets to live comfortably. They're part of the evidence I mentioned, since I recorded all of his orders."

"Well, thank the Almighty for you having a smidgen of conscience."

"I have my limits, Ambassador. And I draw the line at killing innocents. Although it wouldn't surprise me if Juska murdered some of his victims throughout the years. There were mysterious disappearances among the young women who we suspect fell into his clutches during his years as vice president."

Norum nodded, rubbing his chin with his left hand. "Assuming Juska resigns to let me become president, first of all, who do I appoint as my VP? Certainly, no one from the present cabinet. And second, what do you want, because you're not the selfless type. Your payout will be rather considerable, I suspect."

"Surround yourself with people you trust, former Defense Force senior officers whom Juska dismissed. And what's in it for me? Simple. I want the Presidential Guard expanded to a division, with myself as its commander immediately after you take over, and see it gradually replace the Army."

Norum began chuckling. "You want me to pull a Stichus Ruggero? Convert the Army to my regime's Guards?"

DeCarde's laughter at Varik's demand tapered off, and he asked, "You don't know that part of the First Empire's history, do you?"

A puzzled-looking Varik shook his head.

"Stichus was the first of the thrice-damned Ruggero dynasty and, to cement his hold on the throne, he eliminated the Imperial Army and replaced it with Guards who were sworn to his person and his heirs rather than the Constitution."

A light went on in Varik's eyes. "Oh. Well, what's the harm in having Guards instead of an Army? The latter exists to protect the Republic's individual worlds, and my expanded unit will do the same, as well as protect the Republic's government."

DeCarde and Norum exchanged a brief look, then the latter shrugged.

"Agreed. Your regiment becomes a division by presidential order, the day after I take over. Then we can gradually continue expanding it until it covers current Army deployments." Norum studied Varik's reaction, then asked, "Tell me, did you assign Finn as my aide, intending to get me in bed with her?"

A smile crept up Varik's face. "I have to build a dossier on you somehow, sir. Your past is much too clean, and I can't give up my place as kingmaker, to use your term."

"No presidential ambitions of your own, then?"

Varik shook his head. "I'm not suited for high office."

DeCarde let out a gentle snort. "I like a man who knows his limitations."

"Just like you, Currag? I noticed you didn't volunteer to become my VP."

"The Almighty forbid. I'd make the worst vice president in the Republic's history. But I'll gladly return to the Second Empire as the Republic's Ambassador, should this come to pass."

"Speaking of which, when do we activate your plan, Detlef?"

A grin of satisfaction crossed Varik's face. "That's why I'd rather deal with military people, sirs. Once a decision is taken, it's all hands on deck and full hyperdrives ahead. Not like politicians who enjoy wallowing in prevarication for days on end. If only more of you were interested in high office…"

"We didn't say we were interested in high office," Norum replied, "But we are concerned with the Republic's well-being."

"Which is more than I can say for any of the politicos in government right now. I'll arrange a meeting with the president for fifteen hundred this afternoon. That gives him an hour to reflect before the daily sixteen-hundred-press-briefing. It should be enough."

—56—

Derik Juska seemed puzzled by Colonel Varik, Vice President Norum, and Senior Adviser DeCarde descending on his office when only Varik had announced himself. He nevertheless kept his composure and gestured at the chairs facing his desk, although Norum thought he could read a sick realization blossom in the president's eyes. Perhaps he somehow understood that having his three most trusted people in the same room signaled that something unpleasant was afoot.

"Gentlemen, what brings you to my office at such short notice this afternoon?" Juska asked once they sat across from him.

"It's a rather delicate matter, Mister President," Varik said.

"Oh hell," DeCarde exploded, "it's not delicate. Derik, you've lost the confidence of the cabinet and are resigning now!"

As he spoke, he sent a mental explosion at Juska and was rewarded by an intense look of pain in his eyes. The latter raised both hands to his head and placed the fingertips on his temples.

"Is anything wrong?" Norum asked.

"What's wrong, sir," Varik said, "is that your vice president and your senior adviser are both plotting to remove you from power."

Norum and DeCarde turned to Varik, astonishment and anger clearly visible in their expressions. But Juska wasn't listening. His left arm dropped as if suddenly deprived of strength, while the left side of his face drooped.

"I'm —" he slurred, "feeling terrible."

"He's having a stroke," Norum said, reaching for the communicator embedded in Juska's desktop and activating it. "Doctor to the president's office, stat. The president is suffering from a stroke. It looks massive."

Seconds later, the physician's voice replied, "On my way. I'll have a stasis chamber prepared."

Then, while Varik watched in disbelief, Norum and DeCarde gently picked up Juska and laid him on top of his bare desk while the latter shook and mumbled incomprehensibly. Once he was as comfortable as they could make him, DeCarde turned to Varik.

"So, your plan was to rat us out, was it?" He said in a dangerous tone. "Why?"

"My loyalty is to the president. I've suspected you of being disloyal, and our conversation this morning proved it. I was going to expose you to the president and see you removed from office."

"Well, that won't happen, will it? I doubt the president will be in any shape to govern the Republic for a while, meaning Vice President Norum steps up as acting president." DeCarde turned to Norum. "Any orders, sir?"

At that moment, the doctor came through the office door, breathing hard, and headed straight for Juska. He pulled out a medical sensor and scanned the president's head.

"Yep. It's a hemorrhagic stroke. I'll put him in stasis and have him transported to the New Lena Medical Center, where they have the equipment and specialists for a neurosurgical intervention to treat him."

Just as those words came out of the doctor's mouth, a pair of uniformed troopers from the Guard guided a cylindrical stasis chamber atop an antigrav sled into the office and brought it to the desk. There, under the doctor's quiet guidance, they transferred Juska into the chamber, which was activated.

After staring at the chamber's control display for almost a minute, the doctor turned to Norum.

"He's in stasis, meaning he won't get any worse, but you were right, it was a massive stroke. The hemorrhage in his brain is extensive. I can't figure out what caused it. His latest physical showed no weakened arteries. In any case, he's out of commission for a while. Months rather than weeks. The rehabilitation, assuming he survives, will be long. And that means you're the president now. I'll issue the certificate, making President Juska's incapacity to serve official within the hour." He glanced at Varik. "I assume you'll set up the necessary security apparatus at the Medical Center as well as during transport."

"Of course." Varik pulled out his communicator and stepped away from them as he spoke urgently into it.

By then, the president's executive assistant had joined them and was hovering nearby. Norum brusquely speared him with his eyes.

"Get the press secretary in here now and prepare a message for the government advising that because of President Juska suffering a disabling stroke, I've taken temporary control of the presidency."

The slight, elderly man bobbed his head. "Yes, sir." Then, he vanished again, followed out the door by the stasis chamber, the doctor, and Varik, who gave both Norum and DeCarde an undecipherable glance before leaving.

"Currag, want to be interim vice president?"

DeCarde shook his head. "No. Invite Bea Pollan to take the office. I'll replace her as temporary Secretary of Defense and make sure the military obeys any orders you see fit to issue. What do you want to do about Varik?"

"Let him worry about the consequences of his betrayal for now. In the long term, I'd rather merge the Presidential Guard into the Army and pass a law against raising any military or paramilitary force that doesn't come under the Defense Department. It'll keep twenty-four hundred pissed off troopers where we can control them."

A crooked smile lit up DeCarde's face. "You're going to take advantage of this to undo ten years of Juska twisting the Republic to suit his ambitions, aren't you?"

"You bet I am. And my first action will be to shut down the Yotai Re-education Center for good. The inmates are to be freed immediately, along with anyone else held by the OSR for so-called political crimes. Furthermore, the Justice Department will transform the OSR into a Constabulary, an apolitical organization. This Constabulary's only job will be to fight crime, not pursue dissidents.

"Sounds like an excellent start."

"Why do you think Derik had a stroke?" Norum asked in a light tone.

DeCarde grinned. "I'm sure I have no idea."

"As I thought."

Bea Pollan showed up at the door to the president's office forty-five minutes later, face showing no emotions whatsoever.

"Ah, Bea. Come in." Norum made a welcoming gesture and indicated the chairs in front of what was now his desk.

"I understand you've taken over the presidency during Derik Juska's incapacitation."

"I have. And I'm asking you to assume the vice presidency while I act in Derik's place."

A look of surprise broke through Pollan's carefully studied expression of neutrality. "I'm honored, sir."

"Is that a yes?"

"It is. Who'll take over as SecDef?"

Norum indicated DeCarde. "Currag."

"Oh. A good choice."

"I'm glad you approve."

"What's Derik's true condition?"

"It's not good. Even if he survives, I doubt he'll be able to resume the presidency before the end of his mandate, so I'm assuming full powers rather than just keeping his seat warm. Does that pose any problems for you or the rest of the cabinet?"

She hesitated, then asked, "What are your intentions in exercising those full powers?"

"First, I call off this nonsensical war with the Second Empire — which, by the way, is what we'll be calling it henceforth. They dropped the term Hegemony five years ago.

"That's a relief. I never understood why Derik declared war."

"Because an Imperial task force thwarted his attempt at a secret pre-emptive strike designed to kill most of the Empire's population by taking out the secret biolab on Gennari the evening of the grand finale when we all were in the Stadium of the Stars."

A look of incredulity crossed Pollan's face. "Is that what it was?"

"You did not know he was planning on releasing the Barbarian Virus on Imperial worlds?"

"No. If he'd told me, I'd have removed him from office right there and then. No one in the cabinet would have countenanced genocide, and for what?"

"So Juska could become humanity's sole leader and the Republic the sole heir of the First Empire."

"But that's crazy."

Norum studied Pollan for a few heartbeats to figure out whether or not she was dissembling. He concluded her reactions were genuine.

"I'm glad to hear you think so. I'd have been sorely disappointed to find out you or any of the other secretaries knew about the plan and did nothing to stop it."

"We may not be acutely honorable people, but we're not monsters either. However, Derik was rapidly going in the wrong direction. It's a damn fine thing Sister Elana died when she did. She and Derik were feeding off each other's darkness, spurring each other on to see who could take absolute control of the Republic."

"And you were plotting to remove Derik and me."

Pollan shrugged. "Yes."

"Are you still intent on removing me?"

She grimaced. "Not if you're going to reverse Derik's worst policies. I don't particularly aspire to be president at this juncture."

"I will announce a series of policy changes when I go on the newsnets in an hour, the most prominent being an end to persecution of dissidents and a restoration of freedom of conscience."

"Good to hear, sir. If you intend to continue in that vein, you'll have my and the rest of the cabinet's full support. What are your intentions concerning the Presidential Guard and Colonel Varik?"

"I plan on disbanding it and transferring the personnel to the Army, Colonel Varik included. The Marine Corps will then provide a much-reduced presidential protection detail. At least in the interim."

She made a moue. "I suppose you can't simply kick twenty-four hundred highly trained people out on the streets. Might as well use them productively, but even Varik? I don't know. What about the United Stars Bloc movement?"

"In keeping with restoring the freedom of association citizens used to enjoy, it can continue to exist but will no longer have any connection or access to the government of the Republic."

"Wow. You really are determined to shake things up."

"You have no idea. There are ten years of Derik Juska to undo."

A pensive air overcame Pollan. "So, that much-vaunted re-education program by the Sisters of the Void…"

"It doesn't work. At least not permanently. The effects wear off in those who it doesn't kill. But the new Summus Abbatissa already ended it."

"Good. The idea of manipulating a person's brain to fundamentally change it always gave me the creeps."

Her words were heartfelt enough to give even a skeptical DeCarde hope Pollan would be fully on board with the changes Norum was about to unleash across the Republic.

"Glad you feel that way, Bea. As a subject of said procedure, it gave me the creeps beyond anything you might imagine. Now, can you assure me that the rest of the cabinet will support my dismantling of the Juska regime?"

She nodded. "Absolutely. If there are waverers, they'll follow the majority. I'll call a cabinet meeting early tomorrow morning, read them the riot act, and then you come in and take your seat at the head of the table. How does that sound?"

"Just perfect."

— 57 —

"I thought you'd agreed to increase the size of the Presidential Guard, not eliminate it, Mister President." Varik's voice, though calm, covered an undercurrent of anger and worry that Norum and DeCarde heard clearly.

"And I thought you were genuinely going to help ease Juska out of office. Instead, you tried to denounce us to him as he was having a stroke. If it weren't for his stroke, we'd be imprisoned right now and possibly on the way to being disappeared. You're damned lucky I don't have *you* disappeared." Norum's glacial gaze met Varik's eyes, and the latter flinched. "In fact, you're lucky I'm allowing you to transfer to the Army, along with the rest of the Guard, in your current rank."

After throwing the Republic into turmoil the previous day by announcing an end to most of Derik Juska's policies and effectively an end to his reign of terror, Norum and DeCarde had strategized how to deal with Varik and his two thousand four hundred black-uniformed thugs. Both knew it would be a delicate operation. The slightest misstep and they could find themselves with smoking blaster holes in the back of the head.

In the end, they put the 3rd Battalion, 21st Pathfinder Regiment on alert and had them ready to relieve the Presidential Guard's on-duty minders — whether plainclothes or uniformed — within and around the Palace the moment Varik set foot in Norum's office and was out of communication with his people. They should be taking position just about now, sending the Guard troops back to their barracks.

"As I said, Colonel, I have re-designated the Presidential Guard as the Army's 11th Security Regiment, and the Defense Force will reassign it to essential duties. Of course, anyone not wishing to transfer to the Army may request a release from further service, and the military will grant it speedily, wishing them good luck in their future civilian endeavors. The new SecDef will announce this to everyone the moment the Marines from the 21st Pathfinders have secured the Palace and returned the members of the 11th Security to their barracks. From there, those wishing to stay in the Army will be issued the appropriate uniforms and accouterments and eventually be reassigned to various duty stations across the Republic. Some might even find themselves back here as members of the Army's newly created Protection Battalion. The 21st Pathfinders standing watch over the Palace is a purely temporary measure. Then, I will put a law before the Senate banning the creation of any separate military branches. There will be one armed and uniformed fighting entity in this Republic, and that will be the Defense Force."

"Damn you, Norum. You do not know what you're doing," Varik growled.

The president glanced at his SecDef and cocked a questioning eyebrow.

"Do you think Colonel Varik is declining the opportunity to continue serving the Republic as an Army officer? Because that's what it sounded like to me."

He turned his eyes back on Varik, who was visibly thinking about his next words.

"My apologies, sir," the colonel finally said. "I spoke in haste. I would very much like to continue serving."

"Apologies accepted," Norum replied.

"Since the 11th Security Regiment is an administrative grouping," DeCarde said before Varik could speak again, "it will not have a commanding officer. Only its constituent battalions will. You're therefore assigned to Defense Force HQ as a director in the Security Branch responsible for coordinating close protection issues throughout the three services. Go draw a green Army uniform with the proper insignia, in your case, it'll be the crossed flintlock pistols of the military police, and report to HQ tomorrow morning. They'll be expecting you."

"Yes, sir."

"You are dismissed, Colonel. An officer from the 21st Pathfinders will escort you off the Palace grounds. And you are forbidden to enter the 11th Security Regiment's barracks or to communicate with any of its members for the rest of today."

"Understood, sir." Varik climbed to his feet and raised his hand in a crisp salute. "With your permission, Mister President?"

"Go, Colonel. Good luck with your new responsibilities. I'm sure you'll do well."

Once he was gone, Norum let out a small sigh and slumped back in his chair. "That went rather better than I expected."

"Varik's no fanatic. He probably expected a worse outcome for himself. Whether we can trust him with any Defense Force duty remains open to question, but he'll be easy to control at HQ." DeCarde's communicator buzzed, and he fished it from his tunic pocket. "SecDef."

"Lieutenant Colonel Salmin, sir. The 3rd of the 21st is fully in control of the Palace and its grounds. The troops we relieved have returned to their barracks, which we've secured. They'll be ready for you by the time you get there."

"Excellent, Colonel. Well done. I'll be on my way shortly. SecDef, out." DeCarde slipped his communicator back in its pocket. "That was my signal to let the former Presidential Guard know they're in the Army now. I'll be back in about thirty minutes."

Alone in the office, Norum stood and wandered to the tall windows overlooking the Petal Garden. There, he spotted a pair of Marines in full combat armor slowly patrolling the area, holding their carbines at the low port. For some reason, it made his assumption of power over the United Stars Republic real, where the previous twenty-four hours had been like a dream — or a nightmare. And it made him feel safe for the first time since leaving Wyvern.

He did not know how long he stood there, but a brief knock at the door brought him back to the here and now.

"Come in."

Major Magda Finn, wearing the Army's rifle green uniform with blackened buttons, rank insignia, and branch badges, stepped in. The silver aiguillettes she normally wore over her right shoulder had been replaced with the gold version used by the Defense Force, and she displayed the crossed flintlock pistols of the military police at the collar.

"That was quick, Magda! I won't ask how you found out or where you got an Army uniform at such short notice, but it suits you."

"Thank you, sir. You probably didn't know the Palace has a clothing fabricator in the basement. It's very handy. I've come to remove Colonel Varik's surveillance sensor and render this office truly private."

"Oh, excellent. If you'd do the VP's as well, I'd be grateful."

"Already done, sir." She pulled out a scanner and held it up, quickly homing in on Varik's bug, which she dug out of the picture frame hanging on the wall to the right of Norum's desk. "There we go."

"Thanks, Magda."

"Seeing that it's almost noon, would you like me to bring you a tray from the kitchen?"

Norum felt his stomach grumble, but at that moment, DeCarde stepped through the office door. "All done at the 11th Security Regiment's barracks, Mister President."

"Good. If the SecDef is as hungry as I am, I think we'll take our meal in the small dining room, Magda."

"Very well, sir. I'll make sure it doesn't have any of Colonel Varik's devices. Go ahead. I'll warn the kitchen and then scan the room."

DeCarde followed Norum into the dining room next to the presidential office and sat across from him at the dark, polished wood table.

Norum gave his friend an inquiring look once Finn had retrieved the bug and left them alone.

"So?"

"They took it well. I don't think many will ask to be released, so almost everyone should be in Army green with MP badges tomorrow morning. The Army Personnel Office will have a field day processing the reassignments, although we've already identified duty stations for fifteen company-sized subunits on the outer colonies where they're sorely needed. The black ops people among them won't enjoy doing mundane colonial policing, but I've made sure they go nowhere near the Marine Corps units that carry out sanctioned black ops."

"I'd say my assumption of power has gone a lot better than I'd hoped, but then Derik's worst abuses are recent and not so deeply entrenched as to make change difficult."

"And having a battalion of the elite 21st Pathfinder Regiment to back us up didn't hurt either. Especially with a shrewd guy like Jorge Salmin in command. They'd have taken on the entire Presidential Guard and graced them with a thorough spanking had the little, black-uniformed thugs given any lip, and the latter knew it. A couple of companies of fully armed and armored Marines have a way of calming even the more excitable spirits, and say what you want of Varik's people — they are highly disciplined." DeCarde took a sip of water and glanced up at Norum. "On a totally different subject, how open are you to reinstating officers whom Juska forced out or who retired because of him? The Defense Force lost a lot of corporate knowledge in the last ten years, the sort that partially hollowed it out."

"Absolutely. Go for it. Bring them home."

A pair of serving droids trundled in silently and deposited a fragrant dish of rice and fish before them, then vanished again. After swallowing a mouthful, DeCarde looked at Norum.

"You realize you'll have to move fast on every front for the next while, don't you?"

"To keep any potential opposition off balance? Yeah, I know. And I've got an ever-lengthening list of items on which I'll be issuing executive orders. Starting with turning the OSR into the USR Constabulary and firing Charisse Weber. She was too much in Juska's back pocket. I'm hoping you can come up with a solid, apolitical Defense Force Security colonel or general who can assume command of the Constabulary and transform it because I'm not trusting anyone in the OSR to do it properly."

"I'm sure I can."

"Then I need to find a way of re-establishing term limits for senators, the vice president, and the president, as well as re-establishing the Supreme Court's independence."

"That will take half a day. I'm talking about screwing with any opposition for weeks on end, nobody knowing where you'll hit next."

Norum gave his friend an evil smile.

"Don't worry about that, Currag. I've got executive orders lined up like Pathfinders ready for a mass jump from low orbit. By the way, since you're SecDef and I'm not about to let you go, who do you suggest as envoy to the Second Empire? I'd like to reestablish an embassy on Wyvern and assure them the Republic does not have any aggressive intentions."

DeCarde thought about it for a few moments.

"Hermina. Get the Summus Abbatissa to suspend her vows again and send her. She'll be perfect to smooth over Derik's declaration of war."

"Done. I'll ask Sister Quessi when I speak with her tomorrow morning."

"What about Rylo Haggan. Derik made him CDS even though his file contains enough warnings to disqualify him from serving as CNO, let alone CDS."

"I'll let him serve out his term provided he doesn't screw up."

"You're way more tolerant than I'd be."

Norum shrugged.

"I've got to choose my battles because there are not enough hours in the day to let me do everything I have to. But I live in hope he'll screw up badly soon enough."

DeCarde let out a bark of laughter that was both heartfelt and genuine.

"Okay, Mister President. We'll do it your way. But as SecDef, I have serious reservations about Haggan."

"Noted."

"By the way, two items concerning Major Finn."

"Yes?"

"First, no more intimate nights with her. And second, as aide to the president, she should be a lieutenant colonel."

— 58 —

"There you are."

Sisters Hermina, Rianne, and Bree stopped at the sound of Summus Abbatissa Quessi's voice behind them. Knowing they were the only ones in that section of the orchard, it was clear Quessi meant them, and they turned toward her.

As Quessi emerged from the early evening shadows, the three bowed their heads respectfully.

"Sister."

Quessi smiled. "And what is the subject of discussion this fine evening?"

"Whether president Norum's incredibly rapid restoration of the Republic will work," Hermina replied.

"And what's the consensus?"

"It will. Just like your restoration of the Order to its pre-Elana ways is succeeding, proving once again that evil, though appearing insurmountable by despairing souls, has but a tenuous hold on the vast majority of humanity."

"And why is that?" Quessi asked.

"Because being evil, like being good, demands an effort, and most people are content to drift through life without exerting themselves too much in either direction. It's simply a human trait that has always been with us and always will be."

"Perceptively said, Sister. But interesting as philosophical discussions on the nature of good and evil are, I'm here for a much more mundane matter. President Norum has asked me to temporarily release you from your vows, Hermina, so that he may appoint you as the Republic's Ambassador to the Second Empire."

Hermina's eyes widened in surprise. "The president asked for me by name?"

"Indeed. Since he made Ambassador DeCarde as Secretary of Defense, you're the only one left who has experience dealing with the Imperial government on Wyvern. But as I told the president, I will not force you to accept the appointment. You are entirely free to refuse."

"I wouldn't dream of refusing. Did he say when I would leave?"

"No. That is still up in the air. But in keeping with his whirlwind approach to governing, I would expect it to be soon. In the meantime, carry on as usual. I'll suspend your vows the day before your departure."

Hermina inclined her head. "As you wish."

When Quessi had left, a gleeful smile spread across Bree's face. "There is hope for the vision I had many years ago of our star nations growing close."

"And what it took was for you to disobey the re-education orders and leave their minds intact," Rianne said.

"It was probably the finest thing I've ever done in my life."

***

Lucas Morane had been following the newsnets most of his waking hours since the announcement that Farrin Norum replaced Derik Juska after he suffered a severe stroke. Hope, something he'd thought long since extinguished, flickered anew inside him, and he held his breath for the first day after Norum took over the presidency. Then, as Norum signed executive orders proclaiming the nullification of the policies Juska had implemented over the last few years, Morane came to believe the nightmare was finally ending. Eventually, he returned to New Lena, traveling openly aboard the maglev train.

When he arrived, he returned to his former hideout in the city's oldest quarter and, from there, opened a link with the Presidential Palace directly, naming himself and asking the president to be made aware of his call. Half an hour later, his communicator buzzed for attention, and Morane, whose chest had tightened at the sound, touched the control display, opening the connection.

"Lucas? Is that really you?"

Farrin Norum's voice came from the communicator, momentarily stunning Morane.

"It's me. I'm amazed to hear you!"

"I left word with the Palace comms center to warn me about any calls from many old comrades who'd vanished over the last few years, you among the most prominent because of the message you sent me on Wyvern, and which convinced me to come home."

"And you somehow ended up as President of the Republic." Tears were inconveniently forming in the corners of Morane's eyes, but he ignored them, happy this was a voice-only link.

"Yep. It's a long story I might share with you one day, but I'm glad you're coming in from the cold. Currag DeCarde has orders to reinstate all former military personnel forced out by Juska, so if you want to rejoin the Navy at your former rank, get in touch with the closest recruiting office. They'll process you immediately, and you'll be a commodore again by the close of business."

Morane hesitated. Donning the uniform once more had been a dream for a long time after Juska summarily dismissed him. Could he really reintegrate the Service, especially under a man like Rylo Haggan, a contemporary of his whom he heartily detested and thought unfit for higher rank? Then, he shook himself.

"As long as the Navy still needs me."

"It does. Currag is anxious to get most of those dismissed by Juska back to fill the void left by losing so many experienced and highly competent officers. So, what do you say, Lucas?"

"I guess I'm in."

"Good to know, Commodore. I'll warn the Defense Department to expect you in the next few hours at the New Lena recruiting office. Listen, I have to go, but it was great hearing from you. Once you've settled back in, I'll have you over for supper with a few others, and we can reminisce about the good old days."

"I'd really like that, sir."

"Talk to you soon, Lucas." The link went dead before Morane could reply, but he suddenly realized he wore the biggest grin in many years.

An hour later, he walked into the recruiting center, identified himself, and sat for a quick biometric scan. Once his ID was confirmed, the desk petty officer immediately took him to the center's commanding officer, a Marine Corps major.

"Welcome back, Commodore Morane," the major said, climbing to his feet as the petty officer announced him. "You're officially back on the Navy's active list, with the last five years marked as inactive reserve. Will you need uniforms, sir?"

"Yes."

"Let me see if we have your ribbons and qualification badges listed." He glanced at the display on his desk. "We do. If you haven't put on or lost a lot of weight since your last clothing scan, I'll have a set of service and work uniforms manufactured right away. We have a fabricator on site."

"I'm still at a boring eighty-five kilos, exactly the same as I was the last time I wore a spacer's suit."

"Will you need accommodations?"

"Yes."

"Then I'll have the duty car bring you to Joint Base Yotai, where they'll be glad to put you up in the visiting officers' quarters for as long as you need, sir."

Morane was almost in a daze as the major showed him to the staff car an hour later. He carried a case with spare uniforms and wore a working set with the broad stripe topped by an executive curl of a commodore at the collar and a beret with a Navy flag officer's badge on his head. As he returned the major's farewell salute, the unreality of the rapid changes in his circumstances hit him fully, and he closed his eyes as he settled back in the car's passenger seat.

From a fugitive living among society's rougher elements back to a Republic Navy flag officer in less than a day. It had to be a record of some sort.

— 59 —

"The next item will amuse you, Mister President."

Norum made a go-ahead gesture at DeCarde, impatient to finish their meeting because he had two dozen other issues waiting for his input.

"One of our free-ranging corvettes, *Reliance*, stumbled quite by accident on a suspected smuggler in the Isabella system whose registration was dodgy. A small, fast ship with two crew members — a man and a woman. They were lying doggo waiting for *Reliance* to jump elsewhere, but the corvette's sensor chief caught a ghost, and the captain decided that since he had nothing better to do, he'd stick around and investigate. Sure enough, they eventually picked up a trace of the smuggler, lit him up, and boarded him. There were enough things about the ship, *Fedora*, and its crew to raise several alarm sirens in the mind of *Reliance*'s captain that he decided to take *Fedora* to Isabella Station for further investigation on her status and that of the two people aboard.

"Once docked at Isabella, they ran the crew's DNA through the database, and it turns out that the man is well known to the authorities, although the woman isn't. Our friend Hal Paget is back, on a different ship and with a different companion, because the woman isn't Sela Reeve. As soon as Paget was identified, a big red flag went up — one I planted myself with Intelligence and Security just in case either of them showed up again — and both *Reliance* and *Fedora* are on their way to Yotai, not quite knowing why but aware Paget is of great interest to the Defense Force."

Norum let out a bark of laughter. "I wonder what happened when they returned to the Empire. Last we'd heard, the Sisters claimed to have made Paget into a double agent for the Republic."

"All will be revealed in three days, when they arrive in Yotai orbit, but looking at the image of the woman accompanying Paget, I'm almost convinced she's a Sister of the Void."

"Hmm. Paget leaves with a Republic intelligence agent and returns with a Sister. Could it be the re-education he underwent didn't take, and Reeve was arrested as an enemy spy the moment they landed on Wyvern?"

DeCarde nodded. "That's what I hope. So far, every one of those re-educated — at least the ones we were able to contact — has lost that loving feeling for Derik Juska and his former regime."

"And do you think he's coming back for us?"

"I can't see what else would justify sending him when there was a chance he'd get intercepted, identified, and imprisoned. As far as the Empire is concerned, we're still at war with them."

"Well, isn't he going to be surprised when he's introduced to the Republic's new president?" Norum shook his head. "And if it weren't for the Sisters accidentally awakening your family's hidden abilities and you using them against two key people in the previous regime, this reversal of fortune would not have happened. Freedom would continue to be whittled away until the government became the be-all and end-all. I seem to recall a very famous ancient politician who notably talked about the subject. You, with your fetish for history, must remember what he said."

DeCarde sat stock still for a few moments, then slowly nodded. "I believe he said, freedom is never more than one generation away from extinction. We don't pass it on to our children in the bloodstream. The only way they can inherit the freedom we have known is if we fight for it, protect it, defend it, and then hand it to them with the well-fought lessons of how they, in their lifetime, must do the same. And if you and I don't do this, then you and I may well spend our sunset years telling our children and our children's children what it once was like... when people were free."

"Well, we fought for it, now it's up to us to protect and defend what we gained and make sure another Derik Juska never happens again."

"I'm sorry to tell you this, old friend, but the universe throws up Derik Juskas regularly to test our resolve. We just need to make sure the Republic is ready for the next one, because it clearly wasn't for Derik. Speaking of which, what's the prognosis on reinstating the term limits for senators, the VP, and the president?"

"After speaking with the Chief Justice of the Supreme Court, I'll request the Court declare the constitutional amendment Juska rammed through to be invalid on procedural grounds. Since he twisted the process to suit himself, that should restore the status quo ante."

"Why didn't the Court object at the time he did it?"

"Because no one petitioned the justices to issue a ruling, and without someone asking, they don't pronounce. And by the time Juska did his thing, there was no one left willing to risk petitioning the Court."

"That will pain a lot of senators who thought they had a sinecure for life."

"Screw 'em. They let Juska pervert the Republic's foundations to create his paranoid little police state. If I had a way of doing it, I'd dissolve the current Senate and have the citizens elect a brand new one. But I can't, so we'll be stuck with listening to the honorable senators whine about the unfairness of it until the next scheduled election."

DeCarde chuckled. "You're actually enjoying getting the Republic back to where it should be, aren't you?"

"You bet I am," Norum replied with feeling. "I never thought I'd be the one setting it to rights, and I'll step down when my term is up, but until then, I will enjoy every minute of browbeating the assholes who supported Juska and made his fever dream happen."

***

Lieutenant Colonel Finn appeared in the open doorway leading to the president's office and announced, "Your visitors are here, sir."

Norum laid the tablet he was reading on his desk and climbed to his feet. "Please have them enter, Magda."

"Sir."

She stepped to one side and gestured to the people behind her. In came a tall man who bore a faint resemblance to Hal Paget, and a woman who definitely looked like a Sister of the Void wearing spacer's coveralls.

Norum smiled. "Lieutenant Commander Paget, how good to see you again after all this time. And you are, Sister?"

A resigned look briefly crossed her face. "Valery. Am I really that easy to identify?"

"I've spent a lot of time in the company of the Lyonesse Sisters recently." Norum gestured at the settee group. "Please sit."

Once they'd taken their seats, while Finn stood behind the visitors, Norum studied Paget for a few heartbeats.

"The disguise is excellent, Hal. If it weren't for the DNA sample the Navy took during your first visit here, we'd have never ID'd you."

A rueful air settled on Paget's features. "I was afraid that might happen. But how in the name of the Almighty did you end up as President of the Republic?"

"It's a long and convoluted story. Suffice to say, the re-education efforts failed where I and DeCarde were concerned, but we kept up appearances. The entire program disbanded, by the way, never to be reactivated since the Summus Abbatissa who pushed it is dead and her successor is opposed to mind-meddling of any sort. I gather your re-education failed as well."

"It did during the voyage home. I also kept up appearances until Sela and I were in my CO's office, when I denounced her. She's sitting in the New Draconis Detention Barracks these days, wondering why she'd trusted the d'ayvols. Did you really call off Juska's war on the Empire?"

"The moment I assumed the presidency after Juska suffered his disabling stroke. Since then, I've been busy dismantling what he created. And I intend to reestablish diplomatic relations with the Empire. I've already designated an ambassador but haven't sent her out yet. Now that you're here aboard what I assume is another undercover Navy ship, perhaps you can take Ambassador Hermina Ruttan to Wyvern. She was part of the Republic's embassy on Wyvern during President Hecht's administration, and she's a Sister of the Void, but one of the good Sisters, not the sort who got off on meddling with minds."

"I'll be glad to see her again, Mister President," Valery said. "We met back when she was among the Lyonesse Brethren taken from Hatshepsut. And you're quite right, Hermina is one of the good Sisters who'd never enter a mind unbidden."

Norum considered Valery for a few moments, then nodded to himself. "I'm about to propose you remain here on Yotai when Commander Paget returns to Wyvern with Ambassador Ruttan, and act as the Empire's ambassador to the Republic until President Benes designates a permanent envoy. You see, I've been moving at hyperspeed to rid the Republic of Derik Juska's evil influence, and accrediting an Imperial ambassador as soon as possible is a firm step in the right direction. It'll certainly be seen as a return to normal after Juska's lunacy since he broke off diplomatic relations between our two star nations. What do you say? The worst that can happen is you'll be replaced in six to eight weeks. But there's a certain symmetry here — I'm sending a Sister of the Void, even though she belongs to a schismatic branch of the Order and you're one as well, albeit in communion with Lindisfarne."

Valery and Paget exchanged a look, and the latter nodded. "Do it, Valery. I'm sure President Benes will be overjoyed at finding he has an envoy on Yotai when I get home with the Republic's Ambassador."

"Very well. Mister President, I am Valery Chun, the Second Empire's ambassador to the United Stars Republic. However, I have no credentials to present."

"Perhaps President Benes will send some on the next ship from Wyvern. In the meantime, we'll find you a chancery close to the Palace. I suppose you came with the bare minimum of clothing and other articles." When Valery nodded, Norum asked, "Then, would you accept a loan from the Republic's government so you can equip yourself properly for your new status until instructions come from Wyvern?"

"Certainly, Mister President, and thank you."

Paget, with a big grin on his face, shook his head. "You weren't kidding when you said you were moving fast. Does that mean you want me to head home as soon as possible?"

"Yes, and via the most direct route up the Hatshepsut branch of the wormhole network. I'll make sure the Navy is aware of your status — that of a military ship from a friendly star nation carrying our ambassador to her new assignment. I'll see that Colonel Finn brings her to the Guesthouse so you two can meet." He glanced at Finn. "They are being put up in the Guesthouse, yes?"

"Adjoining suites are ready for them, sir."

"Excellent. Thank you. You'll enjoy the Guesthouse, I think. And Ambassador Chun, you can stay there until you arrange permanent accommodations, however long that will take."

"Thank you, sir."

"I have one official and one personal request for you, Commander, and would appreciate you taking them on."

"Whatever you want, Mister President."

"I'll be staying on Yotai, and so will Currag DeCarde. At least for the next few years. Could you ask the Imperial authorities to release Sela Reeve and send her home? I'll have Hermina do it officially, but your asking might have more impact."

"Sure. If there's no war, then keeping her as a prisoner is pointless. What's your other request?"

"Could you get in touch with our partners, Rey Weston and Beth Svent, in New Draconis. Tell them we've taken over the Republic and would appreciate them joining us on Yotai. They're both former Republic Defense Force, so it shouldn't be a big deal. If they can travel on the same ship that'll either bring a permanent envoy or Ambassador Chun's credentials, so much the better."

"I'll run the matter straight up to Admiral Mindar, sir. I'm sure we can have both here within six to eight weeks. Perhaps even Sela as well."

Norum inclined his head. "My thanks."

"You know, sir, my nickname in Intelligence is Imperial Rogue. But I think taking over an entire star nation and dismantling the evil dictatorship that was growing at its heart means you're a much bigger rogue than I can ever aspire to be. And I mean that as the sincerest compliment I can think of."

"You keep your nickname, Hal. I can only be the Republic's Rogue now, but from one rogue to another, we could never have done it without you."

About the Author

Eric Thomson is the pen name of a retired Canadian soldier who spent more time in uniform than he expected, both in the Regular Army and the Army Reserve. He spent his Regular Army career in the Infantry and his Reserve service in the Armoured Corps. He worked as an information technology specialist for several years before retiring to become a full-time author.

Eric has been a voracious reader of science fiction, military fiction, and history all his life. Several years ago, he put fingers to keyboard and started writing his own military sci-fi, with a definite space opera slant, using many of his own experiences as a soldier for inspiration.

When he is not writing fiction, Eric indulges in his other passions: photography, hiking, and scuba diving, all of which he shares with his wife.

Join Eric Thomson at http://www.thomsonfiction.ca/

Scan to visit the site.

Where you will find news about upcoming books and more information about the universe in which his heroes fight for humanity's survival.

And read his blog at https://blog.thomsonfiction.ca.

If you enjoyed this book, please consider leaving a review on Goodreads or with your favorite online retailer to help others discover it.

Also by Eric Thomson

Siobhan Dunmoore

No Honor in Death (Siobhan Dunmoore Book 1)
The Path of Duty (Siobhan Dunmoore Book 2)
Like Stars in Heaven (Siobhan Dunmoore Book 3)
Victory's Bright Dawn (Siobhan Dunmoore Book 4)
Without Mercy (Siobhan Dunmoore Book 5)
When the Guns Roar (Siobhan Dunmoore Book 6)
A Dark and Dirty Wary (Siobhan Dunmoore Book 7)
On Stormy Seas (Siobhan Dunmoore Book 8)
The Final Shore (Siobhan Dunmoore Book 9)

Decker's War

Death Comes But Once (Decker's War Book 1)
Cold Comfort (Decker's War Book 2)
Fatal Blade (Decker's War Book 3)
Howling Stars (Decker's War Book 4)
Black Sword (Decker's War Book 5)
No Remorse (Decker's War Book 6)
Hard Strike (Decker's War Book 7)

Constabulary Casefiles

The Warrior's Knife
A Colonial Murder
The Dirty and the Dead
A Peril so Dire

Ghost Squadron

We Dare (Ghost Squadron No. 1)
Deadly Intent (Ghost Squadron No. 2)
Die Like the Rest (Ghost Squadron No. 3)
Fear No Darkness (Ghost Squadron No. 4)
Violent Fires (Ghost Squadron No. 5)

Ashes of Empire

Imperial Sunset (Ashes of Empire #1)
Imperial Twilight (Ashes of Empire #2)
Imperial Night (Ashes of Empire #3)
Imperial Echoes (Ashes of Empire #4)
Imperial Ghosts (Ashes of Empire #5)
Imperial Dawn (Ashes of Empire #6)
Imperial Rogue (Ashes of Empire #7)